D0802791

HUNTERS OF THE ICE AGE

PASSION AT THE DAWN OF TIME

BROKEN PROMISE

He leaned over and kissed her lips and she felt herself melting once more. "Oh, no," Star moaned and pulled away. "What hold is it that you have over me, Falcon?" she cried.

He stared at her in silence.

She rose to her feet. "I must return to the others." Her hands were shaking as she put on the dress.

"Star." He rose without any sign of the shame that she seemed to feel. "I want to make love to you."

"Well, you cannot."

"You are going to be my wife. It is only natural for a man to want to be with his wife."

"That may be," she retorted archly, "but you seem to have forgotten something."

"What is that?"

"I have not agreed to be your wife! You stole me from my family. And I do not want to lie with you."

Hunters of the Ice Age

Broken Promise

Theresa Scott

LEISURE BOOKS   **NEW YORK CITY**

*This book is dedicated to Vivian Atwell,
modern-day healer of troubled souls.*

A LEISURE BOOK®

January 1995

Published by

Dorchester Publishing Co., Inc.
276 Fifth Avenue
New York, NY 10001

Printed in the United States of America.

With special thanks for technical expertise to:

Andy Appleby, fisheries biologist, Olympia, WA;
Dr. Richard Daugherty, archaeologist;
Christopher Johnson, PA/SA, medical consulting;
Ruby Martin, nurse-midwife, Olympia, WA;
and Daniel S. Meatte, archaeologist, who finds
all the good sites for me.

North America

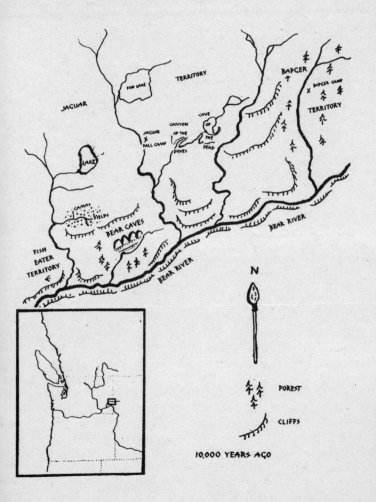

10,000 YEARS AGO

HUNTERS OF THE ICE AGE

BROKEN PROMISE

Chapter One

Autumn, 10,000 years ago
Palouse River area

"Put more mud on your face."

Star obeyed her mother and poured water from a deer bladder onto the dirt and ashes mounded beside the dead fire. She made a thick paste and patted it on her skin. Coarse grains of the charred wood ground into her cheek. She wrinkled her nose at the acrid ash smell.

Blue Jay, her mother, tipped her head critically. "More."

Star picked up a second handful and smeared it across the other cheek, then streaked a glob across her forehead. It felt surprisingly cool and refreshing.

"Now your chin."

Star rolled a dab of mud around her jawline.

When her mother gripped her chin, Star winced and looked into her mother's narrowed eyes.

Blue Jay dropped her hand and scanned Star's face. "Ah, but I despair of hiding your beauty! Those dark brown eyes, those cheeks . . ." Her indrawn breath rattled.

Star stared at her mother. "Surely the Jaguar men cannot be so fierce."

Her mother peered outside the tent, then looked back. "They are," she answered. "I see the Jaguar scout still waits outside Echo's tent. Oh, how I wish our men had not chosen this morning to go hunting. Had they but known the Jaguars were coming, surely they would have stayed. . . ."

She turned back to Star and slid a lock of Star's black hair to one side. Blue Jay cocked her head, frowning thoughtfully. "Every year during this moon, the Jaguars search us out to trade for wives. We have given them women in return for protection against the powerful Fish Eaters, who are even worse than they are. Until now, we have been most fortunate. The Jaguars could not find us for this many years." She held up three muddy fingers. "But alas, our good fortune has ended."

Blue Jay draped the lock of hair in front of Star's face and reached into the ashes. With shaking hands, she rubbed it on the shiny dark hair.

Star closed her eyes, not wanting to see her hair become white, coarse, and gritty.

"The Jaguars will be hungry for women. We must make certain that they do not choose you," said Blue Jay.

"What of the other young women? No one

14

else's mother puts mud on her face and ashes in her hair."

Blue Jay snorted. "A mother does what she must do to protect her daughter. If the other Badger mothers are wise, they will smear mud."

Star tried to rise.

Blue Jay restrained her and pleaded, "Only a little more." She reached for the gray ashes again.

Star smiled tightly and sat back down. "Very well, Mother."

"Your teeth! I must dull your teeth. They are too white." Blue Jay rubbed ash on her daughter's upper front teeth. "There."

Star tried to spit out the foul-tasting substance. Her skin was covered with dirt, her scalp itched from ash, and white dust had drifted all over her yellow leather dress. Always so careful to keep clean and neat, she shivered with repugnance.

"Do not spit it out," warned Blue Jay. "I know you do not wish to walk around like this, but I promise you, it will protect you." She rubbed her hands together. "Now you must stand up so that I can see—" Her gaze darted nervously over the girl. "Oh, no! I had forgotten how tall and straight you are. Oh, what am I to do?" She scanned the tent and picked up a ratty fur the dogs slept upon.

"Here. Hunch over. And put this on."

"Mother! I do not want to wear such a thing. It is—" Star studied the fur. "Why, it crawls with vermin. I can see little tiny things moving. . . ."

"Enough," said her mother. "Here"—she picked up another skin—"Then wear this under it. But hasten. They will be here soon!"

"Mother, I cannot wear that fur!"

15

"Please," begged her mother. "Just put it on. And remember to walk bent over. None of your proud walk, now. That would surely gain the Jaguars' attention."

Star swept the clean fur onto her shoulders. Then with two fingers and a grimace, she picked up the vermin-ridden fur. Several tiny black fleas burrowed into the pelt. She shivered and dropped the filthy piece. "It is for the dogs! I will not put it on." She challenged her mother's narrowed eyes.

"Oh. I understand now. You would be happy to warm the bed of a Jaguar man. How fortunate for you. And he will only beat you now and then. He will take you, my only child, away to live with his people and I will never see you again. Then you will truly be the most fortunate of women! And I, the happiest of mothers!"

Star frowned. "I am not going to join with a Jaguar. I am going to marry Camel Stalker. You know that, Mother. You helped arrange the promising."

Blue Jay sighed. "There will be no joining with Camel Stalker if one of the Jaguar men sees you first!"

"Pah! Jaguar men, Jaguar men! That is all you talk about. Where did they suddenly come from? You never worried about them before."

"You were younger then and I had no need to worry. Now you are fully grown. I worry." She hugged Star. "Ever since your father was killed by the grizzly bear, you have been everything to me, my precious daughter. I do not want you forced to go away with those people."

"You said the Jaguars protect us from the Fish

16

Eaters. How can the Fish Eaters be any worse than our *protectors*?" demanded Star.

Blue Jay sighed and released Star. "It is said, my daughter, that you can recognize Fish Eater territory when you see the rotting heads of their enemies hoisted up on sticks. They are put there to warn of the Fish Eaters' ferocity."

Star shuddered.

"You must remember that many years ago they raided our people for women."

"Yes, you have spoken of them before."

Her mother nodded. "In that raid, there was much fighting and ten of our men were killed. Three of our women were stolen.

"Now, the Jaguars are a strong people who also live in the west. They do not like the Fish Eaters and they promised to protect us against the raids. In return, they demanded three of our daughters as wives. Our headman, Echo, and the other Badger men refused. They thought that we could hide from the Fish Eaters."

"What happened when our people refused the Jaguars' protection?" prompted Star.

"The Fish Eaters raided us again. This time they stole five women and killed five men. I can tell you there was much wailing and crying and gnashing of teeth in the Badger tents that night. So our men sent for the Jaguars, and together they made the agreement. We knew if we did not, the Fish Eaters would kill our people off."

Blue Jay sighed. "But while the Jaguars protect us, they also take from us. I know it is necessary to give brides to them, but I am a selfish old woman. I do not want to give you, the joy of my life, to a

17

Jaguar. I fear that they will take you away and I will not see you for many years, if ever."

When tears rose in Blue Jay's eyes, Star swallowed hard. She clasped her mother's hands. "I love you, Mother. I do not wish to join with the Jaguars, either. They seem no different from the Fish Eaters."

"Ah," answered Blue Jay sadly, "there is a difference. The Fish Eaters steal women and give nothing back. The Jaguars protect us and give us gifts in exchange for joining with our women. Gifts are important."

"They give gifts? Well then, I say we are free to reject the Jaguars' gifts," said Star with a toss of her head. "I, a Badger woman who does not wish to join with a Jaguar man, can tell him so by rejecting his gifts, just as I would do with a Badger man!"

"Unfortunately, it is not that easy, my daughter. The Jaguar men will not accept having their joining offers rejected."

"Pah! A man is a man. No man likes his marriage offer rejected."

Blue Jay's hands fluttered. "Yes, and you would know about this, my daughter. You who have already rejected the joining offers of three of our finest Badger hunters!"

"I did not like the men."

"Gopher is a good man."

"I do not want Gopher. He is a lazy hunter and does not share. He hid his meat from old Grouse when she was hungry and her son was away hunting."

"Hmmm, well, Finds the Marten is an excellent

18

hunter and shares his meat. And I like his mother," said Blue Jay. "She is a very dear friend to me."

"Finds the Marten is indeed an excellent hunter and generous and his mother is very kindly, but he is too quiet. Not once did he speak to me while he was making his joining offer. His mother did all the talking for him. I have no wish to live in a tent with a mute man all my days."

"Wolverine chatters like a squirrel. He is a good hunter and the son of our headman. And he is generous," pointed out Blue Jay.

"True. But alas, I consider him a kinsman. He is related to my father's brother. That makes his blood too close to mine." Star sighed. Finding a good man had proved trying. But she wanted a husband; she wanted a family. She sighed again.

"Well, I am relieved that Camel Stalker is a good hunter and a generous man," said Blue Jay. "He also speaks with great wisdom and he is not related in any way to you."

Camel Stalker would do. He was kind and he was handsome to look upon. Star's confident shrug sent the fur sliding off one graceful shoulder and Blue Jay hastily tugged the fur back up.

"Camel Stalker would not like me to reject his joining offer," teased Star with a sly smile.

Alarmed, her mother met Star's eyes. "Do not reject his offer at this time! If one of the Jaguars should discover you, we can always explain that you are already promised to Camel Stalker." Under her breath, Blue Jay added, "But I fear that a joining promise would not deter a Jaguar."

She dusted Star's forearms with dry ashes.

"Your sleeves should hide your arms, I think. Oh, I do hope this mud and ash hides your beauty. You see, these people are very proud," warned Blue Jay. "They do not take well to being told no. Now, if we were to reject Camel Stalker's offer, why, he would merely be angry with us for a little while. Perhaps even ask us to reconsider."

Star smiled. "I will not reject Camel Stalker's offer. I am pleased enough with him. I think he is the best hunter of our people. And he practices the manly virtues of honesty, bravery, and generosity. Several times I have seen him give meat to Crow." Crow was a widow with two young children.

Her mother touched more mud to Star's temple and smoothed it around.

"Camel Stalker and I will have a happy life together, Mother. I have it all planned! We will be joined soon and have many healthy children and travel the land with our Badger People."

Blue Jay grimaced. "I hope what you say will truly happen."

"It will."

"But first you must evade the Jaguars. I will tell you what will happen, my daughter." Blue Jay stroked Star's ash-grayed hair. "They want all the young women to gather in one place. Then they will choose which women they will give gifts for. The women so selected must leave their families and go away with the Jaguars. If they are fortunate, they will see their Badger families again. But some will not, like my cousin, Fragrance. She was chosen, and I have not seen her for many years." Again, tears welled in Blue Jay's eyes.

Broken Promise

"I would not have a Jaguar for my husband!" cried Star.

"Yes, well, I do not want such a husband for you, either. But remember, the Jaguars take women away as wives. Fish Eaters take women away as slaves. Fish Eater slaves work very hard. They must gather wood, and catch and smoke fish. Tend children. Gather roots and berries. Build fish traps. Weave fishnets—"

"Stop, Mother. I grow weary merely from hearing you speak of the work they must do."

"Living with the Fish Eaters makes a woman into a dog who must work hard and beg for every piece of meat she gets. I do not think you would like to live like that."

Star held up a hand to stop her mother's words. "I think I should go and hide in one of the caves, Mother. There I will be safe. If I stay here, one of the Jaguar men might see past the mud on my face."

Her mother smiled grimly. "Unfortunately that has been tried before, my sweet daughter. And the Jaguars were very angry when they discovered the hidden women! They were so angry that they threatened to withdraw their protection. They even threatened to tell the Fish Eaters exactly where we were located."

"How would they tell them? I thought they were enemies of the Fish Eaters."

"Even enemies communicate now and then. There is a dangerous group of trading men, known as slave catchers, who move freely between the Jaguars and the Fish Eaters unscathed. The Jaguars would tell the slave catchers; then the slave catchers would tell the Fish Eaters."

Star shook her head. "These slave catchers sound like they cannot be trusted."

"They are most treacherous! They hunt for slaves for the Fish Eaters. We Badgers know it was the slave catchers who told them to raid us. There is a story old Granny Dawn tells of the day a trader came and visited us. Shortly after he left, the Fish Eaters raided us for the first time!"

Star considered this. Her thoughts went back to how she could save herself. "What happened after the Jaguars found the hidden women and threatened to withdraw their protection?"

"At first our men were glad. They do not like giving women to the Jaguars. But then Echo, our esteemed headman, pointed out that we do not have enough men to fight off the Fish Eaters. The Jaguars do. The Badger men listened to Echo's wise words. Then Echo gave a most apologetic speech to the Jaguars, convincing them to extend the cloak of their protection once again."

"And they did so?"

"Yes, my daughter. And so now they are on their way to visit us for brides. The Jaguar scout who ran ahead to advise us said they will arrive this day when the sun makes tiny shadows at our feet."

Star hastily slapped more mud on her face. "Do not worry, Mother! No Jaguar will offer for me." She waved a hand dismissively. "Not the way I am dressed and muddied!"

"Your disguise as an old woman should protect you," her mother agreed. "And I will stay close to you, too. We will be two old women together."

"I hope they will make their choices soon. I do not wish to hobble around for long."

"I pray to the Great Spirit that it will be so," said her mother grimly. "But we may have to be patient." Her worried glance indicated that she thought Star lacked that particular womanly virtue.

"Remember: keep that fur over your head. Walk like a bent old woman. Snort occasionally. If one of them chances to speak to you, refuse to look him in the eyes. And I will give you a man's spear to drag around. Use it as a cane and poke at things and people with it. Do anything that you think will discourage a Jaguar man."

"Snort? Drag around a man's spear? Poke people? Mother, you have lost your senses!"

"Better to lose my senses than to lose my daughter."

"Oh, Mother. It cannot be as bad as that!"

"I hope you are correct, my daughter," answered Blue Jay grimly. "I truly hope you are correct."

Chapter Two

When the lone Jaguar runner had announced that his people were on their way to the Badger camp, he had said they would arrive when the sun was at its highest. It was that time now and all Star could see was her tiny shadow. No Jaguars. She yawned and straightened.

"Bend," hissed her mother in warning.

"Oh, Mother, there are no Jaguars. They are late, and perhaps they may never arrive. Perhaps they found some other people to scare—uh, protect." Star felt foolish wearing the furs over her head and mud on her face. "None of the other young women have to wear—"

"Hush!" warned Blue Jay. "Their scout has alert ears, like an owl listening for a mouse. And he may be watching us even now." She glanced in the direction of Echo's tent where Echo's old wife plied the Jaguar scout with ripe red berries.

"Oh, Mother."

"Hunch. Look old," was her mother's only reply.

Having nothing better to do, Star hunched over again, though not as far as she had the last time. Bending for a long time hurt!

"Here," said her mother, handing her an old wooden spear shaft with a missing tip.

Star practiced walking around slowly, using it as a cane.

"Much better," said Blue Jay with satisfaction. Star was staring at the ground so she could not see her mother, or anyone else. Just feet. She straightened a little.

"They are coming." Blue Jay shuddered.

Star's heart sped up. The dreaded Jaguars! At last! She took a quick peek.

They did not look so fierce. She counted the large, leather-clad men whose long black hair hung straight down their backs. She noted that each man carried a spear. There were as many of them as she had fingers and toes.

She unbent a little more to get a better view and heard her mother's sharp hiss, so she stayed frozen at the new level. The pain in her back made her feel truly old.

Star craned her neck to listen as the Jaguars spoke with the Badger headman, Echo. After polite preliminaries were dispensed with, the Jaguar headman said, "We want six women."

Echo looked taken aback. "Claw, we do not have six women to give you." Echo's voice, though shaking, was quiet. "We Badgers number few people. If we were to give you six women of

25

joining age, why, we would have no women for ourselves!"

Star hoped Echo would not give away *any* Badgers to these strangers.

"We have gifts," another Jaguar spoke up. He stepped forward. His leather tunic was dirty and his black hair was tangled. Star frowned at the ground. Who would want to marry a Jaguar? Not she.

Echo said nothing to the offer of gifts and the uneasy silence lengthened. Star peeked upward. Claw, the Jaguar spokesman, a tall, thin man with a protruding stomach, was surveying the gathered Badgers. "Where are your women? I see only old people and little children. And few men," he added in a menacing tone.

It was most unfortunate, thought Star, that the Badger men had chosen this morning of all mornings to go antelope hunting.

"Most of our women are married," said Echo. "And they have children."

"It is good that Badger women are fertile," acknowledged Claw. "That is why they are in high demand by my men."

"We can give you two women," said Echo. "They are beautiful and young. They will give you many children."

"Let us see them." Claw's voice was eager.

Echo coughed and signaled two waiting Badger mothers. The mothers came forward, each holding a shy daughter's hand.

Star straightened a little more, and gave a sidelong peek to see who the young women were. She smiled to herself when she saw the first one.

26

That one needed little encouragement from her mother! Her round face was smiling, her plump body jiggling under her well-tanned leather dress as her mother led her forward. It was Fawn, a middle daughter in a family of six girls. Her mother, Doe, despaired of ever finding enough husbands for all six of her daughters and no doubt saw this as an opportunity sent by the Great Spirit to relieve her of yet another marriageable girl. Doe's remaining unmarried daughters were all too young to give to the Jaguars.

Doe gave Fawn a push in Claw's direction. Star straightened a little more and saw Claw grin at the young woman. Then his expression became serious.

"Who else?" he demanded. "Move aside. Let us see her."

The young woman propelled forward by her mother tried to hide her face in embarrassment. A twinge of pity welled in Star. It was Elk Knees, a recent widow. No Badger hunter had offered to join with her because of her sharp tongue. It was rumored that she had killed her husband with unkind words, but Star knew it was not true. He had suffered a hunting accident. Evidently Elk Knees's family feared that no Badger man would ever promise for her.

"She looks young and strong," said Claw approvingly.

Echo smiled.

It is true, thought Star. Elk Knees is comely, as thin and strong as a young cottonwood. The Jaguars should be satisfied. Now if they would only go home!

"We are very pleased with the two women you have offered, Echo of the Badger People. But I must tell you, we want six Badger women. No more, no less." Claw's words were stern as he held up six fingers.

"We—we have no more women."

The Jaguars milled together, discussing Echo's words. From their deep droning buzz, Star knew they disliked his answer.

Star risked another peek at the Jaguars through her long, ash-covered locks. None of them noticed her and she felt free to study them as they talked about what to do. The Jaguar men were taller than Badger men. They had long legs and broad chests. Her eyes roved over them. They all had long black hair and wore tanned leather tunics and trousers. Jaguar women are skilled in the decorative arts, she thought, for several of the tunics were painted with deer and elk designs, a jaguar's natural prey.

One man had his broad back to her. He sported a wide-winged falcon design on the leather stretched taut across his shoulders. As she stared at him, he swung around, and she saw his face. Her breath caught in her throat. His eyes were black, his face strong-jawed. He would have been truly handsome if it were not for the long white scar that slashed from the corner of his right eye to his unsmiling mouth.

He has suffered, she realized, stirring suddenly. When she saw his eyes surveying the watching Badgers, she dropped her gaze. Her heart pounded. It would not do for that man to notice her. It would not do at all!

"We come to your people for women," Claw said. "We have done this many times. We share grandchildren with you." He named two Badger women who had gone to live with the Jaguars. Star recognized their names. One was Echo's sister; the other was Fragrance, Blue Jay's cousin.

"Yes, and we never saw them again," muttered Blue Jay.

Star stared at the ground. Not to see her family again! Marriage to a Jaguar sounded very lonely. She was relieved she had accepted Camel Stalker's suit.

"You seem to have forgotten our agreement, Echo," said Claw sternly. "We agreed that you Badgers would give us brides in exchange for protection against the Fish Eaters."

"I remember our agreement very clearly," said Echo. "But we have few young women. If we give you any more, we will not have any women for ourselves."

"Six is not so many," argued Claw.

Star gazed once again at the broad-shouldered falcon man she had seen. He was standing, legs apart, calmly surveying the clustered Badgers and Jaguars. He seemed to care little about what went on with the negotiations as he lazily surveyed her people. His long black hair waved in the breeze. She suddenly wondered what it would be like to touch him, to caress those thick black locks.

"Bend," hissed Blue Jay.

Star dragged her eyes away from his rugged face and forced herself to stare at the ground.

Three of the Jaguar men grouped around Claw spoke in low tones. Finally they separated and

Claw said, "We would like to stay at your camp for this night. We are weary from our travels." His bland face gave no hint of deceit, but Star was suspicious.

Echo shifted uncomfortably. Star guessed he wanted to deny the request and was searching for a polite way to decline. If the Jaguars stayed too long, they would soon realize there were more Badger women than those gathered at the fire.

But Echo shrugged helplessly and the Jaguars took his silence for assent. They dispersed through the camp, carrying their belongings and looking for flat places on the grass to set up their tents.

It was to be a longer stay then, thought Star in dismay. If they were going to stay only overnight as Claw had said, they would not bother with erecting hide dwellings.

The Jaguars set up their tents and rolled out bedskins. Star straightened a little.

"Bend," hissed Blue Jay.

The Jaguars finished, and Star relaxed. She and her mother could return to their own home and stay there until these intruders left.

But now that the Jaguars had completed their task, they began prowling among the Badgers and searching the Badger tents!

A Jaguar stopped and peered into a dwelling. A surprised yell came from inside. The man hastily withdrew and wandered on to the next Badger abode.

Several Jaguars were clustered around one particular Badger tent.

"Bend," ordered Blue Jay. "They are getting close to finding—"

A heavyset Jaguar pulled back the flap and reached inside. "Ho!" The Jaguar and several of his fellows laughed heartily. "Look!"

"Oh, no," moaned Blue Jay. "Her mother should have hidden her in the cave or smeared her with mud as I have done."

Star caught her breath, watching as the Jaguar jerked a young woman from the tent. Her long black hair hid her face, but Star recognized the thin form of Chokecherry.

Star bit her lip and ducked her head. Chokecherry had wanted to marry Finds the Marten, Star's silent suitor. Star had thought it a good match because Chokecherry never stopped talking. But the Jaguar held her so tightly that Chokecherry was struck silent with fear. Now Finds the Marten would not be her husband. Instead, she would have a Jaguar man.

Out of the tent crawled Chokecherry's mother. "My daughter is very ill," she moaned, wringing her hands and getting to her feet. "You must let her rest in our tent!"

A brawny young Jaguar pushed her aside, entered the tent, and dragged out a second young woman. Star looked away before she could see who it was.

"Sageflower," whispered Blue Jay as Star kept her eyes on the ground and leaned on her cane.

"Oh, no," muttered Star. Sageflower was a close friend of Chokecherry's so Star was not surprised that they had hidden together. Sageflower was a sweet, delicate young woman, a favorite in the

Badger camp. "Not Sageflower!"

"She is very ill, too," Chokecherry's mother proclaimed loudly. "They are both very, very ill!"

The Jaguars ignored her.

Star suddenly felt grateful for the mud and ashes on her face and in her hair. Blue Jay had known to do the best thing for her, after all. She leaned a little more onto her cane.

The two frightened young women, looking pale but healthy, were led away from the hide dwelling. A thick silence, marred only by the low keening of Chokecherry's mother, descended upon the Badger camp.

The Jaguar spokesman strutted up to Echo. "So, you think to hide your women? That is not in the spirit of friendship between our people. Not at all!"

"Claw looks very angry," whispered Blue Jay in a shaking voice. "And he is mistaken to say that we are friends. Friends do not fear one another like we fear the Jaguars!"

Star squeezed her eyes shut. What would happen now?

"These women are already promised!" insisted Echo. Indeed, Star knew that Sageflower was promised to Echo's son, Wolverine. "There was no need to show them to you. They each have a mate they will join with very soon!"

"Not soon enough," said Claw. "They will have new mates. Jaguar mates. Put them over there with the other two brides!"

Star's heart fell. It was truly most unfortunate that so many Badger men had gone hunting that morning and were not here to defend their brides.

Suddenly she felt a hard grip on her shoulder and found herself peering into a cruel Jaguar face. "Who is this?" demanded the man. It was the one with food streaks on his leather tunic and dirty, tangled hair. At close range he stank. Star opened her mouth, but no words came. She swallowed and tried again.

"She is just my old sister," rang out Blue Jay's alarmed voice. She knocked the Jaguar's hand off Star's shoulder. "Leave her alone!"

The intruder glared at Blue Jay, and Star feared for her mother's life. Then with a shrug and a dismissive glance at Star, the Jaguar turned away. Star's heart slowed to its natural rhythm.

"We will give you gifts for these two women," Claw was snarling at Echo. "We do not steal them from you like the Fish Eaters do!"

"I have not forgotten our agreement," retorted Echo sharply.

Star peeked up and saw the two headmen glaring at each other.

"Down," whispered her mother.

It was unusual for Echo to sound angry. He had been chosen headman by the Badger People because he was so calm. Star guessed that he was angry about the loss of his son's wife, because Sageflower was truly a loss. Wolverine would be heartbroken.

Claw sauntered closer to Echo. Star watched him halt a handbreadth from the Badger headman. "We are taking them," gloated Claw. "You may keep the gifts or not, as you see fit. But we are taking the women!"

The hiss of Echo's indrawn breath told Star he

did not like it. Her heart beat faster. She watched Echo sidestep the Jaguar. Echo paced in a circle, searching the crowded area.

"Do not bother to look for help," said Claw with a sneer. "We have more men than you do."

Echo turned back to his tormentor and stood toe-to-toe with the Jaguar. "You cannot have our women!"

The Jaguar laughed. "You cannot stop us."

Careful to stay bent, Star peered up at them. The two men glared at each other; then Echo's shoulders slumped and he turned away. He had given up. Her heart thundered. If the Badger men would not fight for her and the other hidden women, then she had only the mud and her own cunning to protect her!

Chapter Three

The Jaguars had been in camp for two days, and Star was desperately hoping they would leave soon. Her back hurt from bending over but her mother would not let her linger in their tent because the Jaguars had not given up; they stopped and searched the dwellings thoroughly again and again. So far they had found one more woman, Pine Woman, a lively, dimpled maiden who had been hiding in a cave.

The five captured women stood in a little knot, guarded by two hefty Jaguars. Sobbing mothers huddled around them. Gifts had been offered, but that pretense was as thin as an old worn fur; the Jaguars were stealing the women and no one could stop them.

Star leaned on her cane and wondered where she could go to straighten her back. She was very tired of walking around hunched over. The mud on her face had dried, cracked, fallen off, and been replaced many times, because Blue Jay insisted she wear it always, even at night. Star's hair was buried under the gray ash and her scalp itched. Blue Jay took every occasion she could to pile on more ashes.

But Star had to admit that their efforts had proved successful. Not a single Jaguar had sought out the filthy old woman who hobbled about on a cane.

She often shuffled over to the trail that led to the river, keeping out of sight of the camp, waiting for the Jaguars to leave.

As she hobbled slowly down the trail one afternoon, she wondered where Camel Stalker, Wolverine, and the other Badger hunters were. What was taking them so long?

Well, she thought bitterly, when they finally do decide to return from whatever antelope hunt they are on, they will find I am the only young woman left in camp!

As she shuffled along, Star wished she could get word to the Badger hunters to return and rescue her and the other women from the intruders. Their lone headman, Echo, could do little to stop the Jaguars.

Ah, Camel Stalker. How she wanted a husband, a hearth of her own, children of her own. Her mother loved her, true, and she could always dwell with her, but Star did not want to grow old and live with her mother. She wanted a man. Someone to love and share her life with. Camel Stalker would do well as a husband—if he ever arrived to rescue her.

A copse of cottonwood and aspen bordered the river. The thick screen of trees hid the water from camp. As soon as she knew that no one could see her, she straightened a little and her muscles relaxed in relief. The closer she got to the river, the more upright she became, and the faster she walked. By the time she reached the river, she was running.

She tossed the furs aside and splashed into the water. Ah, how cool and cleansing the water felt on her legs and arms. She put a hand to the small of her back and stretched. How good it felt to straighten! She bent and splashed some of the refreshing liquid on her face. She washed off the dried mud so she could feel her skin once again. Later she would replace the black ooze, but for now how fresh the water felt on her skin, how cool!

She waded out until the water lapped at her knees. Any higher and the fringe on her leather dress would get wet.

Star happily splashed more water on her face, bending over and dipping her ash-caked hair in its coolness. The clean, fresh scent tickled her nostrils. She dragged strands of her hair back and forth on the river's placid surface for a short time, then stopped. If too much of her black hair showed she would no longer look old.

She straightened and glanced around, then sighed. It was so quiet here, so peaceful—the way her life had been before the Jaguar intruders had arrived.

The river was a murky green, and bulrushes grew along the banks. Two ducks settled on the water at a distance from her and she watched them swim and dip for food and gabble quietly with each other. Overhead, a honking sound caused her to glance up. Geese flew by, many of them, in their speartip formation. Winter would soon settle upon the land.

She sauntered back to the riverbank. Carefully, she rubbed fresh mud on her face and hair. When her face was once again weighted down with the thick paste, she retrieved her furs, picked up her cane, and wandered back up the trail. After she passed the cottonwoods, she bent and pulled a fur over her hair as she shuffled along.

Forcing herself to walk slowly, like an old woman, she prayed once again that the Jaguars would soon go away.

Falcon smiled to himself as he watched the woman limp back along the trail. Her disguise was good, very good. It had fooled him and the others, too. He wondered how many more "old" women of the Badgers would prove to be young, comely maidens.

Mud alone could not hide her beauty. It was the bent back that had thrown him off the scent. He had thought her merely a gnarled, skinny-legged heron when he had seen her hobbling about the camp on her cane. Indeed, he had given her nary a thought. But now he knew her secret.

She was tall, too. Tall and well formed and beautiful. He chuckled. These Badgers were wily.

Chapter Four

"We will leave in the morning. There is nothing more to be gained," said Claw. "We have enough women. I am satisfied that they are not hiding more of them. And the ones we have are very comely."

Not as comely as a certain long-legged heron, thought Falcon, grinning.

"We have only five women. We came for six," muttered a man. Several agreed. Claw ignored them.

"What about the Badger men? Where are they?" asked Hooknose, one of the slave catchers. He and his fellow slave catcher, Red Jaw, so called because the lower half of his face was painted in red ocher, had accompanied the Jaguars on their bride quest. So far, the two slave catchers had done no harm, but Falcon distrusted them. They were a deceptive lot.

"Pah, Badger men are no trouble," Claw said dismissively. "There is only one man in the whole camp, and that is the headman. The others have run off. They are afraid of us!"

"Still, we should appoint guards this night," said Falcon. "These people might not be as afraid of us as we think. Badgers, at least the animals, are fighters. They defend their burrows and their young ferociously. It could be that these people are well named."

Hooknose snorted. "They are not fighters. I have never seen a people yield their women so easily."

Falcon shrugged. "And you have had much experience with that, I do not doubt."

Hooknose frowned at him and then turned away to face Claw. "You know that I am looking for slaves to trade to the Fish Eaters along the Great River," he told Claw. "I will take any woman that you do not want and trade her to the Fish Eaters. I want men to trade as well. The Fish Eaters pay well for strong men to labor for them."

"We will not trade these women," answered Claw. "We will keep them for ourselves. As for the men"—he held up his hands, palm open—"as you can see, there are none here. I think that you will have to travel to another group of people for the slaves you seek. Perhaps you will be more fortunate with the Groundsloth People."

Red Jaw, the other slave catcher, protested, "They live too far away!" He smiled a toothless smile. "We can always get a good price for anyone—even a child. I saw several healthy Badger children."

Claw was shocked.

Hooknose eyed him and turned to growl at Red Jaw. "No! We set out on this bride quest with the understanding that we would trade the captured men, and Claw and his hunters would get the women. Forget the children."

Claw nodded, relieved. Hooknose frowned at Red Jaw and shook his head almost imperceptibly, cautioning the other man to silence.

Falcon watched the veiled signals. Another time, when he was younger, before his wife had left him, he would have had nothing to do with men like these slave catchers. Now he did not care. He knew that it did not matter what manner of man one associated with in life. There was no good in life, no good in people. There was no Great Spirit, either; that he knew.

He scanned the field where the Jaguars' tents sat interspersed with the Badgers' tents. Orange flames flickered from the campfires. His gaze rested on one particular fire, where a short, squat woman hovered over a bent, long-legged heron.

"We post a sentry and we leave in the morning," decided Claw.

Falcon smiled. Perhaps he should choose some company on his journey back to Jaguar territory. Long-legged heron company.

Claw caught the smile. "Does that fit with your plans, Falcon?" he asked irritably.

Falcon shrugged easily. He knew that Claw was still jealous of him, thinking that Falcon wanted back his place as Jaguar headman. But Falcon was content to leave the Jaguar leadership to Claw. Claw had made changes, but not any

41

changes that Falcon cared about. What did it matter to him that the Jaguars were edging back into their old ways of stealing women? Perhaps it was in the Jaguar blood. He would soon know, he who was contemplating stealing a woman himself. He had not looked at a woman in a long time. Not since his wife had left him for—

Falcon straightened, driving the thought of his unfaithful wife from his mind. What did he care whom she slept with? What did he care if he stole a woman from another people? What people did, did not matter. What he did, did not matter. Nothing mattered. Not now. He had been a fool ever to think otherwise.

"Falcon?" Claw was waiting for his answer.

It amused Falcon that Claw wanted his approval. "That fits with my plans."

Claw turned to Hooknose. "We will leave in the morning then. It is most unfortunate for you that you have no slaves to sell, but we cannot help that. I warned you before you set out with us that we do not particularly like to take slaves."

Hooknose smiled and bowed. "We are patient men. We will wait."

"It is a fine virtue, patience," noted Claw absently. "When will those mothers stop their wailing? I have heard enough of *that*, I can tell you!"

Indeed, the incessant wailing of the mothers of the captured women was a dirge that accompanied most Jaguar bride quests these days. Falcon was getting used to it. He chuckled to himself that Claw was irritated by it. But then, Claw still had a conscience.

42

Broken Promise

* * *

"It is time to retire for the night," murmured Blue Jay after a big yawn. "I am tired."

"As am I, Mo—" Star stopped. There he was again, the Jaguar with the falcon painted across his broad back. Only this time he did not just stroll past their fire. He prowled right up to it.

Her eyes met his for a heartbeat. He was staring at her, his mouth quirked in an amused half-smile. Her eyes skimmed over him swiftly, gaining an impression of wide shoulders, long legs, thickly muscled arms. He stood just outside the ring of firelight and she had to squint to see him.

Her mother coughed in warning.

Star ducked her head. It was a relief to stare at the ground after meeting those black, black eyes. Her heart pounded and her fingers curled around the cane she held. He had passed by her camp several times this day, but at no time had he been as bold as this.

She gave a thick, hoarse cough. Then she remembered her mother's words. In an effort to disgust him, she spat on the ground. She peeked up and saw that he was watching her. Good. She spat again and waited to see the effect on him.

She thought she heard a chuckle but swiftly decided he had made a sound of disgust. Burrowing into her role of old woman, she scratched one leg lazily with her cane and gave a great burp.

Her mother turned and faced the man. "What is it?" she asked.

"Nothing, Grandmother," he said. "I but wondered how two old women fared on such a cold night. Have you enough furs to keep you warm?"

Star hoped her mother was not fooled by the man's polite tone. He looked anything but polite as he stepped into the light of their fire. And he was watching Star, though his words were directed at her mother.

Star gave another burp and scratched her head and yawned. If he did not leave soon, she would have to wield her cane to drive him away, she thought desperately.

"We do well, thank you," croaked Blue Jay. Star knew her mother was trying to sound very old so that the stranger would go away and leave them alone.

Instead, he took several more steps toward the fire. "We leave in the morning," he told them.

Ah, thought Star, what a relief it will be to see the last of the Jaguars!

"Let me put another piece of wood on the fire for you, Grandmothers," said the Jaguar, and Star wanted to groan. Why would he not just go away?

"Thank you," said Blue Jay politely.

Star wanted to stick her cane out and trip him, but she thought better of it. She contented herself with sitting there and muttering to herself as she had once seen an old man do. Perhaps that would drive him away.

He bent and put the wood on the fire, placing it carefully. Then he picked up another piece and placed it just as carefully. Star wanted to scream her frustration. *Go away!*

Instead of leaving, however, he sat down across from her. She glared at him through narrowed eyes. Yellow and orange tongues of flame leapt between them.

"My cousin lives with your people," said Blue Jay.

Star wanted to tell her mother to be quiet. Talking with him would just keep him around.

"Who is she, Grandmother?" asked the Jaguar politely. "Perhaps I know of her."

Blue Jay shook her head. "I think she is dead," she said. "I have not heard of her for many years."

The Jaguar was silent. Star wondered if he realized that was one reason why her people did not want to go with them. No one ever came back.

"Her name?" he prodded when Blue Jay kept silent.

"Fragrance," answered Blue Jay sadly. "She was very dear to me."

Now it was the Jaguar's turn to remain silent.

"Well?" asked Blue Jay after a while. "Have you heard of her? Do you know how she does?"

The Jaguar shook his head and sighed. "A woman named Fragrance accompanied her husband, a Jaguar man, to his grandmother's people. It is probably she whom you ask after. But they have been gone many seasons and I know nothing more about them."

"I worry about her," murmured Blue Jay.

The Jaguar said nothing to that. Star did not think Jaguars worried much about other people. She yawned loudly and moaned, hoping he

45

would think she was tired and go away.

Unfortunately he did not understand the subtle noises. In fact, he made himself more comfortable and lay on his side, resting his head on one elbow. His eyes narrowed, he observed, "Yon old grandmother does not say much."

Blue Jay cast a hasty glance at Star. "She is old," she said in pretended pity, and patted Star's shoulder. "She does little but drool these days."

Star summoned more saliva to her mouth but could not make herself drool under the lazy gaze of those black eyes. She ducked her head.

"Send her out into the snows, then."

That brought her head up. She glared at him. He was staring into the fire, an amused curl to his sculpted lips.

"We—we do not do such things," said Blue Jay. "Do the Jaguar People?"

He shrugged and yawned. "Sometimes. If an old one is sick or has lost her senses, then yes, my people will send her out into the snows in the coldest time of the winter. Then her food can be given to someone else."

A shiver went through Star and she glared at him. She knew she should stay silent, let his words pass, but she was too angry. He would not be uncontested in his cruelty! "You Jaguars sound like a merciless people," she croaked, hoping she sounded ancient.

"Or practical," he shot back. He reached lazily for another piece of wood to put on the fire.

Star flushed. "Old ones should not be put out to die!" She wanted to rap him with her cane.

He placed the wood on the flames and sparks flew and wood popped.

"Yon grandmother still seems to have her wits about her," he observed to Blue Jay. "Perhaps she is not ready for the snows just yet."

Star ground her teeth.

"She is actually very sweet," murmured Blue Jay, staring hard in warning at Star.

But Star shrugged off the warning. Why, that could be her mother he was talking about putting into the snows! "Perhaps," she said through gritted teeth, "certain hunters should be sent out into the cold."

He stared at her. His lips parted to show even, white teeth. "They would not starve, then, would they? After all, they are hunters."

"Without their weapons," snarled Star.

"Hmmmm." He pondered that. "It might be effective." Then he smiled that white smile again.

Star's hand gripping the cane was shaking. She had never met such an infuriating man! He was truly the worst—far worse than Gopher, her lazy suitor who did not share his meat with anyone!

Blue Jay said nervously, "I think it is best if we old ones retire."

"Yes, that would be wise," answered the infuriating man easily. "Old grandmothers do need their sleep. Yon grandmother seems to be choking on something," he observed solicitously.

Star was indeed choking, choking on anger. She contented herself with gnashing her teeth and glaring at him. She waved the cane in his direction.

"Careful with the cane, Grandmother," he

warned. "You need it for getting around."

He got to his feet and sauntered around the fire, crossing to where Star sat.

She felt his unwanted hand on her arm propelling her to her feet. She shook his hand away.

"Tough old bird," he muttered under his breath. To Blue Jay he said, "I will just aid this old one to her bed." His hand clamped her arm again.

Blue Jay fluttered nervously behind them. "I can help her—"

"She is surprisingly heavy," he observed.

Star's cane shot out and gave him a rap to the shins.

He staggered and almost fell, but he righted himself by leaning on her. Then he jammed his foot between her ankles and jerked one leg out.

Arms waving, she somehow managed to maintain her balance and scuttle out of his way. Her breath whistled in and out in her rage. How extremely rude this man was! Never had she encountered such a creature in all her life!

"There, there, old Grandmother," he crooned. "Let me help you into your tent."

Blue Jay darted here and there, behind them, now ahead of them, trying to hasten Star's entrance into the tent.

"Let me," implored Blue Jay. "I can help her now."

"Only a little farther," he murmured. "A little farther. There. Very good, Grandmother."

Star stood glaring at the tent flap, so angry she did not know what she was doing.

Blue Jay gave her a gentle push. "Go in, go in," she murmured. "Please, just go in."

Broken Promise

Drawing in a lungful of air, Star spun around to face the Jaguar. "Thank you for your help," she gritted.

His white grin flashed in the moonlight. "I am honored to be able to help an old grandmother." He chuckled. "Ah, your cane. You forgot your cane." His eyes held hers as he handed the old spear to her, butt end first.

She snatched it out of his hand, whirled, and disappeared into the safety of the tent.

Blue Jay followed and carefully closed the tent flap.

Behind them, Star heard infuriating laughter as the Jaguar walked away into the night.

Chapter Five

"The Badger men come," whispered the Jaguar sentry.

Falcon scrambled from his bedskins and strapped on his belt with the dangling obsidian knives. He grabbed up his spear.

"They are sneaking through the forest, thinking to surprise us," murmured the sentry before moving on to warn the next Jaguar. "Eight of them."

Falcon ducked out of the tent and saw the shadows of his men moving in the eerie pale light of dawn. Mist swirled from the direction of the river, but in the trees it was quiet and dark. Claw ran up to him and gestured at the forest from whence the attack was expected. Six other Jaguar men swiftly joined them. They held a hasty, whispered conference; then Falcon and the others ran to the forest's edge and slipped silently between the trees.

Broken Promise

All was quiet in the Badger tents. The fires had burned low, and now and then a soft snore could be heard. Once a baby cried, then swiftly hushed.

Suddenly screaming and yelling erupted from the woods as the Badger men burst from the trees and raced to the Jaguar tents to kill the sleeping invaders. But all they found were empty tents. And then they were swiftly encircled as the Jaguars ran up, sharp spears ready to pierce Badger flesh. The Badgers, caught by surprise, tried to rush the invaders, but they were too few in number to fight off the overwhelming Jaguars. They were quickly subdued, for a fight with spears and knives meant certain injury and possibly death for all eight of them, and they knew it. Reluctantly, they threw their spears onto the ground to signify their surrender.

The fight was over just as the sun rose to herald a new day. Eight strong young Badger men were tied up.

The slave catchers were most pleased. "Now we have slaves!" cried Hooknose jubilantly as he and Red Jaw ran in happy circles around the captured men. "Strong slaves for the Fish Eaters!"

The noise of the fight had awakened the Badger women and they crawled out of their tents. When they heard the slave catchers' cries—and the words—they got to their feet. Like a burning fire sweeping the dried grass of a prairie, panic swept among them.

"Our men are captured!" cried one.

"It is the dreaded slave catchers!"

"They are here to capture us, too! Aaaaiiieeeee!"

cried another woman, tugging at her small daughter's hand. They began running, away from the tents, toward the forest.

Hooknose and Red Jaw laughed and shouted and shook their spears at the women. More women began running, carrying small children in their arms. Everywhere Falcon looked, he saw women fleeing to the forest.

"Chase after the women!" Claw screamed. "They are escaping!"

But the Badger women and children had a slight lead and they ran swiftly. Guiding them was a long-legged heron—without her cane.

Hooknose and Red Jaw did not join in the chase. They gloated with satisfaction at the capture of the eight healthy young men and stayed to guard their prizes.

Falcon threw aside his spear and started running. He raced across the trampled grass, passing several of the Badger women who looked at him in fearful surprise as he ran by them. His presence scared them into running faster.

He was rapidly gaining on the one he sought, because she was slowed by her heavier mother. He saw her glance over her shoulder. When she saw him, she pulled harder on her mother's arm.

They disappeared into the forest and Falcon chuckled to himself. She would not get far now.

But when he reached the trees, his smile vanished. It was dark and quiet. They had to be hiding. No one can disappear this fast, he thought.

He spied a different woman cowering behind a bush. She gasped when she saw him, the terror on her face changing to disbelief as he strode right past her. She scrambled for a safer hiding place.

Where was the long-legged one? He stopped and took a deep breath, scanning the trees. He jumped over an old grass-covered log and trotted farther into the woods. He halted again, listening intently.

Ah, breathing. He smiled. His hunter's instincts fully alert, he stealthily treaded on soft-soled moccasins toward her.

Star watched him stalk toward her, pure animal terror freezing her in place. She gulped air in frantic breaths. He must not find her! He must not! Some part of her brain told her he had not seen her.

They were slave catchers. Somehow, the Jaguars were in league with slave catchers!

Palpable dread coursed through her. She glanced wildly around. Her mother was safely hidden in an old rotten log. She would be safe. That knowledge comforted Star a little and calmed her panic. She must remain very, very still in this brush at the foot of a large pine tree. And very, very quiet.

He had stopped. He was listening. For what? The terrible thunder of her heart? The shudder of her breath? What? *What?*

She gripped her hands tightly together; she must not give in to the fear. She must not! She need only be quiet, silent, and he would never find her.

He stalked softly in a large circle and she knew

from his measured movements that he was a deadly hunter. And she was his prey. But he did not know where she was, she consoled herself over the pounding of her blood. He could not know, not for certain!

He surveyed the trees, his head moving slowly around. He stared directly at her and she swallowed convulsively. She prayed the screen of brush protected her from those piercing eyes. Then he started for her.

He does not know I am here, she told herself. He cannot know!

He prowled over and halted next to the tree she crouched beside. She feared that her body's trembling shook the very branches above her. She could not alert him to her presence! Why, she dared not even breathe while he was so close.

She froze when he leaned against the tree. She gave a start when he said aloud, "I wonder where she is?" There was a silence, broken only by her pounding heart, before he added, "Hmmmmm, I wonder just where can she be?"

Star's fists clenched tight. She must not move a muscle.

"She had me fooled. Yes, she did. I thought she was an old woman. But she does not run like an old woman, no. Now, where has she run to?"

Star squeezed her eyes shut, willing herself not to faint in fear. He was so close to her she could hear the soft slither of his leather clothing when he crossed his arms.

"I think," he mused aloud, still talking to the trees, "that perhaps she is a young woman. A beautiful young woman at that. Now where, in a big forest such as this, where would such a beautiful young woman hide?"

She heard him push away from the pine trunk. His soft tread carried him away from her. Hopefully, she opened her eyes. He sauntered over to a clump of pine, the trees grown so close together she could not have squeezed an arm between them.

"Is she in here?" He disappeared into the trees. Several pounding heartbeats later, he reappeared, shaking his head. "No, not in there."

He wandered thoughtfully around the trees and over to a big rock. "Is she behind here?"

He ducked behind the rock and reappeared in the time it took Star to draw a shaky breath. "No. Not there."

He shook his head and reconnoitered the forest. Once again, his eyes fell on the copse in which she hid. He prowled slowly toward it. "Now where can she be?"

Star wanted to get up and run.

He halted in front of the branches that hid her. With a swift motion, he squatted. He peered at her through the branches. "Aha," he said softly. "And what is this lovely surprise?"

Aghast at being found, she could only stare at him in horror. Then she backed out of the brush and turned and ran, careless of the saplings in her way.

Swift as an antelope, he lunged after her.

He caught her to him easily and ignored her kicks and flailing arms. Effortlessly, he threw her over one shoulder. A single swat on the backside was intended to quiet her struggles.

Star sobbed and writhed, but she might as well have been a struggling mosquito for all that he noticed. Cutting through the panic in her mind was one clear cry of silent despair. Oh, Great Spirit, help me! I am going to be a slave!

Chapter Six

When they returned to the Badger camp, Star was able to squirm off the Jaguar's shoulder. He held her to him and she was forced to slide down his hard frame to the ground. Her legs collapsed under her. When he helped her to her feet, his hand on her elbow, she shrugged his touch away and stood straight and defiant, no longer playing the hated role of bent-over hag.

She turned proudly away from him, but unfortunately she could not go far, for he kept a firm grip on her arm. Her ash-strewn hair blew against her cheek and he leaned over to brush the caked strands away. When she turned to glare at him, he stared at her mouth. She swallowed.

All around them stood crying women and children. She averted her eyes from his black ones and cast frantically about for the other Badger women.

Then she saw them, the Badger men. They sat in a sullen, silent group, bound. She took a step toward them, but his hard grip on her arm restrained her. "Easy," warned her captor. "If you go over to them, the slave catchers will think you are theirs to take."

"That is what you plan to do with me, is it not?" she snapped, drawing herself up as tall as she could. She would not beg, even though all her blood throbbed in fear.

"No," he answered, and there was a hateful, amused curl to his firm lips. "That is not what I plan to do."

Claw swaggered up to them. Star turned away, unable to look at either of the victorious Jaguars another moment.

"Who is this woman, Falcon? Where did you find her?"

Star glowered at her captors. Falcon, he was called. Bird of prey. How fitting, she thought angrily. A tiny shiver went through her.

"She is our sixth," answered Falcon, still gripping her arm. "Now we have the six women we demanded."

Claw smiled. "Yes, we do. Very good." Just then he caught sight of Red Jaw hovering near the captured women. "You, there! Get away from those women." He hurried over.

The slave catcher looked guilty and hastened back to his place guarding the captured men. Star's gaze leapt to the bound men and she gasped in fear. "Camel Stalker!"

"You know him?" Falcon tightened his grip.

Camel Stalker's face contorted in rage.

"Perhaps you were promised to him, eh?"

Star clamped her lips shut. She would tell him nothing. Nothing!

"Speak, girl!"

She looked away. He marched over to the Badger men, pulling her with him. Unwilling, she watched in growing alarm as he kneeled beside the bound Camel Stalker. She gave a tiny cry when he gripped Camel Stalker's hair and yanked his head back. He whispered something to the Badger and then pointed at Star. When Camel Stalker did nothing, the Jaguar yanked his hair harder. Finally Camel Stalker's mouth moved but Star could not hear his words. The Jaguar grinned and released Camel Stalker's hair.

Star met Camel Stalker's stricken eyes. In them she read his anger and hurt pride and the shame of his defeat. She wanted to cry. He had tried to help her; all the Badger men had tried. Not cowards, they had returned from their hunt and mounted a raid against the more powerful Jaguars, a raid that had unfortunately failed to free the women.

"I will not forget you," she mouthed silently to Camel Stalker. He regarded her bleakly. Then he dropped his gaze.

He thinks he has nothing to offer me, she thought. No doubt he berates himself; but I know he tried to help me.

She read his self-condemning failure on his worn, bruised, handsome face. "Oh, Camel Stalker," she moaned sadly. Her dreams of a happy marriage to him were as dead as the ashes on her head. "Oh, Camel Stalker . . ."

"He cannot help you," said Falcon. "He goes into slavery with the Fish Eaters. You will not see him again!"

He could be speaking of an animal hunt, so indifferent is he, she thought. No, he would show more interest in a hunt. He does not care what happens to my people!

Then she remembered her mother, hidden in the fallen log. *Thank the Great Spirit that my mother is safe!*

The Jaguar pushed her ahead to the path to the river. "Let me see what you look like without all that mud on you."

They walked in silence to the water, Star scrutinizing the cottonwoods and aspens and brush, looking for any opportunity to escape. But he allowed her none.

She stood stock-still beside the river, unwilling to help him in any way.

"Go in." He pointed at the water.

She took a step.

"Do I have to wash you myself?"

She shrugged, uncaring of what he said or did. Her people were destroyed, her promised husband captured and about to be sold into slavery. Despair settled like a cold hand on her heart.

He waded out into the water with her in tow. She let herself be led. She wanted to retreat to a secret place inside herself and never come out. But he would not let her.

He started splashing the cold water on her, on her arms, on her legs. Finally the cold shock snapped her out of her lethargy and she began to wash the mud off her face. She pushed him away and dipped her head in the water and scrubbed at her scalp. How good it felt to be rid of the mud and ash at last!

When she was done, she waded out of the water, not caring that her dress was wet, that her hair hung in long wet hanks down her back.

He stood on the shore, arms across his chest, and his cold eyes bored into her. She swung away from his avid gaze and took several sauntering steps back to the trail.

He gripped her arm. "Not so swiftly, my Badger maiden," he said. How she loathed that half-twisted smile!

"What do they call you?"

She regarded him in haughty silence.

"Your name?"

She lifted her chin. "I will die before I tell you my name," she said.

He appeared startled at the depth of her anger at him. What does he expect? she thought. That he can take my people into slavery, steal me away, and that I will not hate him for it?

"I will find out," he said, stoniness in his voice.

He can be stubborn, she realized. Well, not as stubborn as I am!

They returned to the Badger camp in silence, Star walking straight and tall ahead of him. She swept into her tent and gathered up her bedskins and sewing needles and her leather hair ornaments. She was about to leave when she spied a woven reed basket. Carefully folded away inside it lay her favorite dress, a gift from her mother. Blue Jay had tanned the pale doeskin to a fine softness, then laboriously sewn on every one of the black and white porcupine quills decorating the breast. Folded under the dress was a pair of matching moccasins, also ornamented with quills. Star had worn the dress and moccasins but once, at her coming-of-age ceremony to announce to her people that she was an adult woman. She clutched the basket to her chest.

"What is taking so long in there?" came Falcon's deep voice.

Hastily, Star threw her needles and hair ornaments on top of the dress. She snatched up a small tanned hide of cottontail rabbit and stuffed it on top of her implements. There! He would not know of her precious dress. To hide it further, she grabbed a small basket of dried herbs used for healing and crammed it under the bigger basket's handle. Now the dress was well hidden. She could not leave her dress behind; she could not! About to be torn away from everyone she loved, she would take this with her into her new life, a reminder of the love she had grown up with.

"Woman!" came the imperious voice on the other side of the tent flap.

Falcon still lingered outside the tent. He is afraid I will escape, thought Star. He is right to fear, for on my first opportunity, I will!

She stroked her hair to one side of her face, calming herself with the gesture, then stepped out of the tent. "I am ready."

She must memorize her last view of the river and the trees. She would return and find her mother, but she had no knowledge of when that would be. For now, she etched the vista of river and grasslands and forest and huge rocks on her mind, searching for and memorizing landmarks so that she could find this place in any season.

The Jaguars were herding the women into a group. She was surprised to see that they were not taking all the women. Only the five they had claimed earlier. And herself, of course. *Do they have honor after all?* The question blew away in the wind when he approached her.

"We leave now," he said.

She averted her eyes and regarded the Badger women who were allowed to remain. Without a word to him, she strode over and spoke to Grouse, her mother's friend who was also the mother of Finds the Marten, now one of the captured men. She was aware that Falcon followed her, though not closely.

"Tell my mother I will return," she told Grouse. The frightened woman nodded and glanced at the Jaguar captor.

Star saw the fear in her eyes. "Tell my mother that I will return!" hissed Star, as if by the force of her words she could make them come true.

Grouse's lips quivered as her eyes focused on something over Star's shoulder. Falcon was standing there.

She felt his hand on her shoulder, jerking her back, away from Grouse, away from her mother, away from her people.

She turned away, not looking at Grouse, not seeing the angry sullen men, and especially not seeing *him*, the Jaguar. But he would not let her go.

"Tell me your name," he said.

She shook her head.

"Tell me your name or I will go to your promised man and force him to tell me."

She glared at him, searching his obsidian eyes to see if he meant what he said. But she did not know him, did not know if he did what he said. She tightened her lips. Let him go to Camel Stalker.

He must have realized that she had no intention of telling him anything because he shrugged and sauntered over to the bound Badger men. Again, he squatted down beside Camel Stalker and said something in a low voice. Camel Stalker glowered at Star and shook his head.

What does he say to Camel Stalker? she wondered frantically. Whatever it is, he lies! she wanted to scream. But surely Camel Stalker knows he lies. Surely he would not believe anything the Jaguar tells him!

Falcon said something else. Camel Stalker shook his head, his lips clamped tight.

Ah, he will not tell, she thought. Camel Stalker protects me! She cast him a trembling smile.

Then the Jaguar pulled out his knife. He held it casually in his hand as he spoke in a low voice with Camel Stalker.

His threat was obvious to Star when Camel Stalker's stricken eyes met hers. Her heart pounded in fear. "Tell him, Camel Stalker!" she whispered. "It is better to tell him my name than to die!"

She waited, mouth dry, hearing only the blowing wind, her eyes locked upon Camel Stalker's.

When his lips shaped her name, she wanted to weep. He dropped his gaze and she felt her tears well. *Oh, Camel Stalker! I understand. You had to do it. But still*—She turned away, anger surging through her at his forced betrayal, and anger at the Jaguar for taking the last bit of dignity from him.

Falcon joined her, a smug smile on his face. "He would have made a poor husband," he assured her. "He gives up too easily."

"You had a knife," spat Star. "What else could he do? Die?"

Falcon shrugged. "I might have used the knife. I might not have."

Star bared her teeth at him. "He did not know that. I thought you would use it."

He grinned. "Probably, I would have."

She glared at him. "I do not understand you, Jaguar. You threaten a man's life with your knife and then disparage him for succumbing to your threat."

"It matters not."

"It does matter." She glowered at him. "It matters very much."

"Nothing matters." His white teeth gleamed and she felt her anger surge anew.

"My life matters!" she answered angrily. "Camel Stalker's life matters. It matters that you are taking me from my home, from the mother I love. . . ." She swallowed, unable to continue as she thought of leaving her mother.

His eyes grew suddenly cold. "Forget her. Forget your people. You will come and live with me now."

"I do not want to live with you!"

He glared at her and took a step forward. "You

will live with me. I won you by my strength! No man will take you from me. Your promised man surely cannot!"

She hated the sneer on his face.

"I will keep you. You are mine to do with as I please. You will work for me, tan hides for me, sew my clothes, cook meat for me, and you will bear my children."

"No!"

His lips tightened, the scar on his face whitened, and a muscle in his jaw ticked. "You have no choice, woman! I have chosen you. You come with me now!"

She saw his blurred image through her tears. "Does nothing matter to you? You know I do not want to go with you. Are you so desperate for a woman that you will choose one who does not want you?"

His hooded eyes watched her out of a stony face. "If I want to."

She shook her head, unable to believe she was being forced away from her mother, from all she held dear. "You know nothing," she said, shaking her head. "Nothing."

He gave her a push in the direction of the sobbing women. "I know that it is only what I can take and hold in my hands that matters. Everything else is fleeting. My life, your life. Your very breath . . . all of it is fleeting. What matters is *now*. What I can take and what *I* want."

Her eyes widened. "What happened to you?" she whispered. "Whatever happened to you that you should think like this?"

They glared at each other.

66

"Understand this, Badger woman," he snarled at last. "I have lost everything. I have nothing else to lose. And nothing and no one will ever mean anything to me again!"

He gave her a push in the direction of the sobbing women and strode away.

She stared after him, pondering his words, dazed. Finally she picked up her basket and possessions and stumbled over to the crying brides. Inside, she felt as frozen as glacial ice. Sageflower reached for her hand to comfort her, and though Star felt the warmth of the other's flesh, it did not reach her heart.

Suddenly there was loud yelling as Red Jaw came running through the camp, a girl and a boy tucked under each arm. Star watched, stunned, as their mother, Crow, staggered after her children. "Give them back, give them back!" cried the distraught woman.

But Red Jaw shook his head and yelled to Hooknose, "Let us leave! I want to sell these ones. They will fetch many shells."

Hooknose laughed and roused the Badger men to their feet. "Come on, you wood rats! Move!"

The tired, humiliated little caravan set off. Crow ran after her children, but Star could see that she had a long red gash in her leg. She must have been wounded in the ill-fated Badger raid because she could barely walk.

Star closed her eyes against the pitiful sight of the mother dragging her leg, holding out empty arms, and crying, "Bring them back. You cannot take them! They are my babies!"

"What is the meaning of this?" demanded Claw,

and hope surged suddenly through Star's frozen breast. "Why are you taking these children?"

"They will fetch a good price," puffed Red Jaw, trying to maintain his grip on the struggling children.

Claw was frowning. "But—"

"I will give you part of the price that I get for them," said Red Jaw. "It will be much. Fish Eaters pay dearly for strong, healthy children such as these."

Claw looked uncertain.

"Half. You can have half," puffed Red Jaw as one of the girl's flailing fists found his soft stomach.

"Half." Claw smiled then and nodded in agreement. Star's hope withered. There would be no help for the children. Her hands tightened on her basket of possessions.

The slave catchers urged the men along at a fast pace and limping Crow soon dropped far behind. Star's last sight of her Badger people was of Crow, exhausted, prostrate, arms outstretched in the dirt, sobbing as she crawled hopelessly after her stolen children.

Chapter Seven

They came to a fork in the trail. Hooknose and his captives would go down the river trail; the Jaguars would follow the sage trail back to their territory.

"Where are you taking those two children?" Falcon asked Hooknose. He kept his tone casual. He wondered why he was even asking. Some vestige of his former noble self, he supposed.

Hooknose's reply was equally casual. "To the Fish Eaters, of course. If you mean which band of them, probably to the Salmon Catchers. They like to work children. Very hard." He chuckled. "They will get plenty of work out of these two."

When Falcon said nothing more, Hooknose prodded, "But why do you want to know? Perhaps you are interested in trading a little something for the children yourself, hmmmmm?"

Falcon saw Hooknose glance at Star.

"Perhaps we could make a trade," continued

Hooknose. "I will trade the two children for your female captive."

Falcon did not like it that Hooknose understood his interest so readily. Seeing the children torn from their mother had given Falcon a vague twinge of regret, remorse . . . something, he did not know what. Just that it did not sit well with him. But what was he going to do about it?

As he had told his Badger captive, Star, he knew that it did not matter what he did. To do good, to do evil, mattered not at all. He had no control over his life. What happened, happened. The best thing he could do was seize any opportunity to do what *he* wanted. And it amused him to find himself in the odd position that he, who could never have what he wanted most—his dead son's life back again—he had the power to decide if a Badger woman was to live or die. He who could not even control his own life, could control hers. What a strange game life is, he thought. There are no rules, so you make them up as you go along, this rule for this time, that rule for another time. And then you throw them all out if it appeals to you, because nothing matters. Nothing.

And as for the two stolen children, for him to help those children would mean as little as if he did not help them. He had learned that lesson well. There was no Great Spirit, so what did it matter what he did? No one was going to judge his actions for goodness or kindness or honesty; no one was going to reward him for any good that he did nor punish him for any cruelty or evil that he wrought. There was nothing. Nothing. If there were, then his son Hawk would never have died—

No! he warned himself. Stop this thinking. No good ever came from churning up the past. He must stop. Now.

"The children?" Hooknose watched him curiously.

Falcon eyed the children. Red Jaw had tied their hands in front of them and then tied the rope to the line of captured Badger men. As the men shuffled along, the children ran to keep up. Even as he watched, the girl fell. Red Jaw kicked her and yelled at her to get to her feet. The girl struggled to stand as the boy reached out his bound hands, trying to help her. Falcon turned away from the sickening scene.

"The woman captive," said Hooknose softly. "Give her to me and you can have the children."

Falcon dismissed the offer immediately. He had no intention of giving Star to this slave catcher. She would lead as miserable a life as a slave as these children would.

Then he caught himself. *What is this wretched softness in me, the kind that yearns for children and a woman? I know all too well how that leads to death and humiliation and despair. No, it is better to care about no one, to care nothing about any living creature.* "No," he answered. "Not interested."

He turned his back on Hooknose and walked over to where Claw and the other Jaguars stood. The women had stopped crying; some looked exhausted from the short walk they had endured. Star, however, was standing straight and tall, her black hair blowing like a thick cape in the cool wind. He wanted to touch the thick mane, as blue-black and as shiny as a raven's wing, but he knew she would not tolerate his touch.

"Why were you talking to Hooknose?" Claw sounded suspicious. "I do not want you interfering, Falcon. Those children will be sold and I will have a share of the price they bring. Red Jaw told me so."

Falcon laughed. "You expect a slave catcher to keep his word to you? You are mistaken to think that."

Claw glanced at the listening Jaguars and flushed in humiliation. "Do not mock me," he warned.

Falcon grinned. He did not care whether Claw was embarrassed nor about what Claw did. Nor about what any of them did. Falcon was merely a breathing, hollow man with no heart left.

He shrugged. "It is nothing to me what you and the slave catcher agreed."

"Good. Then do not interfere with my plans."

Falcon grinned. "I must check on my captive," he said.

"She is one of the brides for the men. When we get to our camp we will decide whom she will wed," said Claw.

Falcon spun around. "I have already decided. She is mine!"

"Now listen to me," said one of the other Jaguars, stepping forward. Lance was a heavyset man. "My two brothers helped me hunt for the furs to give as gifts for a Badger woman. And I gave gifts. I expect a wife. You cannot just come along and take one of the women."

Falcon shrugged. "It is nothing to me what you and your brothers did."

Lance said angrily, "Ever since your wife left you, you have become a different man, Falcon. A dishonorable man."

Falcon's eyes hooded and he reached for his knife. "I captured the Badger woman. I keep her. If you want to fight me for her, do so."

Lance outweighed Falcon and they both knew it. But Falcon had the advantages of height and swiftness. Both knew that, too.

Lance glanced around at the stony faces of his fellow Jaguars. "I will not fight you," he replied at last. "But it troubles me that you behave this way."

Falcon shrugged and kept his hand on his knife hilt. "Anyone else wish to fight me for the woman?"

His eyes drifted over the watching Jaguars in challenge. No one stepped forward.

"Then I will keep her," he said. "And I am not giving any gifts for her. I am stealing her." He moved his hand away from the knife.

Claw said, "But we agreed when we went on the bride quest that we would give gifts—"

"No gifts were given for those children." Falcon pointed at the bound children trailing along behind the departing slave catchers.

Claw glanced at his fellow Jaguars for support. "Nothing was said about children. If the slave catchers want children, well, I—I think it is fine to let them sell children."

"And the rest of you Jaguar men? Do you agree?" Falcon was amused as he waited for

73

their answer. Not having to choose to do good acts any longer truly freed a man, he thought. His knowledge that nothing mattered gave him a whole new view of his fellows and their actions. It was amusing to see which ones tried to behave honorably. Claw, now, sometimes he acted as an honorable, honest man, and sometimes not.

Once Falcon had been an honorable man, but no longer.

Some of them truly struggled with the question. He could see it on their faces. But he also saw that no one wanted to challenge Claw. So much for honor.

Falcon laughed. "You cannot tell me what to do with my captive. Not if you steal sobbing children away from their mothers." His gaze roved over the frowning men. "How many of your wives would allow their children to be taken away? How many of you would let your children be taken?"

Silence.

He turned to Claw. "So. You will get your shells from the slave catchers and be a happy man. I will get my captive. There is nothing more to say."

The men gathered their belongings together. "Come," Falcon said to Star. "You can walk with me. No need to walk with the others."

"I prefer walking with the other women." She drew back coldly.

He laughed. "Do as I say, Star, and we will have a good life together."

"I do not want a life with you!" she hissed.

"You have no choice, woman." He chuckled and pushed her ahead. "You belong to me now."

Chapter Eight

Falcon glanced at Star, unperturbed by the anger emanating from her. Why had he stolen her? he wondered. He had no need of a wife. After the unfaithful Tula had left him, he had decided he did not want another woman in his life—ever. So why had he allowed this woman to interrupt his plans for a solitary life?

He eyed her as she walked beside him. Her knife-straight nose, her flashing dark eyes appealed to him. She tossed her head and her thick dark hair fell behind her shoulders, revealing the strong lines of her jaw. She was tall and slim and strong as she matched steps beside him.

"What will happen to the two children?" Her voice cut through his thoughts.

"They will be sold to the Salmon Catchers."

She did not like that answer. He could tell by

the way she frowned intently and watched her footfalls. "I have known them since they were tiny babies."

What did she expect from him?

"Their mother, Crow, has no other children."

"Perhaps she will have more," Falcon answered. "If she recovers from that bad gash in her leg. Sometimes people can die from bad wounds."

He was amused at her angry glance. Did she think, then, that he wanted the mother dead? Why, this angry beauty thought him worse than he truly was! He chuckled.

"It would be a terrible thing to lose your children," she pointed out.

His smile faded. He tightened his grip on his spear.

"I think it is very wrong to steal children away from their mothers. Or fathers."

He quickened his pace.

"Crow has no husband. Her husband died. She is all alone."

Why was she telling him this? What did he care what had happened to the injured woman and her ill-fated children?

"I remember holding the little boy when he was a baby. Milky is his childhood name because he liked his mother's milk so much. The girl's name is—"

"Silence!" roared Falcon and shook his spear.

Her eyes widened and she halted. He saw that he had frightened her and he struggled to calm himself. "I do not wish to hear any more about those children." He kept his voice firm.

She glared at him, her black eyes burrowing

into his. "They mean nothing to you," she answered evenly. "This I know. They mean nothing to your Jaguar people. But I tell you this. They mean something to me. I love them."

He watched her stride past him in that loose-gaited way she had. He watched her straight spine in her yellow leather dress, her long black hair as it fluttered in the wind.

"Love?" he answered. "Do not talk to me of love. It does not exist!"

She avoided him after that. When they stopped to camp for the night, she gathered what wood she could find for a fire, but she was wary of him and kept her distance.

On their journeys, the Jaguars always carried dried meat for their sustenance. They would sometimes supplement this food with fresh meat if they were fortunate enough to find a deer or elk, but a group of 20 men and six women made so much noise on the trail that it was a hopeless task to hunt unless a man went hunting in another direction and left the main group.

"I want you to stay with the women," said Falcon, after he and Star had eaten their dried meat in silence.

She opened her mouth, then snapped it shut.

"I am going hunting." He answered her unasked question. "I may be gone overnight."

She shrugged, maintaining her silence and her indifference to him.

He got up and walked over to Claw's fire. He told Claw he was going hunting. When Claw glanced at Star, Falcon leaned closer to him and said, "I charge you with the care of my Badger

77

woman. Keep the other men away from her. If anything happens to her while I am gone, I will seek revenge."

Claw tried to hide his fear, but Falcon read it easily in the other's dark eyes. Claw finally nodded.

Falcon returned to the small fire he had shared with the Badger woman. "Get your bedskins and possessions and move over to the women's campfire." He saw that her jaw was set. "I tell you this so you will not be left alone."

She narrowed her eyes at him, then rose to do as he bid.

When he saw that she had found a place by the Badger women's fire, he headed back along the trail they had just traveled. He wondered if deer meat would appeal to a Badger woman's palate.

Chapter Nine

Dawn was breaking. Falcon had hidden his spear farther back on the river trail, so he pulled out his knife and crept quietly through the brush until he was close enough to discern the sleeping forms.

He had not meant to track them, truly he had not. It was just that once he was away from the other Jaguars, he had not thought of deer. His moccasins had set him on a different path, the one to the river.

He peered through a screen of low brush separating him from the slave catchers' camp. Why are you here? he demanded of himself.

But he knew why. A small, shadowed body rolled over and moaned. Probably the girl. Next to her was another small body, the boy. Snores came from the bound Badger men.

Yes, it was the girl. And Milky. He chuckled softly to himself at the boy's baby name. When he became a young man, Milky would try very hard to be a brave hunter; he would do anything to shed that name.

Falcon grew grim. Milky would have little chance to reach manhood if he were sold as a slave.

Creeping closer, Falcon was careful not to waken Red Jaw, who slouched against a pine tree. He has drifted off to sleep on guard duty, Falcon realized in disgust. Hooknose snored on the other side of the fire, tossing now and then. He was the one to watch out for.

Falcon was on his belly now, slithering forward. Carefully he cut the bindings of the girl, then the boy. Neither awoke. He glanced over at Hooknose. Still asleep.

Red Jaw moaned. Falcon froze and waited. Red Jaw relaxed into gentle snores once again.

Falcon crouched and tucked his knife into his twisted leather belt. Then he reached for the girl. Her muffled moans would wake the others, so he put his hand over her mouth and shook his head. Her brown eyes widened. "I will take you to your mother," whispered Falcon. She nodded sleepily and let him pick her up.

He placed her carefully over one shoulder, then lifted the boy and tucked him under one arm. He remembered that his son would have been this age had he not—Stop it! he commanded himself. With gritted teeth, Falcon crept away with his two burdens.

Just as he reached the brush screen, he heard a cry. "Ayyyyyy!" It was Hooknose.

Falcon raced along the river trail, the girl child

bobbing on his shoulder, the boy still tucked under his arm. No time to pick up his spear— he ran fast to save the children and himself.

Footsteps pounded behind him, and Hook- nose's angry screams to stop grew louder. Hooknose had to wake Red Jaw with those cries, thought Falcon, and the younger slave catcher would soon join the pursuit. Falcon quickened his pace.

He ran as fast as he could, but the river trail now sloped upward along a cliff. The children were heavy as he ran and they slowed him. He hoped the steep incline slowed Hooknose just as much.

Falcon reached the top of the hill and glanced hurriedly about, searching frantically for a place to hide the children. Ahead of him, the trail fol- lowed the high river cliff, up and then down. If he ran that trail, he would soon tire and the weight of the children would slow him until Hooknose caught up.

Suddenly Falcon discerned a narrow deer path leading off from the main trail into a forested area. He veered onto the deer path, the children squirming under his arms.

"You must be very still and quiet," he gasped to the children in as calm a voice as he could manage. "Otherwise the bad men will catch you again."

They quieted instantly.

"Now I am going to hide you under that tree." He gestured with his chin. "You must hide there from the bad men. You must be very strong and very quiet. I will lead them away from you. Later

I will come back and get you, so do not move from here."

He set the children down at the base of a large cottonwood. The thick lower branches would screen them from prying eyes.

He wondered if they understood him. It had been some time since he had spoken with a child.

"You must stay very quiet." He glanced in the direction he had come. Hooknose's yells were becoming louder. "Do you understand?"

The girl answered with a soft "Yes." The boy nodded and Falcon pushed them down under the low branches.

"Keep close to the ground," he advised them. Then he set off at a lope, carelessly breaking branches to attract Hooknose's attention. Knife out, he jogged along the deer trail, farther into the forest.

Hooknose gave a yell when he saw Falcon and barreled up the deer path. "You!" he screamed. "Stop! Stop at once!"

Falcon stood on the trail and faced the oncoming, blundering Hooknose. To amuse himself as he waited, Falcon tossed his obsidian knife back and forth from hand to hand. He smirked when Hooknose slowed, then hesitated.

"What did you do with them?" puffed the slave catcher as he searched for his missing property. "Where are they?"

"Who?" Falcon shrugged.

"Do not try to fool me! You know who I mean. The two children you stole!"

Falcon spun the knife up into the air. It sliced down, blade first, and dug into the ground half-way between Hooknose's two splayed feet. The slave catcher jumped back a pace.

His eyes narrowed. "Do not seek to anger me further, Jaguar man," he spat. "I am not a man to make an enemy of."

"Indeed?" sneered Falcon. "And why would I want a slave catcher for a friend?"

Hooknose put his hands on his fleshy hips and stared at Falcon. "I have heard about you, Jaguar. You are the one that Claw spoke of. The one he said did not care anymore. Not about anyone or anything."

Falcon shrugged. Hooknose stepped back another pace as Falcon yawned and retrieved the knife. He flashed the knife up under the big man's nose.

Hooknose stood his ground, though his sagging face flushed. "I would have use for such a man," he said softly. "A man who no longer cared about anyone or anything."

Falcon smiled and waved the knife under Hooknose's beak.

Hooknose did not flinch. "Tell me where the children are. I will share the wealth with you. I know you planned to steal them from me and trade them to the Fish Eaters on your own, but I know the Fish Eaters' ways. I will get us a much better deal." He swallowed. "What do you say?"

Falcon smiled. "No."

"Half. I will give you half of what we get for them."

"No."

83

"You cannot want more! Why, I must have my share. It is only fair!"

Falcon laughed. He placed his knife in his twisted waistband. "I will keep the children and I will not share with you at all."

"You cannot do this!" Hooknose's neck veins bulged in his anger. "Those children are mine to trade!"

Falcon chuckled. "Not anymore." He glared at Hooknose. "They are mine to trade. Now draw your weapon or leave!" Indeed, Hooknose was becoming tiresome with his useless protests.

Hooknose pushed Falcon. Falcon pushed him back. Harder. Hooknose snarled, "Do not think I will forget this, Jaguar man."

Falcon glowered. "I care little whether you forget your own name, slave catcher."

"A man who walks down a deer path alone had better watch his back for wolves!" said Hooknose.

"Those are wise words," agreed Falcon. "You would do well to heed your own proverb."

Hooknose spat. "I do not walk alone," he boasted. "I have friends!"

"And who do you call friend? Red Jaw?" answered Falcon. "Pah, you were ready to cheat him when you bargained with me for the children. Claw? Pah! You were ready to forget his promised share in your eager offer to me. I think," he added thoughtfully, staring into Hooknose's contorted face, "that friendship with you is very fleeting. Like a doe that flees before a wolf."

"You twist my words and insult my good name!" roared the slave catcher.

"I do."

Hooknose leapt upon him then and tried to pummel his shoulders. Falcon wrestled the man to the ground and got a choke-hold on his throat. "Understand this, slave catcher," he grunted. "I care nothing for you or your deals. Now, admit you lost the children. And go away."

He dragged the stout slave catcher to his feet, turned him around, and kicked him in the buttocks, sending him sprawling.

Hooknose got to his feet, his furious face a deep shade of red. "I will not forget this!" His breath whistled in and out and he shook his fist at Falcon. "I will remember you, Jaguar. And I will not rest until we are even!"

"Ever the trader, I see," said Falcon dryly.

Hooknose gave one last bellow of impotent rage, then swung around and marched back along the deer path, muttering dire imprecations. Falcon laughed to see him go.

When he was certain that the burly man had truly disappeared, he returned to the cottonwood tree and pulled the children out from under the branches.

They looked cold and frightened. Falcon took off his fur cape and gave it to the girl to wear, then peeled off his falcon design leather shirt and placed it over the boy's shoulders. The garments were too big for either child but at least they kept them warm. He took each child by a hand. Their hands were cold, too.

"Come," he said. "Let us retrieve my spear and return you to your mother."

Chapter Ten

Once Falcon and the children had put a safe distance between themselves and Hooknose, Falcon gave in to their complaints and let them lie down to sleep. They slept so soundly that it was well into the afternoon before he could wake them. Only mention of their mother served to rouse them enough to get them to their feet. They picked late blackberries off a low, prickly plant, and then, stomachs full, let Falcon lead them onward.

Besides knowing their mother's name, Falcon now knew that Crow's husband had been killed and that another hunter who had been courting her had been taken by the slave catchers in the raid. Truly, Falcon knew everything there was to know about Crow, her children, her deceased husband, and her prospective one, because Milky and his sister, Berry, once started, had not stopped talking. They had chattered on and on. In that

way, at least, Milky did not remind him of his
son. . . .

Falcon had finally told them that he needed
silence so that he could hunt a rabbit or deer to
bring to Crow.

Surprisingly, Berry and Milky were quiet and
Falcon was able to stalk and kill a small doe. But
then, while he skinned the animal, they resumed
asking questions and offering advice. They talked
on as he butchered the carcass and then Berry
insisted that they could both help him carry the
meat to their camp. Falcon let them each stagger
under a load of meat, smiling to himself when
Milky told him that one day he, too, would hunt
and kill such a huge deer.

Falcon felt awkward returning to the place of
the bridal quest. For the Jaguars, it had been successful. For the Badgers, it had been disastrous.
And though the camp looked peaceful, with the
evening sun lighting the rocky black hills behind
the camp and casting a dusty golden glow on the
tents scattered across the dried grass, he doubted
the inhabitants would act peaceably toward him,
a Jaguar.

Smoke from the flickering fires mixed with the
scent of roasting vegetables. The desultory con-
versations of women and children filled the air.
Two dogs barked and circled Falcon and the children, sniffing at the raw meat.

Falcon scared the dogs away. Milky and Berry
had fallen silent at the sight of their home camp.
Then Berry, laden with meat, trotted toward a
tent that Falcon guessed was Crow's. Milky lum-
bered after her.

"Mama! Mama!" Their cries alerted the other Badgers. Women looked up from where they cooked roots by their fires.

Falcon followed, a deer haunch across one shoulder. He halted when a black-haired woman, drawn by the dogs' barking and the children's shrill cries, crawled out of the flap.

She got to her feet, peering around for the source of the noise. When she spied Milky and Berry, she hesitated.

Uncertainly, she started toward them, dragging her injured leg. After several steps she halted, staring, mouth open. Disbelief, then joy, flickered on her face. Arms outstretched, she started forward again, limping as fast as she could go. "My babies! My babies!" she screamed.

The dusty, tired, meat-bloodied children ran into her embrace. When she started crying and laughing and talking all at once, Falcon had to turn away. He could not bear to see such joy, such hope, such love on a parent's face. It reminded him too much of his own son—Stop! he ordered himself. No more of this!

Stiffly, he set the meat down beside a tent and started back the way he had come. He had gone several steps when he heard shouts behind him. He glanced over his shoulder. Milky and Berry were pointing and calling out to him.

With a sigh, Falcon swung around to face them. The two children came running to him, their mother limping slowly behind. When she was abreast of him, she regarded him out of sparkling dark eyes. "Thank you," she murmured, tears streaking the dust on her face. "Thank you for my children!"

He nodded once in acknowledgment, then walked away again.

She limped after him. "Wait! Can I give you a meal? A gift? I want to thank you. . . ."

"No need," he said gruffly. "I expect no gifts."

"Yes, but I want—"

"No." His harshness cut her off and he watched her shrink away a little. Then Berry planted herself in front of him. "My mother wants you to eat with us. Come and eat with us!" She took his hand.

Reluctantly, Falcon let the little girl lead him back to Crow's tent. He sat down beside the fire and Crow bustled about while Berry helped prepare the deer. They left Falcon to his own thoughts. He saw that Crow chattered as much as her children. He smiled to himself. He had probably done Hooknose a favor, saving him from the incessant noise.

Word of Falcon's arrival had spread through the Badger camp and some of the other women came to gape at him. One of them was Star's mother. He saw her watching him out of angry eyes, but her mouth stayed clamped shut in a silent, tense line and she did not approach him. Crow invited them all to stay, and the meal became almost festive, a subdued celebration of Milky and Berry's return. After the meal, the women returned to their own fires.

Falcon rose and thanked Crow. When she pressed him to stay, he murmured, "I must leave this night." Memories of Star made him anxious to rejoin the Jaguars, who were on the trail back to their main camp.

He trotted through the Badger camp, and had just reached the edge of the forest when a loud hissing halted him. He swung around to see a bulky older woman running after him—Star's mother. Wary, he halted and waited.

"Where is my daughter?" she puffed.

"Why would I know that?" he answered. He shifted his spear, anxious to be gone.

"You were with the people who stole her. I know it. My friends recognized you. So do I."

She squinted, coming closer. "You are the one who took her!"

He waited, frowning at her.

"You must give her back! Return Star to me!"

He shrugged.

"You returned Milky and Berry to their mother. Bring my daughter back!"

He looked into dark eyes so like Star's. "I cannot do that."

The old woman wrung her hands. "You took her! You gave no gifts for her! You had no right to take her!"

He shifted, uncomfortable at her accusations. Then he glared at her and shouted, "No!"

Her face was agonized as she stared at him. "It is within your power—"

"I said no!"

She took a step closer. "If I were a man, I would kill you for this!"

He laughed. "If you were a man, you would be one of the captured Badgers on your way to the Fish Eaters by now."

"No," she said. "I would be stomping on your dead body."

He smirked. "Go back home, woman," he advised. "Go back to your hearth where you are safe."

She opened her mouth to speak, then clamped it shut. "You enjoy your power, I see." She paused, assessing him through narrowed eyes. Then carefully, she said, "Please help me. She . . . she is my only child. I have no other. She is everything to me. My life. My—"

"No." He did not care that his voice sounded harsh.

She grabbed his arm.

Affronted, he pulled back.

"Oh," she exclaimed. "I did not mean—" She peered at him, interpreting the look on his face as disgust. "I see that I have offended you. Well, I am an old woman and I am no good at begging. I only want my daughter back. You can help me. You know where she is—you can find her—"

"I cannot help you," he answered coldly.

"But she is in danger! She—"

"No! I cannot help you."

She glared at him. "*Will* not help me, you mean."

He refused to answer.

Frustration showed on her lined face. "Very well. You know where she is. You have stolen her and yet you choose not to help me." She glanced back at the Badger camp, then swung to face him once more. "I do not know why you brought back the two children—"

91

He clenched his teeth until he could feel a tic in his jaw.

"—but you did." She spat. "There must be some good in your heart, but I think it is hidden very deep. I certainly cannot find it!" She glared at him. "You tell my daughter when you see her—"

"I will not see her." Surprising how little the lie bothered him.

"—when you see her you tell her that I love her!"

He frowned at her in consternation. Why would the woman not believe him?

She rocked onto her tiptoes as if trying to intimidate him. "You tell her that I love her. You understand that? Love?"

Irritated, he shrugged and turned away.

"I see that you do not." Her words followed after him like wasps, annoying him and flying around his head.

He left her then. When he last glanced at her from the safety of the forest, she was standing on the trail, hands clenched on hips as she glared after him.

Chapter Eleven

"Where have you been?" demanded Claw.

Falcon ignored him. He scanned the camp, his eyes seeking his Badger captive. When he saw her, relief slid through him. He nodded at her. She swiftly glanced away.

"I said, where have you been? You told me you were going hunting and now I see you return with nothing."

Falcon glanced at Claw. "Not every hunter is fortunate enough to find game."

Claw snorted. "Not every hunter, true. But we speak of you. You get game whenever you want." He eyed Falcon suspiciously. "You have been up to something," he muttered. "I want to know what!"

Falcon tossed his words aside. "How was my Badger captive? Give you any trouble?"

Claw swung his head to glare at Star. "Oh,

you have a fine Badger woman there, let me tell you! First she led the other brides in an escape attempt. Then, when we separated her from the other women, she started an argument between Lance and Red Hawk. Lance wants her for his wife. So does Red Hawk. I had to break up their fight!"

"I returned just in time." Falcon was surprised at the ire he felt rising. Neither Lance nor Red Hawk would have her.

"Yes. You claim she is yours. Very well, *you* keep the other men from fighting over her. I am tired of doing so!"

Falcon smiled and patted Claw's shoulders. "My thanks for keeping watch over her." Truly, he thought, if Claw had not stopped the fight between Lance and Red Hawk, my captive might have been injured!

He sauntered over to where she sat by herself at the fire.

"Escape attempts? Fights? You have been a busy little Badger."

She glared at him and he was suddenly struck by the beauty of her eyes. They were wide and dark and framed with lush, long lashes. As he stared into their depths, he felt himself falling. He shook his head and glanced at her full lips to distract himself. But when she licked her dry lips with her pink tongue, he had to close his eyes and swallow. Oh, what had he done?

It was a mistake to capture a woman this beautiful, he thought. Even now his loins were calling out to him to mate with her. Tearing his eyes away from her, he forced himself to walk past her and sit down on a rock across the fire from her. Her nearness jumbled his thoughts and his senses.

He could feel her eyes upon him but he stared into the fire until he had regained an unaffected mien. When he finally allowed himself to meet her eyes, he felt a jolt run through him. Her eyes mirrored the orange flames, and he watched, fascinated, as tiny fires appeared to dance in her black eyes. "Where do you come from?" he asked in wonder, scarcely aware that he was speaking aloud.

"From the Badger People. You know that," she answered. "You are the one who took me from my people."

He shook his head to dispel the strange feelings that came over him whenever he looked at her.

"Do not deny it," she said.

"I will not deny it. Only I did not remember you as so, so . . ." *Compelling*, he wanted to say. *So beautiful.* He saw that she was waiting for him to finish his words, and the tiny flames looked cold to him suddenly. He shook his head; he must not let her know how drawn he was to her. "What have you prepared for dinner?" he asked, hoping the mundane question would put a distance between them.

"Berries," she answered shortly. He marveled that she seemed unaware of what he felt so strongly.

When she held out a handful of tiny red and blue berries to him, he walked over and stared at her palm as if he had never seen a berry before.

He struggled to focus on what he was seeing. "Is that all? Five berries?"

She shrugged. "It is better than nothing." Then she withdrew her hand and popped all the fruit into her mouth.

He watched her chew. He swallowed. "I want more than berries," he answered.

She shrugged. "Claw did not see fit to provide me with any meat to cook."

Falcon frowned and glanced over at the two other fires. At the closest one, the Badger brides were talking and murmuring among themselves. The smell of roasting venison permeated the air; they were cooking their evening meat. At the other fire lounged Claw, Lance, Red Hawk, and the other Jaguars. Lance straightened a sizzling meat stick that leaned over the fire.

Falcon could hear the hot fat sputter as it dripped into the flames. "The others have meat."

"Yes, they do. A hunter brought in a deer yesterday." He saw that her berry-stained lips were set in a stubborn line. She would tell him no more.

He stalked over to Claw. "Where is the meat for my captive woman?"

"She does not get any meat," answered Claw lazily. "She is troublesome. Troublesome women do not get fed. She must learn this."

Falcon kept a tight snare on his rising anger. "Did you feed her last night?"

"At first. I gave her some meat, but then when she started the fight between Lance and Red Hawk, I took the meat away. After that, she sat quietly. I think she was hungry." He smiled. "That will make her think carefully before rousing the anger of Jaguar men such as myself."

Falcon leaned over and grabbed Claw by both arms and yanked him to his feet. "I told you to care for my captive," he gritted. "That includes feeding her!"

Claw shrugged. "She is troublesome," he repeated. "I think she would be more manageable if she went hungry. That would make her more docile."

Falcon dropped his hands from Claw's arms. Disgust coursed through him. His captive was staring at him. "Look at her," snarled Falcon. He pushed Claw's head in the general direction of the Badger captive. "Does she look docile to you?"

"No," answered Claw. "She still looks fierce. You must starve her some more, I think. That would be my advice."

"Your advice?" snapped Falcon. "I did not ask for your advice! I asked that you care for my captive."

"I kept her alive, did I not?" argued Claw. "And she is still lively. Look how she glares at you, even as we speak."

Both Jaguars stared at the captive. She curled her upper lip in a silent snarl.

"She is not hungry enough, in my opinion." Claw sat back down beside the fire. "Join us for some venison," he offered.

"No," answered Falcon, "I will not join you. But I will take some of your meat." He pulled up two of the meat sticks, ignoring Lance's cries of protest.

Falcon sauntered back to the captive women's fire and handed Star a meat stick. She eyed him carefully before sinking her white teeth into the roasted flesh.

Falcon stared at her as they ate in silence, wondering at the new feelings that rose in him because of her. He had felt nothing for so long that numbness and indifference had been his usual state.

But because of this woman, numbness was being edged out. Taking its place were new feelings: protectiveness, anger, jealousy. He wanted to protect her from Claw's cruelty. He felt angry that she had gone hungry and angry at her for causing a fight between two men. He was jealous that Red Hawk and Lance both wanted her for a mate. Since meeting her, he had even helped two children, an action unlike him ever since his son had died and his wife had left him. What was wrong with him?

Falcon decided he did not like these new feelings. Life was simpler when one's feelings were like the cold, black embers of a hearth long dead.

Chapter Twelve

Falcon watched the sway of Star's hips as she lagged behind the other Badger women. She was taller than the rest; her black hair was thick and long and her legs were slim. He smiled to himself, enjoying the sight of her.

The Jaguar party wound their way single-file along a sagebrush-dotted gravel trail, past tall palisades of black rock. Claw stepped out of the lead and waited while his men walked by. After the Badger women had moved warily past him, he said to Falcon, "We will halt for the night at the Canyon of the Doves."

Falcon shrugged. "The women could probably use a rest."

"They are not very strong," observed Claw with a frown. "Jaguar women can walk faster."

"They will soon *be* Jaguar women," Falcon pointed out.

Claw cleared his throat. "I want the one with the dimples in her cheeks."

"Your wife," answered Falcon, "will be most pleased."

"Uh, yes, my wife. Well, that is, I, uh, I—Well, my wife will understand!" He snapped his mouth shut.

Betafor, Claw's wife, was a large, middle-aged woman with a slow, solid manner. Other Jaguar men shook their heads over how she ruled Claw and every person in his dwelling. Argumentative cries could be heard issuing from their elk-hide tent whenever she disagreed with him. Then Claw would come flying out of the tent and slink around the Jaguar camp until his wife let him back into their home. Even his grown sons and daughters always sided with Betafor, a source of great injury to the headman's pride. In fact, it was rumored in the Jaguar camp that any wisdom Claw showed actually came from Betafor.

"What are you smiling at?" demanded Claw.

"Just thinking how pleased Betafor will be with your new wife."

Claw frowned and appeared to be pondering Falcon's words. As the last Badger captive disappeared around the rocky trail, he smiled unpleasantly. "Almost as pleased as Tula."

At mention of his former wife, Falcon no longer felt like grinning. "I do not care what Tula has to say about my Badger captive."

Claw chuckled. "Oh, she will have plenty to say. You can be sure of that. And so will her husband."

"He will not get near my captive," vowed Falcon.

"Think you not? I would watch Marmot closely, were I you. Unless, of course, you want to lose a second woman to him."

Chuckling, Claw sauntered after the Badger women.

Falcon clenched his fists. Claw's words tore into his gut like a spear. It was true that Tula had left him for Marmot. Everyone in the Jaguar camp knew it. Gritting his teeth, Falcon pushed away waves of anger. Many times he had successfully fought off all feelings where she was concerned until he was numb, a form of peace. He would do so again. What did it matter that Tula had betrayed him when he had needed her most? He had learned from that. Oh, had he learned. Never again would he need anyone, love anyone, rely on anyone. No one—man, woman, or child— would ever have a chance to hurt him again.

Claw pushed past the women. Star stepped out of his way.

Falcon shook his head. He certainly would never let a Badger woman, one with troublesome ways, ever mean anything to him!

When once again he felt numb, felt his own familiar peace, he strode after the line of departing people.

Several small hills of black rock screened the Canyon of the Doves. It was a favorite place for the Jaguars to camp. Water was plentiful from the small creek trickling along the canyon floor. The winds whistled outside the canyon, but inside, the air was still, the leaves of the trees undisturbed.

There was a disadvantage to the canyon: there was only one entrance. There was no chance of retreat if an enemy entered.

Searing memories washed over Falcon whenever he visited the Canyon of the Doves. This canyon was where his beloved father had once taken him as a youth. Together they had climbed the edge of the walls.

When at last they reached the top of the towering precipice, Falcon had to gasp for breath. Standing in the wind, he thought he was ill because he had never had trouble catching his breath before. His father laughed and explained about the thin air.

Then his father raised an arm and swung it in a gentle arc as the two surveyed the land. "It is yours, my son," said his father. "All that you can see is yours."

Falcon shivered as he understood the power of the heritage his father was offering him. His father pointed to the west. "One day you will hunt fat elk in that river bottom."

He pointed to the north. "You will climb that cold ice mountain in your search for long-haired bighorn sheep."

He pointed to the east. "You will kill big deer in those hills."

Lastly he pointed to the south. "You will ambush plump antelope on that grassy plain." Then he turned to Falcon, his kindly black eyes shining. "You are a fine hunter, my son, and all this land is yours to hunt in. I, and my father before me, and his father before him, stood on this exact spot. It is Jaguar land. It is good. And someday you will stand here with your son, a fine strong son, and look out over this land and it will be your turn to show the land to him."

Wide-eyed, Falcon had surveyed the world of his father. And he had believed his father's words.

Alas, he wished now his father was alive so he could tell him how wrong he had been. His life had not been full of the good his father had predicted. Not at all. And his son was dead.

"Good spot to camp," Claw interrupted.

"There is no way out if the entrance is blocked by enemies."

Claw shrugged. "We are many. I am not afraid."

Falcon's mouth tightened and his cheek ticked where Marmot's spear had scarred his face.

"I stopped by to tell you that four of us are going hunting," said Claw.

Falcon nodded, glad to be rid of the man for a while.

"You are in charge if I am gone a long time."

"Ask someone else. I am no longer headman."

Claw glared at him. "Who else do I ask? You know this area better than any of us. You know the trail to take." He shook his head. "I do not understand you, Falcon."

Falcon met Claw's black eyes, daring him to continue.

Claw had never been known for his good judgment, and Betafor—his wisdom—was unfortunately back at the Jaguar camp. "It is time I spoke with you. You have been like this long enough. You are as prickly as a lodgepole pine;

you let none of us, your friends, speak of anything important to you. Your heart is as hard and as cold as a stone. This cannot go on. Your people need you."

Evidently Claw did not see Falcon's ticking scar. "If," continued Claw relentlessly, "it had been *my* wife who had run away with another man, I would be happy she was gone. Who wants a woman who does not want to stay? You are well rid of Tula."

Falcon froze.

"And as for your son, well, I admit that was very sad."

Falcon's grasp on his spear tightened but Claw ignored the danger sign.

"But even you must admit he would never have grown up to be a strong warrior, or even a good hunter. I do not think he could ever have hunted."

"Enough." Falcon's voice sliced through Claw's words like an obsidian blade through a hot deer liver. "It is no concern of yours what I do. I am a grown man. It is not your place to speak to me thus!" Indeed, Falcon could barely restrain himself.

Claw glanced away, beginning to understand that he had goaded a wounded bear. "I go to hunt now," he mumbled. "We need fresh meat."

Falcon watched him stumble away, and his hand grasping the spear shook with the force of his anger. He took several breaths, forcing the anger from him, unwilling to feel anything but the numbness he had lived with for so many seasons. When he calmed, he glanced over at his Badger captive. She was watching him.

Broken Promise

Walking over to her, he took several more breaths to calm himself so that when he reached her, his breathing was even and his cheek scar no longer pained him.

She bent and placed a stick on the fire and he realized she did not want to talk to him. Well, he wanted otherwise. "There will be meat tonight for the evening meal," he said.

She placed another stick on the fire.

"Look at me."

She raised her head and her dark brown eyes met his. As always, a thrill ran through him when he looked into her eyes. How could a mere woman, a captive at that, have such an effect on him? She regarded him steadily; he could read no fear on her face. "I know your name," he persisted.

Her flinch told him he had caught her off guard.

"Star."

Her eyes narrowed and she started to turn back to the fire. Some part of him wanted to prevent that. He wanted her attention on *him,* not the fire.

"I know your name is Star. I know you are a Badger woman. What else is there to know about you?"

She shrugged and reached for a stick. "Nothing."

Irritated, he asked, "Do you know my name?"

Her sly glance made him think that she did indeed. Perhaps she had overheard one of the other men say his name. "No. And I do not care to know it."

"My name is Falcon."

She placed the end of the stick carefully into the flames and prodded the fire with it until it burst into flame. The orange light outlined her beauty and a swift longing lanced through him. He took a breath and let it out slowly, again striving for the numbness, the calm.

"Say it."

She turned away then, as if looking for more wood to feed the fire. He marched around the fire. He grasped her chin and lifted her face. "Say it."

Her eyelashes were thick and a man could get lost in those eyes, he thought, feeling himself falling, falling. . . . No, he would not! "Say it," he said, and the hoarse, desperate note in his voice surprised him.

"Falcon," she snapped. Then, "Falcons are smaller than eagles. And they cannot fly as high." Contempt was in her voice.

He yanked his hand back and stared at her. "Falcons are more powerful than eagles for their size," he shot back. "They have greater courage, too."

"Ha. The female falcon is bigger than the male. He is puny." She sneered.

"Well, we are not falcons, are we? And I am bigger than you." He sneered back.

"Eagles make big, safe nests for their young. A falcon's nest is a rocky ledge. The eggs roll off." She smirked.

"To a falcon, a nest is not important."

She looked taken aback and it was his turn to smirk.

106

Silence stretched between them. He found himself liking her fiery answers. He asked, "Who are you? What manner of woman are you?"

She tilted her head, watching him, and he collected himself. "A Badger woman, of course," he murmured, frowning. "No one but a Badger woman."

She watched him, her dark eyes bright. "What did that man say to anger you so?"

He wondered why she sought out his weaknesses. "He said things he knows not the power of."

She was silent, regarding him.

"And I am not angry!"

She had the impertinence to raise an eyebrow at this. "You are." Then she reached for her digging stick. "I am going to dig roots for the evening meal."

He could detect no censure in her voice. "Very well. I will accompany you."

They set off for the creek.

When they returned, he was carrying his spear and she was laden with dirt-covered wapatoo and bulrush roots.

Claw and the other hunters had not yet returned, but two fires had been lit and several people sat around them.

Falcon walked over to the men's fire. Red Hawk was polishing a spear tip, and Betafor's brother, Slinks Away, was resharpening an already sharp obsidian blade.

Falcon could hear Star trailing along behind him.

When Red Hawk spied Star, he frowned disapprovingly at her armload of leafy stalks and roots and said to Falcon, "You would eat what a Badger woman provides? Ho! Not I. I would fear choking on poison!" He looked around at his friends, waiting for their laughter at his wit. There were a few halfhearted chuckles.

Falcon knew Red Hawk was still angry at losing Star, so he merely shrugged, having no interest in a fight. The walk by the creek with Star had soothed his anger and he felt the welcoming numbness that was so familiar to him.

His captive woman was staring at Red Hawk as though she thought his suggestion a good one.

"Cook the roots," Falcon told her. He did not want her starting a fight between him and Red Hawk. Falcon gave her a small obsidian knife with which to peel the outer skin off a bulrush root.

"Be careful," Red Hawk warned Falcon. "A Badger with a knife . . ."

Falcon waited. "Yes?"

" . . . does not know what to do with it!" And Red Hawk erupted into hearty gales of laughter. After he wiped the tears of hilarity from his eyes, he said to Slinks Away, "You saw those Badger men. They thought to sneak up on us. Well, we tricked them. They are fools."

Star's back was to the men, but Falcon could see her stiffen at what they were saying.

"They should be sold to the Fish Eaters if they cannot fight any better than that," agreed Slinks Away.

"They gave up easily," observed another.

"I jumped out from behind a tree and grabbed one of them," boasted Red Hawk. "A skinny man with a big head of hair. He tried to run away. Would not fight!"

Red Hawk jumped up from his place at the fire and began acting out the fight. "He got away from me and ran. I chased him and jumped on his back," he said. "Then we fell down and I rolled over on him." Now Red Hawk was rolling on the ground in imitation of the great fight. "Then he was on top of me, his knife out—"

The other men were on their feet now, acting out their parts in the fight.

"And I grabbed one!" yelled a Jaguar.

"Twisted his shirt right off his back!" yelled another.

"Took his spear away from him. I still have it; it's mine now!" cried Slinks Away, shaking the weapon.

The Badger woman stopped peeling roots.

"Those Badger men are such cowards!" cried Red Hawk, puffing from his exuberant fight with his imaginary opponent.

Star whirled. "Our men are brave! They were outnumbered!"

Red Hawk froze. "Silence, woman." He glanced at Falcon and demanded, "You must train your woman better than that! She has no place in our stories."

"Except as a captive," observed Falcon dryly, lounging by the fire.

Red Hawk glared at Star. "If she were my woman, I would silence her!" he said with menace.

Theresa Scott

"But she is not your woman," pointed out Falcon.

Reluctantly, Red Hawk returned to his story-telling, but he was less exuberant and cast frowns at Star every once in a while.

She returned to peeling roots. She finished her task and rose. So did Falcon. "Come," he said. "Let us join your Badger women. You have heard enough Jaguar stories."

She glared at him. "I am not afraid of Jaguars! I do not fear their puny words."

He eyed her, amused. "I know you do not. But I would like to hear a Badger story for a change."

She smiled then and it was not a pretty smile. "Oh, you will hear a Badger story," she promised. "And it will strike fear into your cowardly falcon heart. You will then know that you deal with a proud, resourceful people."

Behind him, Falcon heard Red Hawk's gasp of outrage. "Perhaps Red Hawk would like to join us for the story," he taunted.

"No, I would not!" shouted Red Hawk. "I was badly mistaken to think that a Badger woman would make a good wife. I see now that she would not. You have her and you are welcome to her!"

Falcon smiled and sauntered over to the Badger brides' fire. Sageflower smiled at Star and glared at Falcon. Falcon bent and put a stick on the fire to hide his amusement.

"Why did you bring him?" hissed Chokecherry, unaware that her words were overheard.

"I had little choice," Star said with a shrug. "He wants to hear a story." She glanced over her shoulder at the Jaguars. "A Badger story."

She yawned. "Jaguar stories are boring."

Chokecherry snorted, but Sageflower smiled a cunning smile. "Oh, yes, Star, do tell him a story. And when you are done, he will know how wise we Badgers are and how great is our heritage!"

Star's delighted laughter surprised Falcon and he found himself wanting to hear more of it. He chuckled as he stuffed another stick into the brightly burning fire. This Badger woman amused him. To tame her might prove interesting.

Chapter Thirteen

Star gnawed at the meaty venison rib and ignored the Jaguar man who lounged at her side like a great, lazy cat as he listened to the Badger women's chatter.

She sniffed. She pretended not to notice him. Lately, however, she had caught herself watching him whenever he was unaware of it. There was something about him that intrigued her, but she did not know what. Was it his strong body? Was it the wariness with which the other men treated him? Was it those black eyes that seemed to devour her whenever he gazed at her? She dragged her thoughts away from the man lounging at her side. She much preferred her Badger friends for company. Truly she did.

Wild onion and juniper berries flavored the meat that Sageflower and Pine Woman, who was an excellent cook, had roasted, and the deer juices dripped pink. Star closed her eyes as she chewed the meat, savoring every bite.

When she opened her eyes, he was watching her. Holding her with his narrowed gaze, he picked up a hot chunk of roasted meat and popped it into his mouth and chewed. She shivered, wondering if he would chew her up in the same way. He was a ruthless man, a man she must be wary of, and she wished she were not traveling to Jaguar territory with him, and not destined to share a life with him—be it as a slave or a mate or a wife.

Escape is my best choice, she decided as she took another bite off the deer rib. I must escape back to Badger territory and find my mother. She surveyed the other women, counting up how many of them wanted to escape also.

Elk Knees used a rock to crack open a thick deer thighbone. Fawn helped her, anxious to get at the delicious marrow. Neither the comely widow, Elk Knees, nor the giggling Fawn would attempt a second escape, guessed Star. Elk Knees had protested the last escape and Star had barely been able to persuade Fawn to join her.

Chokecherry and Sageflower sat side by side, whispering. They would accompany her, Star guessed, because they did not want Jaguar husbands. Chokecherry had already confided to Star that she longed for Finds the Marten. And Star had heard Sageflower—dear, sweet Sageflower—crying at night, when she thought the others could not hear her. Those tears were for Wolverine, her promised man. But both Wolverine and Finds the Marten were now captives sold to the Fish

113

Eaters. Chokecherry and Sageflower had no hope of rejoining them.

Pine Woman sat by herself, licking meat juice off her fingers. Every day on the trail, Pine Woman laughed and talked with Lance, the hefty Jaguar who had fought with Red Hawk over Star. Frequently, Pine Woman shot Star dark, jealous looks. Pine Woman might warn the Jaguars if she discovered that Star planned to escape again.

Star sighed. Though escape was appearing less likely the farther they walked from Badger land, she could still remember the location of the Badger camp. In her mind, she could see the exact place where the forest, the large rocks, the grass plain, and the river met. Yes, she could find it again, she knew that.

The fire flickered up in a tiny burst. Orange flames reflected on the women's faces. Star stared at the fire. Her stomach full, she sat back with a satisfied groan and wiped her mouth. *Time to put the arrogant Jaguar in his place.*

"This meal reminds me of the time the Ancient Ones held a feast," she said, sliding a wary glance at Falcon. When he merely stared at the fire, she added, "Many times my mother told me about the Ancient Ones and how they killed the seven monsters and held a great celebration."

"Ho. There is little to celebrate at this meal," said Chokecherry with a pointed look at the lounging Jaguar. He yawned.

"Long, long ago," continued Star, "when my grandmother's grandmother walked the earth—"

"Oh, no, it was before that," objected Elk

Knees. "It was in our great-great-great-great-grandmother's time! That is what my mother told me."

"Very well. In our great-great-great-great-grandmother's time there lived a beautiful woman named Darkstar—"

"Whom you are named after," said Sageflower.

Star could feel her face warm. She did not want the Jaguar to know about her.

"Darkstar is the Ancient Mother of our people," added Sageflower proudly.

The Jaguar had an amused smile on his rugged face. It softened the harshness the scar imparted to him.

Star took a steadying breath and continued resolutely, "One day Darkstar went walking by the river. She searched the muddy banks for wapatoo, the large tuber whose milky meat always tastes so sweet once it is roasted. Her hungry brothers and sisters and parents had demanded that she go and dig wapatoo for the evening meal.

"So Darkstar did as her parents bade her. But, alas, her mind was not on the search for the wapatoo roots. As she walked along she sighed many times, for Darkstar's was a lonely heart."

"Yes," chorused Pine Woman and Fawn, caught up in the tale.

"She longed for someone to love," added Fawn. "Besides her many brothers and sisters and her parents and grandparents, of course."

"Someone of her own to love," explained Sageflower.

All five women grew silent and Star smiled to herself when she heard two more little sighs—

Chokecherry and Sageflower. Falcon's eyes were closed and he appeared to be asleep. She frowned at his inattention. At that moment, his eyes flew open and captured hers.

Startled, she continued, "But—but Darkstar could not find the wapatoo roots she sought. She wandered farther and farther along the river, farther away from her people, until the black of night descended and she realized she was lost."

"That happened to me once," said Chokecherry.

"Hush," said Pine Woman.

"Night descended," said Star, "and Darkstar did not know what to do. So she lay down under a pine tree and went to sleep. In the morning, a Badger awoke her. He did a Badger dance and then he said, 'I give this dance to you. Now follow me.'

"Darkstar felt no fear; she knew he was a spirit animal. It would be wise to follow him; perhaps he would lead her home. She followed the Badger to a cave and when he entered, so did she."

"She entered the Cave of the Dead," said Chokecherry.

"Yes, and the light in the Cave of the Dead was poor; she could barely see the Badger moving along ahead of her. At last it got so dark that she had to feel along the walls to find her way. Then suddenly came a terrible shuddering and shaking of the earth. Dirt fell and stones tumbled all around her. When she turned back to run out of the cave, she found the entrance had been blocked by a huge rock."

"This is the fearsome part," said Chokecherry.

"Hush," said Pine Woman.

Broken Promise

"Darkstar was trapped in the cave! She called out to the Badger, asking him to guide her, but no answer came forth. She waited a long time for the Badger, but he never returned from the depths of the cave. She was all alone! Very afraid now, but still courageous, Darkstar felt her way along the rock walls, going deeper and deeper into the blackness of the Cave of the Dead. Once she called out, but only her echo returned to her. She knew the cavern must be vast.

"Suddenly she heard loud grunting noises. Slowly she crept forward and felt her way around a curved wall. There she saw light! It was very dim, but it was light. She moved toward it. There, in the dimly lit cavern, she spied a herd of huge animals—monsters!"

"Aiieee!" cried Fawn.

"Hush," said Pine Woman. "We call them mammoths. The Ancient Ones told many tales of them."

Fawn still looked frightened.

"The monsters were pushing and shoving against the rock cavern. Darkstar crept closer to see what it was they were doing and then, to her surprise, she saw that they were licking the walls! Something about the walls tasted good to the monsters. Later she tasted the walls herself. They were salty."

"I am never going into a cave again," said Fawn.

"Ha," said Elk Knees. "The mammoths are all dead now; no one I know has ever seen one."

"Not in our grandfather's time, either," added Pine Woman.

"I do not care," said Fawn. "I am still not going into any caves."

"Once my uncle saw a monster frozen in ice," said Chokecherry. "He was out hunting for the great sheep that live in the mountains, and he came to a big mountain of snow. As he got closer he saw a head with a long thin leg on it, such as he had never seen before. The head and leg stuck out of the ice. He ran away."

"Aaiiee," shuddered Fawn. The women looked uneasily at each other.

"After a while," continued Star, "the monsters left the cavern and Darkstar followed them. She could see that the monsters knew their way, as if they had been to the cavern many times."

She could feel Falcon's black eyes on her. "When Darkstar emerged from the Cave of the Dead, she saw that the monsters, or mammoths, had gone down to a gravel beach and were drinking from the Lake of Green Waters. She crept after them. She heard them snort and talk among themselves but she could not understand their speech.

"Darkstar followed the mammoth family for many days, eating the same grasses and leaves that they did and drinking from the cold water that ran into the Lake of Green Waters. One day a young mammoth got separated from the mammoth family and suddenly began screaming. Darkstar crept over to see why.

"Hunters were attacking it! Hunters whom Darkstar had never seen before. They wore shaggy bear robes and carried sharp spears. Many times they ran at the wounded mammoth with their spears, trying to kill it. They succeeded and then they saw Darkstar. One of them, a swift runner, ran after her and caught her."

Star glanced at Falcon. Darkstar's predicament seemed too much like her own.

He smiled. *As I captured you,* his knowing smile said to her.

"The—the hunter took Darkstar to live with his people. She stayed with them for some time. They treated her neither kindly nor cruelly."

"I wonder if that will happen to us," murmured Sageflower.

"Then came the winter many died. Great snow-storms and ice mountains covered the lands. The people Darkstar was with began to starve. The shaggy bear hunters could not find enough food for the people. The children cried in the night, their bellies hungry for food. Old people moaned and grew thin and listless."

"Oh, no," moaned Chokecherry. "I do not like fearful winters like that."

"Neither do I," said Pine Woman.

"That is why we dry elk meat and store it away for winter," said Elk Knees practically.

"Darkstar remembered that though these new people were not friendly to her, they had fed her. She pondered this. Finally, she made a decision. She led the hunters to the Cave of the Dead where she had seen the mammoths licking the walls. Silently, they crept into the cave. Inside, licking the walls, were seven monsters. The hunters killed every one of them!"

"Oh," breathed Fawn.

"Now the people had much meat. There was a

feast and singing and dancing. The people had so much meat that the hunters did not have to hunt for the rest of the winter. All the people survived. The children had full bellies and the old people grew fat. They lived in the cave for protection from the cold and they ate the mammoth meat. They painted pictures on the cave walls to celebrate the great hunt."

"Ah," said Fawn.

"The people, the Ancient Ones, were so happy with Darkstar's kindness to them that, in her honor, they called themselves the Badger People. And they gave her as wife to their best hunter."

"To the man who had caught her," interjected Falcon.

Star shifted uncomfortably and stared at his mouth. "Well, yes, it was him."

Chokecherry was eyeing Star and Falcon speculatively.

"They married," continued Star stolidly, "and they had eight children, each one named after the eight points of the earth.

"But this was the strange thing: never again did the Badger People find mammoths to hunt after that winter. It was as if the mammoths had gone far away to another land. After that time, the Badger People hunted only elk and deer. Darkstar taught them to dry the meat, so it would last far into the winter."

"I like to eat elk meat," said Fawn.

"Darkstar lived for many happy years with her children and her husband. And when she died," continued Star, "she turned into a star in the sky—the Darkstar—the one that can only be seen at certain times. But whenever her Badger People have need of her, she appears as a bright light in the sky and guides them to safety."

"We have need of her now," said Chokecherry mournfully.

"Sometimes she sends a badger to help them," added Star.

There was a long silence. Star glanced furtively around to see if a badger hid in the rock crevices. Chokecherry was correct. The Badger women needed help. Desperately.

Chapter Fourteen

Falcon was amused at the Badger woman's tale. So they looked for someone to save them, did they? Well, they could look all they wanted, but they were still promised to Jaguar men. He would have to warn Claw. Star was probably already planning another attempt to "guide her people to safety." They must keep close watch on the Badger brides.

"We arrive at my people's camp tomorrow," he said.

"Oh, no," gasped one of the brides.

"Hush, Sageflower," said another.

Sageflower was slim and had a delicate face. When she smiled, she was beautiful. Once he might have wanted a wife like her. She even reminded him of Tula. He wondered if she had Tula's deceit.

"It is time to rest," he said to the women. "We

will travel a long way on the morrow. The men are anxious to be back at our camp."

All the women, except Star, obediently lay down and covered themselves with furs and blankets. Star glared at him, her dark eyes bright, her black hair hanging in a thick fall down one side of her bosom. A snarl curved her upper lip.

"Come," he said to her. "Let us walk."

The light was fading as they walked away from the camp and into the grass that grew near the creek. Falcon turned away from the entrance to the Canyon of the Doves and headed north, to where giant rocks closed off the canyon's end. Crickets stopped their singing. Frogs ceased their croaking.

"It is a fine evening," he said. The sky was a red and purple and gold roof in the cold clear air.

When Star gazed up at the sky, he said, "It is too early for Darkstar."

She faced him defiantly.

"Do not expect any help," he warned. "What I have taken, I will hold. And so will the other men. You Badger women have no hope of escaping, so do not try it. We will track you and find you and bring you back."

"If it were you that was forced away from your people, would you go willingly?"

He laughed. "No," he answered at last. "Not at all."

"Then do not expect that I will!"

He smiled. "It is different for a man."

"Is it?" she asked, her eyes bright on his.

"Yes," he answered. "A man fights back. He expects to escape, or tries to. A woman, well, a woman must put up with what happens to her."

"Think you so?"

He liked it that her voice was quiet. It showed that she saw the wisdom in what he was telling her.

"Yes. A woman, if she is wise, will go along quietly, tanning the hides, gathering the roots, tending the fire. That is what the other Badger brides will do. They know that they will have a good life with us, that they will have fine husbands, and they accept that. You, however, do not. I warn you not to fight against it. Your life with me will be better if you do not."

"I am not fighting," she pointed out. "I am very calm."

"And that surprises me," he confessed. "I think you plan to run away and take the other brides with you. I am warning you not to do that."

Her smile was cold. "I will certainly consider your warning."

Why did he feel she was not speaking openly with him?

He paused, wondering if he should say what was truly on his mind. She had turned away from him and was idly picking clusters of velvety red sumac berries.

"When we get to my camp," he began, "you will stay with me."

That caught her attention.

"I do not want you talking to any of the Jaguar women," he said.

"Why?"

"That is not for you to know. I want you to stay near my tent. You may speak with your Badger women friends of course, but you must stay away from the Jaguar women. Do you understand?"

"Yes."

She went back to picking the red clusters. He wished he knew what she was thinking. "It will go better for you if you do as I say," he warned.

"I am certain that is true."

She did not look like the obedient kind of woman, he thought uneasily. Perhaps he should see about taking what-was-her-name? Sageflower, yes, that was it. Perhaps he should take Sageflower as wife. No, she reminded him too much of Tula. "And do not go near the other Jaguar men when we get to camp," he added. She must stay away from Marmot, particularly. Marmot stole wives.

"You take me to live with your people and you do not want me to talk to them?"

He heard the bewilderment and incredulity in her voice.

"Do as I say," he warned, feeling foolish. What was it about this woman that twisted him in knots? Before he had ever traveled to the Badger camp on the bride quest, he had no yearning for a wife. But once he saw this woman who hid herself under layers of mud, everything changed for him. Now that he had her, what was he going to do with her?

She inspected a faded cluster of sumac.

"It is our custom," he added after a while. It was not, but if it kept her from speaking to the Jaguar women . . . well, it was better this way. For him.

"Jaguars have strange customs," she said.

He shrugged. "You will get used to our ways."

She frowned at him. "I do not want to get used to your ways."

"No, you do not."

"I am a Badger woman. I come from brave people. I do not want to live with you. Or with your people."

He drew a tense breath. "I do not care what you want. You are coming to my camp; you will live with me. You will sleep with me."

"No! I will not."

He reached for her. She gave a little cry as the berries scattered. He pulled her into his arms, drawing in her scent. She smelled of smoke and leather and something else—woman. And, ah, but she felt good in his arms. "I think you will find it very satisfying to sleep with me," he murmured. He was surprised how hungry he was for her. It had been a long time since Tula. . . .

She pushed against his chest, and her eyes, dark and flashing, met his. "You have a high regard for yourself, Jaguar," she whispered.

He kissed her forehead. "Not so high. It is just that I know how to satisfy a woman. I know how to satisfy you."

He bent and touched his lips to her mouth. Ah, but she tasted sweet. He kissed her long, then pushed his tongue between her lips, but the barrier of her teeth stopped him. He chuckled and held her head, slanting his lips over hers. When she began to pant, he raised his head. "You see how fine it can be?"

She touched her mouth with a finger, her

eyes huge with wonder. He smiled and kissed her again.

"Ugh!" Her knee to his groin caught him unaware. He doubled over and by the time he caught his breath, she had disappeared. "Come back, Badger woman! Come back right now!"

But there was no answer.

Muttering to himself, he ran after her, pausing now and then to listen to her footfalls as she splashed in the creek. He could barely make out her dark shadow as she dodged heedlessly up the canyon floor. Though he had expected her to break and run—it was one of the reasons he had headed into the canyon—now that she was fleeing him, he was exasperated.

"What is it about you that is so difficult, Badger woman?" he muttered.

He rounded a rock-pillared bend, his aching groin still throbbing. He scanned the rocks, listening for sliding rock, for the sound of pebbles bouncing off the rocky walls of the canyon. Nothing but silence. Ah, she had stopped running. She was hiding again.

"Star," he called softly. "It is getting dark. Come out. I will not hurt you, but I do not want to look for you all night."

No answer. His loins still ached from the blow she had dealt him.

"Star?" Where was she hiding now? Probably crouched behind a rock. He hesitated, approaching a large boulder. He peered around its rough edge, his eyes straining to find her in the waning light. "Star."

Not there. He leaned against the rock, wondering what to do. A night spent searching for his reluctant Badger bride held little appeal. "Star?"

He heard a little rustle in the darkness and smiled to himself. He padded softly in that direction. The rustle turned to a hiss and he paused. The woman has a strange way of warning me off, he thought.

Then came a low growl and Falcon's heart started to pound. That sounded more like an animal.

Another low growl cautioned him to halt. The moon came out from behind the clouds and he saw a large, heavy-jawed head and great yellow eyes glaring at him. A jaguar!

He wished now that he had his spear. He felt for his knife at his side. The touch of the sharp blade reassured him.

"Star," he said, keeping his voice low and hoping she could hear him. "Stay hidden. There is a jaguar. I will chase it away."

The big cat hissed at him as it crouched on a rock a little above his head. Falcon estimated it to be the weight of two large men. When it snarled, its sharp white teeth glistened. It shook its head, and its strong neck and shoulder muscles rippled under the sleek yellow fur spotted with black rosettes. A man could be torn apart by such a powerful animal.

"Run away," he said to the cat.

It hissed louder. Jaguars would fight any enemy within reach. But Falcon did not want to fight this jaguar. The Jaguar People did not kill jaguars. They looked to them for protection. In return, the jaguar let its People go in peace. Perhaps this jaguar did not know of the agreement.

"Go away," Falcon said. He waved his knife at the animal. "I am a Jaguar, too. My people are kinsmen to yours. I do not want to fight you."

The jaguar snarled.

"Hsst, Falcon," he heard Star whisper. She materialized at his side. "Here. I have a rock."

He gripped his knife. "I have my knife. Keep the rock."

The beast was the biggest jaguar Falcon had ever seen. Snarling, it crept toward him. He could smell its fetid breath as the animal spat and hissed.

"Get back," he whispered to Star. "Behind me! If he launches himself—"

The animal gathered itself and sprang toward Falcon's throat. Sharp claws fought for a hold on his leather shirt. The cat's razor talons ripped through the skin of Falcon's shoulders as he braced himself against the lunge. Man and cat fell to the ground.

"Falcon!" cried Star.

They rolled over and over, the cat growling and snarling. Falcon struggled to find a place to thrust his knife. The cat raised powerful back feet and tried to rake Falcon's torso to disembowel him. Suddenly the cat yowled and arched around, shaking its back.

Star was pounding at the animal's head with the rock. Falcon stared at her in amazement, then leapt to his feet and attacked the animal again. He yanked the animal to the ground and sank his

129

knife deep in its jugular vein. The cat died with one last snarling growl.

Panting, alert, Falcon watched the beast for any sign of movement. He was ready to fight again should the animal stir. But it was truly dead; its bloody fur ruffled in a puff of evening breeze.

"Falcon?"

He turned to look at Star.

"Falcon, you are bleeding!"

He glanced down at himself. His leather shirt hung in shreds. The thick layer, Tula's last handiwork for him, had protected him from the cat's sharp claws. The thick leather had saved his life. Streaks of blood coated his chest and leather-clad thighs. "It is nothing." It was true; he felt no pain. That would come later.

She took his hand. "Come, let us return to the camp. You need help."

He laughed and pulled off the tattered remnants of his falcon shirt and tossed it aside. It amused him that she thought he needed help. He had only a few scratches. True, they could become inflamed and red, but he had endured much worse.

Star knelt and touched the jaguar's yellow, spotted fur. "Let us skin him and be done," she said. "I am anxious to leave. A second jaguar might appear."

Falcon stared down at the jaguar and wished the beast had heeded his words. When it had refused to leave, he had been forced to kill it! Now misfortune would result.

Falcon skinned the jaguar, but he left the meat.

He could not eat a kinsman.

They wandered back toward the Jaguar encampment, stopping first at the creek.

Falcon waited patiently while Star dabbed water on his cuts. "That does not help," he complained. "It hurts."

"How will you heal if I do not clean your wound?" She glanced about. "I need some special leaves. Ah, there." She waded over to a bushy plant and plucked two leaves. "Here," she said, wading back to him. She dipped the leaves in the water and squeezed them over his bloodied skin. "The juice will help ease the pain," she explained.

Her concentration pleased him. And her attempts to help his skin heal pleased him also. But such leaves were useless. Only a Jaguar shaman and his chants could heal Falcon's deep cuts. "Thank you," he said. "That feels much better."

She met his eyes. "Why am I helping you, Jaguar? I fear I may regret it."

He remembered the feel of her in his arms. "You may regret it," he allowed. "But I do not." Suddenly he felt happier.

She studied him, her dark eyes reflecting the yellow moon. "I help you, Falcon, because you fought the jaguar for me." With that explanation, she turned and headed back the way they had come. He watched the sway of her hips, but he was uneasy that he had killed a kinsman for her.

When they reached the Jaguars' campfire, Falcon saw that the hunters had returned. Red Hawk shook his head when he saw Falcon approach. "What has she done to you, Falcon? You leave to take a walk with her and you return a bloodied mess with leaves sticking to you!"

Several of the other men laughed at the jest.

"Beware the claws of a Badger woman." Red Hawk laughed.

Wearily, Falcon held up the jaguar skin and let it unroll. "It was the jaguar that scratched me, not her."

The chuckles and laughter ceased. Red Hawk's face clouded. Claw stood up. "What have you done?"

The men were staring at him and Falcon shrugged at their alarm. "I had no choice. He jumped at me."

"You know you must not kill a jaguar!" Claw's black eyes flashed angrily in the firelight.

"I know."

The men muttered among themselves. Claw held up a hand. "Falcon," he said, and his voice shook, "this is a bad thing you have done."

Falcon clenched his fists and shrugged.

"You will bring misfortune upon our people!"

"He had to kill it," said Star. "The jaguar leapt for his throat!"

Claw turned on her. "Silence, Badger woman! What do you know of our Jaguar customs?" To the other men he said, "What shall we do?"

"We'd better do something," said Red Hawk. "Otherwise, a jaguar will surely stalk and kill one of our people."

The other men nodded. Lance said, "That is only fair. A life for a life."

Falcon sighed. "No need for a life to be given," he said wearily. "Hawk was taken from me. You all know how he died. Is his life not enough for the Great Spirit? Must there be more deaths?"

Claw frowned. "Perhaps," he said slowly, "we have made a mistake in deciding what this jaguar's death means."

"What are you saying?" Red Hawk looked confused.

Claw said slowly, "Perhaps this jaguar came to you, Falcon, and sacrificed his life because Hawk died."

The others murmured.

Falcon stared at him, wondering if Claw spoke the truth.

"We must consult with the shaman upon our return," said Claw. "But I think that is what happened. Our jaguar kinsmen heard how unhappy you are and how you cause so much difficulty for your people."

The other men murmured agreement.

Falcon flushed.

"They sent this jaguar to comfort you."

"But it does not comfort me to kill him," pointed out Falcon.

"His coat will comfort you," answered Claw. "His skin will keep you warm. Have the Badger woman tan it and make a shirt or cloak for you."

Falcon pondered this. The jaguar's sleek skin that he held was truly a magnificent one, he had to admit. The animal had been at the height of his powers. If what Claw said was true, it had been a very great sacrifice for the animal to leave his life at this time. But then, Falcon's son's death had been a great loss also.

Star said, "I will tan it. Your shirt was shredded. This one will replace it."

Falcon stared at her, wondering if she knew that Tula had made the falcon shirt for him. Now this new woman of his was offering to make him a new garment. He rubbed the jaguar skin thoughtfully.

"Very well," agreed Falcon at last, carefully rolling up the skin.

"It is settled then," said Claw, and Falcon heard the relief in the headman's voice.

The other men returned to their fire, where several haunches of venison roasted. Star wandered over to the women's fire. Falcon stayed with the men awhile and listened to their tales, but he grew bored with them. He wanted to be with Star. And he was tired of her rebuffing him. It was time the Badger woman realized she was his! Thoughtfully, Falcon walked over to speak with Claw alone. "I want your help," he told Claw.

Claw frowned. "I did all I could about the jaguar you killed," he said. "I think only the shaman can help you now."

Falcon shook his head. "This is not about the jaguar. It is about the Badger woman."

The two men spoke together in low tones.

"I will do it," promised Claw with a sly smile.

Falcon nodded and wandered over to the women's fire. Star was lying down. He bent and took her arm. "Come."

"Where are we going?" she snapped.

"Not for another walk," he assured her. "One quiet walk along the creek with you is enough for one night!"

She glanced at the Badger brides' fire. "No one is awake," he assured her.

"Where are you taking me?"

He could hear the nervousness in her voice. "You will see."

He led her a short distance away from both fires. He found a patch of grass near the shelter of a pine tree. The rock side of the canyon was at his back and the stone still carried the sun's warmth. "Here. Sit down."

She scanned the rocks and pine trees nervously.

"You will be safe," he assured her. "There are no more jaguars. They hunt alone."

"It could have been a mother. With half-grown cubs hiding. Perhaps they followed us."

He shook his head. "It was a male. And nothing followed us." She took a step away. "Come," he coaxed, "I wish to rest."

"I do not."

He sighed. The woman was stubborn. Perhaps the Badger people were well named, after all. This one could certainly dig her way into a burrow of stubbornness. He rose, walked over to her, and picked her up, one arm under her knees, the other around her shoulders. She felt surprisingly light in his arms. He ignored her protests and marched over to the rock wall. This time when she gave a little struggle, he set her on her feet. "We sleep here," he said firmly.

"We do not," she answered, just as firmly.

Falcon's muscles hurt from the fight with the jaguar, and he was tired of this woman's resistance. He kicked her feet out from under her and

135

when she fell, he caught her and lowered her to the ground. Then he sat down beside her and gazed into her flashing black eyes. "We do."

When he saw her mouth tighten in protest, he leaned over and placed his mouth on hers.

Chapter Fifteen

Star felt his lips touch hers. The gentleness in him surprised her and she found herself kissing him back. As his lips moved over hers, she relaxed into his embrace. Her heart pounded as his hand moved down her back in a soothing, stroking motion. He lifted his head and kissed her cheek and forehead. "I want you," he whispered.

She grasped his head, her fingers kneading the thick strands of his hair, and she pulled his mouth hungrily back to hers for more kisses. His mouth quested over hers and then his tongue sought entrance. She kept her teeth closed at first but under his insistent probing she soon relented.

His tongue swirled inside her mouth and she felt invaded—invaded and suddenly, wantonly, passionately alive. She clutched him closer.

His hands moved slowly over her back. She

trembled when they reached her breasts and brushed lightly against the sides.

"No," she murmured, trying to push him away.

"Let me," he answered, kissing her. She was caught up in his touch, in his kisses, and she longed to yield to him. He could do what he wanted with her, so good did he make her feel.

Her body felt heavy, her eyelids seemed weighted as though with stones, and the blood throughout her whole body pounded with each stroke of his hand. He slid a palm along one leg and up under her leather dress. Her legs parted of their own will and she felt him stroking, closer, closer to the warm pulse of her womanhood.

He was breathing heavily now and she found the sound intoxicating. That she could make this powerful man tremble as he was doing now was a wonderful revelation.

She moved his hand away from the warm place he sought. "Let me," he murmured, swiftly replacing his hand on her thigh. She tried to move his hand away again, but he held it there and gently stroked tantalizingly closer. She moaned.

"Oh, yes," he murmured, and she clutched him still closer. His kisses were sending her into a swirling oblivion of sensation. She sank back against the warm stone wall behind her.

He followed, pulling her closer, and she found herself clinging to his bare chest, kissing his taut, male-smelling skin. She kissed the tattoo of a black falcon in flight on his shoulder. He guided her mouth back to his.

"Oh, yes," she moaned, "kiss me again."

He chuckled. "It's much better when we remove

our clothes." He tugged at her dress and she lifted her arms to oblige. Once the garment was off, he slipped out of his leather pants. Now there was nothing between them but warm skin. "You feel so good," he murmured, kissing her along the line of her neck.

"So do you," she answered, rubbing her breasts against his hard chest. She loved the feel of him, the scent of him, and everything he was doing to her body excited her. His hands moved up her thighs.

She blushed.

He leaned over and kissed her mouth. He kissed her breasts. His questing lips moved down to her stomach.

"Yes," she moaned. "More," she whispered when he paused in a kiss.

"Falcon? Is that you?"

Star froze.

"Falcon?"

"It is Claw," whispered Falcon. "Say nothing, and he will go away."

"Like the jaguar did?" she answered.

He gave her a warning glance.

As silently as she could, Star felt along the ground for her leather dress. At last, she found it and pressed it to her breasts to cover her nakedness. The air felt surprisingly cool against her heated skin. As they listened to Claw move off into the darkness, still calling Falcon's name, she realized that her good sense had fled. Whatever was she doing sitting naked in the moonlight with this Jaguar man and demanding that he kiss her every place he could find?

139

She raised her arms to put the leather dress back on. Falcon reached out a hand to stop her. "What are you doing?"

"Getting dressed," she answered as calmly as she could.

"Do not do that," he said. "We have just begun."

She stared at his handsome face in the moonlight. The thin white scar that creased his face from cheekbone to mouth stood out against his dark skin.

"We have begun nothing, Jaguar," she told him. Now that her racing blood had cooled, she was glad of Claw's interruption. Why, if he had not come along, she would have been—Well, things would have truly gone much farther. She blushed in the darkness.

He leaned over and kissed her lips and she felt herself melting once more. "Oh, no," she moaned and pulled away. "What hold is it that you have over me, Falcon?" she cried.

He stared at her in silence.

She rose to her feet. "I must return to the others." Her hands were shaking as she put on the dress.

"Star." He rose and dressed in his leather trousers without any sign of the shame that she seemed to feel. "I want to make love to you."

"Well, you cannot."

"You are going to be my wife. It is only natural for a man to want to be with his wife."

"That may be," she retorted archly, "but you seem to have forgotten something."

"What is that?"

"I have not agreed to be your wife! You stole

140

me from my family. And I do not want to lie
with you."

He raised a brow at that. "I thought different,"
he said.

She turned away, not wanting him to know the
truth of his words. He would probably have her
down and moaning on the ground very soon if
she did not get back to the Jaguar fire swiftly.

"Falcon? Oh, there you are." Claw stumbled out
of the darkness. He paused and eyed the two of
them with suspicion. "What are you two doing?"
he asked, peering at them.

Star would not answer. She thought that Claw
could see for himself what they had been doing,
especially as Falcon was taking his time tying the
waist of his leather pants.

Claw laughed. "Well, well! You could not wait
till the wedding, eh? Nothing like a tasty sample
before you are married!" He laughed heartily and
leered at Star. "Falcon! Now that you are done
with her, it's my turn!"

Falcon lifted an eyebrow. "Too late, Claw. Her
legs are closed."

Star gasped.

Claw chortled and pounded Falcon's back as
if Falcon had done a wondrous thing. Falcon
winced.

"Let us go back to the fire and I will announce
the good news to all the camp!" cried Claw.

Falcon looked suddenly guilty and turned
away.

Star frowned. "What news?"

Claw chuckled. "Ask Falcon."

Falcon finally met her eyes, and when he did,

141

he smiled a distinctly predatory smile.

"What news? Will one of you please tell me?" Frissons of alarm were skittering up and down Star's spine.

Claw danced giddily in place.

"The news that Claw is going to announce," said Falcon, "is that you and I are now married."

"What do you mean?" Star was aghast.

"Why, my dear one, just that. We are now married. By Jaguar custom, as Claw knows so well, if a man beds a woman, he is obliged to marry her. Especially when someone else has witnessed it."

"But, but—"

"Yes," interrupted Claw, "and I witnessed it. Do not try to tell me any different!" He shook a playful finger at Star.

She was mortified that Claw might have seen her. Then she reassured herself. *It was dark, Claw was out walking around the canyon, he could not see—And Falcon and I did not truly join our bodies! Surely that must mean we are not married. Not yet. I am not ready for marriage to this man. I need time . . . time to escape!*

Falcon watched her, a grim smile of amusement twisting his mouth.

Star was not amused.

"Our marriage customs are very clear," explained Claw. "A man and woman must wait until after the marriage feast until they, uh"— he shot a laughing glance at Star—"uh, go off by themselves."

"But, but—"

"Sorry, wife. No doubt your Badger customs are very different, and I wish our Jaguar ones were also," said Falcon smoothly, looking as if he wished nothing of the sort, "but there is no help for it. We are married. It is done. Are you happy, dear one?"

"You know I am not!" she snapped. "And we did not do—we did not have—"

"Come, come," said Claw. "Enough of this arguing. You will have all your wedded life to argue. And there will be plenty of that, I can assure you, if your marriage is anything like mine." He turned to Star, his mien suddenly serious. "I do wish you well, Badger woman."

Star drew herself up. "I thank you, but your well wishes are far too early—"

"Come, wife," said Falcon, dragging her along by an elbow. "We must return to the camp."

Star let him lead her away, too dazed to protest. She kept tripping, her legs were so weak and shaking. Each time, Falcon hauled her up to regain her footing.

I am married! To a stranger! This cannot be! I am supposed to marry Camel Stalker. We were going to have children. We were going to live with our Badger people. We were going to grow old together! Now I am married to a stranger! Oh, what will become of me . . . ? She stumbled once again.

Chapter Sixteen

Star let Falcon lead her closer to the women's fire. She spied Chokecherry snoring under a beaver fur. The other women, also bundled under furs, slumbered out of reach of the sparks. Star tried to tread softly so as not to awaken them.

"Now that you are my wife," said Falcon, "your place is by my side this night."

"But I do not feel like your wife," answered Star. This had happened too swiftly for her.

Jaguar customs were not anything like Badger customs. Among her Badger people, a man and woman were joined after a long courtship and the giving of gifts to the families.

The Badgers did marriage the proper way. A man's mother or aunt would approach the woman's family and suggest the two have time to get to know one another, a time of courtship. If this request were well received, then the young couple visited together under the watchful eye of an old grandmother or uncle. If the two got along well and marriage was decided upon, then the man gave a gift of a well-tanned hide or hunted for an elk or antelope, whatever the bride's family requested. Sometimes, if the bride's family did not like the groom, they tested him by demanding a fierce wolf or bear.

The woman's family gave bone awls and needles and baskets and hide scrapers to the man's family. Some of those gifts would start the couple off in their new life together. And of course the woman's family always provided the vegetables and roots at the marriage feast while the man's family always provided the meat.

But with these Jaguars everything was done in haste and none of it made any sense to her. That a man and woman could be married off because someone thought they had slept together bewildered Star. Why, all it took was one person going around a camp saying this man and this woman slept together and that man and that woman slept together and soon he would have the whole camp married off! No, it did not make sense.

"We will sleep here," said Falcon, spreading a camelskin on the ground.

Star glanced around, glad to see that they were still near the women's fire and only a little distance from the Jaguar men's.

He sat down. "Come here."

Star shook her head.

"What ails you, wife?"

A moan came from the women's fire. One of

the brides was waking. Star whispered, "It is too sudden. I do not want to be married."

"Well, you have little choice. You have known all along that you were to be married to me. I do not see why this should suddenly bother you."

"You do not see—"

"Shhh," complained Pine Woman. "You are waking me up with your noise."

Star lowered her voice. "You do not see why this should bother me! Well, let me tell you! First you steal me and the other women from our home."

"We gave furs for you."

"Not for me!"

He was silent.

"You steal me from my home," continued Star. "You sell my promised husband to the slave catchers."

"Your promised husband was caught attacking us."

"But you gave him to the slave catchers!"

"The slave catchers were there, true. . . ."

"You steal me from my people and you expect me to marry you!"

"There is nothing more to say. We are married," he answered calmly. "Claw has told you that."

"Claw saying that I am married does not make me married."

"Oh, yes, it does," Falcon answered. "Under our customs we are now married. And every man here will accept Claw's word that we are married."

"I do not want to be married!"

Falcon looked amused.

"Can we not get out of it?"

"Certainly."

She smiled for the first time as relief coursed through her. It was all a mistake. A horrible mistake. "Good! Then let us undo the marriage."

"Jaguar men can unjoin from their wives if the wife cannot have children. Or if the man no longer wants to be married."

Star waited, the smile fading from her taut facial muscles.

"That is all? Barrenness or that the man no longer wants to be married?"

"That is correct."

"What about the woman? How can she unjoin from the man?" A suspicion was growing in her that the woman had few choices.

"She cannot."

"The woman must stay with the man?"

He nodded. "Unless he gets tired of her."

"Why, that is foolish!" cried Star. "I have never heard of such a foolish custom. Among the Badger People—"

"Please," murmured Fawn, yawning. "You are keeping me awake. I want to sleep. I am very tired."

Star lowered her voice. "Among the Badger People, a woman can leave the man any time she wants! She merely takes his spear and she breaks it in two and discards the broken pieces outside their tent. When he comes home and sees his spear so desecrated he knows that he is no longer welcome in her tent and the marriage is over."

"I do not think much of that," answered Falcon with a frown.

147

"Surely there is some way I can get out of the marriage."

He regarded her for a long time out of solemn black eyes. "There is," he said finally.

"What is it?" She held her breath.

"You could invite another man to your bedrobes. That would unjoin our marriage." His eyes were unreadable as he watched her.

She stared at him. "I do not want another man in my bedrobes!" she shrieked. "I do not want *you* in my bedrobes!"

"Quiet," complained Elk Knees. "You are too noisy over there."

Star gritted, "I do not want to lie with you and I do not want to marry you! Do you understand?"

Falcon seemed to relax. He yawned. "Uh huh. I understand." He lay down and pillowed his head on his arms and gazed up at the night sky.

Star waited. "Well?"

"Well what?"

"I am going to tell Claw that we are not married!"

"Hmmmmm. You can tell that to Claw," he answered lazily. "Or any of the other Jaguar men. But I must warn you: by now, Claw has already told them we are married. If you go and tell them something different, they will think you are not well in the head." He touched the side of his head for emphasis.

"And I suppose you Jaguars hate people who are not well in the head," she snarled.

"No, we like them. Very much."

Hope sprang anew. "Perhaps I will do that." She rose.

148

"Before you go to Claw, you must know what we do with people who are unwell in the head."

"What do you do with them?"

"We make them our shamans."

"Oh." She sat down again.

"Will you please go to sleep?" complained Chokecherry. "All this talk is keeping me awake."

Star whispered, "I do not want to be a shaman."

Falcon shrugged. "Shaman is a difficult job," he agreed.

Tula had been so certain that their son, Hawk, would be a shaman when he grew up. Falcon remembered Hawk would have strange fits and fall down on the ground. His whole body would quiver and shake. He would toss and thrash his limbs and cry out. Sometimes he would lie still for a very long time. One day when another of the strange spells had overcome Hawk, Tula had begged Rapt, the shaman, to help Hawk. Rapt had squatted down and chanted for a long time beside the boy. Then Rapt had gone into a trance to retrieve the boy's spirit, which obviously had gone wandering off. When Rapt returned with it, the boy awoke. Rapt rose to his feet and announced to Tula that Hawk would one day be a great shaman of the Jaguar People.

But Rapt was wrong. Tula was wrong. A strange sickness swept through the Jaguar People and Hawk, sick, precious Hawk—with his twisted legs, his dull eyes, the son that Falcon loved, the son whose face he stared at day after day, willing him to get well, willing him to be as other boys, willing him to grow strong so that Falcon could teach him to hunt—Hawk had died. So had two other strong Jaguar hunters. Those three were the only Jaguars to die from the strange sickness.

After Hawk's death, Rapt told the People what had caused the strange sickness. He had been advised about it in a powerful dream. In the dream, he saw a little mouse chewing and spitting on Hawk's bedskins. Then the mouse defecated on the bedskins. Poison red worms from the mouse's spittle and feces flew through the air from Hawk to the two strong hunters and crawled up their nostrils and poisoned them. Rapt reported that the only way to save the remaining Jaguar people was to burn Hawk's diseased bedskins.

When the two hunters' families heard Rapt's dream, they grew very angry at Falcon and Tula. They demanded that Hawk's furs be burned. Tula cried as she watched her son's remaining possessions being thrown in the fire. Falcon watched with a stony face.

Then, still angry, the families demanded that Falcon bring them back two mountain sheep in payment for the loss of the hunters. So, in the midst of his own grief about his son's death, Falcon had to leave the Jaguar camp and go far into the mountains to kill two mountain sheep, one for each family. Only when he brought the dead, shaggy beasts back were the families satisfied.

And it was when Falcon returned from that hunt that he discovered Tula had moved into Marmot's tent. Marmot had been one of her suitors when Falcon first courted her. But Falcon had won her, or so he thought. But after Hawk's death, Tula took everything from their tent—her baskets and her awls and all the clothes she had made for Falcon. She took everything except the falcon shirt he had been wearing.

Hawk's death left a gaping hole in Falcon's life. He had loved Hawk, but all his love could not make Hawk whole, could not keep him alive, could not make Tula stay.

Sorrow swamped Falcon as he remembered, and he turned his back to his new wife. He had planned to take Star to his bed this night. He had even arranged with Claw to discover them. But now the sad memories of Hawk and Tula had intruded and stanched his desire for Star. He could not let her see how overcome he was whenever he remembered his son.

Falcon closed his eyes and gritted his teeth, willing the pain away. When he no longer felt the sorrow, when his heart had become numb and peaceful once again, he rolled back to face her.

She sat with her back to him, staring at the sleeping women and the sputtering fire.

"Come here," he said gruffly. He put his hands on her shoulders and drew her to him.

He was glad that she yielded and obeyed him this time. He was too heartsick for an argument. She let him pull her close.

"We will sleep now," he whispered. He did not want any trouble from this new wife. His old one had caused him too much. His heart was sick from the trouble she had caused him and from the death of his son. All he wanted to do now was sleep.

He gently pulled Star to him. He felt grateful suddenly that she did not protest his holding her.

He breathed in the scent of her that lingered in her thick hair. He could feel the heat of her body through the leather dress. Perhaps he could grow to have some feeling for this new wife. . . .

He yawned and they fell asleep that way, Star curled toward the fire and Falcon curled around Star.

He woke himself crying her name aloud.

Chapter Seventeen

Star, her new husband, the brides, and the bridal quest party all walked into the main Jaguar camp the next afternoon. The Jaguar People had chosen a campsite situated in a broad, open field of grass dotted with an occasional pine tree. The field gradually sloped down to a placid river that rounded a bend some distance away. On the other side of the river rose sheer black rock cliffs.

Erected in the tall grass were many brown elk-hide tents set over thin poles. Black-haired women worked near the tents, feeding wood to the flickering fires, cutting meat, tanning hides, and swatting at flies. Children raced around the camp, chasing each other and throwing sticks at the camp dogs. Several men ran over to greet the returning bridal quest members. Claw smiled proudly at the hearty congratulations he received.

153

"Fine batch of Badger brides!" complimented one man.

It took some time to tell the story of how each bride had been caught. Star wanted to put her hands over her ears because, with each telling, the Jaguars became braver and finer and the Badgers became more pitiful and useless. Awed listeners asked so many questions about the cowardly Badgers that Star wanted to scream at them to go away. She opened her mouth to do so, and was promptly propelled away by Falcon.

"Do not say anything, wife," he warned. "Now is not the time to start telling them stories about the heroic Darkstar saving her people. My people will not stand for it."

Star raised an eyebrow. Ever since they had been married he had not missed a single opportunity to call her "wife." When she had awakened in his arms that morning, it was to the stares of the other Badger brides. He had called her "wife" then. Elk Knees gave an amused smile, Fawn giggled, and Pine Woman looked relieved and pitying at the same time. Sageflower and Chokecherry both looked shocked. And now here she was at his people's camp and he was still calling her "wife."

Many of the Jaguar People were staring at her curiously.

"Who is this one?"

The man who asked had a pinched look on his face. "How was she captured? Whom does she belong to?"

"She is mine, Marmot," said Falcon, placing himself between the inquiring man and Star.

There was a note in Falcon's voice that Star could not interpret. "No need to concern yourself with her."

A beautiful woman walked up to join Marmot. Her lovely face was further enhanced by a wide swath of white hair that grew at her forehead and swept back over her long black hair in two white streaks. Star stared, never having seen such a striking woman. On her back, the woman wore a thick hide and out of the top peeped a baby with bright black eyes.

"Greetings, Tula," said Falcon.

The woman sniffed contemptuously. Marmot puffed up his chest. "Do not speak to her. She wants nothing to do with you."

Tula met Star's eyes. "Who are you?" she demanded.

Before Star could answer, Falcon said, "My bride."

Tula gasped and her eyes narrowed assessingly.

Marmot scowled.

Falcon grimaced.

Star squirmed. Something did not feel right about this conversation.

Tula glared at Star for several heartbeats. "Are all Badger women so ugly?" She sneered.

"I am not ugly," answered Star calmly, though she did not feel calm inside. In a confused turmoil, she wondered, Why is this woman so hateful to me?

Lips set in a stern line, Tula said, "Come along, Marmot," and marched over to assess the other Badger brides. The baby on her back turned and stared at Star.

Marmot licked his lips. "Oh, but I do like Badger women," he said. Then, laughing at Falcon's reddened face, he hurried after Tula.

"Who was that?" asked Star.

"That wood rat of a man is Marmot, Tula's husband." Falcon's scar throbbed white against the surging red of his face. "And Tula is my former wife."

Star blinked. He had not mentioned a wife before.

"I do not want you talking to her. She is trouble," gritted Falcon. "I cannot have you speaking with her."

"I have nothing I wish to say to her. And she does not talk kindly to me." Indeed, Star needed little encouragement to avoid the woman.

"I do not want you talking to any of the other Jaguar women!"

"So you have said."

They must have much information about him, thought Star. I wonder what he is trying to hide?

"Do not believe anything Tula says."

"How will I hear anything from her if I am not talking to her?" Whatever he is trying to hide, it must be important, Star thought. But is it important enough to seek Tula out?

She let Falcon lead her over to a place where the grass was flattened. "We will set up our tent here," he said.

Star set down her basket and possessions. Falcon unrolled a thick, wide mat of many elk hides sewn together. "This is my tent," explained Falcon.

He dug two deep holes and placed a stout,

forked stick in the hole. Then he filled in the dirt until the stick stood firmly planted. He did the same with a second forked stick. Next, Falcon cradled a third stick across the two forks, like a crossbar. Together, Star and Falcon lifted the heavy, sewn elk hide and placed it over the crossbar. The two sides formed the tent walls. Falcon walked around the outside of the tent, weighting the tent flaps down with round boulders so that the tent would not blow away in a strong wind.

When they were finished, Star stepped back to admire her work. A hunting scene was painted in red ocher on each side of the tent. On one side, the scene showed a falcon swooping down to attack a huge deer with many-branched antlers. On the other side of the tent, the scene showed a falcon flying off, a dead rabbit grasped in its deadly talons.

Star shivered. She knew how the rabbit felt. "Did Tula paint the pictures on the tent?" she asked.

Falcon shot her a pained look. "No. My mother did."

"Ah. Your mother is a very good artist."

"Yes. She was. She is dead."

"Oh."

Judging from the strained silence, Star decided not to ask anything more about his mother.

"She died soon after my son was born." Falcon's lips were tight, as though he forced the words out.

"Your son?" floundered Star. She stared at him. "You never said anything about a son." Or about a wife, either, she wanted to add.

Falcon glared at her. "If I wanted you to know about my son, I would have told you about him."

"Is—is this your way of telling me? Is that your son on Tula's back?"

"No!" He walked over to the back tent opening and draped a wide, tan-colored camel hide over it. Then he walked to the front end of the tent and placed a white, thickly furred mountain sheep hide over it as a doorflap.

Star waited for him to speak but he said nothing more. Evidently he did not want to talk about his son. Perhaps she *should* talk with Tula . . . or one of the other Jaguar women.

Falcon did not know why he had told this woman so much. A swirling confusion of feelings invaded him as they always did whenever he thought about his son. Love mixed with guilt and disappointment and grief assailed him. Pain as though from a spear lanced through his heart and he gritted his teeth to keep from crying out. My son, he cried silently. My son! Ah, Hawk, I loved you so much. . . . Why would the Great Spirit not hear my prayers and let you live? Why were you taken from me?

A terrible agony shook Falcon and he had to stop his efforts to drape the tent. If only his son had lived, if only the Great Spirit had answered Falcon's prayers. He had done everything a man could do to make his son survive. He had paid the shaman to sing strong chants over Hawk. He had fed him invigorating broths. He had hunted for the best, the strongest animals and fed the most powerful parts to his son: the lion's heart to make him brave and want to live, the elk's liver to give him strength, the fox's brains to give him the wisdom that Tula insisted he had. But none of it—none of it—had done any good.

During the last days of his son's life when Hawk had fallen suddenly deathly sick, Falcon had been on his knees praying, begging the Great Spirit to let the boy live. And had He? No, He had taken the boy. Taken him away to wherever it was the dead went. Taken him and left a broken man and a bitter, distraught woman. Together they had destroyed what little was left of their love after their son's sickness had come. And now there were ashes in Tula's heart for him, and ashes in his heart for her, where before there had been only love. His son's death had taken everything worth living for in Falcon's life: his marriage, his son, his hope that one day his son would stand beside him, strong and healthy and whole. Everything, every one of Falcon's dreams for his life had been burned to ashes.

That was what the Great Spirit had done by taking Hawk.

Even Hawk's baby name was different from the other children's. When Falcon was a child, his baby name had been Hawklet and he had named his son after himself. But though he had bestowed a powerful name upon Hawk it had done no good.

Tula's insistence that Hawk was a special child, destined to be a great shaman someday, had not helped. When Falcon had watched Hawk fall down in a foaming fit, when he had looked at Hawk's twisted legs, and seen his scrawny body grow slowly year after year, Falcon had hoped that Tula would prove correct, that the Great Spirit did have special plans for his son, that He wanted Hawk to be a great teacher or healer for the Jaguar People.

But it had not turned out that way, thought Falcon. He felt the bitter legacy of his son's death invade his throat. Tears! A grown man with tears over a son's death.

What a weakling I am, he thought. I should be done with tears. I should know that tears make no difference. That there is no meaning to life. If there were, my son would have lived. And if there is truly a Great Spirit, He would have heard my pleas, my father's cries! He would have seen the love that I bore my child and he would have let him live. But He did not. So I know there is no Great Spirit. It is all lies that the shaman told me, that my mother spoke to me when she taught me to pray to the Great Spirit. All lies that my father showed me that day when we stood on the Canyon of the Doves and he told me that someday my strong, healthy son would look out across the land with me and see the animals and know the land. All lies! He gritted his teeth until his jaw ached and his scar twitched.

His new wife was watching him closely, and he wanted to turn away from her gaze. He could not tell her what had happened. The pain was too raw.

"Stay away from Tula," was all he could get out. He stumbled away, leaving Star staring after him.

Chapter Eighteen

A huge fire burned on a round, flat spot that sloped gently to the river. That morning, two Jaguar hunters had brought in the last of the six deer and there had been much shouting and laughing. Now the Jaguar marriage celebrations could begin!

Star watched as men and women warmed themselves near the fire. The Jaguar women visited and talked with each other and sometimes pulled roasted roots out of the hot dirt pits they had dug and lined with leaves beside the huge fire. The Jaguar men clustered in small groups, also talking.

Several baskets and platters of food were laid out in a neat line. There were baskets of dried blueberries, baskets of dried blackberries, and baskets of dried red huckleberries. There was a leaf-lined platter of freshly picked mushrooms.

Split sides of staked salmon roasted at the edges of the fire. Mounds of bear meat and elk meat sat heaped on wooden platters. The delicious scent of steaming camas roots wafted through the air.

Excitement throbbed in the drumming. Three old women beat skin drums using sticks cushioned with soft leather on one end. Two old men sang hunting songs. When they finished, a third old man slyly broke into a song about a hunting party that hunted only brides.

Two little boys grabbed up handfuls of tasty, spiced bear meat from a platter, while a camp dog sniffed at roots set out to cool. A little girl ran over and chased the dog away from the food.

Everywhere Star looked there was somebody laughing. People chatted excitedly. Happiness was rampant—among the Jaguars, that is, thought Star morosely. But among the Badger brides, whom she stood with, some were happy, and some were not.

Star was not. She glanced down at herself. Once she had learned that the marriages were to be celebrated this day, she had forced herself to put on her new dress, the soft white leather one that her mother had made. But now the sight of the dress and her lovely moccasins only brought tears to her eyes. Many a winter night she had watched her mother sew the black and white porcupine quills on the dress. Many a night they had talked in quiet voices by the fire, planning her life, planning what they would do when she was married to Camel Stalker and Blue Jay was a grandmother.

Star would live happily in the tent of Camel

Broken Promise

Stalker. Her mother, Blue Jay, would dote on her grandchildren, all three of them. Star knew she would sit on long winter evenings sewing tiny moccasins for her children's feet. In the summer she would take her children to the river to swim and play. She would tell them stories and sing them songs and guide them, as Blue Jay would continue to guide her.

How carefully Star had planned her life! How confident she had been that she knew just what to do, just what man to marry. She had known exactly how she would live and just what would happen to her!

And now here she was—married to a Jaguar man that she did not know and about to celebrate that same marriage with a feast among people she did not know. Her life was not working out at all as she and her mother had planned!

Suddenly Star yearned for her mother. Tears filled her eyes. How she wanted to be held in her mother's arms and comforted! How she wanted her mother to know that her life had changed forever. Cruel memories of her dashed hopes and dead dreams flitted through her brain.

Ah, but is my life so bad? came an unbidden thought. I have a strong, handsome husband. One who sends shivers through my body whenever I look at him . . .

"So. You have already married the Jaguar they call Falcon." Elk Knees's voice held an amused note that jarred Star out of her tortured thoughts.

"He married me. I did not marry him!"

"Oh? Is there a difference?" Elk Knees laughed openly.

Star said nothing. Anger and embarrassment washed over her; she was irritated, too, that Elk Knees should find her terrible predicament so amusing.

"I will tell you something," said Elk Knees, coming closer. She set down the basket of dried berries she had been carrying. "First I must know, did you mate with him?"

"What?" gasped Star. "How dare you ask me such a thing?"

Elk Knees shrugged. "No need to be offended. It is of some consequence," she answered. "I merely wanted to know."

Star turned away.

Elk Knees blocked her path. "I ask you this for a reason, Star. I do not ask it to hurt you."

Star met Elk Knees's eyes. Indeed, the woman seemed sincere.

"What I wanted to tell you is this: once a man has mated with a woman, he wants her again and again. At least most men do."

Star blushed and glanced down at the ground.

"I see I have embarrassed you," said Elk Knees. "That was not my intent. My husband, before he was killed, could never have enough of mating. I wanted to warn you about that. It will probably be that way with your new husband."

Star felt her cheeks grow hot.

"It is best if you do not let him mate with you too often. That way he will not expect so much and you will have many opportunities to rest. It goes much easier for you."

Star wanted to stop up her ears with her fingers.

"Of course," continued Elk Knees, "once you are pregnant with your first child then he must leave you alone. And for the three years that you nurse the child, you will be free from his attentions."

Star gaped at her. "But—but it feels so wonderful. . . ." she blurted.

"Wonderful? Girl, have you become crazed? It is not wonderful. Why, it hurts; they care little for the woman. . . ." She frowned. "Why do you shake your head?"

"Because," murmured Star, "it was not that way for me. When he touched me, it felt wonderful. I—I wanted to melt into him."

"Pah! We do not speak about the same thing, I think," said Elk Knees. "It has never been like that for me. I think you lie."

"I do not lie, Elk Knees."

The two women stared at each other.

"A woman needs a man," said Elk Knees slowly. "I know that. She needs a man to hunt for her, to give her children, to protect her from fierce animals. But she must endure in the bedskins, not enjoy. That is the only part of marriage that I do not like. I want a Jaguar husband but I do not like—"

"Come! The feast is about to begin!" Pine Woman ran up, breathless with the news. "They are calling for us down at the fire!" She straightened her clothing and touched her hair. "Do I look pretty? I am going to marry Lance!" She hugged herself in delight.

"Oh!" cried Fawn and did a little dance of excitement. Her body quivered in the smooth yellow doeskin dress she wore. A necklace of dried red berries bounced on her breast, and tiny white flowers peeked out of her shining black hair.

Chokecherry and Sageflower regarded each other with dread. "I do not want to get married," moaned Chokecherry. Her black hair was tangled and a huge spot of grease darkened the middle of her leather dress.

Earlier, she and Sageflower had been out gathering roots for the feast and Sageflower's bare legs were still muddy up to the knees. The two women clung to each other.

Elk Knees gave Star a knowing glance. "Soon you will understand what I mean." Then she sauntered off after a capering Pine Woman.

Star smoothed her dress one more time and slowly followed the others. Her heartbeat quickened as she remembered the feel of Falcon's lips, the touch of his hands.

When she reached the fire and joined the other brides, she caught sight of Falcon and she gasped. He was clad in brown leather trousers. The leather thongs of his moccasins crisscrossed up to the knees. Over his broad naked chest he wore a black-spotted skin vest. Around his neck he wore a bear-tooth necklace. The teeth were huge, bigger than any Star had ever seen before, and she knew they must have come from a giant bear. Star marveled that Falcon had killed such a huge beast, for no one else but the hunter would have the right to wear such teeth.

Missing were his knives at the waist and the spear he usually carried everywhere.

Broken Promise

On both his wrists he wore thick leather bands decorated with painted black falcon designs. Draped down one side of his hair, white against the shining black, was a line of feathers that fell past his shoulder.

He had painted three slanted red lines of ocher on the smooth skin of each of his upper arms. She knew the ocher meant good fortune. It troubled her to see this sign of hope on the man that she was marrying. Did he have hope then for the marriage they had embarked upon? Such a notion did not fit with the man she knew.

He was listening to something one of the men said and he threw back his head and laughed. She saw his strong jaw, his white teeth, his black hair that drifted past his shoulders. Suddenly she wanted him.

She forced the feelings away. She must not want him! He was dangerous!

He caught sight of her then. He stopped laughing and stared at her. Star could hear nothing, see nothing but him. His beauty, his strength. By the Great Spirit, there was something in him that called out to her and she was powerless against that call!

She swallowed and took a step toward him. He walked over to her, holding her eyes with his black ones.

"You look very beautiful on your wedding day," he whispered. A hush fell around them, one that might have been only in Star's mind. But she saw only him, felt only his hands as he clasped both of hers in his. How long they stared at each other she did not know.

Claw broke the spell. "Bring the brides over here." He pointed to where six deer heads were set out on a bristly, brown bear hide. Each deer head was the groom's promise of abundant meat for his bride during his lifetime.

Standing behind the deer heads, in a row, were five grooms, all dressed in their best leather finery. Star recognized Lance and Red Hawk, but not the other three men.

Pine Woman and Fawn danced over to where Claw indicated. Chokecherry and Sageflower stumbled after them, each supporting the other. Elk Knees sauntered past, amusement flitting across her face.

Ah, but Star, she floated, led by Falcon. He gently squeezed her fingers and smiled at her. There was a light in his eyes, a flashing happiness that she had never seen there before. Tentatively she smiled back as she took her place across the bearskin from him.

The shaman arrived, dressed in his powerful shaman costume. Two long white feathers dangled from each ear where they were looped. He wore a vest made of finely scraped doeskin scattered with speckles of gold. He glittered whenever the sun caught his movements. He wore heavily furred brown bear leggings tied at the ankle. The leggings still retained the shape of the bear they had been taken from. His bare feet were painted with red ocher. Both his hands were painted with red ocher up to the elbows. Above the elbows, his bare arms were painted black. A streak of red ocher went down one side of his face and black paint down the other side of his face.

He carried a handful of juniper branches mixed with sage that he shook vigorously.

As he shuffled around the six brides, he shook the foliage over each of their heads and called out to the Great Spirit for blessings upon them. When he raised his arms an expectant hush fell over the throng.

Facing north, the shaman sang a chant. Then he swung to face the east, singing a different chant. He swung to the south and then to the west, chanting the whole time. Star did not understand the words and she wondered if it were an ancient language he spoke.

Next the shaman shuffled around the bearskin. Shaking the foliage over the head of each groom, he named him and called great blessings down upon each.

Then he faced the four directions again, chanting each time.

The women stood facing the men shyly. Star looked into Falcon's hungry black eyes, Pine Woman smiled at Lance, and Fawn giggled at Red Hawk. Sageflower and Chokecherry fidgeted across from their new spouses. Sageflower's husband, a tall, striking man, was called Deer Summoner. From his name, Star guessed he was an excellent hunter. Chokecherry's husband, Cat Lurks, was a short, muscular man whose thick hair fell only to the tops of his shoulders. His trousers and leather shirt appeared to be made from the tanned hides of cougar and bobcat.

Elk Knees smiled her amused smile at the man standing across from her. He was an older hunter, graying at his temples. The shaman called him

Horn. Star did not recognize Horn from the bridal quest but she had seen him around the Jaguar camp, often with two small children, a girl and a boy, clinging to his leather-clad legs. Elk Knees would now be the mother of two children. Perhaps she would like that.

Star suddenly felt eyes upon her. It was Tula. When Star stared back, Tula sniffed and looked away.

Star wondered at the woman's animosity. Just then, she felt Falcon's measured gaze upon her. The look in his eyes was hot and possessive and Star felt a little thrill of excitement run up and down her spine.

Now the shaman had the women join hands with their respective men. Falcon's hands were warm to her, his clasp firm as he captured both her hands in his.

Chokecherry and Sageflower refused to hold hands with their soon-to-be mates. The shaman halted his speech and stalked over and placed Chokecherry's hands within the grasp of Cat Lurks's, and Sageflower's hands within those of Deer Summoner. Admonishing the two women to behave themselves and chiding them that this was an important ceremony, the shaman then marched back to his place at the head of the bearskin.

Demure Sageflower stared down at her hands, and Chokecherry looked miserable. Star felt their misery as her own and suddenly wanted to tug her hands free from Falcon's warm clasp. He sensed her intent, however, and his fingers closed firmly over hers. When she tugged again, wanting to run, she saw the warning light in his eyes. Her trembling hands were locked in his.

She closed her eyes. She was marrying a man she did not know; marrying a stranger whose hot looks and warm hands aroused her so. She should be marrying Camel Stalker!

When she opened her eyes, guilty tears blurred the ceremony for her. She could not meet her groom's eyes. She could not see the other women, but she heard a sob come from Chokecherry. Chokecherry's sobs set her friend Sageflower to crying and soon both young women were sobbing uncontrollably in front of the whole Jaguar camp.

Star tightened her lips, not wanting to show her pain, though she heartily understood the crying women's sorrow. Pine Woman gave them a warning hiss, but that did not halt their piteous weeping.

The shaman stalked over once again and waved the handful of juniper and sage over Chokecherry's and Sageflower's heads. Still they wept on.

Exasperated, the shaman took to chanting loudly, drowning out the women's weeping. The crowd of Jaguars looked relieved when he finally came to the end of the ceremony. He scattered white duck down over the heads of the brides and their new husbands.

The tiny white feathers clung to Falcon's black hair and vest. He picked one up and gave it to Star. "To bring good fortune in our marriage," he said, and there was that same mystifying happy glow in his eyes that she had seen earlier.

"I do hope your marriage to this Badger woman yields you good fortune," interrupted Tula, effectively dampening Star's reply. "Anything will be better than what we had!"

Star's eyes widened at the woman's effrontery. Falcon's eyes narrowed to slits. "Leave us, Tula. What I do is no longer any concern of yours!"

Tula glared at him, her mouth working. Before she could say anything more, Marmot stepped between her and Falcon. "I do not want you bothering my wife," he snarled.

"Then tell your wife to mind her own concerns."

"I was merely giving my good wishes for the success of their marriage," protested Tula, her black eyes flashing in anger.

Marmot glanced from Tula to Falcon and back again. "Come, Tula. We will leave this man to his life."

"But I was only trying to wish my best—"

"Tula. Enough." Marmot brooked no further protest. He dragged her away, the baby on her back bouncing with every hurried step she took. Star let out a breath of relief.

Falcon watched them go. Star watched him. Tension lined his face and there was a slump to his shoulders that had not been there earlier when he had participated in the marriage ceremony.

She wondered at him, wondered what secrets he hid. Wondered what secrets stood between him and Tula.

He turned back to her. "Do not let Tula upset you," he counseled.

Broken Promise

"She did not upset me," denied Star.

"No?"

"No." *Only a little.*

Falcon looked as if he did not believe her. He took her hand. "Come, let us walk."

Star nodded and let him lead her past people talking and eating and piling food onto platters. Chokecherry and Sageflower, eyes red from weeping, huddled together. Then Chokecherry started crying again and her new husband, Cat Lurks, glanced around, embarrassed.

When Sageflower joined in with her sobs, her husband, Deer Summoner, angrily swept her up into his arms and marched off to a nearby tent. The two disappeared into the tent. Chokecherry sniffled. Cat Lurks grasped her by the shoulder and shook her.

Star could not watch any more. The drums began once more and this time it was a laughing song that the old women sang. This type of song was merely an excuse to tell jokes about different people in the camp. The chorus of the song was stylized laughter. The first old woman sang about this hunter and that. She sang about the time that Lance sought shelter one night in a cave and how in the morning he awoke staring into the angry eyes of a cave bear. Star chuckled.

The second old woman sang about a certain Jaguar woman who went digging for camas bulbs. Instead of choosing a bulb with a purple flower as every woman knows to do, she picked a white-flowered plant, dug up the bulbs, took them home, and fed them to her family. Her family all got sick. Now the woman was not allowed to dig for camas bulbs on her own. Star laughed.

The third old woman, with a sly glance at the brides, began to imitate Chokecherry's and Sageflower's sobs. The old woman clearly enjoyed her role, crying louder and harder with each verse. Star felt her face go red; she pitied Chokecherry and Sageflower, who would henceforth be forever mocked in the songs of the Jaguar People.

"Come," whispered Falcon. "Let us get away before they spot you and make up a song about you."

"Or you," answered Star.

"Me? There is nothing to say about me!" He chuckled.

"Perhaps," suggested Star, "I should give the old women a gift and ask them to sing a joke about Tula."

"That is not funny, Star."

Star smiled. It was.

They walked past groups of people sitting and eating the abundant repast set out. Star was too nervous to eat, but the food looked delicious.

They walked down by the river where several large cottonwoods and willows hid them from the festivities.

They stood on the bank and Falcon pointed across the water. "Ducks," he said, as two birds rose and flew off. Star watched the sure, swift flight. Suddenly a loud honking drew her attention. A huge flock of geese came flying out of the north.

"My people will be hunting them in the next day or so," said Falcon, eyeing the birds.

"I know how to make duck nets to catch them with," volunteered Star.

"Good."

There was a silence between them and Star stared at the sky, pretending she was intent on the geese. But what she was truly intent on was Falcon. She was alone with him; they were married now. I am a wife, she thought and shivered, wondering what that would entail with this man.

He took her hand. "We are married now," he said, echoing her very thoughts.

She glanced down at her hand, shading her eyes from the bright sun. She gave a little tug to remove her fingers from his grasp. He tightened his grip. She met his dark eyes, hot with wanting.

A tremor went through her. "What do you want of me?" she whispered.

"You," he whispered back. "Only you."

He lowered his lips to her mouth and kissed her. He smelled of smoke and leather and tasted of man. She tried to move her head back, but he grasped the thick hair at the back of her head and pulled her into the kiss.

"How I want you," he murmured.

She could feel his hands tremble as he cupped her face. Why, he was as moved as she was! She closed her eyes and leaned into his kiss. She sighed in bliss and relaxed. How good his kisses felt.

Soon he wanted to do more than kiss; she could tell because he was tugging her to the ground, to a soft grassy patch warmed by the sun. Unsure of how to proceed, she let him take the lead.

His kisses were so sweet, so enticing, that a few more could not hurt. She snuggled into his arms and spread her fingers over his warm chest. How good he felt, how strongly his heart pounded beneath her hand. He was moving his mouth over her face now, then her neck, her shoulders. Her breath came in gasps, as did his. Excited, she ran her hands over his shoulders, wanting to feel his strength, to caress the newness of him.

"Here. Let me." He shrugged off his vest.

His large chest felt muscular under the smooth skin. With one finger, she touched the tattoo in the hollow of his shoulder. Then she kissed it.

"That is my coming of age tattoo." His words seemed to be breathless. She kissed the design again.

"It is," he gasped, "a falcon."

"Mmm, yes, it is," she agreed.

"A black falcon," he explained with that same breathlessness that was so exciting to her. "Diving on its prey."

"Mmm."

"A vision . . ." He could no longer get the words out, it seemed, and he pulled her down onto his chest.

She lay on top of him, looking down at him with narrowed eyes. "I have a tattoo, also," she said, kissing his nipples.

He raised her head and met her mouth, his tongue plunging in and meeting hers.

The sensations were wonderful, she thought, wanting to melt.

"I did not know that Badger women wore tattoos," he gasped when the kiss ended.

When she could get her breath, she answered, "We do." She had to gulp some air. "I wear a star."

"Of course," he murmured, meeting her lips once more. When the kiss was done, he said, "Show me where your tattoo is."

"No."

She laughed when he rolled her over and sprawled on top of her.

"Show me where your tattoo is or I will tickle you."

She laughed again and then when he started tickling her, she giggled and squirmed. "I—I cannot!" she gasped.

"Try," he urged.

"Stop! Stop! No more!" she panted, still laughing from his tickling. Then she drew up one side of her dress, exposing the top of her left thigh. "Here it is."

"Ummmm." He pretended to bite it, but instead, his lips touched the tattoo gently and he kissed it. "It is very pretty," he murmured.

Indeed, she was very proud of it, a star with eight points on it. "It is the Darkstar," she murmured. "My ancestress." Old Granny Dawn had drawn the design with much skill and rubbed in the ash and fat carefully.

Falcon's lips began to wander from the tattoo. "Back," she whispered, moving his head back to the top of her thigh. Her hand lingered in his hair and she caressed his head.

"Ah, yes," he murmured, "how foolish of me. I was supposed to be kissing your tattoo." After a few moments, he raised his head and said, "Your

177

dress is in the way. It has to go."

She pretended to pout.

He sighed. "I see I shall have to tickle it off you."

She laughed. "No. I will help." She lifted her arms and he pulled the garment off and tossed it aside. She watched it land on the grass. "My mother sewed that," she said in a warning voice.

"She did make a beautiful dress," he whispered, but his eyes were not on the dress. They were on her, roving over her, and she began to feel a little afraid.

He smiled and bent to kiss a breast. "I am hunting," he said. His warm lips moved to the other breast and he made gentle, sweet love to that globe, suckling the tip.

She closed her eyes. How good he felt! "Hunting for what?" she managed to gasp. His kisses on her breasts quite took her breath away.

"I"—he was kissing his way up her neck—"am hunting"—now he was turning her around and kissing her along her shoulders—"for tattoos."

She giggled. "You will not find any more." She had to gasp as his lips worked their way back to her front and now he was kissing her stomach. "That is the only tattoo I have."

"I do not"—he was licking her navel—"believe you."

"It is," she protested with a squeal as his tongue swirled inside her navel. "I only have one! Oh!"

"I shall have to continue my hunt," he said solemnly, his lips moving down her stomach, quite ignoring her thrashing legs.

"Here!" She grasped his head and pushed him

over to the eight-pointed star. "Here. Be satisfied!"

He chuckled as he kissed the tattoo again. "Never."

Now his tongue was moving over to the very center of her femininity. She giggled as his lips moved through the curling hair protecting her. "Oh, Falcon," she moaned. "What are you doing to me?"

He did not answer but his lips moved closer to the bud of her womanhood. When he touched that soft part of her, she thought she would scream with delight. She gave a little moan and quivered as his tongue swirled over and around her. Then a sweet rushing feeling overcame her and she arched up, meeting his lips with her upthrust hips. "Oh, Falcon! Oh, help me!"

He pressed her to him then and held her until her shaking and quivering subsided.

She ran her fingers through the black mane of his hair. "Oh, Falcon, what did you do to me?" She smiled at him, satiated, replete with contentment and well-being. New feelings stole over her as she smiled at him: awe, gratitude, soft caring.

He moved up over her and kissed her gently on the nose. "That is what people do," he whispered. "That is what a man can do for a woman."

Then, carefully spreading her legs, he entered her. She felt him move inside her and pulled him closer.

"You can wrap your legs around me if you want," he encouraged. She did so and held on to him.

He thrust into her, his black eyes holding hers

as he moved. She smiled at him and when he tensed and closed his eyes in evident pain, her own widened. Was something wrong? Had she done something to hurt him?

"Falcon?"

He froze, clutching her to him.

"Falcon?" She wanted to thrash wildly but he was holding her too tightly.

Then he sighed and collapsed on top of her.

"Falcon?"

He opened one eye. "Yes?"

"Are—are you hurt?"

He shook his head. "That is what it is like for the man, Star."

"Oh." She hesitated. "Are you certain it does not—hurt?"

He opened the other eye. "No, wife. It does not hurt. Not at all." He lifted himself onto his elbows and looked down at her. "It feels very good."

She smiled at him, relieved. "It feels wonderful to me, too."

He kissed her on the nose again. "Now," he said sternly. "Are there any other tattoos you must tell me about?" He reached for the sole of her left foot. "Is there one here?"

"No!" She laughed.

He reached behind a knee and tickled. "Here?"

"No. You know I do not have any more. I have none to hide from you!"

He went still at that and a solemn light shone in his dark eyes as he regarded her. "No," he agreed at last. "You have nothing to hide from me, Star." He bent to kiss her lips. "And I am glad of that."

She wondered at the seriousness in his voice; then she shrugged and yawned. "I am tired. I want to sleep."

He chuckled. "And I."

They fell asleep then, Star snuggled in Falcon's arms. When they awoke, the sun had set and a chill breeze blew.

He patted her naked buttocks. "Come, let us get dressed, wife. I hear the drums and singing. They are dancing."

"I like to dance," she said.

"Do you dance as well as you make love?" he asked as he put on his leather pants.

"I dance about as well as you hunt for tattoos."

"Ah, that must be very well indeed. I cannot wait!"

When she was fully clad, he took her hand and they started the walk back to the fire. They had taken but several steps when he halted and swung to face her. "Star?" He ran his hand along her hair, his fingers gentle, then along her cheek, his eyes searching hers for something.

"Yes, Falcon?"

"I—" He hesitated.

She waited. Instead of speaking, he continued to caress her face and her hair.

She ceased his movement by taking his hand in hers and moving it to her lips. She kissed the back of his hand softly.

He stared at her, and she felt herself becoming lost in those black eyes.

"I—"

He looked lost to her as well, as though hope and fear warred within him. She reached up and

181

touched the long scar that marred his face. "Tell me," she whispered.

He flinched then and drew back. "I cannot."

He bent and kissed her. A jaunty smile was on his lips, but there was still that lost look in his eyes. "I thank you," he said. "I thank you for what you gave me back there."

"And what did I give you?"

"You gave me a beautiful gift. Your virginity. I am your first man." Then he suddenly seized her by both arms and held her firmly. "And I will be your *only* man. Do you understand?"

Puzzled, she searched the depths of his eyes and saw a tortured look therein. "What is it, Falcon? Why do you hold me like this, as though I would run from you?"

He laughed, but there was no amusement in the sound. "I do not fear your running from me because I will hunt you down if you flee me."

She shivered suddenly at his words. "What do you fear then?"

He laughed again. "Nothing," he said at last. "I fear nothing."

She did not believe him.

After several heartbeats, he dropped his hands from her arms. "Come," he said, "let us join the dancers."

Her heart pounding, she followed him up the path to the Jaguar festivities. What had just happened between them?

Chapter Nineteen

Star poked her head out of the tent and looked around for Falcon. Where was he?

She stepped out of the tent, yawned, and stretched. How good she felt this morning after a night of tender lovemaking with him! It had been that way ever since that first time. She counted on her fingers. Yes, ten days ago. It seemed so long ago that the Jaguars had given the huge feast to celebrate the new marriages.

Unwillingly, her eyes skipped to the tent where Chokecherry stayed with her new spouse, Cat Lurks. For many nights Star had heard sobs coming from that tent. In the daytime Cat Lurks walked around looking haggard. In the nighttime Chokecherry cried out for Finds the Marten.

Star shook her head. Poor Chokecherry.

In the distance a woman was walking down to the river, carrying a basket. Dread coiled in

Star's stomach. It was Tula, her baby cocooned on her back.

In the time that Star had lived with the Jaguars, she had had ample opportunity to observe Tula. From what she had seen, Tula was a very unhappy woman, and she was making everyone around her unhappy. Star had learned to avoid her.

Where was Falcon? Had he gone to the river for a swim? Even though the leaves on the trees were turning to yellows and reds, and Star found the river water too cold for her liking, she knew that Falcon liked to swim in the chill water in the mornings.

Careful to keep a good distance between herself and Tula, Star wandered down the path that led to the riverbank. As she entered the screen of trees that hid the path from the encampment, she heard a little cry and saw a flicker fly to a branch. The red stripe on the bird's cheek reminded her of Falcon's scar.

She was about to step out into the open along the riverbank when she caught sight of Tula. She must have taken another trail to get to the river, thought Star. I must hide. I do not want her to see me.

Then Star gasped. Standing naked in front of Tula, his body glistening with drops of water from his swim, was Falcon. Star frowned. While many Badger men customarily went naked from time to time when hunting or swimming or in hot weather, it unsettled her to think that Falcon would appear that way in front of his former wife. But Falcon did not seem to mind; he was too involved in his conversation with Tula.

Broken Promise

Jealousy pricked Star. Squashing the protests of her conscience, she crept closer, shielded from their view by scraggly bushes.

"Do not think I care," Tula was saying.

"I know you do not care," Falcon answered, crossing his arms over his wide chest.

Star swallowed. He looked so handsome standing there. Oh, why was he allowing Tula to gaze upon his nakedness?

The baby started to cry, drawing both Falcon's and Tula's attention. Tula swung the baby off her back and cuddled him in her arms.

"You have your son," said Falcon stiffly.

"I do." Tula brought out her breast and put her nipple in the baby's mouth. He stopped crying.

Falcon was staring at Tula's naked breast. Star's fists clenched.

"If you had not left me, I could have given you a son," said Falcon.

Star gasped.

"Ha! You give sickly sons!" retorted Tula.

Falcon flinched. Star could see his scar throb.

"We had a sickly son. Remember?" Tula's face grew ugly and she spat on the ground. "I was the one who rubbed his legs with medicine leaves. I was the one who sat beside him at night. I was the one who called for the shaman when my son fell into a thrashing fit! I was the one who loved him!"

Falcon looked as though she had struck him. "You think I did not love him? I loved him! I paid the shaman with antelope meat whenever he brought Hawk's spirit back from its wandering!"

"You hated Hawk! You wanted a whole, healthy

boy. Many times I saw you look at him, contempt upon your face."

"I never said—"

"You did not have to! I know how you thought! I saw it! You hated him! You wanted a boy who could run, who could talk like other boys—"

"I did," yelled Falcon. "I admit it! Many times I prayed to the Great Spirit to heal him. To take the strange look from his eyes. To give him understanding so that he would know our words and know me, his father."

"Ha. The Great Spirit would not listen to words from such a man!"

"That may be. He certainly did not answer my prayers."

"Ah, but he did." Tula's face grew cruel. "He took our son, just as you wanted!"

"I did not want our son to die!" Cords stood out on Falcon's neck. Star wanted to run away, but she was frozen. If she moved, they would see her.

"You did! He was not perfect. He was not strong and healthy. He would not grow to be a fine hunter. He was not good enough!"

"I knew he was sick." Falcon drew in a deep breath. "I accepted that. I did not like it, but I accepted it."

"No, you did not! You wanted nothing to do with him!"

"I hunted for him. I brought him the best meat I could. I gave him lions' hearts to make him strong. I fed him the meat from antelope legs so he could run swiftly. I gave him the brains of foxes so he would grow wise. I did everything

186

I could to help him. I wanted him to grow strong and powerful. What is wrong with that?"

"It was not what he was supposed to be," screamed Tula. "He was supposed to be a great shaman! When he would fall down on the ground and kick and froth at the mouth, that was important work for being a shaman. Rapt told me that!"

Falcon's chest rose and fell with each word. "Well, Rapt told you lies! He said our son would grow to be a great shaman and you believed him. But our son is dead. Our son is dead!"

"And it is all your fault," screamed Tula. "You are the one who killed the bear! It was my father's animal. He saw the grizzly in his vision quest when he was but a youth. You should never have killed that bear! The bear's spirit told the Great Spirit to take our son!"

"I had to kill the bear," cried Falcon. "You were pregnant, you had tripped, you were lying on the ground! The bear was going to kill you! I had to do something!"

"You could have chased him away!"

"That bear was not afraid of me! He was laughing at me. It was only my spear that saved you that day, saved our son." Now Falcon's voice grew deadly. "It was not my fault; it was *your* fault. You are the one who fell while carrying my son. It was your clumsy fall that crippled Hawk."

"I did not!" screeched Tula. The baby at her breast started to cry. Tula shoved the nipple at him and Star heard the baby's muffled protests, but Tula did not seem to notice. "I did everything I could. I almost died giving birth to that baby! It

187

was long and agonizing. Many times during that birthtime I cried out your name! It was so cruel that you should give me a baby that took so long to be born!"

Falcon glared at her and her son.

"Now Marmot's son, this baby," said Tula, beaming at her child, "his birth was swift and smooth. Was it not, my little butterfly? Oh yes, it was, it was." She lifted her head and glared at Falcon. "It was all your fault."

"It was yours!"

They glared at each other. Star wondered if she could just tiptoe away.

"You were unfaithful," snarled Falcon.

"I could not stay with a man who did not love his own child!"

"I loved Hawk! I did everything I could—"

"You did nothing! I did it all! I put the leaves on his legs, I—"

Falcon held up a hand. "We are beginning to repeat ourselves," he said wearily. "There is no winner in this fight between us."

Tula's mouth was tight. "Yes, there is," she cried. "It is I! I have a healthy son! I have a husband who loves his child, who loves me!"

"Marmot stole you from me!"

"Marmot did not steal me! I went willingly. He is more man than you."

"He is a sly, sneaking wife-stealer."

"Well, I love him. He's better than you. And he is better under the bedrobes than you are!"

Falcon snorted. "Do not try to provoke me, woman. The Badger woman has no complaints."

Tula's lips curled in a snarl. "She is a dog-girl.

188

Broken Promise

A slave. She is ugly. I do not know why you chose her. Never have I seen such a tall, ungainly, ugly woman in my life! She is just right for you!"

Falcon's lips set in a bloodless line. "She is not your concern. You leave her out of what is between us, Tula."

"I will not! I cannot stand the sight of her, I can tell you that!"

Falcon turned away. "Go, Tula," he said. "Get your water and leave. I wish to be alone."

The baby began to cry.

Tula hushed him and then swung him to her back and tied the blanket securely to hold him. She bent and scooped water into the tightly woven basket lined with clay; then she hurried off.

Star tried to duck into the bush when she saw Tula headed her way, but she was too slow.

"Aha!" cried Tula triumphantly. "Look what we have here!"

Her black eyes glowed as though she were hungry and had found a cache of meat. "Oh, Falcon," she said in a singsong voice, "do come here. I have something interesting to show you."

Falcon was swimming in the middle of the river. "Go back to your husband," he called. "I do not want to talk with you any longer."

Tula ran back to the riverbank, her baby bobbing on her back. "It is your dog-girl! The Badger! She heard every word we said! Ha ha!"

Falcon said nothing, only stood looking at the two women on the riverbank. He struck out across the river and swam with vigorous, powerful strokes to the other side.

189

"He knows," said Tula to Star. "He knows you were spying upon him, dog-girl!"

Star blushed. She was too embarrassed to speak.

"Let me tell you something, girl-who-scratches-fleas-and-sleeps-with-the-dogs." Tula came so close that Star could see her left eyelid twitch. "He will never love you." Her eyes shot to Star's flat stomach. "Or any child you give him."

Her expression was triumphant and malicious. "He cannot love anyone. He hated our son!" She turned to watch Falcon as he swam. "Good fortune in your marriage, Badger woman!" she said breezily and laughed. Then she walked back up the river path and disappeared.

Star choked back tears and sat on the riverbank to await Falcon.

Chapter Twenty

Only when his muscles were sore and aching did Falcon wade from the river. He walked over to where Star sat twisting a piece of bulrush grass in her strong, slender fingers. She stared at the ground. Tula must have said something particularly cruel to her. He took a breath and said, "She lies, you know. I did love my son."

Star lifted her head then, and her beautiful dark eyes looked hurt. "You still love *her*."

He had to laugh at that. "No. I do not." Could his new wife not see that for herself? Tula caused him great pain. He shook his head. If Star could watch Tula and him argue and scratch at each other like hissing bobcats and not understand what she had seen and heard, then it was no fault of his. "It matters not."

"It does matter!"

He liked the flash in her eyes when she was

191

angry. He shrugged to goad her with his indifference.

"It matters whether you love her or not—"

He wondered if she knew how lovely she looked. "Why? Do you want me to love *you?*"

He almost laughed at the red flush that spread across her face. So she did want him to love her, the little Badger. Huh, but all women were the same, anxious to entrap a man within their closely woven nets of love! But it was not love they craved, oh no. It was control. That was what they all wanted. To control a man, to make him do as they wanted.

Well, he had played that game with Tula. He had pretended that his sick son would get better, he had hunted the meat to pay the shaman for his useless advice to Tula. He had listened to Tula's dreams of how her son would one day be a great shaman of the Jaguar People. He had even prayed to the Great Spirit to heal his son, to make him whole in his mind and his body, and when that did not work and the Mouse Death-Sickness struck Hawk, Falcon was reduced to begging the Great Spirit that his son would live. But the Great Spirit saw fit to ignore his prayers and Hawk swiftly died.

Well, Falcon was not going to play any more deceitful games with anyone. Not with Tula, and not with Star, either. He knew that nothing mattered, and he would no longer pretend that anything did. As for women, they were all the same. He would have a woman, take her in the bedrobes when it pleased him, but never again would he love one. Love. Ha! He wanted to spit.

All love brought a man was pain and betrayal!

He met Star's eyes. "Will you come and swim with me?"

She shook her head, her long black hair fluttering in the breeze.

With a sigh, he sat down and took one of her hands in his. "What is between Tula and me is none of your concern."

His words would hurt Star, but there was no other way to make her understand. "What happened between us is finished and I will not discuss it. Nothing good ever came from talking about the past." How well he had learned that! Why, if he talked about what had gone on with his son and Tula, he would be reduced to weeping like a woman here on the riverbank. No, it was better to leave that pain alone. Better to feel the welcoming numbness than the turmoil of feelings that could unman him. "I do not want you to talk about it, either."

She frowned. "I am confused about you and Tula. You say that you do not love her, yet you protect her. From me."

"I do not protect Tula! I want nothing to do with her!"

"You protect her with your silence."

I protect myself with my silence, Badger woman. He rose and stood looking down at her. "If you insist upon questioning me about my life, I will leave."

Her eyes narrowed and she shrugged. "Then leave."

He stomped off. Now he was deprived of her company because she was so stubborn. Two wives he had and each of them stubborn. Great Spirit, spare me from stubborn women, he thought, before he remembered that there was no Great Spirit. Or, if there was, He was uncaring of what happened to anyone, especially a man named Falcon.

He decided to go hunting. Perhaps a solitary hunt would soothe him and bring back the numbing peace.

Star wanted to cry. The grass she was twisting into a basket blurred in front of her fingers. She closed her eyes, and tears ran down the bridge of her nose. Oh, what had happened to her? She had spent the past ten days learning to love her new husband. And just as she was beginning to realize she loved him, he taunted her with it, and then left her alone when she would not be silent. "But how can I be silent," she muttered aloud, "when it is his life with Tula that keeps intruding on mine? I did not ask to be taken from my people! I did not ask to be married to this man! I was not here when their baby died; I had nothing to do with it! Why, then, must I bear his anger, and hers, too?"

She sobbed, then wiped her eyes and brushed the tears from her cheek. "Neither of them knows what they are doing," she muttered. "Tula wants both Marmot *and* Falcon, though she will not admit it. And Falcon wants to be left alone. He cares nothing for me and his anger at Tula keeps drawing him back to her, but he does not admit *that*." She buried her face in her arms. "Oh, what am I going to do?"

194

Broken Promise

She lifted her head and stared out at the water. It flowed past at its familiar slow pace, gurgling where it bubbled against the low riverbank.

After a while Star rose and plodded back along the trail to the camp. She passed Tula's tent and saw the Jaguar woman sitting outside in the sun, nursing her baby. When Tula caught sight of Star, she hissed.

Star sighed. If she did not leave the Jaguar camp soon, it was going to be a long, cold winter. *Perhaps I will go and talk with Chokecherry. She is unhappy, too. We can make plans together, plans to return to our Badger People.*

Chapter Twenty-one

At the time of the evening meal, Falcon walked into camp with two large rabbits, gutted and skinned, slung over his shoulder. Relief swept through Star. She had not seen him all day since he had stridden away from the river, and she had secretly worried that he was going to stay away hunting for several days because he was so angry with her.

But now that he was back, she shrugged off her relief and kept scraping at the deer hide. She had to remove the thick fat from the inside of the skin before it could be worked into soft leather for clothing.

Falcon placed the rabbits by the fire and sauntered over to her. When he was quiet, Star glanced up at him.

"So. You decided to return." The coldness in her voice was not feigned.

"I went hunting."

She said nothing to that obvious statement but kept scraping at the hide.

"Is that hide you are scraping going to be our next meal?"

"No."

He glanced around at the neat baskets laid out with her scraping implements and her awl and needles. Fall berries and freshly dug wapatoo roots were in the other baskets. Star was proud of her work, work that she had done while worrying and wondering where he was, she thought angrily. Her lips tightened.

"I did not return from hunting just to watch my wife labor at tanning a hide while I am hungry."

She carefully set aside the scraping stone, unfolded her legs, and got to her feet. She gave him a level look. "I did not like it that you left without telling me where you were going."

He shrugged his broad shoulders. "I went hunting."

"I know you went hunting," she answered patiently. "But next time you go hunting, please tell me. Then I will not fear for you."

"Fear for me? You?"

She wanted to wipe the astounded look from his handsome face. "I did not know where you were," she answered doggedly. "I worried that you might have gone hunting for many days, or been lying hurt in a ravine somewhere."

He frowned and appeared to be pondering her words. "I was safe."

She snorted. "Do you Jaguar people not tell others when you go hunting?"

"Yes, we do. It just did not occur to me. I knew I was not going to be gone long."

"Among my people," she answered, "we tell one another these things. How long we are going to be gone. Which ravine or part of the river we are going to hunt, or dig roots at."

He nodded. "I will do so next time."

His answer surprised her. She had expected he would tell her it did not matter. Perhaps there was a part of him she had yet to learn about. Remembering his gentleness whenever they made love, she flushed and reached for the rabbits. "I will prepare these for our meal."

His hand brushed hers. His dark eyes met hers. "Very good. I do not like to eat tanned deer hide."

She chuckled. "Surely you can cook rabbits."

"I can if I have to. But then, that is what I have a wife for."

The smile left her face. She raised the dead animals and looked at the pink flesh. Then she let them drop to the ground. "Cook them yourself!" She picked up a water bladder and strode away.

When she reached the river, she was so angry her hands were shaking. *First he stomps off because he does not want to talk about whatever is truly bothering him; then he stays away all day without telling me, and now, now he brags that he has a wife to cook his meals for him. As if that is all I am good for! No wife would put up with such poor treatment*, she scolded herself. *No Jaguar wife, no Badger wife, and certainly not me!*

She carried the full water bladder back to the tent and was surprised to see that he had put both rabbits on sticks and that they were roasting

198

over the flames. She frowned. Roots were missing from her root basket. He must have buried them in the hot ashes to bake. She grimaced. If he was trying to show her that he was a practiced cook and could get by without her help, that was fine with her. Let him do all the cooking!

She entered the tent and fidgeted with the baskets, hiding from him.

"Meat is ready," he called out, and reluctantly she left the safety of the tent.

The meat was overcooked and dry. The roots were also overcooked: mealy inside and thickly charred on the outside. He had tried to make the meal tasty, she noted. He had rubbed aromatic leaves inside the rabbits to flavor the flesh.

She gnawed at a leg bone, pondering. It would not do to discourage him from trying to cook. Why, he might even learn to be better at roasting food than she was!

She tossed the leg bone in the direction of a skulking camp dog and leaned back against a rock near the fire.

"Did you like my cooking?"

"It was very good," she said with a show of reluctance.

He grinned smugly. Star had to hide a smile.

Just then Horn and Elk Knees wandered past. Falcon called out to them, "Come and sit and visit."

Obliging, the two walked over to the fire. They stayed and talked for some time, the men discussing hunting prospects, the women talking about roots. While Falcon and Horn were caught up in a heated exchange about how to make the best spear tip, Elk Knees rose and said to Star, "Let us go for a walk." After the women had wandered a short distance from the tents, Elk Knees asked, "Was it not as I told you?"

"What are you talking about?" asked Star.

Elk Knees glanced back to where Horn and Falcon spoke, heads together. "About mating. Was it not as I said? And I think a Jaguar man wants to mate even more often than a Badger man."

Star shifted uncomfortably. Horn did not look like a man who thought of nothing but mating, but how would she know?

"I hope you are keeping him from your bed."

"Are you keeping Horn from yours?" asked Star pointedly.

Elk Knees nodded. Star raised an eyebrow. She could try to keep Falcon from her bed. But she did not want to. The time between the bedrobes was too precious, too wonderful. . . .

"It is time to go, Elk Knees," called Horn. "The children will be crying out for us."

Elk Knees smiled her amused smile as they returned to the fire. Star watched as Elk Knees put her hand on Horn's arm and dutifully fell into step beside him as they left.

When Star turned back to the tent, Falcon was staring at her, a small, cruel smile playing about his mouth.

"What is it?" she asked.

"Do not think to leave me for Horn."

"Horn?" she sputtered. "Horn? Why ever would I want to leave you for Horn? He is happy with Elk Knees and she with him."

"No. He is not happy with her."

"What do you mean? Elk Knees is a good woman; she is an excellent cook."

Falcon laughed. "A man needs more than an excellent cook. A man needs a woman who will be his companion. In the bedrobes," he added.

"Oh. Does Elk Knees—" pried Star delicately.

"No, Elk Knees does not."

"Oh." She stared at him, pondering.

"That is, not often enough for Horn's liking." He eyed her. "Horn asked me if you turned me away in the bedrobes."

Star's eyes widened. "I will if I want to. Tonight might be a good time to start."

He laughed. "Not tonight. But that is what I told Horn. I did not want him to get interested in you. I do not need another wife stolen."

So it still hurt that Tula had left him. How long would he love his former wife?

Falcon prowled over to her and took her in his arms. He plunged his hand into her hair and held her head still. His eyes glittered. "You will not leave me for another man. Do you understand?"

She met his tortured look. "Yes," she whispered.

The pain vanished from his eyes then and he kissed her on the forehead. "Good. You and I will deal well together, wife. This I know."

He led her into the tent then, but as she followed she wondered what he would think of her when she left him and fled back to her Badger People.

Troubled, she knelt on the bedrobes and fidgeted with the baskets, arranging and rearranging them. He would be very angry with her when he learned she had escaped. She knew that. Ah, but he was tantalizing to her. She was beginning to see that there was more to him that she did not know. Like tonight, when he had tried to please her by roasting the meat and the roots. She stared down at the furs, pondering. *He seems to be a man who hides his hurts. . . .*

"Come here, Star," he commanded.

The hunger in his eyes sent shivers through her. She held his gaze, then smiled happily and went into his arms.

Chapter Twenty-two

"Do you want to return to our Badger People?" whispered Chokecherry.

Star picked a handful of late fall berries and put them in her berry basket, all the while carefully thinking how to answer Chokecherry. Star did not want to be overheard by the several other women, both Jaguar and Badger, who picked berries in the brush of the ravine. And crouched on a rock above them, Horn stood guard against the big cats and wolves that stalked the hills. Star did not want to be overheard by him, either.

Chokecherry sidled closer and reached past Star's nose. "You missed one," she said and popped the big, round black fruit into her mouth.

Star murmured, "I know you are not happy here, Chokecherry."

Her companion spat out the berry. "I will not stay here any longer!" she hissed. "I do not like

Cat Lurks and I do not like the Jaguars! I want to go home!" She suddenly looked ready to cry.

"Hush," murmured Star. "The others will hear you."

Chokecherry lowered her voice. "I want to go back. I want to see Finds the Marten."

"Finds the Marten is gone. He was stolen by the slave catchers. Remember?"

"I remember," answered Chokecherry bitterly. "But I want to go back."

"He will not be there."

"I know that. But he may escape. He may return to our people and if I am not there, he will be very unhappy."

"Chokecherry," said Star, alarmed that her friend seemed to be making up a dream life, "Finds the Marten is gone; he will not come back." She stared hard at the other woman, wanting her to understand the truth. "If you return to our people, it will be to live alone, or with your parents."

"That is still better than living with Cat Lurks."

"Is he so bad?"

Chokecherry would not meet her eyes. "He is very bad."

Star swallowed. "What—what does he do?"

Chokecherry shook her head and would not answer.

Feeling sad for her friend, Star picked another handful of berries and put them in Chokecherry's basket. "Here."

Chokecherry looked blankly at the fruit, then at Star. "You have not answered."

"Answered what?"

"Do you want to return to the Badger People?"

"Sometimes," answered Star honestly. "A few days ago, I was going to search you out and ask you if you wanted to return to our people. I thought we could leave together."

"Good plan," approved Chokecherry.

"Today, however," answered Star slowly, "I am not so certain."

Chokecherry picked at a berry bush. "What changed your mind?"

Star sighed. "Ah, it is that I do not know my own mind. Some days I want to be with Falcon; other days I want to flee him. I am all confused."

"Ha! That Jaguar man of yours sounds like a man who is much trouble."

Secretly Star liked it that Chokecherry called him "that man of yours." Aloud she said, "He is not my man."

"Ha! I have seen how he looks at you. How you look at him, when you think he is not looking."

Star blushed.

"Huh!" said Chokecherry. "I can see that you do not want to flee with me."

"It is not that. Many times after we were brought here, I thought of nothing but escape. But I find that as more time goes by, I feel less and less like fleeing."

"Except for a few days ago," said Chokecherry dryly.

Star shrugged. "Some days he is more difficult to be with. Some days I am."

Chokecherry was silent for a time as she picked. After a while she offered, "Sageflower has been my best friend since we were young girls."

Star nodded and kept picking.

"But Sageflower does not want to escape with me. She likes her new husband." Chokecherry's voice was bitter.

"Deer Summoner seems to be a kind man," observed Star.

"Too kind. Sageflower dotes on him."

"It is unfortunate that Cat Lurks is not a good husband," probed Star delicately.

"Cat Lurks," said Chokecherry, "is not a good husband at all. He is not a good man. He is like a—a—slave catcher. Yes, that is it. He is like a slave catcher."

Slave catchers were the worst kind of people. "Surely he cannot be so bad," murmured Star.

"He says he will trade me to the Fish Eaters if I do not do what he says."

"What does he say to do?"

Chokecherry picked berries and ignored Star's question. When Star realized her friend was not going to answer, she asked, "Are any of the other women willing to flee with you?"

Chokecherry shook her head. "Elk Knees and Pine Woman are happy with their mates. Fawn giggles over Red Hawk, though I do not know why. And as for Sageflower and her Deer Summoner, well, Sageflower is no longer my friend!"

Star gasped. "Surely you are still friends!"

Chokecherry shook her head. "No, we are not. She does not understand how it is for me. She thinks that if I but act in the proper manner to Cat Lurks then everything will be fine. But it will not. She tells me to feed Cat Lurks this tasty morsel or that. To talk sweetly to him. All the things

206

she does that work so well with Deer Summoner. But Cat Lurks is not like Deer Summoner. He is not like Finds the Marten, either. He—"

She saw Star watching her and suddenly clapped her hand over her mouth. "I have said too much."

"Chokecherry," answered Star, "you have not said enough. I still do not know what it is about Cat Lurks—"

Chokecherry shuddered. "You must not know, either. But, oh, Star, you must help me escape." She clamped her hand on Star's arm. "Even if you do not wish to escape, say you will help me!"

Desperation lurked in Chokecherry's brown eyes and Star could not deny her friend. "I will help if I can," she promised. "Though I wish I knew—"

Chokecherry shook her head and fear contorted her face. "No. You must not pry. I cannot tell—" Tears pooled in her brown eyes. "I am too ashamed—"

"Chokecherry! What does he do? Tell me! If he hurts you—"

Chokecherry shook her head, her lips a tight line. "I cannot—"

She took her hand off Star's arm then and staggered over to a tree, where she sat down, her back to Star. Fortunately, the other women had drifted farther up the ravine in their hunt for the late-fall berries and there was no one but Star to see the pathetic huddle that was Chokecherry.

Star dropped her basket and ran over to her friend.

Chokecherry's thin body shook from her silent

sobs and Star wanted to cry with her. She put her arms around the other woman and hugged her. Still Chokecherry cried on, violent sobs shaking her body. Star held her and knew that something was very, very wrong in her friend's life. Chokecherry wanted to escape whatever misery it was that she lived with.

Star patted the weeping woman's shoulder in an attempt to comfort her. At last Chokecherry raised a red, sad face. "I cannot live with him anymore," she choked out. "I do not know what will become of me if he continues to—" She sucked in her breath and shook her head mutely.

"We will try to get you away from here." Never had Star seen practical, easy-to-laugh Chokecherry in such a state. "Do not despair, my friend. We will try to get you back to our Badger People, where you will be safe."

Chokecherry sobbed as she held tightly to Star. "I just want to go home to my mother!"

After a while Chokecherry's sobs softened and Star asked, "What are you going to do?"

"I thought you could tell me." Chokecherry sounded so pitiful.

"I do not know what to say to you, Chokecherry. I do not know what is most important to you."

"To get away from Cat Lurks." Chokecherry scowled as she said her husband's name. "I loathe him!"

"Well, if you are able to escape the Jaguars, then you can return to our Badger People."

"Yes, that is what I want! But I cannot go alone."

Star glanced around. "If I help you, that means I, too, must leave these people."

"It is dangerous," moaned Chokecherry. "There are wolf packs. There are bears."

Star patted her hand. "There, there, I did not mean to alarm you. I was but thinking aloud."

"I want you to come, Star. I fear the journey alone. And it is such a long way." She sniffed. "When shall we run away?" Her brown eyes fixed trustingly on Star's.

Star shook her head. "I do not know."

"I want to leave soon! Tonight!"

Star's eyes widened. "That is too soon."

"Why?"

"We will need food. We will need warm clothes, and furs to sleep on at night. We need knives for protection."

"Pah, I can get those things!"

"We need to choose the right time, when no one is watching us."

Chokecherry glanced at Horn, who was guarding the women. He was staring off into the hills.

"Pah, we can sneak away. Easily."

"We must take water with us."

Chokecherry eyed her. "You do not want to escape, do you?"

Star glanced away. Was that why she was listing all the things they must do before they escaped? "No," she admitted at last. "No, I do not want to leave."

Chokecherry smiled bitterly. "You are my last hope, Star. If you do not help me, I will run away by myself. And if I die trying to get back to our Badger People, it will be all your fault!"

Star gasped. "Chokecherry!"

"It is true! Sageflower will not help me; none of the other women will help me. I cannot stay and let Cat Lurks do—" She broke off and waved the silence away. "You are my only hope!" Her brown eyes were pleading.

"Why can you not stay with Cat Lurks?"

"I cannot tell you."

"You must."

"I do not want to."

"I know that." Star shrugged impatiently. "But you are asking something very difficult of me. You know I do not want to leave."

"Today, you do not. But what about tomorrow? You may want to leave him then."

Star did not like having her indecision thrown back at her. "I need to know if you are truly in danger from Cat Lurks. Only then will I be able to tell you if I will go with you."

Chokecherry stared at her, eyes ablaze. "Very well! You want to know my shame?"

Star flushed in anger. "It is not that, Chokecherry! It is that I am reluctant to leave Falcon."

"But you will do it?"

"Perhaps." He had forced her to marry him, after all. She had chosen Camel Stalker. Falcon had ruined her plans for her life.

"Cat Lurks forces himself on me."

Star gasped.

Chokecherry's voice was dull with pain. "Every night I tell him I do not want to mate with him. Every night he forces me. I do not know what to do. I cannot stay with him."

"Have you told him to stop?"

Chokecherry nodded her head. "Yes. Many times. He does not listen. Or care. He does what he wants to do. He says that because I am his wife he can do this thing to me. That I have no say! I—I do not like it. My body hurts— very much. I cannot live with him."

At last Star said slowly, "I will help you, Chokecherry. You should not have to live like that. And I do not want you to die trying to escape alone."

Chokecherry smiled sadly. "Thank you, Star. I—I had hoped you would help me."

Star nodded, wondering what to do. She did not want to leave Falcon, but she did not want her friend to be forced to mate with Cat Lurks, either. And the journey back to the Badger People was a risk; there were wolves and bears and cougars wandering the hills. Alone, Chokecherry would be in grave danger.

The younger woman was watching her. Star patted her hand. "We must get the things together: water bladders, furs, warm clothes. Winter will come soon and if we get caught in the snows, we must be warm."

Chokecherry nodded. "Let us leave soon. Before the snows come."

"That would be best," Star agreed. She helped Chokecherry to her feet, all the while pondering what to do now. If she fled with Chokecherry, she could never come back to Falcon. From the little she knew of him, her flight would greatly anger him and set him against her. Yet if she did not help Chokecherry, the younger woman would surely flee and possibly die in the hills alone. Oh, what to do?

211

"I am glad you are going with me," Choke-cherry was saying. "It will be good. We will surely find our Badger People. You have good eyes for searching the land."

"Yes." Star was beginning to wish she had not promised to help Chokecherry.

"I think we should leave at night, when every-one is asleep," said Chokecherry.

"That would be fine." Yet if she did not help her, Chokecherry would lead a life of misery. Oh, what to do?

"Do not tell anyone. I do not want Cat Lurks to find out we have disappeared until long after we are gone."

Star nodded, too dazed by what she had just promised to answer. Dread twisted her vitals. She had just promised to leave Falcon.

Chapter Twenty-three

Star hid the strips of dried camel meat in a basket. The meat was intended for her journey back to the Badger People. She felt guilty hiding the meat from Falcon, whom she was becoming more and more reluctant to leave.

He was visiting Claw at his campfire and the two men were discussing where the Jaguar People should move for the winter.

Star lowered a fur over the basket so that Falcon would not discover the small cache of meat she had stored away.

And he was being so kind to her. He had overcooked two more meals and she thought he would never learn the correct amount of time needed to roast a bird. But he was trying. For her.

Star rose and peeked out of the tent, wondering when he would return. She groaned to herself when she saw Chokecherry ducking between the tents and heading her way.

Every day since ten days ago when Star and Chokecherry had first planned their escape in the ravine, Chokecherry had told Star some new part of the plan.

Now the younger woman hummed softly as she walked along. Guilt swamped Star as she watched Chokecherry's approach. Guilt that if she went, Falcon would be hurt and angry. Guilt that if she did not go, Chokecherry's life would be unbearable.

Not only that, yesterday afternoon, Chokecherry had told Star that she must flee soon because Cat Lurks had increased his threats to trade her to the slave catchers.

Chokecherry arrived at the tent. "Come, Star," she called out. "Let us go down to the river and fetch some water."

Star dutifully got out the deer bladder she used for carrying water and followed her friend down the path that led to the river. As they passed two of the tents, Star caught a glimpse of Falcon. He was sitting cross-legged at Claw's fire. Horn, Red Hawk, Lance, and some of the other Jaguar men were there too. Relaxed and talking, Falcon looked young and handsome. He threw back his head at something Claw said and his laughter drifted over to her. How she loved to hear him laugh!

Chokecherry watched her with a sad look.

Star hastily swung into step behind her.

"Cat Lurks forced himself on me again last night," said Chokecherry. She held up one bruised arm, where blue finger marks were clearly visible.

Star winced. "I have not forgotten that I promised to go with you."

Chokecherry dropped her arm.

Star was silent while they filled the bladders with water and walked back. Chokecherry, usually talkative, was also quiet. They came to Star's tent. "I suppose I must return to my tent," said Chokecherry.

Star nodded.

"When will it be?" asked Chokecherry. "When will we leave here?"

"Soon," promised Star.

"I cannot take any more of this," said Chokecherry. She glanced over to where Falcon sat with Claw and Betafor. "I know you want to stay with him," she added sadly.

Star shrugged, not knowing what to say. It was true. Yet Chokecherry could not escape alone, either. Alone, she was too vulnerable to the bears, cougars, jaguars, and lions. And she might get lost if the Badger People had moved camp since the Jaguar bridal quest.

"You like it here with the Jaguars," said Chokecherry.

Star nodded. "I like it with Falcon," she whispered.

Chokecherry looked miserable at this admission. "Star, I—I need your help."

"I know," answered Star softly, feeling as miserable as Chokecherry looked.

A sly look came over Chokecherry's pretty face. "How could you forget Camel Stalker so easily?"

Star was taken aback. "I did not forget Camel Stalker."

"Yes, you did. He loved you. He wanted to join with you. Just as Finds the Marten wanted to join with me." Chockecherry's voice trembled.

"Chokecherry," said Star softly, "they are both gone. Taken and sold to the Fish Eaters. There is nothing we can do to help them."

"There is," said Chokecherry sternly. "We can return to the Badger camp and be there when the men return."

"The men are not going to return! They are gone! Why are you so stubborn?"

"I am not stubborn. I am faithful. Faithful to Finds the Marten's memory."

Star shook her head, but Chokecherry's words raked her guilt anew. Indeed, she had been willing to forget Camel Stalker. "He is gone," she repeated, hoping to convince Chokecherry.

The other woman shook her head. "He will return. I know Finds the Marten. He will not be content as a slave. He will do everything he can to escape!"

Star listened uneasily. What if Chokecherry spoke the truth? Camel Stalker would hate slavery, too. Surely he would try to escape. If he still lived.

"Come with me," coaxed Chokecherry. "They will return to us. You will see."

Star did not want to go with her. She did not want the men to return. That is, she did not want to marry Camel Stalker if they returned. She was happy with Falcon. The direction of her thoughts stunned Star for a moment. She was truly feeling content with Falcon! Whatever was the matter with her?

"Star? What is the matter? You look strange."

Star shook her head. "I was thinking."

"About our escape?" said Chokecherry hopefully.

"No."

Chokecherry sighed. "Well, we must leave soon. The snows will be here."

"Chokecherry," said Star slowly, "I think that I will not—"

"Well, well, well. Who do we have here? A gathering of the Badger dog-girls. How sweet."

Star glanced at Tula. Her cruel tone belied her lovely face and attractive white streak of hair.

Chokecherry frowned. "Who are you?"

"Me? Why, I am Tula. And I know all about you."

"You do?"

Star said, "I think I will leave now."

"Oh, no, you will not," said Tula, shifting her baby in the cocoon on her back and stepping in front of Star. "Hear me out, Badger woman."

"Why?"

"Because I have something interesting to tell you." Tula's eyes sparked with a malicious gleam.

Star held her breath.

"Horn told me that you two are making little plans to escape."

"Horn?" gasped Star. "How—? Ah, that day at the ravine!" He must have overheard her and Chokecherry talking. "But he was so far away—!" Star's stomach clenched in dread.

"You are both fools," said Tula with contempt.

217

Theresa Scott

Star felt sick. If Tula knew, she would tell Falcon. And he would hate Star for planning to leave!

Chokecherry looked pale. "Do not tell—"

"Do not tell me what to do," crowed Tula, rounding on her. The smaller woman eyed Chokecherry. "Oh, I know what you go through. I know Cat Lurks." She smiled a tiny smile.

"Then you know why I cannot bear it!" cried Chokecherry. "You know that he hurts me! I must escape him. I must!"

Tula smiled. "Must you?" The baby on her back gave a hiccup. She jiggled him up and down until he quieted. Then she turned to Star.

"And you? Why must *you* escape?" Her voice was gentle. Even. Kind.

Star warily shook her head. She would tell Tula nothing.

Tula frowned. "Let me think. It would have something to do with my former husband, would it not?" She laughed.

Chokecherry eyed Tula and Star. "Former husband?"

"Falcon was married to Tula before he married me." Star hoped her terse words gave no sign of her racing heartbeat.

"I hate him!" spat Tula. "I would do anything to see him destroyed!"

Chokecherry glanced at Star, eyes wide, but a cunning smile crept to her lips. She said, "Well, if you help Star escape, that will upset him. I doubt it will destroy him, but it will annoy him."

Star gasped at Chokecherry's betrayal.

Chokecherry shrugged. "I want to go home," she explained guiltily to the ground.

218

Broken Promise

Tula smiled. "And you will. I will see to it myself."

"You?" asked Star. "Why should you help us?"

"Because if it will get rid of you"—Tula's eyes narrowed—"and if it will hurt *him,* then of course I will do it." She smiled sweetly.

Star did not trust the woman. Not at all. Tula help her? No, there was danger in it somewhere.

"I see," said Tula, "that you do not trust my words."

"No, I do not," answered Star truthfully.

"No doubt Falcon has told you many lies about me—"

"Falcon has told me nothing about you. He will not speak of you or anything that happened between you."

Tula looked dumbfounded. "He hates me."

Star shrugged. "Believe what you will."

Tula eyed her, then continued, "In two nights' time there will be a feast to celebrate the choosing of the new winter home."

Star nodded.

"That night there will be singing and dancing and much eating. I will put some herbs in Cat Lurks's food and in Falcon's food."

Star grimaced.

Tula laughed. "No need to alarm yourself, Badger dog-girl," she said to Star. "It will not kill him. If I had wanted to poison him, I would have done it before now."

Star thought of the food she had eaten while at the Jaguar camp. Dried meat she had accepted from Falcon. Dried meat Tula had prepared. She gritted her teeth.

Tula laughed at her. "Escape will be very easy that night." She beamed at them, triumphant.

"How do we know that you and Horn will stay silent about our escape plans?" Star was still suspicious.

"Simple. I will not tell anyone, and neither will Horn."

"Is he your lover?" asked Chokecherry. "Is that why you are so certain of his silence?"

Tula gave her a withering stare. "He is my brother, you jackrabbit-without-a-brain!"

"Oh."

Tula turned to Star. "That is the best plan I can think of for your escape."

"It is very good," admitted Star. Now what was she going to do? Tula was helping her escape, so success was assured. Chokecherry needed her on the journey home. And Falcon would hate her the rest of his life for leaving him.

"What is the problem? I hear it in your voice. There is a problem." Tula glared at Star.

"She does not want to go," said Chokecherry.

"Ah. Is that right?" purred Tula. She laughed. "Well, I would say she has no choice."

"That is what I would say, too," agreed Chokecherry.

Chapter Twenty-four

It was the night of the feast. Falcon was out visiting and Star glanced around the tent nervously. Tonight she would escape!

She managed to hide 17 more strips of dried meat in a basket before Falcon returned. She was just covering up the basket with a deer hide when he entered their tent through the front doorway flap.

"Would you like some meat?" she asked, moving carefully away from the basket. She picked up the oil lamp, a stone bowl holding rendered elk fat with a twisted wick of sage bark, and placed the lamp in the center of the tent. "It is late and you must be hungry."

Falcon shook his head, his black hair sweeping his shoulders. "Betafor and the other women graciously fed the men and myself this evening's meal."

A twinge of jealousy surprised Star. "I roasted plenty of roots," she encouraged. "I thought you would like some."

Falcon shook his head. "Not this time." He glanced around and his gaze fell on the baskets lined neatly against one side of the tent. Star held her breath when he walked over and sat down on an elk hide near the basket with the fur covering— the one holding the dried meat for her escape.

Star watched him nervously, suddenly fearing he would lift the fur off the basket. She tried to concentrate on weaving dried bulrush leaves. "What did you talk about with the men?"

"This winter we Jaguar People will live in the Bear Caves above the Bear River," announced Falcon. "Grizzly bears winter in those caves."

"Grizzly bears?"

He nodded. "Before the women and children come to the caves, the other men and I will go into the caves and drive out any bears that have started to nest there for the winter."

"You must be careful, Falcon. Grizzly bears are very dangerous!"

He was looking at her oddly.

"Did I say something strange?"

He studied her intently.

She wanted to douse the flickering light of the stone lamp so that he could not see her, so hard was he staring.

"The Bear Caves," he finally continued, "are warm and well protected from the freezing cold winds. That is why the grizzly bears favor them for winter nests. Hunting is good in that territory, too. The bears know this. Elk and deer come down from the deep snows on the hills. They drink at the river and brush aside the snow, looking for grass. Sometimes my people catch fish in the river. It will be a good winter. You will see."

Star could not meet his eyes. I will not be with you in the winter, Falcon, she thought sadly. I will not see the Bear Caves. At last she was able to look at him. "I have wintered in a tent before," she said, "and it was very cold. Three of our people died that winter."

"Caves are better." He eyed her. "It is a good thing that you are married to me. You will be warm this winter."

Her head jerked up at that.

He smiled, confident, his even, white teeth gleaming in the dull lamplight. Star sucked in her breath when their eyes met.

"You think well of yourself, Jaguar."

"I do, yes." He waved a hand. "And why should I not? I have a woman who works industriously. You dry meat for the winter. You weave baskets. Many baskets." He laughed, indicating the line of them. "You tan hides. You are even making me a jaguar cloak. Why should I not think well of myself?"

Guilt made her cringe inside. If he were to look in that one basket . . .

He pulled a basket over. "See? Dried berries. You are very industrious."

Her hands fumbled with the bulrushes. "Falcon—"

He reached for another basket. "Bone awls. Your wedding dress. White moccasins. All neatly

223

packed away. You are a good wife, Star. You keep my home tidy."

Her lips trembled to keep from crying out.

"And this." He dragged over the basket with the fur covering it. He idly stroked the deer fur that draped the large basket. "Why, I think you must be the hardest-working wife in the whole Jaguar camp. You tan hides swiftly and cleanly; your cooking is very tasty." He rested his hand on the fur as he stared at her. "Any man would be proud to have you as his wife, Star," he said softly.

Star met his bright eyes with a sick feeling. "I—I—" Words failed her. At last she managed, "I am pleased that you like my work." She wove the bulrushes with hands that shook.

He set the basket aside. The fur covering started to slide off. He caught it just before the contents were revealed and carefully replaced it on top of the basket.

Star went limp with relief.

"Come here, Star."

She gave him a sidelong glance through the black curtain of her hair. Now that the danger had passed, she could relax. A little.

"I want you, Star. Now."

She gasped at his blatant command. *And I want you.*

He reached over and put his hand on her breast, claiming possession of her. "Come here, my Badger wife, my industrious woman, my sweet-smelling flower."

She smiled as he pulled her to him. He cradled her close and began kissing her neck. Shivers ran down her spine. "Ah, Falcon," she moaned. How

Thrill to the most sensual, adventure-filled Historical Romances on the market today...

FROM ⫸ LEISURE BOOKS

As a home subscriber to the Leisure Romance Book Club, you'll enjoy the best in today's BRAND-NEW Historical Romance fiction. For over twenty years, Leisure Books has brought you the award-winning, high-quality authors you know and love to read. Each Leisure Historical Romance will sweep you away to a world of high adventure...and intimate romance. Discover for yourself all the passion and excitement millions of readers thrill to each and every month.

Save $5.00 Each Time You Buy!

Six times a year, the Leisure Romance Book Club brings you four brand-new titles from Leisure Books, America's foremost publisher of Historical Romances. EACH PACKAGE WILL SAVE YOU $5.00 FROM THE BOOKSTORE PRICE! And you'll never miss a new title with our convenient home delivery service.

Here's how we do it. Each package will carry a FREE 10-DAY EXAMINATION privilege. At the end of that time, if you decide to keep your books, simply pay the low invoice price of $14.96, no shipping or handling charges added. HOME DELIVERY IS ALWAYS FREE. With today's top Historical Romance novels selling for $4.99 and higher, our price SAVES YOU $5.00 with each shipment.

AND YOUR FIRST FOUR-BOOK SHIPMENT IS TOTALLY FREE!

IT'S A BARGAIN YOU CAN'T BEAT! A Super $19.96 Value!

⫸ LEISURE BOOKS A Division of Dorchester Publishing Co., Inc.

Get Four Books Totally FREE— A $19.96 Value!

was it this man could do so much to her with only a kiss?

"Do you like that?" he murmured.

"Oh, yes."

"What about this?" He kissed her neck again and ran his hands up and down the sides of her stomach. Soon his hand was inching around to the soft juncture of her thighs.

"Let me take this off," she whispered, reaching for her dress.

He helped her pull the garment over her head, then shrugged out of his own leather shirt and trousers.

Star was clad in nothing but a thin leather breechcloth. It was something she knew Jaguar women wore. It barely covered the curling hair he was staring at. "Ah," he breathed. "You are so beautiful, Star."

She smiled coyly. "Do you think so?"

He chuckled and kissed her forehead, folding her under him. When he sprawled on her like that, she thought she would melt into the elk robes.

He braced himself on his elbows to take some of his weight off her. "I think," he said, looking down into her eyes, "that it is a good thing you came into my life, Badger woman."

Star went still, struck by guilt again. I will soon be leaving your life, she thought. And you will hate me for it. Oh, Falcon, what shall I do?

He traced her nose, her cheeks, her lips with a finger. When he pushed his finger into her mouth, she bit it.

"Ow!" He chuckled and bent his head. His

lips covered hers and she could feel his tongue demanding entrance into her mouth. She kept her teeth clenched until he started tickling her in the ribs. Then she giggled and opened her mouth and he came into her. Their tongues swirled in a mating dance.

"How I want you," he murmured. He clutched her head, his hands entwined in her hair, and held her still. He stared at her, and she felt sad suddenly. This is the last time we will make love, she thought. The last time I will hold you, the last time . . . She had to close her eyes to keep her tears from falling. *Oh, Falcon, what have I done?* She turned her head to the side.

"Star?"

She shook her head, unable to answer.

"Star? Are you all right?"

She swallowed, her throat tight. Her arms went around his neck and she pulled him closer. "Yes," she whispered, and her voice was husky with unshed tears. "Just love me, Falcon."

He yanked off her breechcloth and parted her thighs with his hand. Then he surged into her, claiming her in one swift stroke. She clung to him as he moved within her. Suddenly his kisses became fierce as he pressed his mouth everywhere on her face. He was brutal as he kissed her neck and she thought that if he had been a jaguar animal, he would have pierced her jugular vein, so forceful was he.

But she welcomed this ungentle taking. Welcomed it wholeheartedly. It was how he would take her if he knew that she planned to run from him . . . it assuaged the terrible guilt she felt.

The strength of him as he pushed within her, the force of his thrusts, ground her into the elk hides. And still she clung to him, demanding more and more. And he gave her more.

When the explosions in their bodies came, she soared to the heavens and fell back to earth with him. He collapsed on top of her.

Gently, she pushed aside a lock of his black hair that fell across his forehead. "Ah, Falcon," she murmured.

His face was buried in her shoulder. His grip on her tightened. "You are mine, Star."

She smiled sadly at the roof of the tent. She closed her eyes to shut out the one lie she knew she must tell. "Yes." That was all. Just one lie: yes.

He lifted his head and searched her eyes. *For what, Falcon? The truth? I cannot tell you, though my heart cries out for you.*

"I will not let you go, Star." His firm hold on both of her upper arms surprised her. She smiled to calm him. Surely he did not suspect—?

"Remember that, woman."

"Why, Falcon, I—" His kiss stopped the second lie she was about to tell him. *I cannot help it, Falcon,* she wanted to cry. *Tula in her envy, and Chokecherry in her desperation have forced me. They will do everything they can to ensure my escape. I cannot stop this. I want to, but I cannot!*

She squeezed her eyes shut and then the tears came. She clung to him, silent sobs shaking her whole body.

He rolled over onto his side and kept her in

his strong embrace. He kissed her hair, her face. "Star," he whispered. "What ails you?"

She shook her head, afraid to speak, because she knew if she did, she would tell him everything. Everything, including her growing love for him.

He patted her awkwardly on the back. "We will talk about it in the morning," he assured her. "You will feel better then. And I—" He yawned and then touched his forehead. "I feel strangely tired. . . ." He was asleep in a heartbeat.

Tula's medicine, she realized and took a ragged breath. But I will not be here in the morning, Falcon. Tonight I must flee and leave you forever. Oh, Falcon! This is far more bitter for me than I ever thought it could be!

Chapter Twenty-five

When Falcon awoke, Star was gone. He swiftly dressed and glanced around the tent. In the eerie light of dawn he could see that two deer bladders of water were missing—and the hide-covered basket.

He smiled grimly. Horn had told him of the planned escape. At first Falcon had not believed his former brother-in-law. Had not wanted to believe it. He thought Star truly cared for him and wanted to stay with him. Even last night, in her arms, he would have sworn to the Great Spirit that she cared for him. He was even willing to believe her lies despite the dried strips of meat he'd seen hidden in the basket. Oh, yes, she had made a fool of him!

How Horn would laugh at him this time! Tula's brother had always liked to joke. He had been a good hunting companion, too. He and Falcon had been close friends, but after Tula left Falcon, their friendship had withered like an old berry. Falcon had kept his distance from Horn, knowing that Horn's first loyalty would henceforth be to his sister, Tula. Horn once told Falcon that he disapproved of his sister's choice of second husband, Marmot.

Horn had just done Falcon a good turn. One he would remember.

Falcon picked up his spear and shrugged into the newly made jaguar cloak that Star had tanned and designed and sewn. Good! It was fitting that something she made for him would keep him warm as he hunted her down.

As Falcon left the tent, Cat Lurks hailed him. Cat Lurks prowled toward him, dressed in warm leather clothing and carrying his spear.

"You look like you are going on a hunt," said Falcon.

"Hunh," grunted Cat Lurks. "My woman ran away." His face was grim; his eyes held a cold, stony anger.

"As did mine," admitted Falcon sheepishly.

"When I get that woman back, I will beat her," said Cat Lurks.

Falcon raised an eyebrow. "A woman's strength is less than a man's. I think it is a bad thing to beat a woman."

"Stay out of my concerns," snapped Cat Lurks.

Falcon shrugged. He guessed that if Cat Lurks beat Chokecherry, she would run again. As for himself, he had his own plans for Star once he recaptured her, and they did not include beating her.

"Did any other women flee?" asked Falcon. He had been so certain she would stay. . . .

Cat Lurks shook his head. Falcon fell into step beside him and the two hunters left the camp, heading east in the direction of the old Badger camp.

Because basalt rock gravel covered most of the ground, it was difficult to find the women's trail. But Falcon's and Cat Lurks's persistence was finally rewarded when Falcon spotted a freshly broken twig on a ravine path. He smiled. They had traveled this way.

Later, Cat Lurks spied a footprint in the dirt on a trail over the cap of a hill. They followed the trail to a narrow creek. There, a single feminine imprint in the mud pointed at the water. "They are clever," murmured Falcon. "They stayed on the basalt gravel so that we could not find their footprints and now they hide them by wading in the water."

"I will beat Chokecherry," muttered Cat Lurks, his fists clenching.

"You are poor company," complained Falcon. "All you talk about is beating your woman."

"Silence!" snarled Cat Lurks. Falcon had grown up with Cat Lurks, the spoiled only son of a strong hunter and his first wife. Though the second and third wives had produced two offspring each, because they were daughters, the father had always seemed to value Cat Lurks the highest. He gave him the choicest meats, and interfered when his son played with the other boys so that Cat Lurks got favored treatment. During his childhood, Cat Lurks had been given everything he wanted and he did not like to be thwarted in his wishes.

They followed the trickling creek for some distance, watching the mud for telltale footprints. "Those women walked a long way in the freezing water," observed Falcon. "Their feet must be very cold by now."

"I will beat her," snarled Cat Lurks.

Falcon grimaced at him. "I am tired of hearing about how you will beat her when you find her. Stop telling me that."

Cat Lurks glared at Falcon but he kept silent.

They walked up to the top of the hill above the creek. When they reached the crest, Falcon gazed out over the brown, scarred mounds. The hill he stood on towered above those around it and great fissures sloped down to the main river. Some of the fissures hid tree-covered ravines laced with trickling creeks like the one the fleeing women had waded through. The creeks flowed downward to the single wide river, the one his people called Bear River.

Upstream, a waterfall poured over a rock wall and Falcon watched the white water plummet down. The crashing sound of the waterfall masked any sound made by Falcon and Cat Lurks.

Suddenly Falcon saw a movement—a brown blur. "There!" He pointed.

"It is they," said Cat Lurks in excitement. "I see Chokecherry!"

Falcon glanced at him. Perhaps Cat Lurks felt something tender for Chokecherry after all, a feeling beyond anger. "If you beat her, she will not like you," Falcon warned gently. "She will not want to stay with you. If you treat her kindly, she will stay."

That cold gaze surveyed Falcon in contempt. "Do not tell me how to keep my woman when your own woman flees from you!" He pointed his spear at the two brown blurs slowly working their way to the main river. "And it is none of your concern!"

Falcon turned back to watch the two women. He had been mistaken to think that Cat Lurks wanted anything more than to punish the woman who thwarted him.

"They are trying to reach Bear River. It is easier to walk along its banks and they probably know it will lead them back to their Badger camp."

"She will not make it to her Badger camp," said Cat Lurks through clenched teeth. "I will see to that!"

"They are a little distance away from us," observed Falcon, "and they have yet to see us. We will catch up with them soon."

Cat Lurks began striding down the hill toward the distant figures. With a sigh, Falcon followed.

The two women rounded a hill and disappeared into a ravine. When next they emerged, it was beside the wide river's bank.

Falcon and Cat Lurks continued their swift pace, and Falcon judged they would reach the women very soon. The waterfall drowned out the noise of the approaching men, though neither woman watched for pursuers.

"They seem confident we cannot track them," said Falcon in amusement. Indeed, Star was taking off her leather dress and Chokecherry was kicking off her moccasins.

"They are going to swim in the river!" exclaimed Cat Lurks, baffled.

"It is the best way to rid oneself of the ticks," observed Falcon.

He watched Star wade out into the slow-moving current not far from shore. Her smooth brown back enticed him ever closer. Cat Lurks, too, was staring at Chokecherry as she yanked her dress over her head, tossed it on the riverbank, and walked out into the water. He frowned and gripped his spear tighter, growling softly to himself. Falcon pitied Chokecherry.

The men entered the small ravine and wended their way through the wind-sculpted thicket of trees. Just as they emerged from the ravine, Star glanced up. She screamed and threw herself into the deeper water and began swimming frantically. Chokecherry looked up and her face showed her fear and surprise. Then she, too, launched herself in the water, arms flailing.

Falcon and Cat Lurks ran along the riverbank, keeping even with the swimming women. "They cannot swim faster than we can run," said Falcon.

"And that cold water will stop them soon." Cat Lurks had a cruel smile on his face, as if he enjoyed the women's suffering.

Chokecherry was beginning to tire, Falcon saw. She was behind Star and her strokes were weaker than Star's. Soon she would have to come ashore.

While the current was slow not far from shore, it was steady and the women were carried along. Out in the middle the water flowed more swiftly.

Chokecherry's head went under and Falcon began to fear she would drown.

Star's black head bobbed farther ahead of Chokecherry. "Wait!" screamed Chokecherry. Then she went under once more.

"We must save Chokecherry," said Falcon. "She is weakening rapidly. If you do not swim out and save her now, she will drown!"

"Let her!" Cat Lurks had that cruel smile on his face. "She should not have run from me. This is what happens when she defies me!"

"I fear she will not learn your lesson in time," said Falcon. "She will be dead."

Cat Lurks shrugged. "I care little what happens to her. Let her drown!"

Falcon shook his head in disgust and quickly shed his clothes. In his haste, he left his knife belt on with two obsidian knives dangling from it. He dived into the water and swam at an angle until he reached Chokecherry. She looked exhausted, barely able to keep her head above water. "Help me," she gasped, reaching for him. She latched onto his neck.

Her desperate groping pushed Falcon underwater and he had to fight to get to the surface for air. He managed one gulp of air before her struggles pushed him under again. Her panicked grasp would drown him!

His feet felt the bottom of the river and he thrust himself upward. When he reached the surface, he unwrapped her arms from around his neck. "Float on your back," he commanded.

She thrashed wildly, frothing the water around him. Fear contorted her face.

"Float on your back," he said again, willing his voice to stay calm. When she still did not heed him, he deliberately pushed her under, then brought her up again. With wild eyes, she bobbed up, gasping for breath.

"Listen to me," he said. "You must do as I say or we will both drown." Something of what he said finally reached her. She stopped struggling and gaped at him. "Float on your back."

Relief flooded through him when he saw that she understood. She moved onto her back, letting the water support her. Falcon held her between the middle of her shoulders and towed her through the water.

Cat Lurks stood onshore, hands on hips, a malicious smile welcoming them.

Falcon ceased his swimming, turned, and began swimming to the opposite shore. "Listen carefully," he said to Chokecherry. He hoped the dazed woman would understand him.

"I am setting you free," he told her as they moved with the current to the far shore. "If you go back to Cat Lurks, he will beat you. Or kill you. You must escape alone. Do you understand?"

Onshore, Cat Lurks raced back and forth, screaming Falcon's name.

Chokecherry nodded feebly. They reached the shallow water and Falcon helped her to shore. "Here," he said, handing her an obsidian knife from his belt. "Use this knife to protect yourself." He wondered if the naked woman, armed with a mere knife, would ever survive the trek back to her people. But to return her to Cat Lurks would seal her death.

"Go," he commanded, setting her on the riverbank. Across the river, Cat Lurks shook his spear and ran along the bank. His face was black with rage. When she saw him, Chokecherry gave a little cry and staggered off along the muddy riverbank.

"Run!" Falcon told her.

Then he dived back into the river to pursue Star. He reached the middle of the river and glanced around. She had disappeared.

He strained frantically to see her while the current carried him ever forward. Ahead was a bend in the river. He swam with an occasional stroke, but the swifter current in the middle of the river pulled him along. *Where is she?*

He scrutinized both banks of the river, but he could not see her. Had she drowned while he was helping Chokecherry? His gut tightened. Chokecherry would have drowned if he had not helped her. Yet to lose Star—! Had he misjudged the strength of her swimming skills?

The water felt cold suddenly and he wondered how long she could survive its freezing hold.

"Star?" He shouted her name several times, but the only sound he received was his echo bouncing off the tall basalt cliffs near the bend.

The current was very swift now; he need do nothing but stay afloat as he passed the riverbanks with swift ease. "Star?"

Once he had rounded the bend, he suddenly caught sight of a black, bobbing head swimming slowly toward the shore. Relief surged through him and he propelled himself forward with strong, swift strokes.

He could see that Star was tiring. As she waded onto shore, her shoulders drooped, her body heaved with each breath. When she reached shore, she glanced back once and saw him. She ran and darted into a thicket of trees.

She is alive! Falcon's heart sang as he swam to shore. She is alive!

When he reached the shallows, he raced for the thicket. "Star!"

She had vanished. He heard branches breaking and he laughed inside. He would soon catch her. Most important, she was alive.

Chapter Twenty-six

Star paused, breathing heavily, listening for sounds of Falcon's pursuit. *I must escape, I must!* Exhaustion from her swim crept over her, but she urged herself on. *Run! Hide! He must not find me!*

She found a small place to secrete herself, in a crevice under a rocky overhang. A snarled tangle of branches and twisted trees hid the crevice.

Two birds flew off a branch as she rushed by them. Their shrill cries sounded loud to her ears.

She strove to quell her panting breaths. Falcon must not hear her. She knew him well now; she and Chokecherry had been so certain that their footprints could not be seen, yet he had tracked them. And Star had thought to escape him by swimming swiftly away. Yet still he followed her. She must not be lulled into thinking he would give up easily.

She put a hand to her pounding chest. *And where is Chokecherry?*

Fear for her friend made Star's heart pound faster. Chokecherry had always been a poor swimmer; even as a child, she had preferred to stay on the riverbank and poke at roots and catch frogs rather than join the other children frolicking in the water.

The sound of breaking branches told Star that Falcon was close by. She held her breath, listening to his footfalls. She wanted to scream her despair when he walked up to the crevice and reached down for her. She shrank back, trying to hide further under the overhang.

"Come out, Star." His voice sounded weary—and something else. Relieved?

He gripped her arm and tugged. Star slowly crawled out from under the crevice. She ignored the relief that thrilled through her at his touch.

Without a word, he marched her through the thicket, back toward the river. He ignored the slapping branches, but Star could not. She felt their occasional sting.

When at last they reached the entrance of the ravine, he pushed her ahead of him. She stumbled and almost fell on the grass but he caught her and righted her.

"Let me go!" She jerked her arm from his grip.

They stood there, face-to-face, both naked, he wearing only a single knife on his belt.

Star crossed her arms over her breasts and glared at him. He grinned at her. For a moment her breath all but ceased as she gazed up into his handsome dark features. His dripping wet hair was slicked back, his broad chest lifting and falling with each breath.

"You fooled me," he said.

She frowned. He spoke as though it were a game they played. "I tried to," she snapped.

He put his arms around her then and kissed her. The kiss was so sweet, Star wanted to close her eyes and kiss him for a long, long time. When at last she opened her eyes, he was smiling down at her, his brown eyes warm. She shrugged off the strange lethargy she felt and pulled back from him. "Where is Chokecherry?"

He pointed. Star craned to see what he pointed at. Alongside the bank ran Cat Lurks. Far across the river, she saw a thin brown flash. A woman!

"Chokecherry!"

He nodded. "Hurrying back to her people."

"As I should be," she said, observing her friend run. A yearning to go home to her Badger People swept through Star. "I should be with her!"

"You are with me."

She spun to stare at him. "Not by choice."

He shrugged, not at all bothered by her irritation.

After a time, Star asked, "Will she be safe?"

"She has a knife. She will find her people."

"I should be with her," murmured Star, but secretly she felt relieved she was not. The man standing so close to her had a power over her that she did not understand.

He frowned at her. "I did not expect you to flee."

She laughed. "You think I must stay with you, Jaguar? At your whim? I wanted to flee you."

Her conscience pricked her at these words. "I—
I wanted to return to my Badger People!"

He glared at her, his face becoming distant
and stony before her eyes. "Your place is with
me now, woman. Accept it."

"No!"

"Yes!"

"No!" She glowered at him.

He glowered back.

"I will escape you at every opportunity!"

He gripped her upper arms. "You will not! You
will stay with me. You will not run away again!"

"What can you do to stop me?" she taunted. A
frisson of fear went through her that she dared
bait him like this; she felt like a hunter teasing
an angry bear. But she could not help herself.

He dragged her to him and kissed her brutally
on the lips. She pushed at his chest, struggled in
his grip. When at last he let her go, they were
both breathing heavily. "That!" he snarled. "That
is what I can do!"

Her hand flew to her bruised mouth. "That will
not keep me from running away!" she screamed
in anger.

He grabbed her again and she fought against
him. They fell to the grass. His weight on top of
her was crushing.

He was kissing her again. She moved her head
from side to side to stop his lips from seeking
hers. But he held her head still and kissed her,
plunging his tongue into her mouth.

Her eyes widened at this blatant invasion and
she tried to buck him off. She could not move
him.

He growled and kissed her again.

She pushed at his shoulders, trying to get him off, but he let his weight fall against her and her arms buckled. She kicked out at him, but he laid his legs over hers, effectively stilling them.

She pounded his back with her fists. He grabbed them in one hand and held them over her head.

She felt something warm and hard against her thigh. Knowing what it was, she arched her body, trying to move away. He laughed and pulled her closer. Soon she felt him nudging against her very core.

She struggled harder, but he entered her in one swift stroke. She felt helpless and excited as he took her, thrusting strongly inside her. A yielding lethargy overcame her and she could no longer fight him. Instead, she joined with him in the movements and they clutched each other. Their joy blossomed together; his power crushed her, hers caressed him. Panting, spent, they lay there.

At last he lifted his head. "I can do that," he growled, "to keep you."

She met his triumphant gaze. "You can," she agreed happily.

Chapter Twenty-seven

Star watched as Falcon pulled the elk hide off the wooden tent frame that had been their home for a short time. I feel sad to be leaving this place, she thought in astonishment. She glanced over at the stream. Behind the aspens and cottonwoods, she glimpsed Sageflower and Pine Woman filling water bladders for the impending journey.

Half of the Jaguar People had already left, following the lead of Old Antelope. They had decided to winter farther back in the hills at the shores of Fish Lake, where the waters teemed with fish. They would meet up again in spring with Claw's people.

Star did not know any of the Jaguars who followed Old Antelope. They seemed to be closely related families and were not given to socializing with others.

She thought it good that the Jaguars had

reduced their numbers this way. It would be easier to feed fewer people through the winter.

"How long will it take us to reach the Bear Caves?" she asked Falcon.

"Eight sleeps." He placed the painted elk hide on the ground, skin side up. Then he placed the possessions they were taking with them in the middle of it.

"It is far then?"

He shook his head. "Not so far. It takes some time to get there because we are carrying so many things."

A black mortar bowl and black pestle, several chunks of black obsidian, and a sleeping mat, folded, were in the center of the hide. Star already had her biggest basket crammed full with bone awls, scrapers, porcupine quills for decorating, dried meat, her wedding dress and moccasins, a wooden comb that Falcon had made for her, and her smallest basket full of dried berries. She had two medium-size baskets full of dried camas roots and wapatoo roots.

"I will go to the river and fill the water bladders," she said.

He nodded and held up one of his spears to examine the blade. She noticed that Falcon was careful to keep his weapons in good repair.

On their journey, he would carry the full water bladders over his shoulders so his hands would be free to carry his spears. The men were ever on the alert for predatory animals.

Star would carry the burden of baskets and the folded-up elk hide.

As she wandered down to the river, Star thought

245

about the time she had spent at this camping spot. It had been where she first lived with Falcon, and it held special memories for her because of that.

The wild sound of honking geese caused her to glance up. Geese flew low overhead. Her gaze followed them until they were tiny dots in the clouded sky. They were on a journey to their winter grounds, too.

A chill breeze ruffled Star's hair. She shivered, glad suddenly of the warm bison cloak she wore. Falcon had killed the bison after it had become separated from its herd and wandered, lost, in the forest.

She wondered if Blue Jay had such a warm cloak for the winter and if Chokecherry had managed to return to the Badger People. Star sighed sadly. She would never know what had happened to her mother or her friend.

A few yellow leaves flickered at her on the cottonwood and aspen trees that grew near the river, but most of the leaves had fallen off the trees and their naked branches were another reminder of the coming winter.

Star filled both water bladders. She stepped back from the water and turned, only to halt. Tula blocked her path. Her son slept in the blanket tied to her back.

"It is too bad only your friend escaped and you were left behind." Tula tossed her head, her white hair as dramatic as ever.

Star had not spoken to her since her own recapture. She shrugged. She enjoyed Falcon, so she was not going to protest too hard against his bringing her back.

Broken Promise

"When will you try again?" Tula's face held such hope that Star wanted to laugh.

"I will not," she answered, to annoy Tula.

Tula's lovely face contorted into a glower. "You must!" she hissed. "How else will you get home to your people?"

"I will visit them when I wish to." Truly, Star did not know when that would be, or even *if* it would be, but she was not going to admit that to Tula.

"Ha. That man will never take you to visit them."

Star knew she meant Falcon and she thought that probably Tula was correct. Ah, but it would be so good to see her mother. . . .

Tula's eyes narrowed. "Are you pregnant?"

Star was taken aback and could not answer.

"If you are, I think you should leave swiftly. He will not love your child. He will not love you."

They both knew who *he* was.

"And no one in this camp likes you," continued Tula. "They all think you are ugly. Why you stay here is beyond what I will ever know. Why do you not just leave?"

Star flushed as though struck by a cruel hand. Tula's words hurt. "I do not believe you," she answered at last. "I have many friends here. Pine Woman, Elk Knees, Sageflower—"

"Pah!" Tula waved a hand as though swatting away a fly. "They are as the dry dust on the hillside. Badger dog-girls, all of them! No, it is the real people I am talking about. The Jaguars. That is who I speak of. None of them like you."

Star smiled menacingly. "Falcon likes me."

Tula went pale. She gritted her teeth. "He does not!"

"Oh, yes, he does. He likes me. Very much."

Tula stuck her chin in the air. "I care nothing for what you say. You know nothing."

"Oh, I know a few things," answered Star. She studied the graceful, delicate woman in front of her. "I know," she said slowly, "that you still love him."

Furious anger leapt into Tula's wide brown eyes. "I hate him. I would grind him to dust in my mortar and pestle. I would scrape his hide with my scrapers. I would pour him out as though he were dirty water. I would burn him like camel dung at my fire! I hate him, I tell you!"

Star had been in the Jaguar camp long enough to overhear some of the people talking. "I do not see why you are so upset, Tula," she ventured. "It was Falcon who lost so much. You have another husband, another baby. It was he who was left alone. He whom the Jaguar People whisper about behind their hands."

Tula sneered. "That is as it should be. After what he did to me, he should be left alone. He should have no one to love him!"

Star's eyes widened as she heard why the woman was so anxious to drive her away. Tula wanted to punish Falcon.

"What did he do?" Star demanded.

Tula's mouth tightened. "I do not know why I am talking to a dog-girl such as you. You have nothing to—"

"What did he do?"

"Yes, Tula, what did I do?"

Broken Promise

Star jumped at the sound of Falcon's voice. He had come upon them on silent, hunter's feet. He stood on the trail, arms crossed against his broad chest, feet planted on the path, blocking both women.

Tula glared at him. "You know what you did! It is all your fault that Hawk was born as he was! All your fault that he did not grow properly! It is all because of you!"

Falcon shook his head. "I had nothing to do with it."

"You killed the bear!"

"Your father's animal, I know," he said wearily. "But that did not cause Hawk to—"

"It did!" she shrieked. "It did! You hated him. His spirit knew it and ran away. That is why his body refused to grow!"

"Tula, Tula," said Falcon, taking a step closer to the enraged woman and holding out a hand to her. Her baby started to cry softly.

"Do not touch me," she screamed. "You will hurt me. You will hurt my baby!"

"I do not want to hurt you or your baby," he answered.

"You do! You hate us, just as you hated Hawk!"

Falcon's brow darkened. "I did not hate Hawk!" he snarled.

"You did! I saw your face when you looked at him! Hawk would have been a fine baby but for you!"

"Hawk would never have been well," Falcon protested.

"He would have! The shaman said—"

"The shaman was wrong!" Falcon roared. "He

249

made false promises that Hawk would be a great teacher and healer."

"Hawk would have been! He would have! The shaman knew—"

"The shaman knew nothing!"

"He gave me hope!" cried Tula. "He told me that our son would heal and teach—" Suddenly she bowed her head and started to cry.

Star stared at the agonized look on Falcon's face. He loves her, she thought. He still loves her and wants her. Oh, what am I doing here?

Tula's sobs ripped through the silence surrounding them. "I—I loved him," she gasped. "That was more than you did!"

"I loved him, too," said Falcon, and his voice broke.

Tula shook her head. "No. No, you did not. You only say that. It is a lie you tell yourself!"

"Not as big a lie as the ones you told yourself," he answered coldly. "You lied to yourself every day when you said he would get better, that he would grow into a whole man. You saw him, day after day, you touched his withered legs, you looked into his eyes that showed no understanding. . . . And then you lied to yourself—and to me."

Tula's bent head bowed under the blows of his words. "I loved him," she cried. And in that cry, Star heard a mother's howl of pain and love. Tears rose in her eyes for Tula and the terrible loss of her firstborn son. Slowly, carefully, Star reached out a finger and stroked Tula's white streak of hair.

Tula jerked her head up and her flashing brown

eyes met Star's. "What are you doing? I want nothing from you, Badger woman! I do not need your pity!" And stuffing her fist in her mouth to stem the sobs, she staggered away up the path.

Star and Falcon watched her go. Falcon let out a breath. "Come," he said. "It is time to go."

"But, but Falcon . . ." Star wanted to talk about what had just happened.

He took her arm and led her along the path. Star tried to push his hand off her arm. "I—I see now some of Tula's pain. . . ."

"Tula and her pain are none of your concern. Or mine."

His grip was firm as he pulled her along.

"But Falcon, do you not see that she—"

"I see nothing!" he growled. "This does not concern you and I will not talk about it!"

Star halted in the middle of the path and refused to take another step. "Falcon. You brought me here. You married me. I am part of this, whether I want to be or not."

"I should have left you with your mother," he snarled.

"You should have," she agreed. Hurt by his words, she wanted to hurt him back. "Then you could live your lonely life. No one would speak to you and you could go your silent way. Except for the occasional yell at Tula, of course."

His white scar was ticking; his jaws clenched. "You are quick to believe her words, Badger woman."

"Does she lie?"

He was silent, regarding her, his black eyes burning with a heat she could not understand.

"Does she lie, Falcon?"

Still he would not answer.

"Does she lie? I would know."

"Tula says many things," he answered at last. "But to my knowledge, no, she does not lie."

"Then you did not love your son."

She did not understand the sadness she saw in his black eyes.

"Believe what you will, Badger woman."

She stared at him, willing him to tell her more.

But he only took her arm. "Come. We leave now on our journey to the Bear Caves."

Star stumbled after him, lugging the dripping water bladders. But her heart was uneasy at what had passed. There was a new distance between them now, something that had not been there before, and she did not know what to do about it.

Chapter Twenty-eight

Star trudged along, her heavily laden baskets hooked through a leather strap that looped around her forehead. The baskets dangled down her back and hit her hips with every step. Her arm muscles ached from carrying the folded elk-hide tent. Her nose hurt from breathing in the musty smell of the hide. For ten sleeps, not the eight Falcon had predicted, she had carried her burden of baskets and tent hide. She was exceedingly tired of the journey to the Bear Caves.

But in the voices of the Jaguar People around her, she heard little cries of excitement and her spirits lifted. Pine Woman staggered by, her face hidden by the armload of possessions she carried. "My husband says we are close to the Bear Caves!" she cried as she tottered along. Star hoped she was correct; perhaps this would be the last day of the long trek to the caves. She quickened her faltering steps.

Her weary eyes sought out Falcon as he loped alongside the straggling Jaguar People and Star envied him his ease. All he has to do is keep watch for wolves and jaguars and lions, she thought, while I have to lug these heavy baskets!

"Tonight we reach the caves!" said Claw, jogging past. He gave a jaunty wave of his spear. Behind her, Star heard Betafor's heavy panting. Betafor, Claw's wife, carried a very heavy load of baskets and hides, but she was aided by her three grown daughters and their children.

Star wished *she* had someone to help her carry her baskets, or even someone to talk to. Ever since Chokecherry's escape, none of the other Badger women accompanied her, for fear their new Jaguar husbands should think they wanted to escape also. And of course, none of the Jaguar women sought her out.

She wished that Falcon would help her carry something, even a basket, but he was too busy darting here and there, watching for predators. All he had to carry were his spears. And two small, very light water bladders.

Star licked dry lips. Her last drink of water had been in the early morning.

The long snaking line stretched out over the brown hills and every woman in that line was loaded with possessions. There were baskets crammed with dried roots and berries for winter and tanned hides for making winter clothing and bedrobes.

Star trudged along. The Jaguars wound their

way through a dry creek bottom and the walking became easier on her dusty, sore feet. She wiped sweat from her forehead and plodded on.

The sun was low in the sky and the Jaguar People had just emerged from the dry creek bottom when Claw at last cried out, "Stop! We will rest here for a short time." Star halted and set down her possessions with a sigh of relief. She rubbed her forehead where the wide leather band had pressed into her skin.

They had halted at the base of another brown hill—one of many that surrounded her in this hilly country. Between the hills were the ravines, where twisted trees grew, their branches gnarled from the wind that whipped across the hills. She caught a glimpse of sparkling blue to the south. It was a river, cutting through black layers of rock.

"It has been a long journey," said Sageflower shyly, walking over to stand near Star.

Star nodded. "Too long. I will be glad when we reach the caves."

She watched Sageflower set down the huge basket she was carrying and wipe her brow. When Sageflower glanced around at the men who wandered the hills, Star knew she looked for Deer Summoner.

Star smiled at Sageflower, glad that the younger woman's marriage, at least, had proved to be happy.

"I wish Chokecherry were here," said Sageflower softly.

"I miss her, too," answered Star, "but Chokecherry could not be wife to Cat Lurks."

255

"I think she did not try to be amiable to him," said Sageflower.

Star shrugged. Evidently Chokecherry had not confided in Sageflower the true problem of her marriage. There was no point in correcting Sageflower now that Chokecherry was gone.

"I wonder if she made it back to our people safely."

Star heard the wistful note in Sageflower's voice. Star, too, had wondered that. "I think she did," Star answered. "Chokecherry was always brave. I think she would have survived until she found our people."

"Perhaps." Sageflower's eyes followed Cat Lurks as he prowled along a hilltop. "But I wish she had stayed."

There was nothing Star could say to lift the sadness in the other's voice.

Falcon came trotting up from the dry creek bed. He grinned at them as he approached and Star's heart drummed a triple beat. How handsome he looked, how strong and robust and exciting! She touched her bosom to slow her rapidly thumping heart.

Falcon nodded deferentially to Sageflower, but it was on Star that his eyes lingered. She flushed.

He glanced at the baskets and elk hide on the ground, then at Star. "I, too, will be glad to reach the caves."

"How many bears must you drive out before the Jaguar People can live in safety?" asked Star.

Falcon shrugged. "Two or three. Not many."

Sageflower said a polite farewell and dragged her baskets over to where Elk Knees sat with her new daughter and son. Star tried not to watch the easy exchange between the two women. She sighed, wondering when the Badger women would speak freely to her again. She felt grateful to Sageflower for their brief conversation.

"You will like the Bear Caves," said Falcon, apparently not seeing Star's sadness. Or if he did, he chose—as usual—not to talk about it.

Star nodded and sat down. "I think I would like anywhere where we can winter in safety."

Falcon squatted beside her to rest, but she noticed he still surveyed the hills; he was always alert.

Tula walked past them, her baby bouncing gently on her back. She did not even glance at Star and Falcon. Falcon's eyes followed Tula and desperation rose in Star. Would he ever forget her?

"Did—did you stay at the caves last winter?" Star could not stop herself from blurting out. "With Tula?"

Falcon's narrowed gaze met hers. "Tula left me two winters ago," he said; then he got up and walked away.

Star sat there miserably, wondering when she would learn never to speak of anything important to Falcon. Only then would he stay with her. She stared out at the slice of blue sparkling water and it blurred through her tears. She blinked them away and held her face up to let the biting wind dry her tears.

The men left shortly after that, Claw leading them to the caves. Betafor went from this group of women to that. When she came to Star, sitting alone, she said, "We will wait here until the men return. They have gone to drive the bears out of the caves."

"Is—is it dangerous?" asked Star.

Betafor shrugged. "Sometimes a hunter gets hurt." Star's alarm must have shown on her face for Betafor added hastily, "But there are many hunters. Only a few bears." She grinned and moved away.

Star worried. She sat there for a long time, thinking about the bears. She had not told Falcon something that frightened her about bears: her father had been killed by a grizzly bear. She had grown up hearing again and again how fierce grizzly bears were, how her father had tried to kill one, but the animal had snapped his spear and batted him with a huge paw. While her father lay stunned on the ground, the bear killed him.

Now she pictured Falcon facing a huge grizzly emerging from a dark cave—the bear upright on its hind legs, teeth gnashing and arms flailing as it chased Falcon from its home.

She thought of her dead father. She imagined Falcon trying to kill the huge, thrashing bear with one of his puny, thin spears.

At last she could stand it no longer. Falcon was in trouble. She knew it. He needed her.

She left her baskets and elk hide and started running in the direction the men had taken.

"Come back!" she heard Betafor cry, but Star kept running.

She heard several more cries from the women, urging her to return, but once she rounded a hill, their voices ceased.

Ahead of her, she had a better view of the river. On one side of the river, sheer cliffs reared up from the rocky banks. On the other side, a gradual series of wide ledges terraced the bank.

On one of the ledges she saw a line of dark holes burrowing into the cliff. The caves!

She started running toward the caves but she was too tired from the day's long march. She had to slow to a stumbling walk.

As she neared the rocky ledges, she glanced up to see how close she was to the caves. To her surprise, the men were sliding down the gravel, returning from the caves. And two of the men carried a prone man between them.

"Falcon!" she cried, and despite her fatigue she found the strength to scramble up the loose, gravelly slope. "Falcon!"

The gravel slid under her feet, but she kept climbing, her heart pumping wildly. "Oh, Falcon," she moaned. By now, the men had reached a terrace and were carefully laying the prone man down.

"Falcon!" she cried, running up to the injured man. "Is he—?" She dared not say it. She dared not ask if he was dead. "Oh, Falcon—"

The injured man opened his eyes. "Get away from me!"

Pale, her hands clasping each other in tortured wringing, Star stared at the injured man.

"Cat Lurks?" she whispered.

"What do *you* want?" Ever since Chokecherry's escape, he had borne her a particular ill will. Star saw it on his face now.

"I—I thought—" She faltered.

259

"Star! Why are you here?" Falcon walked over to her. "Why are you not with the other women?"

"Oh, Falcon," she cried, throwing herself into his arms. He caught her easily and held her to him. "I—I thought you—"

Cat Lurks was snarling at her. She buried her head in Falcon's shoulder. "I thought it was you that was hurt. I came to help you!"

He patted her awkwardly. The men around him appeared to be looking avidly in any direction but at the two of them.

"You did not need to do this, Star," he said, and she warmed to the kindness in his voice. "I am quite able to fight a bear without your help."

Several Jaguar men snickered at that. When Star glanced up, none of them would meet her eye.

She stepped away from Falcon, wondering suddenly if he was embarrassed at her display of concern for him. "I—I will return now that I know you are safe." She dragged her eyes away from his, whirled, and fled down the hillside, the snickers of the Jaguar men ringing in her ears.

"Star! Wait!"

But she would not wait for him. Let him laugh at her, laugh at her concern for him. What did she care? Let them all laugh at her; she did not need them. Her face aflame, she slid to the bottom of the slope and quickened her pace to return to the other women.

Once, she glanced back and saw Falcon running as fast as he could toward her. "Star!" he cried. "Wait! Do not go! There are—"

Mortified at how she had thrown herself at him on the ledge for all the Jaguar men to see, she swung around and started running.

And came face-to-face with a lion.

Chapter Twenty-nine

Star froze.

Behind her, Falcon cried, "Do not move, Star. Stay still."

She could not move, even had he told her to. The lion's yellow eyes held Star's in a grip that announced her impending death.

"There are two of them," said Falcon softly as he came closer. "Male and female. There may be more. Lions have big families." His voice was a cautious whisper. Still, the lion held Star frozen.

The great tawny beast with the tawny mane crouched to spring. To her right, she could hear a low growl. The second lion!

Without moving her head, her eyes darted to the side.

A snarl from the male lion jerked her eyes back to him.

His fur is the color of the sand and gravel

around him, she thought. That must be why I did not see him until too late!

Falcon was beside Star now and his presence lent her courage. "What should I do?" she whispered, her lips barely moving.

"Move behind me," he directed. "Move slowly so you do not alarm him. He is already angry. We disturbed him. Perhaps he has a kill nearby."

Cautiously, Star forced her legs to move. Somehow, she found herself behind Falcon, peering at the lion over his shoulder. "Watch the second lion," gritted Falcon. "If she moves, tell me."

Star glanced at the second lion. The long, lanky lioness seemed content to sun herself on a rock and leave the fight to her mate. "She only watches you," whispered Star.

"Esteemed lion," said Falcon in a soothing voice to the crouching, growling male. "You are strong and noble. A very worthy opponent. I have no wish to fight you. You may have the delicious kill that you made. I will seek other game. See? I am willing to move away and let you have your meat."

Star reminded him, "Falcon, it did no good to talk to the jaguar."

"Sometimes it helps," whispered Falcon.

The lion stopped growling. He stared at Falcon. Star held her breath. "We will back away, esteemed lion," promised Falcon in that same even, droning voice. "You may have the food all to yourself. All for you and your family."

Star carefully took a step backward, feeling the rough ground with her feet. To trip now would prove fatal.

Falcon backed into her. She took another backward step.

Making slow movements, careful not to scare the angry lion, Star and Falcon backed away.

When they had gone a little distance, Falcon said to Star over his shoulder, "Return to the other hunters and warn them of the lions."

While Falcon continued to watch the lion and back away from him, Star hastened up the talus slope to the Jaguar men. But they had seen for themselves what had befallen Star and Falcon and they waited on the ledge.

Star stood with them, fists clenched, the silence taut until Falcon was finally beside her. Only then did she release her breath.

"We cannot get back to our families," said Claw. "We must wait for as long as those lions stand between us and our women and children."

Down on the gravel flats, the lion continued to crouch and watch them. Now and then he snarled. His mate sunned herself.

"Will the women and children be safe?" asked Star.

Falcon nodded. "There are many of them. Lions fear a large group of people, even when the lions have a kill nearby. The shaman and two of our hunters stayed behind. The women will be safe."

Star sat down to watch the lions.

Cat Lurks moaned, his eyes closed tight.

"We must get him back to the shaman," said Claw, and Star heard the fear in his voice.

She peeked over at the injured man and saw for the first time that his stomach bore deep, bleeding gashes. She closed her eyes. Stomach injuries were very difficult to heal. The Jaguar shaman must be very skilled indeed.

The lion now looked as if he were sleeping. "I do not want to stay here all night," groaned Cat Lurks.

"Shhh, the lion sleeps," cautioned Claw.

After some time, Cat Lurks gave a loud cry. "If I do not get back to the shaman, I will die!"

His loud shout woke the lion, who gazed up at the men and snarled. It was getting darker now and it was not as easy for Star to see what the lion was doing.

The lioness was gone from the rock where she had sunned herself.

"Perhaps he will leave," she suggested.

"If the wind shifts, the smell of Cat Lurks's blood may draw him," said Falcon. "We hope the lion will go away and not scent Cat Lurks."

Star glanced down at the groaning man. "I wonder how much longer Cat Lurks will live?"

"Not long, unless the lion moves away," answered Falcon.

They waited for some time but the lion remained crouched. Cat Lurks had fallen into a deep sleep.

At last Claw said, "If we go down there shouting and talking loudly, perhaps the lion will run away. I do not like to leave our families alone for so long. Remember, we killed two bears in the caves, but the third escaped. He could be wandering around and find the women and children."

The men murmured among themselves and finally it was decided to do as Claw suggested.

Red Hawk and Lance picked up Cat Lurks

to carry him. The wounded man groaned in his sleep.

By the time they reached the place where the lion had been, the animal was gone. Star stayed a scant three steps away from Falcon the whole time they hurried through the gathering night. An occasional groan from Cat Lurks speeded their steps.

When they reached the other women, there were several fires burning and the smell of roasting meat filled the air. Betafor waddled up to them.

"What took you so long? How many bears were there?"

Claw told her. She eyed Cat Lurks's prone form. "Call Rapt," she ordered one of her grandchildren. The little girl ran off to fetch the shaman.

When Rapt arrived, he was dressed in his ordinary garb except for a few feathers stuck askew in his hair. He approached Cat Lurks and walked around him three times, shaking his head all the while. Star guessed he thought Cat Lurks would be difficult to heal.

"Come," said Falcon. "We will let the shaman help Cat Lurks."

They moved away but Star glanced over her shoulder one last time. "The shaman does not look hopeful," she observed.

"No. He does not. That bear gave Cat Lurks a mighty swipe. He may die."

She touched Falcon softly on his tattooed shoulder. "I am glad that you are safe. I feared for you."

"Yes, you came to the caves to help me," he

said. "Why did you do that?"

She busied herself digging through her baskets, looking for some dried meat for their evening meal. She did not want to answer.

"Star?"

When she maintained her silence and business, he said, "You often accuse me of not telling you about how it is for me. Yet now you do not tell me. You keep your secrets, too."

She did not like that. "Then I will tell you, Falcon, but in return, I will have some answers from you. Is it agreed?"

He busied himself gathering twigs. "We need a fire. It is cold out this night."

"Aha, you do not want to tell me anything about yourself! Very well, we will both keep silent."

They worked side by side, Star rolling out the elk hide to sleep on and Falcon making the fire. "I go to Claw's fire," he said and left.

Star fumed. How like him to walk away rather than tell her anything! Just as she was talking to herself about the foolish ways of men—Jaguar men and one Jaguar man in particular—Falcon returned carrying a branch with a burning tip. He touched the branch to the small twigs, and tiny flames leaped up.

Star warmed herself at the fire and gazed overhead at the indigo canopy of sky. White stars shone in the clear, cold air. The nights were colder now.

"Looking for Darkstar?" he asked.

She raised an eyebrow at him but refused to answer. Let him think what he wanted. In truth, she had forgotten about Darkstar, forgotten about finding someone to lead her and the other Badger women to freedom, and she no longer knew if she wanted to escape. Certainly the other women did not. Oh, there were times when she longed for her mother, for the old ways, even once in a while for Camel Stalker, but she thought she had accepted her new life with the Jaguars.

"Darkstar will not help you," he said.

He is trying to provoke me, she realized. Would he rather argue with me than tell me what he really thinks? Probably, she answered herself wryly. "You asked me why I came to you today to help you," she said.

He put a twig on the fire. "I did ask," he said at last.

"I will tell you then." She took a breath. "I came to you because . . ." Because I love you, she wanted to say, but she could not say the words that would make her vulnerable to this man. " . . . because I feared for you."

"I guessed that." When she was silent, he said, "You have not told me anything I did not already guess." He threw the stick on the fire. "I do not think talking helps us. But, unlike you, I will try again. Do you fear that I cannot fight bears?"

She stared at the flames. "No. It is not that, Falcon. It is that my father was killed by a grizzly bear."

When she looked up, he was staring at her. "Ah. It is a fearful thing for you then, fighting grizzly bears."

"Yes, it is."

They were silent as they both stared at the flames, but Star felt a new closeness to him.

Broken Promise

"When I was five summers old," she continued, "my father went hunting and never returned. He was killed by a bear. From then on, my mother always warned me about the dangerous grizzly bears. Fear is in this burden basket that I carry with me."

"I have a few burdens myself," Falcon observed.

She smiled at him sadly.

He rose. "But talking about them will not help," he said. "It only makes the burden heavier."

He walked over to the elk hide. "It is time to sleep," he said, and she heard the underlying excitement in his voice. He wants to make love to me, she thought. But how can I lie with a man who tells me nothing of who he is? Of what he thinks? Of what he fears? How can I love a man I do not know?

Chapter Thirty

When Falcon reached for her, Star rolled away. "Oh, no," she said. "I do not want to make love to you."

"You do not?" She heard the disbelief in his voice.

She stared up at the stars, wondering how to tell him her strange new feelings and thoughts. "It is not easy to let a man into my body when I do not know that man."

Falcon leaned over her on one elbow. "You know me. We are married. Have been for some time. You cannot say you do not know me!"

"Ah, but I can, Falcon. For truly I do not know you."

He growled. "What is this you say, Star? You would deny me my rights as your husband?"

"I would."

"You cannot."

"I just did."

"Star!"

She turned her head to look at him. He looked angry.

"Will you force me, Falcon? As Cat Lurks did to Chokecherry?"

"That is why she left him?"

At Star's assenting nod, he said, "No wonder Cat Lurks was so furious."

There was an awkward silence between them. "Star," he said in a wheedling tone, "why not forget these little things you are saying? I want you; you want me. Let us just enjoy each other."

She stared at him, wishing she could see his eyes in the dark. She could only guess his reaction from his voice. "And what then, Falcon? After we have satiated ourselves on one another, what then? I still will not know you. Not truly know you. You do not tell me about yourself, about what has happened to you, about anything."

"There is nothing to tell!" His voice rose in anger.

"There is everything to tell."

He pushed her shoulders, pinning her to the elk hide. "I could take you now. Like this."

"You could," she agreed steadily, her heart pounding. Her mouth felt dry. She had pushed him too far—and for what? An elusive, frustrating, unknown feeling that she wanted to know more about him. "But I do not want you to."

"What you want matters naught." He was back—the old, uncaring Falcon who cared about no one and nothing. Oh, why had she started this?

271

He moved on top of her. She felt him fumble with the bottom of her dress, felt the cool air as it hit her thighs. "No, Falcon," she murmured. "Not like this!"

"Yes," he groaned. "You cannot deny me."

She pushed at him. "Do not do this, Falcon." She heard the note of pleading in her own voice as fear swarmed over her.

"I can do what I want," he said.

His voice was harsh against her neck, his breath warm. She felt him nip her neck with his teeth and she winced. "Falcon? Please. Do not do this. Stop!"

She felt him hard against her thigh. She tried to close her legs, but he put his hand between them. Desperate, she grasped his head with both hands, her fingers plowing through his thick, long hair. "Falcon! Listen to me!"

His ragged breathing almost drowned out her words.

"Falcon. Do not do this. It is wrong."

He laughed cruelly. "Why should I care? Why should I care what you want? It does not matter. Nothing does."

"Falcon!" She pulled his face down to meet hers. They were a breath apart. "If you do this thing . . ."

He pushed tauntingly against her.

She felt him touching the center of her womanhood. Her breath came faster. "If you do this thing . . ."

"You will do what? Leave me?" A taunting note had entered his voice now. "You cannot leave me, Badger woman. I own you."

272

She shifted her back, trying to get away from that intimate part of him pressing, pressing against her.

He reached up and took her hands and pulled them over her head. He laughed into her face. "I own you. Like I own my spear. Or my tent. You are mine, Badger woman. To do with as I want." He pushed against her, his manhood sliding through the curls that offered no protection for her. "And I want you." His lips hovered over hers, and his warm tongue entered her mouth. As his manhood would enter her . . . very soon, unless she fought him.

Star felt his tongue swirl through her mouth, giving, taking, plunging. She tried to lift her hands to push him away, but her wrists were pinned. He lifted his head. "It will do you no good, Star. You cannot get away. You are mine."

"I am not!" she cried. "You cannot do this."

"Ah, but I can," he said smoothly.

She clenched her legs, but she could not shut him out. She tried to pull away from him, but his weight held her in place. She tried to wiggle out from under him, but he pressed into her. "No, Falcon! No! Do not do this! I cannot love you if you do this—" The rest of her words choked in her throat. Great, racking sobs shook her body as she realized her own powerlessness.

At what moment he began to hate himself for what he was doing, Falcon did not know. But it must have been when he heard her say the word "love" and heard her wrenching sobs.

What am I doing? Why am I forcing myself on this woman who is too weak to stop me? Am I so desperate to have my own way that I will hurt her?

Shaken, he let go of her wrists and rolled off her. He had not penetrated her, but he had come very close. He lay, chest heaving, staring up at the stars. What have I become? he wondered. What has become of me that I choose to hurt this woman rather than stay my hand? Have I lost my humaneness, the essence that makes me a man?

He pondered this as he stared at the winking stars, so calm in the distance. Around him were the night's soothing sounds: the croak of frogs, the whine of crickets. But in his heart was a terrible turmoil. He had come close to forcing himself on a woman who did not have the strength to stop him. He turned to look at Star and saw that she had flung one arm across her face and was sobbing. "Star?"

He did not expect an answer.

He lay there, listening to her sobs, and he wondered for the first time if some things truly did matter.

Chapter Thirty-one

Star glanced around the cave in satisfaction. Their bed of elk hide was topped with furs. Baskets she had carried sat full of stored roots and dried berries. Two of Falcon's spears leaned against the rock wall. Star's digging stick lay against another wall. An array of household knives and needles and awls, all neatly laid out, completed their possessions.

And she had even lined the empty fire circle with rocks.

She was fortunate that they did not have to share this small cave with any other family. Some of the Jaguars were living three and four families to a cave, but because Falcon's parents were dead and he had no sisters or brothers, there was no one else to claim the same living quarters with him. Of that, Star was glad.

But since that first night they had come to the

Bear Caves, she had avoided Falcon. And he, her. Oh, they had slept upon the same elk hide every night, but they had not made love and they had barely spoken. Star felt haggard, and wondered how much longer she could live like this.

It was true that Falcon did not treat her badly, nor did he try to force himself on her again. But he was distant to her and she was becoming very lonely.

When Star was younger and she and Blue Jay had planned her life on those wonderful, peaceful evenings, Blue Jay had confided about how happily she had lived with Star's father. Blue Jay and Star's father had laughed together, loved together, and spoken of their thoughts and feelings. Star had expected that it would be the same with her and her husband, Camel Stalker. But, ah, how her life had changed! Camel Stalker was not her husband. And the man who was did not wish to laugh and love or share any words with her at all.

Star stared sadly at the mortar she held in her lap. The black bowl had been shaped smooth and round from many seasons of pounding herbs. She held up the black pestle, worn long and smooth by grinding in the bowl. She frowned at the implement. Was it Tula's? Then she shrugged. No. If it were, Tula would have taken it with her when she left Falcon. Star threw the pestle into the bowl, tired of squashing the juniper berries for flavoring meat.

What should she do?

Star sighed. Her life was lonely among these

Jaguar People. Among her own people, the Badgers, Star had enjoyed visiting and talking with the others in camp. Her mother had provided good companionship; she had told Star stories and taught her tanning and sewing and decorating and food preservation. And Blue Jay and her friends were always visiting back and forth. The Badger camp was always bustling.

But here in the Jaguar cave it was quiet, too quiet. Star felt left out of everything. Falcon did not want to talk with her or be with her. The Jaguar People she was with did not seek her out to speak with her. Even her friends, the Badger women, did not want to visit with her very often for fear their husbands would disapprove.

This was not the life she had planned for herself. How could everything a woman had planned come to naught, like the fluff that blew from cottonwood trees in the spring? And yet that was what had happened to her. Her life was not at all the way she had thought it would be. She was not married to the man she had expected to marry. She was not living with the people she had expected to live with. Nothing was turning out as she had planned. Nothing!

She rose and left the cave. Falcon was away hunting. The men were trying to bring in as much meat as they could before the long, cold days of winter settled in. In winter, snowy blizzards blew across the land, and when that happened no man or woman would leave a safe home to hunt. The preserved meat saved lives then.

She padded down the trail to the river; the ground under her feet was cold. Tomorrow she must wear her moccasins to keep her feet warm.

She reached the river and sat down. She had even forgotten to bring a deer bladder to fill with water, so sad and lonely was she. She glanced around, half prepared to climb back up the path. Then she shrugged. It mattered little if she got the water. One more trip up or down the cliffside mattered little. She sat staring into the water, feeling empty.

She cried softly then, thinking about her Badger People, and missing her mother. She missed Blue Jay, missed her mother's good humor, missed her mother's love and concern. She suddenly realized how fortunate she had been to grow up in a home knowing such love. How happy her childhood had been with people all around her, talking and laughing and telling stories and singing songs! Yet not once when Star had lived with her Badger People had she thought about that, about how it was the love and caring among her people that made her life so good, so precious. Not once had she realized that her happiness stemmed from being with people she cared about.

But here among the Jaguar People she did not have that love and concern in her life day after day. And, oh, what a loss it was!

She dried her eyes and realized suddenly that if she had stayed with the Badger People, it would have taken her a long, long time to realize how precious her mother was, how powerful and good were the feelings between herself and those she lived with in the Badger camp. It would have taken her a long time to realize she was truly happy.

But here, with the Jaguars, she belatedly recognized her earlier happiness, for now she was truly miserable.

She had no one to love her, no one to care about her, and no one to talk with. She could admit that there were some people she cared about—Falcon and the Badger women—but they wanted little to do with her. Star felt as though she had wandered thigh-high into a river of despair.

At her feet, the real river gurgled. She stretched out her leg and stuck her foot in the water. The cool liquid felt soothing on her foot. When it became too cold, she withdrew her foot.

What was she to do? How was she going to make her life matter—to herself and to those around her?

How was she going to give her life meaning?

A little bird flew down from a branch and cocked its head at her. She watched it pick at the dirt, searching for food. I have enough food, she thought. But I need more than food to have a valuable life. What do I need?

The little bird flew off and she watched it disappear into the distance in several graceful swoops.

She stared at the river. Out a little way from shore, a fish's fin broke the surface. *Oh, salmon, what have you come to tell me?*

She stood up and peered into the water, trying to understand the salmon's message. He was a large male; his red, molting skin indicated his spawning time was due. A female swam by, smaller, and the male swam after her.

A mate? wondered Star. Is the salmon telling

me to look for a mate? But I already have one, she thought in dismay. And he does not want to be with me. . . .

She waited at the creek bank for more advice from the animals and birds, but only a soft breeze caressed her cheeks and fluttered through her hair. *What is there for me in life?*

Was there something about her time with the Jaguars that could give meaning to her life? Perhaps she should look for what was good about her new life with the Jaguars.

She stared at her fingers, then tentatively touched one finger as she thought of the one good thing she *did* have in this new life of hers. It was her husband. Though Falcon and she were not doing very well at present, at least he still stayed with her, brought her meat, and shared the cave with her.

A thought struck her and she touched the next finger: she did have an opportunity for some companionship in that she lived with other people, the Jaguar People. She was not alone out in the barren hills.

Excitedly, she realized another good thing: even though her mother resided far away, and perhaps Star would never see her again, yet Blue Jay still lived and Star was glad of that.

Star's eyes blurred and she had to weep for a little while. She missed her mother. When she finished wiping her eyes, she looked at her fingers. Tentatively, she touched her little finger; she did have Badger women friends nearby, or at least they used to be friends. And Sageflower still seemed friendly.

Star drummed her fingers together, wondering if she had overlooked anything else good in her life with the Jaguars. Ah, yes, there was! Thumb: there were a few Jaguar People who seemed kind, Betafor for one. Perhaps Star could make friends with her, or with one of Betafor's daughters. They seemed to be a fairly happy family.

She went back over her advantages: she had Falcon; she lived with other people; her mother was still alive; she had Badger women friends nearby; and there were some friendly Jaguar people in camp.

Staring at her fingers, she wondered if a woman could make a rewarding, happy life out of those five things.

The water gurgled at her feet, whispering yes! yes! and Star gave a little bark of laughter.

Then she wondered if she should even attempt to plan her life this time. Perhaps not. Perhaps she should just live a day-to-day existence with no hopes, no expectations, no dreams . . . and no love? No, she could not do that! She had to have love in her life. She had to have love to survive.

"Where do I start?" she whispered to the wind. "Where do I start to find love and meaning in my life?"

But no bird flew down to tell her. No fish came swimming close to her feet. Only the breeze caressed her cheek. And gave her no answer.

Chapter Thirty-two

Falcon knew he was spending too much time away from Star. A part of him longed to be with her, yet still he played the coward and went off hunting. He could not face his own woman. What kind of a man was he?

Something was happening between them, a change, and he did not know what it was. Worse, he was uncomfortable with her, very uncomfortable.

No, it was better to stay away from her and hide here, in the hills. He could pretend he was hunting.

The Jaguar hunters had been very successful after they had reached the Bear Caves and had killed most of the meat they needed for winter. The meat from the two bears had been dried and cached away, and then they had the good fortune to slay 17 deer and two big elk. Falcon was the only hunter who had objected when the shaman, Rapt, had stepped on each of the elks' necks and made the claim that the elk had come to their spears because *he* had called them.

Why, that shaman could not even call a meadow mouse, thought Falcon in disgust. Rapt was feeling boastful because Cat Lurks had recovered. After so many failures, Falcon told himself bitterly, Rapt's single success of a cure had made him crow and boast to whomever would listen. And Falcon had not missed the admiring glance on Star's face when Rapt had claimed the elk. She thinks shaman are all-knowing and all-powerful too, he thought. She is just like Tula!

After he had realized that, Falcon did not want to be around Star. And an unaccountable despair had settled upon him.

He glanced around at the lonely, windy landscape. Not a single animal had come down to drink at the water hole he had been hiding near. He knew he was in the hunting territory of the male lion and his mate, but since the day the Jaguar People had taken over the caves, the lions had not shown themselves. Perhaps they had found other hunting territory. Falcon hoped so. That would explain the successful hunting the Jaguars had enjoyed. No lions for competition.

If Star was just like Tula, mused Falcon, then he faced a miserable life. And had he not already been through more misery than most men? He had endured the loss of wife to another man and the loss of his child to death. What more could a man put up with?

He stared at the barren landscape again, willing

an antelope, a deer, anything to appear so that he could hunt it and kill it and relieve the feelings building inside him. Anything was better than this terrible brooding.

But as so often happened, Falcon did not get what he wanted. If there had been a Great Spirit, he would have shaken his fist and screamed his anger at Him. But there was none. None!

The cold wind took its toll on him. His limbs were chilled. Night was coming on. The other hunters would probably have returned to the caves. What was it that pinned him to this barren, windswept spot waiting for deer? Nothing but fear, he decided, getting to his feet. Fear of his own wife.

Time to hunt down that fear and vanquish it.

When he reached the cave, a comforting sight greeted him. The fire burned with welcoming flames; the smell of roasting vegetables wafted through the air. His woman, Star, sat beside the fire, the lovely, angular planes of her face lit by the orange flames as she bent over her sewing. Her long black hair draped her shoulders and he saw the calmness settled on her face.

Behind her he could see their possessions laid out neatly; the baskets, the spears, the elk-hide bed. Wherever she went, she made a home, he thought. And she had made a home of the cave.

Suddenly a wave of fear coursed through him. She was a woman; she was just like Tula! She would make a home and then destroy it, destroy every part of it and him until nothing was left but ashes and hate. The thought flashed through his mind like a bird's wing seen out of the corner of his eye that if he destroyed everything now, destroyed this home, then he would be safe.

"What have you done?" he roared.

She looked up, startled. He threw down his spear and kicked dirt over the jumping flames. He must put out the fire that falsely promised home and hearth and food and love.

"What—?" Star lifted her arms to protect her face as dirt flew past her.

As soon as the fire smoldered, stinking, under the dirt, Falcon ran to the elk hide. He yanked out his obsidian knife from its place at his waist and grabbed up the elk hide. With several swift strokes of the knife, he cut through the hide, leaving it in tatters.

"What are you doing?" screamed Star. He turned and saw she had both hands pressed to her cheeks, her mouth open, a horrified look on her face.

He ignored her and grabbed up the baskets, spilling their contents. Berries and roots rolled everywhere and he kicked dirt over them. He tried to pull the baskets apart with his bare hands but they were too tough, so he slashed at them with his knife. He reached for the white deerskin dress that had spilled from the basket and raised his knife to slash it to tatters, too, but Star snatched the garment out of his reach. She ran out of the cave.

He saw a blur of white on the dark floor and slashed up the white moccasins. In a fury of rage, he picked up a tanned fur and threw it at the cave wall with all his might. It slid to the ground in a crumpled heap. He picked up a second fur and did the same. Then he ran over and stomped on the furs, pounding them with his feet, his teeth gritted in rage. He fell to his knees and used his knife to make deep, jagged cuts through the furs. Then he jumped to his feet.

She will not do this to me! went through his brain over and over. She will not lull me to sleep with gentle ways and then turn on me and destroy me!

"I will destroy everything! Nothing will be left for her to hurt me with!" he howled at the cave roof.

He whipped around, chest heaving, searching for anything he might have missed. Baskets, elk hide, fire, all destroyed!

He seized his two spears leaning against the wall and tried to break the wooden shafts. He pounded them against the rock wall, he tried breaking them with his knee, but they were too strong. He threw them on the ground in disgust. Grabbing up Star's digging stick, he threw it out of the cave's entrance.

A black bowl caught his eye. The old mortar and pestle, passed down from his mother, quickly followed the digging stick as he threw it out of the cave's mouth. He heard the crashing sounds as they rolled down the gravel slope below the caves.

His breath coming in gasps, he glanced around. Destroyed! Everything must be destroyed!

Everything was. Where before there had been falseness: quiet and neatness and contentment, now there was truth: dirt and smoldering wood and tattered rags.

He had done good work. With a last, guttural cry, he whirled and ran out of the cave.

Chapter Thirty-three

The next morning Star stood among the ruins of her cave home and stared about her. He had severed her baskets with his knife and cut up the furs she had worked so long on tanning. He had stomped on the dried berries and scattered dirt over the dried vegetables. Why had he done this? Why? And what were they going to eat when winter arrived?

Thank the Great Spirit she had been able to spend last night at Sageflower's cave. Though it was crowded with Sageflower's husband's people, still they had made room for her. Star had cried herself to sleep, her sobs muffled in the unfamiliar fur she'd been silently handed by Deer Summoner's grave mother.

As for Falcon, wherever he was, he had not shown himself. Not last night, not this morning.

Why had he done this? Why?

She moaned to herself, wondering what to do now. She stepped over to the ring of rocks. The fire was cold. Should she light it again? Sageflower would give her a light from their hearth fire. Star shivered as a cold wind brushed her. Winter was near. And now she had no food. What was she going to do?

She had tried to show him there was hope in her heart for them. She had thought she would start with making herself a fine home. That would show him and others that she valued herself. That her life held meaning. That she could make it have meaning. Falcon would see she valued him, too, and he in turn would want to be a part of her life. That was how she had planned it.

Well, another of her plans dashed. She had tried to make him a fine home, one he would feel proud of and welcome in. She had set out the things they owned and used. She had done all she could to make it a home. And now this.

Gone. Destroyed. Utterly, utterly useless.

The wind whipped at her fur now in harsh reminder of the winter that was surely coming. What should she do?

She wiped away a tear that dribbled down her cheek. Why had he done this? Did he not want her? Want their home?

She heard a scratching sound behind her and turned. Her heart sank.

"What a tidy home you have here," sneered Tula.

Why had she chosen this morning of all times to stop by?

Tula grinned smugly. When she swung to the

side to better observe the destruction of Star's home, Star could see her baby's little round face. He yawned.

"Falcon never did this while *I* was married to him."

Ah, so Tula had heard. Star should have known that word of Falcon's deed would travel swiftly through the Jaguar caves.

"When he was *my* husband, we had a fine home. A fine home, indeed."

Star gritted her teeth.

Tula sauntered over and halted when she was a handbreadth away. "I would say he does not like you." She looked pleased. She gave a light laugh and sauntered over to where the torn furs lay on the cave floor. A long, jagged cut in one fur gaped obscenely, like an open mouth.

"I would say he does not like the way you tan furs."

She kicked at a broken basket. "Do you think he likes your basket making?" She smiled sweetly, then gave a tinkly laugh. "No, I think he does not."

Her baby made snuffling sounds as he rooted for a breast. "Go to sleep, little one," she murmured over her shoulder. She shot Star a wide smile. "Such a mess," she murmured and made little clucking sounds.

Star said nothing. She felt too humiliated. Why did it have to be Tula who saw her at her worst, standing amid the ruins of her home?

"Well, it has been most pleasant, but I must go."

Relief swept through Star.

Broken Promise

Tula shuffled over to the cave entrance. The baby on her back was beginning to cry softly. Tula was just about to step outside the cave when she stopped and said, "Why do you stay here? Go home to your people, Badger dog-girl. No one wants you here. Not even Falcon!" Then she gave a low, delighted laugh and strode away.

Star began to cry.

She gave in to her despair, and great tearing sobs ripped from her throat. She sat down and buried her head in her arms. Her whole body shook with the force of her sobs. It was true: she was not wanted. No one here wanted her to stay. Not Falcon, none of them. She sobbed for a long time.

Suddenly she felt a nudge on her shoulder. Star slowly raised her head.

Betafor stood looking down at her. "Here." She held out the black mortar bowl. From behind her, hanging on to her dress, peeked one of her little granddaughters. In her tiny hand, she held the pestle.

Star stared at the bowl in a daze; then slowly she reached for it. She clamped her fingers around the cold, hard stone. The little granddaughter came over and plopped the pestle into the mortar, where it rattled. Then she scurried behind her grandmother once more.

Betafor glanced around the cave and shook her head. "I do not know why that boy did this."

Star blinked and it took her several heartbeats to realize Betafor meant Falcon. "I do not know, either." After so much crying, her voice sounded like the croak of a frog.

Betafor gave her a kindly glance. "What will you do?"

The little granddaughter, her black eyes shining, peeked out at Star. When she saw Star watching her, she shyly buried her face in the back of her grandmother's leather dress.

Star shook her head, still dazed. "I do not know."

Betafor gave her a tiny pat on the shoulder and then, as if afraid she had done too much, quickly withdrew her hand. Star's lips trembled at the loss.

Betafor shook her head. "Well, I will talk to that boy for you, but I do not know if any good will come of it." She sounded doubtful.

Without thinking, Star touched Betafor's arm to stay her. "No. Do not. He will not welcome it." She dropped her hand at her own presumption. "He—he does not like to talk."

Betafor nodded. "Very well." She glanced around the cave again. "Still, to let him do this—"

Star stared at the dead fire, humiliation washing over her. "I could not stop him."

"Of course not, child," murmured Betafor. "I did not mean it was your fault. I only meant— Well, I suppose I meant that he should give you some explanation."

"I do not think he will," whispered Star.

Betafor walked over to where the two spears lay. Her granddaughter clung to her every step like a second shadow. Betafor picked up the spears and leaned them against the wall. She reached for one of the baskets, examined its sorry condition, shook her head, and set it back down. She wandered back to Star, her granddaughter still a part of her leg. "Do you wish to come and join us at our fireside?"

Star shook her head. "No, but thank you for your kindness. I—I will stay here. . . ."

Betafor nodded and reached around and pried her granddaughter off her leg. She took the child's hand and led her toward the cave's mouth.

As Star watched them leave, she suddenly felt grateful for the other woman's visit. Betafor had come to her when no one else had and she had tried to be kind. "Thank you," she called after them. "Thank you for returning the mortar and pestle."

Betafor gave a little wave. Then she and her granddaughter disappeared from the entrance. Star heard the crunch of their steps receding on the gravel. She was alone again. "Now what do I do?" she muttered aloud.

She stared around the cave and shifted to her knees. "Am I going to let this discourage me?" She stared down at the mortar and pestle. Her hand closed over the cold stone handle of the pestle as she thought of Betafor and the little grandchild returning the implements. "No," she said aloud. "I will not let this stop me. And I will not let Tula scare me off. I will rebuild my home."

She got to her feet and began to pick up the tattered remains of her possessions.

While she was working, Sageflower stopped by. Deer Summoner was with her and the two worked over the dead fire at the circle of rocks.

They scraped back the dirt, gathered twigs, and relit the fire. Finally the tiny flames crackled and leaped up, throwing grotesque shadows on the cave walls.

Star glanced up from where she had gathered up the discarded food. She saw the two and wiped at her face and hair. She had been so lost in her thoughts, wondering how she was going to face the winter, that she had not even noticed their presence. "Sageflower," she said politely, coming over to where the handsome couple stood. "My thanks for your help. And Deer Summoner's also."

The two nodded. Deer Summoner, as always, looked dignified.

"I—I did not expect you to—"

"Hush," said Sageflower. "Of course we would help you."

"Falcon—" Oh, how it hurt to say his name. Did he not want her? "Falcon—" She could not get the words out.

Sageflower touched Star's arm. "We know Falcon did this. But we do not know why. It is a serious thing he has done. Do you have any food left for winter?"

Star shook her head. Deer Summoner and Sageflower regarded her solemnly. Star flushed under their pity-filled glances. "I—I must get back to cleaning and repairing," she murmured. "Thank you for your help with the fire."

After they left, she shook her head, amazed. To have the Jaguar People pity her was worse than to have them dislike her.

She went out and broke a pine branch from a

scraggly tree that grew in the shelter of a big rock near the caves. She brought the branch back to her home and used it to sweep the floor clean.

While she was sweeping, Elk Knees stopped by. She carried a bowl of hot venison stew. "I brought it for you," she said shyly.

Star set the stone bowl aside. "I do not feel hungry," she confessed.

Elk Knees glanced around the cave. "Why did he do this?"

Star shrugged. "I know not."

Elk Knees fidgeted and shifted from one foot to the other. Finally she blurted, "I have come to tell you that I was wrong."

"Wrong? About what?"

Elk Knees leaned closer. "You were correct. Lying with a man can be very wonderful!" Then she whirled and dashed out of the cave.

Puzzled, Star pondered her friend's words. Then she chuckled to herself. Elk Knees and Horn were enjoying their time in the bedrobes!

Feeling better, Star nibbled at the venison stew. Its delicious taste nourished her body and soul. The stew finished, she rose and, humming to herself, examined the baskets. They could not be mended. But the two furs and the elkhide could be repaired with careful stitching, she thought. She took some hope from that.

She had to throw out most of the food, but a few roots had remained in one basket and she managed to brush the dirt off a handful of dried berries. It was not much, but it was food.

She glanced out the cave entrance and saw the sky was still light. There was still enough time left in the day to go and dig roots.

She walked out of the cave and was climbing down the gravelly slope when she spotted her digging stick. She clambered across the gravel and retrieved it. Ah, all was not lost. She could work, and she could rebuild her home. With a little smile on her lips, she set out with her digging stick to find more roots.

Chapter Thirty-four

Falcon took two steps into the cave and stopped as suddenly as though he had come up against a rock wall. Everything looked just as it had been before he had destroyed it to save himself.

Aghast, he surveyed the cave. The elk hide was in the same place. Set out on a freshly woven mat were his mother's mortar and pestle, a few bone tools, and two awls. He was relieved to see there were no baskets, but then he spotted the two furs. No sign of his knife's slashes showed on the hides. Worse, there were now two great bunches of aromatic herbs hanging from a new pole set in the dirt of the cave floor.

And beside the flickering fire sat Star, calmly weaving a basket.

She had restored everything, he saw. It was as if he had done nothing to save himself.

Despair settled over him like a thick winter cloak.

When she looked up at him, he wanted to run out of the cave. "Are you going to destroy this, too?" she asked, and he wanted to cringe at the calmness in her voice. She did not understand. She did not understand anything!

"Why did you not leave?"

"Did you want me to?"

No! he wanted to say. He could not meet her eyes, so he squinted through the smoke at the hanging herbs. He pointed at them with his spear. "What are those for?"

"To make our home smell pleasant."

She understood nothing! "We have no home."

She shrugged. "Perhaps you do not. But I do."

He took a step forward. He swung his spear to include all the cave. "This is not to be a home. Do you understand?"

"No."

He could see by her defiant eyes that indeed she did not. "What must I do to make you understand?" he mused aloud.

She set aside the partially woven basket and got to her feet. She walked around the fire until she stood in front of him. He could smell her, smell the scent of smoke and herbs that drifted to him from her skin, her hair. He leaned closer, closing his eyes and inhaling her scent. Ah, she smelled so good.

"What is it you want me to understand?"

He opened his eyes and stared into hers. She watched him, and he felt a quiver of pain at her wariness. He took a breath. What could he say without telling her of all the pain he carried inside?

298

"I am listening."

He saw that she was alert, wary. She waited.

He hesitated. Then he caught sight of the elk hide, whole, unshredded, and the taste of defeat entered his mouth.

"I do not want a home."

"Ah, I see. You are truly like the falcon, then. The bird that lays its eggs on a ledge. He makes no nest."

He smiled, relieved. "Yes. I am like that."

She smiled back. "You are well named indeed."

He was glad she understood.

"But Falcon, I am not like that. I want a home, family."

His smile disappeared. "We cannot have that." He glanced away. "I—I should never have taken you from your people."

Her smile wavered and he saw her lips tremble. But she held his eyes with her bright black ones. "You may do what you want, but as I am here, I will make a home."

Powerlessness entered him then. She did not understand; she would never understand, and they were pitted against each other like hunter against lion. He glanced around the cave again and he realized that even were he to tear it all apart, she would merely go out and get more herbs, more rushes, and make more baskets. She would never see how it was for him. He felt as though he were stepping off a cliff and falling, falling through the air. And he knew the only thing that would stop his fall was death: his death.

"So be it then," he said softly, setting his spear

down. He took her in his arms. He could not fight it. He could not tell her all the feelings that roiled in him, but he could seek solace in her arms. That would hold death at bay for a little while.

She clung to him and he was surprised at the strength of her hold. He kissed her trembling lips. Desire for her flared in him. "Let us go to the bedrobes," he suggested.

She took his hand and led him past the fire to the back of the shallow cave where the elk hide was. They sank to the bed and he helped her out of her dress. She helped him shed his clothes and then they were lying naked, her heated skin pressing against his. He took her then, and only when he was inside her could he forget the overwhelming despair that he fought day and night. She is like Tula, came the taunting little voice in his mind. She will destroy you and your son, too!

He shook his head to dispel all thought and pushed harder into her. Soon came the all-encompassing, intense, life-giving burst as he drove into her, and it blotted out all his fear, all his pain. He held her and buried his face in her neck, inhaling her sweet fragrance. He would stay with her, he would live with her, in this cave home. And when it came time to die, he would go willingly, gloriously, if only he could hold her like this every night.

Chapter Thirty-five

Winter

Star sat by the fire, wrapped in a huge, warm
beaver fur, and stared out at the thickly falling
snow as it blew past the cave entrance. It was the
second day of the blizzard and she was glad that
she and Falcon were safely ensconced in their
cave home.

She had never told him where the extra food
came from. No doubt he thought that their stores
had just mushroomed on their own. But it was
Betafor who had parted with two bundles of dried
cakes made from pounded roots, saying that her
daughters had been most diligent and provided
more than enough roots for this winter. She gave
no explanation when she handed a bundle of dried
meat to Star.

Sageflower had stopped by to visit and given

Star, baskets and all, dried berries, dried meat, and dried mushrooms. Pine Woman and Elk Knees had both appeared at Star's cave entrance, carrying a basket of pine seeds and a basket of dried blueberries each. Over Star's weak protests, they had insisted that they could spare such food for her. Even Deer Summoner's grave old mother had visited Star's cave when Falcon was out and silently handed Star two giant, warm beaver pelts, one of which she wore this moment.

Star brushed away a tear as she thought about how kind the people had been to her. Not just the Badger women, but the Jaguar women, too. It had been so generous of them to part with the food they had saved for their families, and they had done so graciously. For her. And for Falcon. She was starting to feel accepted by these Jaguar People.

She slanted a glance at Falcon. He sat wrapped in the other large beaver robe and stared moodily at the fire. Waiting out a blizzard was difficult for him to do, she thought as she burrowed further down in the warm robe.

The snow was falling swiftly now and had piled up thigh-deep outside the cave's entrance. The path along the ledge to the other caves was covered in snow, but the Jaguar People could outwait the blizzard.

Later that night, Star heard the wind howl as the snowstorm raged across the land. She snuggled up to Falcon and he, sound asleep, pulled her closer and held her. She smiled to herself and fell back to sleep.

The next morning when she awoke, the snow

had stopped. She and Falcon broke their fast with strips of dried meat.

"I will go hunting," he said.

She nodded, understanding that he could not linger for many days in the cave without becoming restless. "Perhaps one of the other men will go with you," she answered. "Then if a snowstorm comes, you will be safer."

He stared at her as he always did whenever she suggested that she wanted him to stay safe. Why is it such a surprise to him? she wondered. Sometimes she saw disbelief cross his face and she thought then that he did not trust her words. She sighed. Would she ever understand this man? No, she answered herself. Not until he himself explained what went on in his soul.

"I will ask Horn if he wants to go," answered Falcon.

She nodded and went over to kiss him. He gave her an answering kiss; then he grabbed up his spear and hurried off. She shook her head and went to sit down by the fire. She picked up her sewing and stared at it. She stared but did not see the bird she was designing on the newly made leather shirt, the one she had made to replace the leather shirt the jaguar had shredded in the attack so long ago. But whenever she looked at the falcon design she had drawn, she thought it paltry and childish compared to the magnificent design he had once worn. The one Tula had made.

With a dissatisfied sigh, Star set the sewing aside. Now she was the one feeling restless. Perhaps she could go hunting with Falcon. He found that soothing; perhaps she would, too.

She put on her long moccasins, then wrapped a fur around her torso and tied it with a leather belt. She headed out into the snow.

The path along the ledge that led to the other caves was well trodden and she soon reached the cave that Elk Knees and Horn lived in. Unfortunately, Star had forgotten in her haste that they shared the large, comfortable dwelling with Horn's sister, Tula, and Marmot and their son.

"What do *you* want?" Tula greeted her at the entrance.

"I am looking for Falcon," answered Star as reasonably as she could. Why did she feel like screaming and throwing things whenever she saw Tula?

"He is not here."

"He said he was coming to visit Horn."

"No. He is not here. Go away."

"Who is it, Tula?" Elk Knees's voice came from the back of the cave.

"No one," snapped Tula.

But Elk Knees was coming forward to see for herself. "Oh, Star." She smiled. "Welcome." Was that a blush on her dusky cheeks?

Star liked the way that Elk Knees ignored her sister-in-law's angry grunt. She let Elk Knees propel her past the glowering Tula and guide her back to where her small family sat. The little girl was weaving a tiny basket and the little boy was carving the handle of a toy spear. "Where is Horn?" asked Star.

"He has gone hunting with Falcon," answered Elk Knees.

"Oh." Star stared at the little family, trying not to show her disappointment.

"You just missed them."

Star nodded. "Perhaps if I hurry I will catch up to him."

Elk Knees nodded. "If you hurry. They seemed quite anxious to hunt. Sitting around in caves does not agree with men."

Star took her leave and walked back past Tula and Marmot's sleeping place without saying anything. She could feel Marmot's eyes on her the whole length of her walk, and Tula muttered at her angrily when she passed. Star kept going, head down.

"Badger dog-girl . . ." The whispered curse followed her out of the cave.

She stood on the ledge and gazed out across the snow-clad land. She could see the two men making their way slowly across the landscape. They wore snowshoes. Crestfallen, she glanced at her feet. She did not have snowshoes. There would be no hunting for her this day.

Slowly she went back to her little cave. She took off the robe and pulled off her moccasins. She carefully placed some wood on the small fire, then sat down beside it to begin her lonely vigil. She gave a sigh, picked up the leather shirt, and stared at it. Then she started to draw a falcon upon it once more.

She was dozing by the fire when stamping footsteps outside the cave awoke her.

"Falcon!" She jumped up and flew to him. She threw her arms around him and hugged him. "I am so glad you have returned!"

He stared at her, then shrugged, accepting her enthusiastic hug. He set aside his spear and dragged in the deer he had killed.

"Oh! Oh! A deer!" She clapped her hands in glee. "You were most fortunate!"

He stared at her again as if he thought she were in danger of losing her wits.

"It was so quiet here all day," she explained. "I had no one to talk to, nothing to do. I am so glad you have returned."

He nodded at that.

"Oh!" she exclaimed again, seeing anew how large the deer was. "All that meat! We must have a feast!"

He was looking at her strangely again.

"I want to invite Betafor and Claw, and—and Elk Knees and Horn and their family! And Pine Woman and Sageflower and their husbands! And, oh, yes, Deer Summoner's old mother—"

He held up a hand. "We will have no meat left for ourselves."

"That is correct."

"And will you tell me why we are going to give away all our meat?"

"Yes. We are going to store it in our friends' stomachs."

"Hmmm. I suppose this is a Badger custom."

"Oh, yes. It is considered very wise to store one's food in other people's stomachs. Then when you need food, they will store some in yours."

"I see."

She clapped her hands in excitement. "It has been so quiet in this cave. I have been wanting to talk to someone, anyone—and now I have a wonderful chance—"

"Star."

"Yes?"

"Just tell me why we are going to store our food in their stomachs."

"Well, that is being friendly." She looked at him brightly. "You want to be friendly, do you not?"

He yawned. "I do not care if I am friendly or not. Friends do not matter."

She felt the old despair rising and she tamped it down. She would not let him get to her with his "nothing matters" ideas. She would not. . . .

"Since it does not matter to you, I will run and invite the guests." She was halfway to the entrance when his hand gripped her shoulder and stopped her.

"I do not want to have a feast. I want to rest. I am tired."

She swung to face him. "Well. You are tired. Too bad." She took a step forward and leaned into him. "If it were not for your friends, the ones you do not care about, you would be so tired you would be dead!"

"What do you mean?" He stared at her blankly.

"I mean," she gritted, "that it was Betafor and Elk Knees and Sageflower and Deer Summoner's mother who fed us. They made sure we had warm furs for the cold winter. And why did they do that, Falcon?"

He did not answer but his eyes narrowed.

"Aha! You *do* know why! It was because you destroyed every piece of food, every fur we had saved for the winter. That is why! Without their gifts of food and warm furs, you and I would both be dead. Frozen under a blanket of snow! *Now* do you understand why I want to give them a feast?"

He flinched at her words. At last he answered in a surly tone, "Invite them then."

She tossed her head. "I will." And she stomped out of the cave.

When she returned with her guests in tow, she found that Falcon had added more wood to the fire and had started to cut the meat in chunks for roasting on sticks. She smiled at him and waved, chatting happily with her guests all the while.

She tried not to stare when he politely offered the first cooked chunk of meat to Deer Summoner's old mother.

Much later, when all the guests were holding their full stomachs and staggering out of the cave, she turned to him and smiled. "Thank you so much for treating my guests so well."

"They were my guests, too," he pointed out, but then she saw his black eyes twinkle.

She leaned forward and touched her forehead to his. Her nose touched his, too. "Falcon?"

"Hmmm?"

"That was a fine feast you gave."

"We gave," he corrected.

"We gave," she agreed happily. Then she took his hand and pulled him along to the back of the cave where the elk-hide bed was.

Soon they were happily rewarding each other for a feast well given.

Chapter Thirty-six

Falcon stamped the snow off his snowshoes and undid the leather thongs that tied them to his feet. He set them aside and walked into the cave.

"Welcome back to our home," greeted Star.

He stared at her. Did she realize what she had just said? Home? Was she trying to torment him?

He grunted in answer as he took off his fur robe.

"No animals?" she asked brightly.

He shook his head. "All the animals were hiding from the cold."

"As you should do," she chided.

"I do not like lying around the cave all day," he retorted.

Her face softened and she answered, "I know you do not, Falcon. You are a good husband. You hunt often for us and you are always very generous with the meat you kill. You share what you have with others."

He bent over to take off his moccasins so that she could not see how much her words and voice undid him.

"It was not my idea to share," he retorted gruffly. "It is you who insists on giving away the meat."

"Ah. I do not believe you, husband," she answered, and he felt himself soften inside when he saw how her brown eyes danced in the firelight.

She continued in that voice that sent shivers of desire down his spine, "I saw you give Old Widow a deer haunch yesterday, when you thought no one was looking. She has no one to hunt for her, but I suppose you knew that."

He turned his back to her and peeled off his leather shirt. "Horn feeds her. So do the other hunters."

"Perhaps you should send her out into the snows," suggested Star.

He whirled. "No! We will not send her out into the snows!" he thundered.

"Good," Star answered meekly. "I remember when you first visited my Badger camp so long ago, you said that your people send the old ones out into the snows."

He stared at her, remembering that time he had once teased her and her mother at the Badger camp. It seemed like many seasons ago now, he thought wearily. He turned away from her. "Old Widow will find a new husband in the spring. There is much life spirit left in her yet. One of the young men will surely offer for her."

When he glanced at Star to see how she

reacted to his answer, he saw that her lips had tightened. Trying not to laugh, the little Badger, he thought.

Indeed, the idea of Old Widow marrying again did seem funny. She was the oldest woman of the Jaguar People and her counsel was occasionally sought by Betafor so that she could better advise Claw before he advised the rest of the Jaguar People. But everyone knew that Old Widow was content to stay unmarried. And the hunters were always generous with their meat to her; she never lacked for food. One day she would be among the fortunate ones and just die quietly in her sleep.

"I should put you out in the snow," he said, marveling to himself that he had tried to make a joke. It seemed he had not laughed in a long time.

But he saw that his wife understood his joke; she made a wry face at him. He smiled back, liking the slight banter between them. Was this what it was like to be married then? he wondered. Was this happiness that seeped through his chest what it was like to live with someone you truly loved?

He froze. Loved? There was no such thing as love. He had best remember that. He did not love Star. He loved no one.

His wife must have read something on his face, for she went back to her sewing. He walked over and looked down at what she was doing. "What is that?"

She turned the leather over as though she did not want him to see it. The little Badger, he thought. What is she trying to hide?

He reached down and turned the leather back

311

so he could see it. "What *is* that?" he asked, perplexed. "It looks like a prairie hen or some such. . . ."

She snatched it away from his hands. "It is nothing!" she announced.

"It is, Star. It is something. Give it to me."

But she refused to hand the leather over to him. He held out his hand. "Give it to me, Star."

"No." She ducked her head.

"I want to see it."

"No!"

"Star . . ."

When she bent herself around the leather to hide it from him, he could not resist. "Give it to me," he insisted, trying to get at it, "or I will tickle you!"

She began to giggle as his fingers found her ribs and underarms and started wiggling. She began to laugh so hard from his tickling that her grip on the leather loosened and he snatched it away.

"Aha!" he exclaimed in triumph. "I have it!"

"No!" She came at him, her hands out like claws trying to get at the garment.

He held her off with one hand while he shook out the soft, crumpled leather with the other. "Why, it is a shirt!"

She shrieked and dived at him. It took all his strength to hold her off with his one hand, and then he started to laugh because now she was tickling him under the arm.

"Give it back to me, Falcon!"

"No!"

"You must! You must!"

He was laughing too hard to hold on to the

leather and she snatched the garment back.

He grinned at the discomfiture on her face. "It is a fine prairie hen, Star," he assured her.

"Ooh!" She snorted. "It is not a prairie hen!"

"It is not? But it looks like a prairie hen."

"It is a falcon!"

He could not help himself. He started to laugh. He had to hold his stomach, he was laughing so hard.

When he could finally choke out some words, he said, "Of course it is. Why could I not see that?"

"You fool," she gritted, and she was not laughing anymore. "I was doing it for you!" Then, clutching the garment to her, she ran out of the cave.

He sat there staring at the fire, wondering what to do now. Perhaps he would go hunting again. Old Widow could always use the meat.

He was just strapping on his snowshoes when Star returned.

"Where are you going?" she demanded.

He eyed her. She held the leather shirt close to her stomach, protecting it from him. Her lips were tight and her eyes narrow.

"Time to go hunting," he answered.

"You just got back from hunting! And now you are going again?"

He heard the dismay in her voice and he shrugged. He did not want to go hunting, but he wanted to stay around the cave with an angry woman even less.

"So! You think to run away again."

313

"I am not running away."

"You are going hunting. That is running away!"

"Silence, woman. I said I am going hunting."

She stepped out of his way. "Very well," she answered. "Go hunting."

And she sauntered into the cave. He could not help but notice the sway of her hips. He glanced back at the cold, snow-clad hills. Then back at the warm fire and the woman, taking her place to sew beside it.

With a sigh, he took off his snowshoes and tramped back into the cave. "I changed my mind," he said.

She smiled.

He smiled back.

The fire cracked and popped and he put a few twigs on it. "We will have to get more wood soon," he said.

She nodded. "We could go together and bring some back."

"Very well." They got up and put on their fur robes and headed out into the afternoon cold.

When they returned, each bearing an armload of branches and wood for the fire, it was almost dark.

"I will get the evening meal," she said, and he nodded. He stamped his feet to keep the blood running. He breathed into his hands to warm them.

The fire kept them warm that evening and the dried meat and berries tasted good.

When they sat beside the fire, he ventured, "I thought it was a very well drawn prairie hen, Star."

She glanced at him. Finally she said, "It is not well drawn at all. And it is supposed to be a falcon."

"Let me look at it."

Reluctantly she handed the leather shirt to him. It was indeed a pitiful drawing—it looked like neither a prairie hen nor a falcon. He bit back his chuckles before they could erupt and offend her.

He handed the shirt back to her, keeping his face as solemn as he could.

"It is supposed to replace the beautiful shirt you had—the one the jaguar shredded," she explained, her dark eyes sad.

"Ah. It is good of you to make me the shirt. You do not have to decorate it."

"Tula did."

"Ah." So that was it. Tula had made the other shirt and Star knew it.

"Yes. I wanted to draw a falcon as beautiful as she did."

He started to laugh. He could not help himself. He rolled on the floor, roaring with laughter while his wife looked on with a hurt expression.

"I—I—" He could not get the words out, he was laughing so hard. "She—she—"

"When you are done laughing at me, you Jaguar fool"—he could hear the blizzard of ice in her voice—"you may go hunting."

He kept laughing so hard he thought he was going to die. He laughed so hard his stomach hurt. Finally he gasped, "She did not draw that falcon. Betafor's oldest daughter did."

"What did you say?"

315

That got the little Badger's attention. "It is true. Betafor's oldest daughter is a very skilled artist. It was she who drew the falcon on my shirt. Not Tula."

Star looked suddenly relieved.

"And Tula cannot sing, either," he added generously.

Star smiled. She snatched up the leather shirt. "I am off to visit Betafor and her family. Do not wait up for me."

He chuckled to himself. Having a wife was proving very entertaining. And one advantage to having this Badger wife was that she could not go back to her people. She could not leave him. Ever. She was his.

He smiled at the fire, feeling more relaxed and happy than he had in a long, long time.

Chapter Thirty-seven

Spring

They had survived the winter, thought Star happily. The Jaguar People had used their stored foods and the men had hunted and they had all done very well. It helped that there had been only two blizzards—a mild winter. Star remembered one winter she had spent with the Badgers when the snows had raged fiercely for many days and nights. She was thankful that had not happened this time.

And while the Jaguar People were kind, she thought they should have been better prepared for the coldest time. Perhaps she should speak with Betafor and suggest they start preserving roots and bulbs earlier this year.

Star stood at the cave entrance. Behind her, Falcon still slept. She had crawled out of their warm fur robes and made her way to the entrance of the cave, lured forth by the shrill morning cries of little birds.

Before her lay a vista of gravel and hills and she could see the green of grass blades starting to push up here and there on the hills. Sage grass was growing once again. Yesterday she had seen a bear and two cubs. Spring was truly here.

She yawned and stretched easily in the warm spring sunshine. A new day had come and with it a happy feeling. She smiled to herself. Something very special had happened this winter. She was growing a baby.

She knew she was because Sageflower, who now waddled with a huge stomach on her and knew all about pregnancy, had assured Star she was indeed pregnant. No blood these past three moons, lethargy, even the vomiting, had all been signs, according to Sageflower, that Star was pregnant.

She had not told Falcon yet. She wanted to surprise him.

She hugged herself as she listened to the birds. It was truly a wonderful day. She had made a life for herself with the Jaguar People. She had made a home, she had made friends with most of the Jaguar women, and she and Falcon had enjoyed their time together. She loved him and he was a good husband to her. All was well with her.

And perhaps once Falcon knew they were expecting a child, he would be so happy he would let her visit her mother. Then everything would indeed be wonderful.

Humming a little song to herself, Star went

back into the cave and yanked the fur robes off Falcon. He groaned.

"Get up, sleepy one," she sang.

He opened one dark eye and looked at her. "You are like a chirpy bird this morning."

She smiled. Today she would tell him the happy news.

"Get up. It is spring! It is time for men to be up and about."

He groaned and rolled over and put one muscular arm over his head. "Go away. It is too early." They had both become accustomed to sleeping late into the morning in the winter.

She snickered and picked up a corner of the elk hide. "Get up! Get up or you will regret it."

He moaned and put his other arm over his head.

She lifted the elk hide, trying to roll him off, but he was too heavy and her trick did not work.

Suddenly a hand clamped on her ankle. "Come here," he said gruffly. He pulled her down beside him and rolled over on her.

She stared up at him and smiled. "Time to get up, dear one."

He kissed her. "Not yet. I have something else to do."

His questing hands told her what that was. She giggled. They made sweet love. Afterward, as she lay satiated and lazy and thinking about burrowing under the furs once more, he jumped up from the bedrobes. "Now who is the lazy one?"

She watched him, amused that he thought he had bettered her. She stretched, feeling good in

319

every part of her body. "Falcon."

"Hmmm?"

"I have something to tell you."

He was putting some twigs on the fire to revive it and he did not answer. Then he retrieved some pieces of meat from a basket and brought one over to her. While chewing on a piece, he handed one to her. "You'd better get up and get us some water, woman. We have none."

She smiled. "We can go to the river together."

"Oh ho. Not me. You will not convince me to scramble down that slope to the river. I will stay here, where the fire is."

She laughed and rose. She handed the meat back to him while she dressed. When she went to retrieve it, she found him chewing the last of it. His eyes glinted. She held out her hand. "More meat," she demanded.

He chuckled and went over to the basket.

She followed him over. Three pieces left. "Looks like you had better go hunting," she observed as he handed her the largest piece.

He stretched and nodded. "Some of the other men will want to go, too," he agreed.

After he dressed, they walked down to the river and drank the refreshing water. "What was it you were going to tell me?"

How his smile warmed her. She loved him so.

She moved closer to him and took his hands in hers.

"Something has happened," she said. At his wary look, she laughed. "Something very good."

He looked relieved. She chuckled. "We," she announced, "are going to have a baby!"

Broken Promise

She laughed aloud, delighted at surprising him.

He went very still; then he dropped her hands. When he stepped away, she stopped laughing. "Falcon?"

He turned to face her. His face looked grim.

"Falcon? What is wrong?"

He shook his head. "It is naught."

"Are you not happy?" She could barely get the words out.

He stared at her, his black eyes growing cool before her eyes. "Are you?" he asked cautiously.

"Oh, yes! I am very, very happy!"

She thought he tried to smile, but then he looked away and she could not tell what he thought.

When he turned back to her, his face was solemn. "I must go hunting now, Star."

Her mouth dropped open. "Now? But—but—"

"I need time to think about this."

"Time?"

"Yes. I must think about what this means."

"But Falcon, it is wonderful! It means we will have a child!"

He looked at her and his eyes glinted with pity. "Yes, it does mean that."

Then he turned and walked away, leaving her standing beside the river and holding the dripping water bladders. "Falcon?"

But he did not hear her.

Chapter Thirty-eight

It had been a handful of days since Falcon had learned that Star was going to have a baby—his baby. Throughout those long days, Falcon still could not bring himself to express the joy that she so readily showed. If only she were not pregnant, he thought desperately. Then everything would be good again.

But she was pregnant. She was growing his child.

He lay on his stomach in a small ravine, hiding under a twisted oak tree and waiting for deer to come and drink at the tiny stream. He had speared a deer here once before and he hoped the trick would work again. Also, it gave him time to think.

Seeing no deer, no coyote, nor anything else moving, he rolled onto his back and looked up at the blue sky through the twisted, budded branches of the oak. He sighed. He remembered how happy Tula had been when she had become pregnant with his child. And he had been very happy, too.

But he did not feel happy about Star's pregnancy. He felt sick with dread. He rolled over once more and buried his face in his arms, heedless of scaring away an animal.

Tula had a healthy son now. So the problem was not with her. It was with him. Deep in his heart he knew this. He, the father, was the reason that Hawk had been so sick and his body grown so twisted. Falcon could never admit this to anyone.

And now, how could he look into Star's beautiful, eager, brown eyes and tell her that her baby would be born as sick as Hawk? How could Falcon go through the terrible agony of watching another of his children sicken, watch him waste away day after day until death claimed him, knowing there was nothing he could do to help him. How could he do it?

He could not do it. He could not!

And Star—what about her? After the baby came and she saw how slowly he grew, she would lose her hope that he would ever heal, just as Falcon had. Then she would grow to loathe her husband, as Tula had done. To see Star change from her loving ways to spiteful, hateful ways would undo him. And when she left him for another man, it would finish him. There would be nothing left in his life worth doing. He would be a dead man with no soul.

Star had already been cruel in an unknowing

way: she had revived hope in him, hope that he could have love. He did not want to admit that to anyone, either. But since he was alone under the oak tree, he could admit it to himself. Just this one time. She had brought love to him again. He had known happiness in the time she had been with him. After Tula had left him, he had thought he would never be happy again, but Star had revived him.

He clenched his eyes shut. What could he do to stop the terrible fate hunting him down? With each passing day the child grew, and with each passing day Falcon wanted to hold Star tighter to him, knowing that one day he would lose her; she would turn away from him and never come back. What could he do?

Over and over again, he thought of how Tula blamed him for their child's death, of how she had left him for Marmot. And he knew the same thing would happen with Star. His stomach clenched with the dread of losing her and their child.

He knew only one thing: he could not go through such terrible losses again. He could not.

"Welcome back to our home," greeted Star.

Falcon stared at her wearily out of hooded eyes. Did she know how her words mocked him? Their "home" was about to be destroyed, far more completely than the mere destruction of a few furs and baskets which he had wrought before.

He grimaced as he sat down beside the fire. He had tried to stop Star from making a home. He

324

had known deep in his heart that he must stop her, stop the love, stop the hope. He had failed. But now the baby would destroy everything for them. No, not the baby, he corrected himself. It was he, Falcon, that was the source of the destruction that would fall upon them all.

She smiled at him as she handed him a roasted camas bulb. He ate it, not even tasting the spring delicacy.

"I went digging camas today with the other women," she said cheerfully.

He grunted.

"I see you return with no meat. You will do better tomorrow."

He stared at her. She thought something as paltry as returning without meat bothered him? He snorted.

She nibbled at a cooled camas root she held in her hand. He could feel her watching him, but he kept his eyes on the flames.

There was a long silence between them, one that Falcon felt too despairing to break.

"Horn stopped by. He wanted to go hunting with you on the morrow."

Falcon shrugged. He cared little what he did on the morrow.

He caught a look of concern on Star's face. He managed to say, "I will go with him."

She looked relieved at his answer. The deep dread in his stomach sat there with the camas and he wanted to sink into himself. There was nothing he could do to stave off the doom he saw ahead for himself. And for her.

She patted her stomach and beamed at him.

He swallowed the bile that rose in his throat. Fear and dread warred in him.

"The baby flutters." She smiled. She took his hand and placed it on her gently rounded stomach. "Would you like to feel it?"

He felt a twinge under his fingers. He yanked his hand back as swiftly as if he had placed it in a lion's mouth.

She looked hurt. Anger rose in him. How could she expect him to be happy after what had happened to him?

He rose to his feet. "I go to talk to Horn." He left the cave.

"Falcon? Falcon, come back! We must talk—"

He hurried around the corner of the cave entrance so that her words were cut off. He hunched over to protect himself against the sound of her voice behind him. He must do something to stop the fate that stalked them all. But what?

Chapter Thirty-nine

Star tromped along with Sageflower to the camas fields. Though the fields were at a considerable distance from the Bear Caves, the Jaguar women considered it worth the trek to obtain the tasty bulbs. Blue-flowered camas plants grew in a huge field near a river. The plants thrived in damp, black soil.

It was the second day the Jaguar women had gone to dig the small bulbs out of the ground and Star wanted to be sure she harvested enough to save for next winter.

"Do not walk so fast," panted Sageflower.

Star laughed and waited for her friend. "I know you must walk slower with that big belly of yours," she said affectionately.

Sageflower gave her a wise glance. "You will have a big belly soon. Just wait."

Star patted her slightly protruding stomach and

smiled. "It is difficult for me to wait. I want to see my baby now!"

Sageflower chuckled. "Yes, it is a wonderful thing we do: growing new life within us."

Star nodded, but some of her exuberance faded. "I do not think Falcon is as happy about the babe as I am."

Sageflower looked so aghast that Star wished she had not spoken. "I am sure he will be happy once the babe comes along," she added hastily. But even she could hear the doubt in her voice.

"Deer Summoner is very excited," confided Sageflower. "He rubs my back for me and sings hunting songs to our baby at night." She giggled. "He wants his son to be a strong hunter."

Star's lips trembled. "He—he does a very fine thing for his son."

"What does Falcon do?"

Star bit her lip. "He goes hunting often," she hedged. She could not tell Sageflower how distant Falcon was becoming. It was difficult to get him even to speak with her. At times, she caught him staring at the fire, and the look on his face was so sad she wanted to cry. No, to tell Sageflower such things would only squash her friend's joy.

"He hunts to give you meat so you grow a strong child," observed Sageflower.

"Yes," said Star glumly.

"Cheer up, friend," said Sageflower blithely. "Jaguar men love their children. You will see."

Star looked away. Sageflower had been wrong about Chokecherry and Cat Lurks, too.

Suddenly Star halted. "Sageflower," she whispered. "Look!" Slowly she raised her digging stick and pointed.

Sageflower gasped. The stocky, flattened body and shaggy, silvery gray fur on the animal was unmistakable. "A badger!"

Both women glanced at each other. What did this mean? Warily they watched the animal.

"I think Darkstar sent it," said Sageflower.

Star shrugged. "Whatever for? We have no need of her help now. We needed her before, when we were first brought to Jaguar territory and wanted to escape. But not now when we have accepted our husbands. I do not understand—"

Mystified, the two women watched as the animal dug its way into the ground, throwing up great handfuls of dirt and sand as it swiftly retreated into the ground. Within heartbeats, it was gone.

Sageflower's pretty face wore a thoughtful frown.

"What can it mean?" pondered Star aloud. "Why would Darkstar send her helper to us? I do not want to escape. Do you?"

Sageflower shook her long black hair. "No." She stared at the spot where the badger had disappeared. "Perhaps it is a sign of good fortune for us. Perhaps it means that Darkstar is wishing us much happiness with our growing babes."

"Perhaps," agreed Star. A cloud passed overhead, shutting out the sun. Cloud shadows flicked across the hills. She felt chilled suddenly. She continued to watch the burrow where the stocky creature had disappeared, but he did not reappear. "I do not like it, Sageflower," she whispered.

Sageflower glanced nervously about. "Let us catch up with the other women."

"Yes," agreed Star readily. The two women hastened to join the Jaguar women who were some distance ahead.

Star spent the rest of the afternoon prying into the wet ground with her digging stick. She dug up many camas bulbs despite the uneasy feeling that settled upon her. Once she asked Sageflower if she felt anything amiss, but the younger woman merely held up her basketful of bulbs and smiled happily.

Star returned to her digging, but she could not rid herself of her uneasiness.

When next she glanced up, she saw that the sun was low in the afternoon sky. Already the Jaguar women were gathering up their baskets and digging sticks and starting the long walk back to the Bear Caves. They did not want to spend the night in the camas fields.

Star picked up her basket and fell into step behind Betafor and one of her daughters, the one who had so kindly drawn the falcon design on Falcon's new shirt.

As she walked along behind Betafor, Star mused to herself. Something is going to happen, she thought. Darkstar sent the badger for a reason. But what?

Chapter Forty

Falcon watched Star enter the cave. She carried the heavy basket of camas bulbs and at first did not see him in the dim light of the cave.

When she spotted him, she dropped her basket and rubbed her arms. "It is cold."

"I will make a fire," he said, getting to his feet. He headed to the entrance to get more wood.

As he passed her, she put out a hand to stop him. "Falcon?"

He paused. Slowly, carefully, he turned his head until his eyes met her dark brown ones. Such a sorrowful look on her face, he thought in surprise. "What is it?"

"Is—is something the matter?"

He shrugged her hand off his arm. "What could be the matter?"

Her hand curled into a fist and then relaxed. "Will you never tell me what is on your mind?"

"No." And he stalked out of the cave to get the wood.

When he returned, she had already scraped some wood peelings for the fire. He went to Claw's cave and brought back a branch with a burning tip and lit the shavings.

As the flames sparked to life, the silence between them was dark and heavy.

"I will go and get some cooked camas bulbs from the other women," she said and left the cave. She returned with several hot, roasted bulbs on a wooden platter.

They ate in that same suffocating silence. When their meal was finished, she said, "You do not want this baby, do you, Falcon?"

He heard a deep sadness in her voice.

He shrugged. "The babe comes whether I want it or not." And a three-day-long, torturous birth it will be, dear one, he thought, shifting a little so he did not have to look at her. I would gladly spare you the suffering that Tula bore at our son's birth, if only I could. I would have gladly spared Tula that pain, too. He sighed. Star had no idea of what lay ahead of her. Bearing his child would be a bitter thing for her and then she would turn against him.

"But it is as Tula said, is it not? You did not love your first son and now you do not want this child."

How can she think me so uncaring? he wondered as he gazed at her. Her brown eyes shone bright with tears. Her voice sounded dead, like a stone. "Tula has nothing to do with this," he answered gruffly.

Star leaned forward. "Tell me what happened with Tula. Tell me why you do not want this son."

He shook his head. He could not put in words what filled his heart with dread.

She hesitated. When she touched his arm, he forced himself not to cringe. He looked into her eyes and for a moment he felt lost. Everything in those dark eyes called to him. She loves me, he thought, and an exulting happiness filled him. She loves me and she is telling me so with her eyes. Then dread swiftly intervened.

And if she loves me now, then how much more will she hate me when, after a long, painful birth, she holds our poor, sick son in her arms? She will realize I can only give her sick children. And when she turns to another man, I will die.

He carefully peeled her hand off his arm and glanced away from those love-filled eyes. He rose to his feet. "I am going hunting."

Her jaw dropped. "Now? At night?"

"Deer like to drink at the river at night. I will catch one."

"But—but we have no need of meat. You killed a deer but yesterday—"

"Hush, woman. I will hunt, whether you agree or no."

Her face was shuttered as she said, "Very well. Go hunting."

He picked up his two spears and stalked past her. Suddenly she jumped to her feet and ran ahead of him. She swung around and stopped, placing her hands on his shoulders, blocking him from leaving the cave. "Stop! **Do not go!**"

333

He stared at her. "What is this? What ails you, Badger woman?"

"I do not want you to go! I want you to stay. I want to talk with you about what has come between us."

She peered up at him and he hissed in alarm at her desperate look. He tried to push her away, but she stood fast. "I go hunting."

"No," she said.

Her stubbornness angered him. "Step aside, Badger woman."

"No!"

"You cannot stop me."

"I want to!" she cried.

He cooled his heart to the pain he heard in her cry. Perhaps if he did not care for her, he would not get so hurt. "I go hunting and no puny woman is going to stop me!"

He set her aside. She swung around and threw her arms around him, clinging to him like a bird clings to a branch.

"Do not go!"

"Wife! This is unseemly!"

"I do not care! You are my husband. I do not want you to go. I want you to stay here. With me!"

He frowned. "Never has a woman behaved this way to me," he said angrily.

"We must talk!" she cried. "If we do not—"

"Talk? What is there to talk about?"

"Our baby!" Her howl echoed in the cave, echoed in his ears, and he wanted to put his hands over his ears to shut out the terrible words.

334

"No." He was proud of the coldness in his voice. This woman was too forward. She did not know her place. *This is what comes of marrying a Badger woman.*

He spoke without thinking. "I will take you back to your Badger People in the morning."

She gasped and her face went pale—an oval moon in the dim light. "What?" Her voice was the croak of a frog.

"I said I will return you to your people."

Her hands went to his face, pleading. "I—I do not want to return—"

"You have no choice. I have spoken." He realized suddenly that his hasty words provided the best solution for them both. Once she was with her people, they would help her. As for him, he could not watch a wife go through another arduous birth. He could not watch another of his children waste away for many seasons, and he could not watch another beloved wife spurn him.

Yes, it was best for them both this way. Were she to stay, he would love her, love the child, and his life would be destroyed. This is what comes of love, he thought savagely. This is what I tried to prevent that day I tore apart our baskets and slashed our furs. Why did you not heed me then?

He had to turn away from the anguish on her face.

"No, Falcon! No!"

The look he'd seen on her face almost unmanned him. Fear, desperation, loss—he knew not what it was, only that it hurt to look upon her.

"Do not do this," she cried and sank to her knees. "Please, do not do this!"

She clutched his legs. He looked down at her dark head and tried to push her away. "Do not do this, woman," he said. "You bring shame upon us both with your begging."

She looked up at him, her face tear-covered. "Falcon, think! Do not send me away. I love you. I carry your child. By all that is right and honorable, do not do this thing!"

"I have decided," he said and set his jaw. "You will go." Welcoming, peaceful numbness came upon him now. Nothing she could say would move him because he could not feel. He was safe.

"Nooo," she wailed and clutched at his legs all the harder.

Star hugged him to her. Could he not understand that she loved him, that she would do anything to stay with him? Their child, so precious to her, fluttered even now in her womb. "You cannot," she gasped. "You cannot just send me away—"

"I can. I will." His hard voice sent chills through her.

"Falcon, tell me why you say these things! Why can you not tell me?"

He opened her fingers from where she clutched him. Star held on all the tighter, but his grip, though gentle, was insistent.

"Falcon!"

"Do not bring further shame upon yourself, Star!" His voice was stern as though she were a child and he chiding her.

She jumped to her feet and flung her arms around his neck. She kissed his face everywhere her lips could reach. "Falcon! Do not do this! I love you! Let me stay—"

He peeled her hungry arms from around his neck. "Stop it, Star."

She kept kissing him, hoping he would understand the depth of her love for him. But his strength was greater than hers and she could not hold him for long. "Falcon! If you do not love me then think about our child! He needs you! Needs his father—"

"I *am* thinking about our child," he said grimly, his mouth set in a narrow line. "And what I do is for the best. For him, too, if you but knew it!"

"No! What you do destroys everything between us. Our home, our love—"

"There is no home. There is no love." His voice sounded dead.

How do I fight against this? she wondered frantically. How do I reach the man behind the dead voice?

He was staring at her, his chest rising and falling with each breath. "You will go, Star," he said. "You will leave in the morning. I have spoken." He left the cave.

"Falcon! Come back! Falcon!" When only silence greeted her desperate cry, she fell to her knees, put her slumped head in her arms, and sobbed. "Come back, oh please, Falcon, come back. . . ."

Chapter Forty-one

Star woke in the morning and her face was swollen from her tears. Falcon was not beside her. He had not returned in the night. Dully, she climbed out of her bedrobes and began packing her things in a big basket: her wedding dress, the slashed, then repaired moccasins, a few awls he had made her, a comb. In a separate basket, she put some cold camas bulbs from the night before and strips of deer meat, sustenance for the journey back to her Badger People. When that was done, she sat in the cave beside the fire, which had died in the night. She felt as dead as the ashes; a dull numbness invaded every part of her body. She was going back to her people.

"Ho!" cried out a voice at the cave's entrance.

Star turned and blinked, the bright morning light at the entrance blinding her momentarily. "Who is it?"

But the person did not answer, merely entered and walked toward her. Star recognized the sauntering gait. Tula.

Star did not even have the desire to jump up and chase the woman away. She just wanted to sit by the dead ashes of her dead fire in her dead home.

"So," sang out Tula as she sauntered closer. "Your husband is throwing you away. What a terrible, terrible thing to have happen!" And she laughed.

Star turned away from the vicious woman and gazed at the rock wall. "You have come to gloat, Tula. Do so and get out."

"Tsk tsk." Tula gave a little hiss. "You are not so sweet now, are you, second wife?"

Star did not answer. Of what use was it to engage in a fight of words with Tula? Tula could never understand anything but her own pain.

"I knew he would tire of you," said Tula. She turned and glanced around the cave. Star peeked over at her. The baby on Tula's back was asleep. Tula turned back to Star.

"Take everything," she warned. "I do not want to see you leave anything behind."

"This is not your cave, Tula," said Star wearily. "Falcon is not your husband. And what I leave behind is no concern of yours." It is my heart I leave behind, she thought.

Tula smiled and sauntered closer. "Did you know that Claw entertains visitors?" she asked.

Star glanced up, perplexed. What was Tula up to now?

"Oh, yes. He has guests," Tula cooed.

Star shrugged. She had no time or inclination for Tula's strange play.

"So." To Star's regret, Tula sat down, cross-legged, across the dead fire from Star.

"Please leave," said Star.

"Oh, no," said Tula. "I have waited too long for this. I want to savor it." She smiled.

Star sat silently. If the woman wanted to be objectionable, she was succeeding.

Tula smiled and leaned forward. "Falcon is telling everyone in the caves that he is taking you back to your mother."

Star's face felt carved of stone.

Tula hugged herself in delight. "He is shaming you before everyone. All the Jaguar People are talking about you. They think you a fool." She laughed. "Oh, I am so happy!"

Star glanced at her. "It is a sad thing when another's pain brings you happiness."

Tula frowned. "I will not worry about your paltry words, Badger dog-girl. You know nothing."

Star was silent. Did Tula truly think that Star cared about what she thought?

"So, tell me," continued Tula. "Why is your husband casting you aside?"

When Star refused to answer, Tula grew impatient. "Tell me, dog-girl! What is it that causes your husband to treat you so?"

"Why do you wish to know? Is it not enough that I am humiliated in the Jaguar People's camp?"

"I can never see you humiliated enough." Tula smiled as though they were having a normal talk.

340

Broken Promise

Star shook her head, baffled. She had never known anyone like Tula.

"Did you burn the food too often? Did you refuse him your bed? Did you take a lover?" Tula chuckled at her last question. "He hates other men, you must know that."

"I think he hates Marmot," acknowledged Star. "Not other men."

Tula grimaced. "Marmot is a good man. He has helped me. We have a healthy child."

Star glanced at the sleeping child. "Yes, you do," she acknowledged. "In all the time I have been here, I have yet to learn your child's name."

Tula stared at her. "You are a wicked woman. I will not give you my child's name. You will try to hurt him."

Star sighed. "I do not want to hurt your child," she murmured. "Please, leave me."

Tula frowned. "I see you are not going to tell me why he is casting you aside."

Star felt a perverse delight in Tula's obvious disappointment. How pleasant it was to thwart the woman in this one little thing! "No. I am not."

"Very well. I will go." Tula tried to rise but the baby on her back unbalanced her so that she could not get to her feet.

Star felt goaded out of her lethargy. She rose and went to aid Tula to her feet, shaking her head in disbelief all the while. *Why am I helping this woman?*

Tula's hand felt cold as Star clasped it. She braced Tula and helped her up. The moment Tula regained her feet, she dropped Star's hand. "I did

341

not need your help," she said haughtily.

Star towered over the smaller woman. "Please leave."

Tula stared at Star, up and down. Her eyes lingered on Star's gently rounded stomach. Tula ran a hand through the white streak of her hair. "Now I see why your husband is leaving you."

Star had had enough. "Perhaps you can explain it to me then," she snarled.

Tula laughed. "Aha, so even you do not know why he is throwing you aside. How amusing! I must be sure to tell the others." She tittered behind her hand.

Star was shaking with anger. Would the woman never leave?

"It is very simple." Tula chortled. "He is leaving you because you carry his child."

"That makes no sense to me!" cried Star, but deep inside her, Tula's words did make a strange kind of sense.

"Did you not know?" laughed Tula. "Falcon can only father very sick children. He cannot make healthy babes!" She started to laugh, but then, as Star watched her, Tula's laughter suddenly became choked and turned to a horrible sobbing.

Tula's hands covered her eyes and she wept. Tears rose in Star's eyes as she watched the other's contorted, sobbing features. Slowly, gently, she reached out to touch Tula's shoulder and comfort her.

Instantly, Tula's sobbing halted and she lifted her head to glare at Star. She brushed Star's hand off. "You will pay," she ground out. "You will pay for carrying his child!"

"But, Tula." Star recoiled. "He is no longer your husband. You did not want him. You chose another man!"

Tula gave a quick shake of her head as though to deny Star's words. Then her shoulders sagged. "I did," she muttered. Once again, she lifted her head and her eyes met Star's. "But you will pay for seeing me cry!"

Star protested gently, "I cry myself. I do not think the less of you for that—"

"You do! I cannot stand your pity!"

Star shook her head. "Believe me, Tula. What I feel for you is not pity." *Anger, fear perhaps, sometimes hatred. But not pity.*

Tula's fists were clenched at her sides. She gritted her teeth. "You will pay, Badger dog-girl! No one must see my weakness!"

Did Tula mean that Star had seen that she still loved Falcon? Or did she mean that her tears were a weakness? *She cannot be reasoned with,* Star realized. *Whatever wounds this woman has cannot be reached. Not by me.*

Tula moved toward the cave entrance, her body as stiff and as straight as a wooden branch. Star hurried after her.

They reached the cave's mouth and Star blinked several times as her eyes adjusted to the bright daylight.

Gravel crunched under Tula's dainty feet as she walked away. Star watched her go, and an unexpected sadness for the other woman welled in her heart.

Suddenly Tula swung around and screamed at

Star. "I will hurt you!" A long, hideous laugh tore from her throat.

Gone was every trace of the sobbing, hurt woman who had stood in Star's cave and cried.

Star turned away.

But Tula was not done. "Claw's visitors are the slave catchers!" she cried out, and a note of triumph rang in Tula's voice. "And they are always looking for new slaves!"

Fear spiraled through Star before she was able to stop it. Tula cannot hurt me, she told herself over and over. I will be leaving these people and there is nothing she can do to hurt me. I must remember that!

But it was a difficult thing to remember with Tula's raucous laugh echoing in her ears.

Chapter Forty-two

Falcon passed Tula and her baby as he walked the path that led past the caves. Tula did not glance at him, but he noticed she had a smug look upon her face. He wondered whom she had been hurting.

When he reached the cave, Star sat huddled by the unlit fire. "Come," he said heavily. "It is time to leave."

He had informed Claw and Betafor that he was taking his wife back to her people, that the marriage was over. Many people had been coming and going and visiting at Claw's, but Falcon felt he had been discreet. Claw and Betafor would tell the other Jaguar People after he and Star left. No need to shame her before his people.

And it was too bad that two of Claw's guests were the slave catchers. Hooknose and Red Jaw had both snarled at Falcon when they had seen him enter Claw's cave. Though he did not fear them, Falcon hoped that Claw sent the brutal slave catchers away soon. Wherever they went, their deceit brought trouble.

His eyes swung back to Star as she got slowly to her feet. Her every movement looked as though it were painful. He jerked his eyes away from her protruding stomach.

She lifted her baskets and waited, not looking at him. He swallowed and glanced once more around the cave. When he returned to his Jaguar People, he would not live in this cave. He could not face the memories.

They left then, Falcon in the lead, Star stumbling along behind him. After they had traveled some distance, Star halted and set down her baskets. "I forgot my digging stick."

"You can get another one from your people," he answered.

She winced at his words, at the reminder that he was taking her to her Badger People. Her pain troubled him not at all; he was proud of how cool his heart felt toward her.

Wordlessly, she hefted her baskets once more and set out behind him. They walked all that day, stopping only to drink water from a clear-running creek. As evening approached, he called a halt to their march. While Star sought twigs and branches for the fire, Falcon mused upon how she was able to travel such a good distance while pregnant. She was a strong woman, he decided, and felt some relief. She would need to be.

After a silent meal they each lay upon their furs, backs to the fire. Star kept away from him. Once he awoke in the night and thought he heard her

crying, but when he crept over to her, he saw that
he was mistaken. Her eyes were closed, her lashes
thick and dark on her cheek as she slept.

The next morning they were on their way after
a short breakfast of dried deer meat. She must be
anxious to return to her people, he thought when
he saw how eager she was to be on the trail once
again. Something inside him felt sad at this but
he quickly squashed it. His heart was cool, like
a glacier stream. He must remember that.

The journey continued in a blur of numbness
for him. He felt a twinge of surprise that it
should be so easy to return her to her people.
Once, when they had lived in the Bear Caves, he
had fooled himself into thinking that he loved
her. He shook his head, glad to be rid of that
delusion. For he had discovered the truth: love
was only a delusion. Nothing substantial, nothing
real or true. Love meant nothing and it surely did
not last. Not love for a mate, not love for a child.
And it never survived death.

Strange how a twinge of pain should pierce his
chest just then.

Star glanced at him when he groaned aloud.
"Falcon?"

He clutched his chest and rubbed it. Shook his
head. "It is nothing, Star." He remained silent, the
pain gone as suddenly as it had come.

Star glanced away from Falcon's cold, handsome face. Everything was ashes for her, like a
dead fire. Her love for him was gone, her hopes
for the baby, everything was gone. Destroyed.

She wondered if Blue Jay would be able to
give her life again. What an onerous task for a

mother, Star mused. To birth a babe and then, when she was grown to adulthood, to give her a reason to live, to fan the flame of life once more. For surely that was what Star needed. It felt as though her soul had flown to some other place, so deadened inside did she feel. How did one learn to live again, to love again after such a devastating blow? How could he cast her aside? Did he not understand that she loved him?

She almost laughed aloud when she remembered the badger she and Sageflower had seen that day they had dug camas bulbs. Little had she known then that Darkstar was warning her about the trouble to come: her beloved husband was about to cast her aside. Ah, yes, Darkstar was right to send a messenger. The only problem was, no messenger could help Star now. No one could. Not when her life lay in ruins.

That night they stopped to camp beside a small stream. She stole peeks at him as he built up the fire. When he handed her a strip of dried deer meat, his handsome face appeared as though carved in stone. After their meal, his dark eyes were cold, even as he wished her a good night's sleep.

She retired to her robes as swiftly as she could. Why could he not understand that she loved him and wanted to be with him?

She sobbed silently into the warm fur beneath her face. She did not want him to hear her crying in the night, for she knew now that her tears would leave him unmoved and only add to her shame.

Broken Promise

For nothing she did could reach him. She carried his child, yet that meant little to him. She'd pleaded desperately with him, yet her pleadings went unheeded. And now her tears would avail her nothing, either. This man had gone too far away for her to reach.

Chapter Forty-three

They had found a camp. Star sat waiting, hidden behind a small cluster of pine trees, her baskets spread around her on the dried brown pine needles. From where she sat she could see ten or more tents set out among the spindly trees of a pine forest. A little distance away she could see the sparkle of water on a wide river. Blue smoke drifted through the trees.

Falcon had left her to wait while he crept close enough to the tents to determine if they were indeed her people's. Star listened, but no sentry gave a cry to alert anyone. Falcon must not have been seen yet, she thought, when all of a sudden he was back and standing in front of her. "Your mother is there. It is your Badger People's camp."

Star glanced at him, but the sun was at his back and she saw nothing but the darkness of his form.

She could read no reassurance, no caring on that strong visage, nor hear it in his voice.

She rose to her feet and picked up her baskets. "I will go to them," she answered. If he expected more pleading and begging, he was wrong.

He fell into step behind her, carrying his spear loosely, but she knew him now and knew those black eyes missed nothing. They were approaching her mother's tent before a warning cry from the Badgers went up. Star ignored Falcon's snort of derision which implied her people were easy to sneak up on.

When she saw Blue Jay, Star began to run. "Mother!"

Her mother whirled and dropped the spoon she was holding. Her jaw gaped and she moved away from the fire, peering through the smoke in Star's direction.

"It is me, Mother!"

Blue Jay's face split into a happy grin and she started to move toward Star. The two women embraced, laughing and crying, and Star held on to her mother's bulky arms tightly. She pulled away for only a moment to say, "Oh, Mother, I am so happy to see you!" Then she hugged her mother again. She wanted to stay in her mother's loving arms and never leave.

When their laughing and crying had subsided into the murmurs of conversation, Star glanced up to see Falcon standing, arms folded across his broad naked chest, watching them. "Mother," she said carefully, "here is Falcon."

Her mother stiffened. "I see him."

Star's heart ached for the pain in her mother's

voice. It had been difficult for Blue Jay while Star had been gone and her mother's voice told her that now.

"He is welcome in our camp," Blue Jay grated out.

Star's lips tightened. How welcome would he be when Blue Jay found out that Falcon was casting Star aside?

Echo, the Badger headman, came up. He regarded Falcon warily, but to Star he gave a nod. "It is a happy day for us that you have returned."

Star nodded politely. "I am glad to be back."

There was an awkward silence as more Badger People came to gather around the visitors. Falcon was the only one who did not seem to notice the tense silence.

"Star!" It was Chokecherry. The two women hugged.

"Oh, Chokecherry, it is so good to see you!"

"And you, Star!" They hugged again.

Suddenly two children came running up. The two, a girl and a boy, threw themselves at Falcon. The other Badger people gawked.

Star gaped while Falcon picked up the girl and swung her high while the boy clutched his leg. "Greetings, Berry!" He laughed.

Then he set her down and unwound the boy from his leg. He lifted him up and met him eye to eye. "Have you been a help to your mother, Milky?"

"Oh, yes!" the boy assured him. Falcon laughed and put him back on the ground. The two children clung to his legs, beaming.

Star was not the only one who stared. When Crow limped up, she pretended to scold her children but she did not drag them away from Falcon. All the Badger People were watching the children and their mother and then, one by one, they greeted Falcon.

Seeing Star's befuddlement, her mother moved closer and whispered, "He brought Berry and Milky back after the slave catchers stole them away. That is why the children and their mother are so happy to see him."

Star's eyes met Falcon's and he grinned. Her heart leapt when she saw that grin, so long had it been gone from her. She wanted to cry right then, in front of all her people, at seeing him so relaxed and unguarded. Oh, why do you not want me? her heart cried out.

He turned away then to listen to something that Milky was telling him, and the moment was gone. So close, she thought. It is the man I love, but for only a heartbeat. Oh, Falcon, where have you gone? What have you done?

Echo raised his voice to announce a feast to celebrate Star's visit. Star glanced away, embarrassed. How could she tell her people that this was not a visit, that her husband was returning her because he did not want her? Never mind, she scolded herself. Enjoy the feast. They will find out soon enough that I have returned to stay. And though her lips trembled, she kept a smile on her face.

Grouse approached, and Star turned aside when her mother's old friend asked how she had fared with the Jaguar People. Star was trying to think of an answer when her mother cried out, "Star! You are pregnant! You bear my grandchild!"

Star saw her mother's beaming face and she wanted to cry again. She stifled the urge, nodded briefly at her mother, and made up some nonsense answer for Grouse, but her mind was not on what she told the old woman. The painful humiliation of returning to her people, alone and pregnant, her husband not wanting her, bore in upon Star and she wanted to fall to the earth and weep. Instead, she gritted her teeth and smiled.

Falcon was watching Star so closely he could see her lips quiver. He smiled sadly and turned to speak with Blue Jay so that Star would have a moment to regain her calm. "Have you other grandchildren?" he asked Blue Jay conversationally.

"You know that Star is my only child," answered the old woman, her lips white.

Falcon shrugged. Of course. He had forgotten that one of the reasons the old woman had been so furious with him for stealing Star was that she had no other children to keep her company. Well, she would have plenty of Star's company now. He grimaced at the thought.

Blue Jay stepped closer. "My daughter does not look happy, Jaguar man," she hissed. "What have you done to her?"

Only saved her from a terrible fate, he thought. Or tried to. He looked at Blue Jay, saw the anger on her wrinkled face. You will not understand what I do, he thought.

"How long will my daughter be here?" she hissed at him.

"Ask her."

"I ask you."

Clearly, his wife's mother had little liking for him. The thought caused him amusement for a moment. "A long time."

Blue Jay relaxed somewhat at those words. "You may stay in my tent," she offered graciously. "I will stay with my friend, Grouse."

"No need," he answered gruffly. "I will not be staying more than this night. I return to my people on the morrow."

Blue Jay beamed. "It is to be a very long visit then?" She gloated happily. "I insist you take my tent," she offered even more graciously, if such a thing were possible. She was about to walk away when she stopped. "It is very decent of you to bring her for a visit. I thank you."

Guilt swept over Falcon. But not enough to blanket the relief he was feeling. *Tomorrow I will be gone and she will be starting her new life with her people. She will have her mother and Grouse and Echo and they will help her with her long labor and her sick baby. I can do nothing.* Indeed, there was so much turmoil in his breast now that he thought he would burst. Tomorrow, he told himself. Tomorrow I can get away and leave all this behind. She will be safe with her people and they can help her.

If all was well, then why was he feeling this turgid dullness? Why had the raging turmoil been replaced with a deadened feeling? What was wrong?

355

He watched Star walk away, the throng of people around her talking avidly now that she had returned. They love her, he thought in surprise. Then he realized what he was thinking and he corrected himself. *There is no such thing as love.*

"Come," beckoned Blue Jay upon seeing him standing alone. "This way to my home." She turned her back on him then, evidently expecting him to follow.

With a shrug, he trotted after her.

Chapter Forty-four

Star sat by the fire and stared at the river while her mother mixed up a paste of dried nuts. She patted the paste on large, flat, heated rocks in the fire. The smell of baking nut cakes filled the air. Ever since Star was a child, her mother's nut cakes had been her favorite food. But this morning she could not force herself to eat even one.

Falcon was taking his morning swim in the river. He had told Star's people last night that he would leave this morning, and Star did not know what to do. Should she let him go? Should she demand that he take her with him? Should she tell the headman, Echo, and demand that he demand that she go with Falcon? Should she tell her mother and have her demand—

"What is it that sorely troubles your mind this morn, daughter?" asked Blue Jay.

Star stared at the river. She could see a head

357

bobbing in the middle. Long black hair. Falcon.

"Daughter? What ails you?"

Star swung to meet her mother's gaze. The concern on her mother's face made her want to cry and warmed her at the same time. Here, at least, was love. And her Badger People, too; she must not forget them. Several of the women and children had expressed their happiness at seeing her. Most of the men, of course, were gone—slaves.

Star sighed. "My husband does not want me anymore."

Her mother gasped. "How can this be? He stole you away. Now he brings you back and dumps you like an old deer carcass! What is the matter with the man?"

Star shook her head. "I do not know, Mother. I do not know."

"And you bear his child!" exclaimed Blue Jay. "How does he explain that?" Her eyes narrowed suddenly. "It *is* his child, is it not?"

Her mother's blunt talk annoyed Star. "Oh, Mother! Of course it is."

Her mother slapped another nut cake on a hot stone. Star listened to the sizzle.

"Then why," demanded Blue Jay in a loud voice, "does he want to throw you away?"

Star shook her head. "I know not."

"Is he planning to take a second wife?"

"I am his second wife."

"Did you not get along with the first wife then?"

"His first wife left him some time ago. She remarried."

"Ah. So perhaps he hates women because of her."

"Perhaps. It would be easy to do," admitted Star. "His first wife is a very difficult woman."

"So." Blue Jay's hands were on her ample hips as she stared at Star. "What are you going to do?"

"I do not know. Stay here, I suppose."

"You suppose? Of course you can stay here. This is your home. We love you. We will help you."

Her mother's blunt talk sounded fine all of a sudden and Star began to relax. "I have nowhere else to go," she said in a small voice.

"Go where you are wanted, girl," said her mother. "And you are wanted here."

Star touched her stomach. "And the babe—"

"Of course we want the babe! What foolishness is this? He will be my grandchild."

"Perhaps it is a girl."

"Whoever it is, she will be loved," promised Blue Jay.

Star reached for one of the nut cakes. Her appetite had suddenly returned.

If he did not look so handsome, none of this would hurt, thought Star. If he were ugly and squat and short and had a mean temper, none of this would matter. But he is not ugly or squat or short with a mean temper. He is tall and handsome and, when he is not trying to cast me aside, very pleasant, even playful.

He came up to them and stared at the nut cakes.

Blue Jay, hands on hips, said, "Get away from those nut cakes, Jaguar man. The man who throws away my daughter will not eat my cooking!"

In disbelief, Star saw a smile start to curl at one corner of his mouth. He thought it was funny, did he? Let him go hungry then.

She bit into a nut cake and chewed it slowly, ignoring him. "These are delicious, Mother," she announced.

Blue Jay frowned. "What are you going to do about the babe?" she demanded of Falcon.

Star took another bite of the nut cake as she awaited his answer.

"What do you mean?" He was watching her. She chewed very, very slowly.

"You fathered it. You take care of it."

Star sat up in alarm. Her mother had promised that the child would be taken in with the Badger People. What was going on?

"You want me to take care of the babe?"

Star wanted to laugh at the sheer incredulity in his voice.

"Someone must teach the child to hunt. To snare birds. To fight. If you do not teach your son, who will?"

Sometimes her mother's blunt talk was a blessing from the Great Spirit.

Falcon's jaw was set and Star could see his scar flicker. He was silent.

But his eyes met Star's. Tell me, she said silently. Tell me you will help me raise our child. Tell me you will not cast me aside. She waited, uncaring that her eyes pleaded with his.

But his dark eyes were cold and he turned away.

So, she thought. He will not take responsibility for his child. So be it.

"Well?" Blue Jay was still waiting.

"Enough, Mother," said Star. "If he chooses to leave me, leave his child, let him." She stood up and walked over to him. "I will stay with my people." She thought her heart would break as she said the words.

Falcon looked sadder than she had ever seen him. Star's chin came up. "I cannot force you to stay. I cannot force you to love me. Or our child. It is best if you go."

"It is best," he whispered.

She could hear her mother move up behind her. "I love my daughter," said the old woman. "I do not understand you, Jaguar man. I think you are a lazy fool to treat my daughter like this!" She spat on him.

Star watched in shock as the spittle dripped down the scar on Falcon's face. He brushed it off. He stared at her, stolid.

"Just tell me, Falcon," Star burst out, unable to stop herself, "just tell me you want me as your wife. I will stay with you!" Hope beat in her breast. Did he realize now how much she loved him? Would he grasp for their love? Or would he let the promise of their love, their marriage, be broken?

He remained silent.

Blue Jay stepped in front of Star. She lifted her hand and pointed to the trail leading away from the Badger camp. "Go," she said. "And do not come back."

Falcon's dark eyes locked on Star's. "Please," she begged, over her mother's shoulder. "Do not leave me. . . ."

"I must." He whirled and loped down the trail. He was going out of her life. Forever.

Sobbing, she ran to her mother's tent.

Chapter Forty-five

Falcon glanced around the forest. What was he doing here? How had he gotten here? He had been so dulled to the pain of leaving Star that he had wandered, unknowing, wherever his legs had seen fit to go. And so he was here, staring out from the forest at the top of a cliff, down, down at the churning water below.

He had done it. He had taken Star home to her Badger People. He had found a place for her, with people who would help her more than he could to give birth, to raise their child. Why then did he feel as if he had cut off his spear arm? Why then were the bird calls gone from the forest? And the brightness gone from the sun?

How many days had he been wandering, lost? He shook his head, trying to remember. He thought it must be his third day of wandering. He drew a breath as he stared down at the churning white water below. He must get back to his people. He must return to them or he would wander and become lost from them and die.

Somehow the thought did not scare him. If he died, who would care? The wolves would still run in the forest. The birds would still call to their mates. There was no Great Spirit to receive his soul. He had no soul. None. Only a man with no soul could do what he had done: cast aside his pregnant wife—the wife he loved.

The white water below him called out his name. "Come down and play," it called. "Falcon, Falcooon, come down and play."

He shook his head to clear it. Something was wrong with him. The water could not call to him. He glanced around. It was getting dark in the forest. He should build a fire, make camp for the night. He should not be leaning over this cliff listening to the water calling him.

More ominous now, "Falcon, come and swim. You were always so good at swimming. Come and swim in my white depths. Foreeeverrr . . ."

He leaned over, the better to see who was calling him. White mist rose and he could feel it kiss his face. "Falcon, Falcon, cooome . . . come into my aaarrrms. . . ."

He leaned over a little more. "Yesss, come . . . No more painnn . . ."

He fell into the swirling depths and took no breath as his head sank below the boiling surface.

Chapter Forty-six

Falcon blinked, struggled to open his eyes. "What—what happened? Where am I?" He squinted, could make out the caves up on the hill.

The shaman's wrinkled face hovered above him. "Red Hawk and Horn pulled you from the water. You almost drowned. They carried you back here. Some of us thought you had already gone to join the Great Spirit at his camp."

Falcon closed his eyes. "There is no Great Spirit," he whispered.

The shaman laughed and shook his head in amusement. "Good joke."

The shaman began to gather up his things, and Falcon turned his head to see what he was doing. There were several dull green, leafy plants and two colored rocks and eight small sticks and feathers with some black sticky substance on them. "Ho," said the shaman. "Do not look upon these things. They have great power."

"There is no Great Spirit," retorted Falcon, his voice stronger now.

"You should know," said the shaman, and by his voice Falcon thought the man was trying to humor him. "You went to visit him, not I."

"I—I did not visit him," rasped Falcon. It hurt to speak.

The shaman stopped stuffing his precious items into a leather sack and he stared at Falcon. "You are a strange man," he said at last, then resumed putting away his implements, shaking his head as though baffled.

Falcon turned away. "I must get up," he muttered.

"You do that," said the shaman and walked away.

Falcon pushed himself up and rested on his elbows. He was lying on a bedrobe. Horn came up to him. He squatted down to meet Falcon's eyes. "I am glad you live, Falcon," he said soberly. "Red Hawk and I thought we were too late to save you. You were very limp and cold when we dragged you from the water."

Falcon did not answer. He was trying to remember how he had come to be in the water in the first place.

"Here," said Horn. "I will help you up." He helped Falcon to his feet just as Claw arrived.

"Falcon! You are alive!"

"I am," answered Falcon wryly. "You had given up hope on me, Claw?"

"We all had," the headman answered. "Even

Betafor. Only the old shaman kept chanting and praying. The rest of us went home to our caves."

Falcon frowned. Now he owed his life to the shaman. "Why did he bother to save me?" muttered Falcon.

"What did you say?" asked Horn.

"It is nothing," answered Falcon. He did not feel like explaining his feelings to Horn and Claw.

With a man propping him on each side, Falcon staggered up the gravelly hill to the caves.

Horn led him over to the cave that Falcon and Star had shared.

"No," murmured Falcon. "Not there."

The other two men looked puzzled, but Falcon would not explain. "Very well," he said at last. They helped him inside and set him down on the elk hide beside the cold hearth. Falcon felt weak and dizzy.

"I will bring some food," said Claw and left the cave.

"Will you be all right?" asked Horn in concern.

Falcon nodded. Horn glanced around the cave. "I will light the fire for you." He built up some wood and then scattered some wooden shavings over it. He hurried off.

He returned with a lit brand and touched it to the shaved wood. Tiny flames leapt and crackled.

Claw entered carrying a stone bowl. "Here is some deer stew," he said and set the bowl down beside Falcon.

Falcon glanced at it, but he was not hungry.

"Is there anything else we can do?" asked Horn.

Falcon shook his head. The two men waited

around for a while but when Falcon merely continued to stare at the fire, they left.

Now what? thought Falcon listlessly as he slumped by the fire. The fire is lit. I have food. He glanced around the cave. All signs of Star were gone. There was no pain when he thought of her. Only a dull calm.

He thought about his fall into the water. He had leaned forward, heard the water's voice calling him, and fallen. . . .

I tried to kill myself, mused Falcon. If it had not been for Horn and Red Hawk, and the shaman, too, he added wryly, I would be dead. The thought brought him no pleasure, no pain, just a dullness.

He stared at the fire. The dullness persisted in the very center of him. I have nothing to live for, he thought. Nothing at all.

Chapter Forty-seven

Summer

Star smiled at Blue Jay, who sat across the fire making baby clothes for Star's soon-to-be-born babe. By Star's reckoning on her fingers, it would be another four full moons before the little one arrived. She smiled to herself in anticipation and patted her stomach gently, reassuringly, to the little one nestled inside.

It was not quite what she had planned, this life back among her Badger People. Her mother and she were getting ready for the birth, and that she had always wanted and planned. But she had no husband, and there her plans had gone awry. A man had always been part of her dreams, a man who wanted to be with her, to share the joy of a family.

But what she had learned so late in her life was

that things did not turn out as one planned. Oh, she could make choices, but those choices did not necessarily come to fruition. Something else made them happen, and she thought it must be the Great Spirit. And so far, the Great Spirit had not seen fit to bring Falcon back into her life.

But He had seen fit to bring Camel Stalker back. When the young man had first appeared in the Badger camp, worn, thin, but with his eyes ablaze with freedom, the Badger People had gone wild with rejoicing. And when Finds the Marten appeared, staggering out of the forest behind Camel Stalker, Chokecherry's screams of happiness could be heard echoing in the distant mountains.

The two men had escaped the Fish Eaters and hidden in the forests during the days, walking the trails at night until they had found their Badger People.

Star was glad for Chokecherry, for now her friend was being courted by Finds the Marten. There was a quiet glow in her eyes every time Star looked at her, and she was very different from the haunted woman she had been as Cat Lurks's wife. Perhaps she would have a happy marriage, mused Star. She certainly hoped so.

As for Star, herself, Camel Stalker had started to court her, but she was reluctant to be alone with the young man. If anything, his sojourn among the Fish Eaters had hardened him, and he was pressing his marriage suit very strongly.

"I invited Camel Stalker to eat with us tomorrow eve," said Blue Jay.

Star's lips tightened as she sewed a fine seam

on the soft deerskin covering she was making for the cradleboard.

"I think he is such a fine young man," added Blue Jay. She sliced at the sinew with a knife, then knotted it again. She was sewing a tiny deer design on a blanket covering for the babe. "He would make such a good husband."

"Yes," murmured Star, as she had murmured every night for the last seven, which was when Blue Jay had first learned that Camel Stalker had started his joining suit. She had learned it because Camel Stalker had sent over his old aunt to tell her so.

"He is a very good hunter," continued Blue Jay, undaunted by Star's listless response. "The woman he marries would never go hungry. Neither would her children."

The baby gave a kick and Star winced.

"He would make any woman happy."

She had been made happy once, thought Star. She did not need to be made happy ever again. "No, thank you," she muttered.

Blue Jay raised one brow and went back to sewing the deer design. "I think I will have the fawn lying in the soft grass," she mused, holding up the hide blanket. "That will look pretty."

"Yes," murmured Star dutifully.

Just then Camel Stalker walked by, wearing a long cloak of tanned hide that his mother had made him in honor of his return from the Fish Eaters. He had told very few of the Badger People what had happened to him when he was a slave. Finds the Marten, too, spoke little of it, though it was known in camp that both men suffered bad dreams and cried out in their sleep.

Camel Stalker stared hard at Star, then continued his walk through the camp, stopping to visit at Finds the Marten's fire. Camel Stalker was tall, well formed, and prior to his slavery, he had been gently spoken. But now Star thought she did not know him as well.

Truth to tell, she was feeling a little afraid of his pursuit. He had followed her to the river twice, each time reminding her of their previous agreement to join. She tried to explain that she still felt married to Falcon, but Camel Stalker had laughed cruelly and reminded her of how she had been cast aside.

Star did not talk to him after that and two days later he had come to her at her mother's tent and stiffly apologized. She had accepted his apology but she still did not feel comfortable around him.

"His mother would be very happy if you two joined," prodded Blue Jay. "Grouse's old sister is my old friend. We would be related." The old woman sighed.

"Grouse's old sister must be the only woman you are not related to in this encampment," snapped Star. "Pleasing Grouse's sister is not important to me."

"Star!" gasped her mother. "How you have changed!"

"Yes, I have," she answered with more spirit than she had felt in a long time. Since she had been left by Falcon, in fact. And it felt good. "It is my life, Mother, and I will choose whom I marry."

"Better not wait too long," advised Blue Jay. "Or your child will be grown and gone."

"That is unlikely."

"They grow fast," warned Blue Jay. "They eat much, too, once they are weaned. You will be hard-pressed to provide food."

Star stabbed at the cradleboard covering. She picked up a porcupine quill and jabbed the needle into the hide.

"Do not take such huge stitches," cautioned Blue Jay.

Star wanted to scream in frustration.

Camel Stalker wandered by, this time the other way. Again, he stared hard at Star. She clenched her jaw and stabbed at the deer hide, hoping he would not approach her fire and add to her woes. Her mother was enough to contend with this night. And Star had thought sitting and sewing for her children with her mother would be so wonderful! Ha!

"Greetings, Camel Stalker," called out Blue Jay, and Star groaned. The young man took the greeting for encouragement, which it was, and veered toward them.

Star groaned again.

"Silence," hissed Blue Jay. "You will scare him away!"

Star groaned again, louder.

"Hush," warned Blue Jay. To Camel Stalker, she asked, "And how is your old mother this evening?"

"She does well."

Star could feel Camel Stalker's eyes on her. When she peeked up from her sewing he was

373

staring at her. He nodded stiffly.

"Your babe grows," he said, his eyes dropping to her stomach.

Star gasped. Blue Jay studied her sewing intently.

Camel Stalker squatted by the fire and absently poked at the flames. "I did not like living with the Fish Eaters," he said. "But I learned from them. One thing I learned was that each day of life is precious."

"That is most wise," murmured Blue Jay to her sewing.

Camel Stalker met Star's eyes. "When a woman has been left by her husband, I would think she would know this, too. Each day is important."

Star shrugged. "I suppose so." She had not actually thought of life like that.

"I know what I want," continued Camel Stalker, "and I will not let things, or people, slip out of my grasp."

"Oh." Star attacked her sewing with her awl, drilling the hole too big. Now she would have to disguise it with a design.

"Yes." He rose to his feet. "Good evening," he said to Blue Jay. To Star he nodded and walked away, heading in the direction of his tent.

"He is like a strong wind that whips across the hills," observed Blue Jay. "Think you that you can hold such a one off for long?"

Star stared at his disappearing back. She would have to. For a while, at least.

Chapter Forty-eight

"What do you think is the matter with Falcon?" whispered Claw.

His wife shook her head. "I do not know. I have not seen such a thing happen to a man."

"He just sits by his fire day and night," muttered Claw. "If the fire dies, he does not start it again, oh no. He just sits there. If someone lights the fire for him, he still just sits there. He does not care if he is warm or cold. He does not care if he has food or not. If you did not bring him food every day—"

"He only eats a little of it, too," mused Betafor.

Claw lapsed into silence.

"Perhaps we should talk to the shaman," said Betafor.

"Perhaps," acknowledged Claw. "It would be better than watching Falcon sit and do nothing."

They went to the shaman's cave and found him

sorting herbs into leather sacks beside his fire.

"We are concerned about Falcon," said Betafor. "We want to help him."

The shaman set aside the herbs and nodded. "I have stopped by his cave several times. I see that he just sits."

"Yes," agreed Betafor.

"Is someone feeding him?" asked Rapt.

"Yes," she answered.

"Does someone light the fire so he can stay warm?" asked Rapt.

"Yes," said Claw.

The shaman was silent. "Where is his wife?" he asked at last. "I thought she carried his babe."

"He sent her away," said Claw. "He does not want her anymore."

"What does Tula do?"

"Nothing. She does not help him. Nor does Marmot. They do not like him. Horn helps him sometimes."

"What do his friends say?"

Claw shrugged. "He does not have any except Horn and myself and Betafor. He has driven his other friends away. Ever since his child died . . ."

"Ah, yes," murmured Rapt softly, "his child . . ." He was silent a long time. "I think—" he said at last, then fell into a reverie.

Betafor and Claw waited expectantly. After some time, the shaman spoke again. "I think," he continued slowly, "that his soul has gone away."

"Hmmm, gone away. That is very bad," said Betafor.

"Can you bring it back?" asked Claw.

"I must think about it," answered Rapt. "It is not an easy thing to do, to bring back a wandering soul."

"We must do something," said Betafor. "Otherwise he will die."

"I will give you a deer if you help Falcon," said Claw.

The shaman's bright eyes snapped. "It is a most difficult thing when a soul as strong as Falcon's wants to go away. It takes much work to bring it back."

"Two deer," said Claw.

"It will take some time," warned the shaman. "His spirit may have wandered far, far away."

There was a silence. Betafor nudged her husband.

"Three deer," said Claw.

"He still has some friends, I see," remarked the shaman.

Betafor and Claw nodded. The shaman regarded them, his wrinkled face pensive. More time passed.

"Four deer," said Claw.

The shaman chuckled. "I will do it," he said, getting heavily to his feet, "for three deer." He left the cave.

What does the old man want? wondered Falcon. If he were not so filled with despair, he would tell the shaman to leave the cave. As it was, it took too much effort. Not worth it. Nothing was.

The chanting would have annoyed Falcon if he had let it. As it was, he just ignored the old man and his smoking herbs and his foolish songs as he sat beside the fire.

The smoke from the herbs irritated Falcon's eyes. "Go away," he croaked at last.

"Ah," said the shaman. "You have come back."

"I did not go anywhere," said Falcon. "I have been sitting here."

"Your soul, man. I talk about your soul."

"I do not have one."

"Everyone has a soul. The Great Spirit gave you one."

"Well, since there is no Great Spirit, how can He give me a soul? Tell me that, old man with your stinking herbs," said Falcon, beginning to grow angry.

The shaman shrugged. "Sometimes the soul falls asleep," he muttered. "Perhaps that is what happened to yours. It did not go wandering; it fell asleep."

Falcon scoffed. "I am wide-awake now. Get out of my cave."

The shaman rose. "It does not go well for a man who denies his own soul, a gift from the Great Spirit."

"There is no Great Spirit! I have no soul! Now get out of my cave!" Anger was washing over Falcon now and it felt good. He felt alive. He cast off the robe he had wrapped himself in to keep off the cave's coolness. His legs trembled with weakness as he got to his feet.

The shaman tottered ahead of him toward the cave entrance. Falcon followed him and bellowed, "You could not help my son. You cannot help me!"

The shaman whirled. "That is what this is about. It is your son, is it not?"

"No!" screamed Falcon. "It is not my son!"

"You are correct," said the shaman. "He is dead. It is you."

"No! It is not me!"

"Tula then?"

"No!"

Falcon prowled up to the shaman. "Listen to me, old man," he growled, jerking the shaman by the front of his vest. "You poisoned my wife's thoughts. You said my son was important. That he would be a great teacher!" Falcon glared into the shaman's black eyes. "Well, you were wrong, you lying old man! My son is dead!" And he howled his anguish and pain at the cave roof.

The shaman shrugged out of his grasp and straightened his vest but he did not step away. When Falcon's howl had echoed through the cave until all was silent once more, the shaman said, "I did not lie. It was revealed to me that he was a healer."

"You old fool! How can a boy whose eyes are dazed, whose body is so sick he cannot walk, whose mind wanders at will, be a healer?"

The shaman shrugged. "I do not know," he admitted.

"Then why," raged Falcon, "did you tell my wife such foolishness?" He wanted to throttle the old man where he stood. All the problems of his first marriage, all the foolish hopes, the unreality of it, could be laid on this man's skinny shoulders.

"Because it was the truth."

379

"Bah! There is no reasoning with you!" cried Falcon. "Leave my cave!"

The shaman did.

After he had gone, Falcon marched up and down beside the flickering fire, muttering to himself. Finally, the excitement and energy of his rage-filled encounter with the old man spent itself and he slumped down beside the fire. And this time, when the despair came, it was a yawning dark hole that swallowed him up.

Chapter Forty-nine

When Falcon awoke, the old man was sitting beside the fire, eyes closed, breathing slowly. Falcon gave him a kick in the leg. "Get out of here, old man. Let me be!"

The shaman opened his eyes. "I see you are back."

"We disagree, you old liar. I did not go anywhere. Do not play your games with me."

"Falcon? Rapt? Are you there?"

"Who goes?" asked Falcon, blinking against the light of the cave's entrance.

"It is I, Claw's wife," said Betafor, edging into the darkness. She walked up to them. "I came to see how you are faring."

"I would fare better if this old man were out of here. Who pays you?" he addressed the shaman. "Not me, I can tell you."

The old man shrugged. "Your friends."

Falcon spat. "I have none. Leave."

The shaman got slowly to his feet, nodded at Betafor, and left the cave.

They watched him go. "You are very rude to that old man. He tries to help you."

Falcon sighed. "I suppose it is you who pays him?"

She did not deny it, but sat down heavily on the robe beside the fire. Finally she said, "Yes, Claw and I and Horn pay him. We want to help you. Are there any other friends you have?"

Falcon grunted. "No."

They sat quietly for a while. "Is it you that brings the food?" asked Falcon.

"Yes."

"Oh."

There was another long silence broken only by the snapping of the fire. "Do you—do you ever wonder about Star?" asked Betafor.

Falcon glanced at her. "All the time."

"Why do you not go to her then?"

He laughed bitterly. "Why should I? What woman would want the man who casts her aside when she is pregnant?"

"You regret it?" asked Betafor with a hopeful note in her voice.

"No." He sighed heavily. "I did it for her. And the babe."

She was silent for a long time. "That does not make sense, Falcon."

He glared at her. "Do not ask me to tell you any more, old woman."

"I see that you will not."

"No. I will not."

There was another long silence. At last Betafor said, "I do not know why you did what you did. You must have your reasons. But I think that Star is a good woman. She would not hurt you."

He gave a guttural laugh. "She is like Tula."

"Oh? How so? Tell me, for I did not notice the likeness before this."

He sighed. "After her long labor and the delivery of her sickly child, she will turn against me and blame me. And," he said hoarsely, "she will be correct to do so. She will hate me."

"Ah, just like Tula."

"Just so."

There was a long silence. Falcon spoke up. "And I, I will not be able to help her."

"Mmmm. And so you got rid of her before this could happen?" asked Betafor.

"What man would not? What man would choose to watch his child die and his wife leave him? What man would choose to go through that again?"

Betafor stared at the flames thoughtfully. "No man," she said at last. "No man."

A glimmer of hope entered Falcon's breast. "So you see why I did it."

"I do."

For the first time in a long time, Falcon relaxed. "You see then that the shaman is wrong. My soul is not wandering or asleep. I am doing what I should do. I am trying to stop another tragedy."

"You are trying to stop the pain to yourself, too," said Betafor.

Falcon glanced at her sharply, but her bland face was watching the fire.

"I am trying to protect Star," he said.

"And the babe, too."

Guilt stirred in him. "I cannot help the babe. I have been through a sickly son's death once. I cannot bear it again."

"No. Let Star bear it this time."

When he gazed at Betafor, she was still watching the flames. "That does not sound so good," he said slowly. "You make it sound as if I am thinking only of myself."

Betafor glanced at him. "Are you?"

"No."

"Well then, what is the worry?"

"None," he answered hastily. "None at all."

She nodded.

The only sound was the hissing of wood burning low.

"I have been trying," said Betafor, "to think how alike Tula and Star are. I fail."

"What do you mean? Of course they are alike. They are both women."

He caught Betafor's amused glance. "I understand you are a woman, too, but you are different."

"I suppose," said Betafor.

"Tula blamed me," he said bitterly. "She thought I hated my son. Wanted him dead. But I loved him. I did everything I could to help him survive."

"Yes."

The simple statement reverberated inside Falcon. At last someone believed him. "She left me before she could even know the truth."

"And you think Star would do the same?"

Broken Promise

"Yes."

Betafor was silent.

She is a smart old woman, thought Falcon. I will ask her. "Do you think Star would have left me?"

Betafor glanced up at him. "What I think does not matter. Whether she would or not, I do not know."

Falcon's heart sank. "That is no answer, Betafor."

"It is the only honest answer I can give you."

Falcon stared at the fire, feeling the grim despair creeping up on him again. For a short time, he had felt hope, felt there was a way out of the yawning blackness. But he had been wrong. As he had been so many times before.

"But I do know this," added Betafor slowly. "You will never know until you ask her about this."

He laughed bitterly. "You sound like Star. She always wanted to talk."

Betafor met his eyes and smiled for the first time. A little while later, she rose to her feet. "I go now," she said. "I can bring you back some stew, if you wish."

It seemed he spent so much of his time staring at the flames. "That is good," he said. "I am hungry."

After she had brought the stew and left, he thought about her words. Would Star tell him any different? If he asked her, would she be honest and tell him that she would leave him when their babe was born sickly? Was there a chance that she would tell him she would *not* leave him?

What is it I truly want? he wondered. Do I want to know how she would behave after the babe is born? Or do I want to be assured that she loves me? He froze at the thought. Love? Is that what I truly want?

Strange how hope suddenly stirred within him again.

Chapter Fifty

"Where are you going?" asked Betafor one evening as Falcon tottered out of the cave. She peered at him in the deepening twilight.

She held a stone bowl filled with deer stew, his evening meal that she had been about to give him.

He took the bowl from her, slurped down the hot stew, and wiped impatiently at the juice dripping down his chin. "I go."

"I know that," said Betafor, taking the bowl from his hands. "But where?"

"Canyon of the Doves."

"That is a long way."

Even in the dark he could see her concern for him. He wanted to push her away and run off. People caring for him were just a burden. Why did she bother? Nothing mattered.

He took a few more tottering steps, using his spear for a cane. His strength was not what it had been. Sitting around a cave weakens a man, he thought. Then he thought, what does it matter? He had no one to hunt for. Not even himself. It did not matter if he lived or died.

"Why are you going to the Canyon of the Doves?"

He glared at her. "You ask too many questions."

She sighed and nodded. "I do."

He relented a little. "I must stand on the walls. Like my father before me."

His words made little sense but he cared nothing for her understanding. He did not want to talk to her. Whenever he did, he said too much. "Farewell," he said and started forward.

"Farewell," she called after him softly.

It was better this way. Leaving in the dark. None of the Jaguar People would see him or follow him.

It took him three days to find the Canyon of the Doves. And that was because he was so weak from sitting around the cave, thought Falcon viciously. He had forgotten to bring food with him, but he had not felt hungry after the first day. He drank water from creeks he crossed.

As dawn approached, he sat up. He'd had a restless sleep this past night. He had dreamed of Star and she had called him. "Go away," he had answered. "Leave me alone." And so he awoke, feeling mean and alone and full of despair.

Above him was the slope of one side of the canyon. "I will climb it," he said aloud. "I must do this thing."

Broken Promise

He did not know why he had come to the canyon. Only that he must. Once he had tried to end his life. But he could not do it in the churning white water of the river, and so now he would see if his life held anything more for him.

He felt drawn to the slopes of the steep canyon where his father had taken him when he was but a youth. His father had shown him the land and said that the animals and everything he saw were for Falcon's use. And his father had further promised that one day Falcon would stand there and show all he surveyed to his own son.

What a lie, thought Falcon angrily. Everything is a lie. My father's promise was a lie. Tula's love was a lie. My son's life was a lie. Everything. Star is a lie, too—she and her "love!" He gave a snort of disgust, yet he rose from the bedrobes and started the ascent.

It took him the whole day to climb to the top. The gravel slopes were difficult to scale in his weakened state and he slid so many times his feet and legs were bleeding. But he cared nothing for that.

He finally reached the top, puffing, and sat down. Below him, back the way he had come, was a gravel slope. On the other side of him, the wall dropped sheer into the canyon. Night was approaching and he could see very little of the country. "I will see what tomorrow brings," he thought. "I am too tired now."

He thought about lying down to sleep but it was a precarious position he held and in his sleep, he might roll down the slope. So he sat and nodded, finally falling asleep with his head slumped on his knees.

What awoke him he did not know, but suddenly he was awake, with the kind of alertness that comes when a hunter hears something.

He glanced around but all was quiet. The moon shone full. Below him in the canyon he could see a yawning blackness. On the slope, he could see the gravel. What woke me? he wondered.

He got to his feet, the better to survey. He clutched his spear. It was very unlikely a wildcat would scale the canyon's side. Yet he had heard something. . . .

Only silence greeted his straining ears. As he stood there, he felt suddenly as if he stood at the top of the world. Alone.

As he stood there, he felt surrounded by the soft darkness and his fear at being awakened receded. It was only he and the darkness and the moon and his memories.

He held his spear defiantly. "I am here," he said. "I am alive." He shook the spear. "Do you hear me, Great Spirit, if you even exist? This is my life and I will do what I want!"

There was no answer. He became bolder.

"If you exist, I tell you that you are a destroyer, Great Spirit!" he cried. "You have destroyed my life! And I blame you for it all! You gave me a son who was crippled, a wife who was faithless! You gave me a second wife who would be equally faithless! What is the matter with you? Why do you torture me so? Have you nothing better to do at your camp behind the sun than throw evil upon us?"

There was no answer.

"I am angry at you, Great Spirit! I am angry at you beyond anything I can do or say! Life is all lies! It is not good! Fathers lie to their sons! Women leave their husbands! Sons die! What kind of a world have you created? I do not want to be part of it! Do you hear? I do not want it!"

Again, silence.

Rage reared up in Falcon, a mixture of grief and sorrow and pain at all he had suffered in his life. He gave a huge, tearing scream. When the scream died out, silence reigned again.

"I am angry at you! I am angry at Tula! I hate her! I am angry at my son! How dare he die when I wanted him to live! I hate Rapt! I hate everyone in the Jaguar camp! They are all fools! I hate everyone!"

He thought about that. Since the Great Spirit was not answering him, Falcon could say anything he wanted. He felt marvelously free.

"I am being truthful with you, Great Spirit! You are a sham! The shaman lies about you! People lie about you! You do not create, you destroy! I have seen enough to know this! You destroyed my son and my first marriage! And now you are waiting for me to destroy myself!"

Again, no answer.

"What does it take to move you, Great Spirit? What does it take for you to answer me? I stand here a broken man. Broken in body, broken in spirit. Will you still give me no answer?"

Silence.

"Have it your way then, Great Spirit! You are not great. You are puny. I spit on you! I am angry at everyone you have sent to me in my life! I am angry at everything you have done in my life! But most of all, I am angry at you! You are uncaring about the death you deal us! You do not care about me! You do not care about anyone. Not my son! Not my wives! Not me!"

Silence. He glanced down into the yawning darkness on the canyon side of the wall.

"Have it your way, then, Great Spirit," he said wearily and sat down to wait for the dawn.

Chapter Fifty-one

Falcon stared out across the yawning maw of the canyon and watched the sun come up behind the distant mountains. As it cast its yellow glow, disgust welled in him. He had received nothing but silence from the Great Spirit. Tula had betrayed him; his father had made false promises. His beloved son had died. His life was a mess. He was alone, and no one was there to help him. No one.

He watched the rays of light grow brighter and expose more of the land and he found it difficult to hold on to his anger. The sharp hills and river valleys were bathed in gold as the sun rose.

Falcon's heart softened at the beauty he saw. He wondered if his father had ever sat here on the high slope and watched the sun rise. Perhaps he had; he had been enthralled with this place when he'd brought his only son to see it.

Falcon thought about his father, how his father had taught him to hunt, how his father had tried to guide him. He had done what he could for his son and Falcon had grown up to become a fine hunter. He was glad of the skills his father had taught him, for he seldom went hungry.

But his father had been wrong about Falcon and his own son standing here someday. Falcon realized now that he had badly wanted his father's prediction to come true, felt that he would please his father by taking his own son here. And it was not to be. His father's experience was not to be his.

He wondered if his father would have understood that. "I tried, Father," he whispered. "I tried to raise a son that I could teach to hunt as you taught me. I would have brought him to this wall and shown him the vast land. But I could not do it!" A sense of failure rose in Falcon, failure that he had not lived up to his father's hopes and dreams for him. He had the sudden realization that he had lived with that failure for a long time.

A whisper of wind blew on the canyon wall. Was it his father saying he understood? For some reason, Falcon thought it was. A rare peace descended on him.

He sat there for a long time, thinking of his father, realizing the hopes he himself had carried, which he could not fulfill. Perhaps it was time to let them go.

There was a sadness in him as he watched the sun rise. A sadness, but an acceptance, too. He sat with those feelings inside him as the sun came up.

And then something odd happened. In this land of dryness, of long periods of time of drought, a strange thing happened.

It began to rain. Little, light, sprinkling drops landed on Falcon's face and hair. Rain was always greeted reverently by his people, for rain brought life to the land.

Falcon lifted his face and felt the sweet drops skim his face and he wondered if perhaps the Great Spirit had heard him after all.

He rose and let the rain pelt him as he descended the slope. Going down did not take as long as going up. By the time he reached the bottom of the slope, it was raining heavily. He needed to find shelter. He passed by the entrance of the canyon. He knew from past explorations that though the canyon stretched back for a long, long distance, nowhere in it was there a place to shelter himself. He must look elsewhere.

When he passed the canyon, he started up a small ravine, the rain and wind driving him before it. The sun was long gone and all the sky was a dark gray. It would rain all day, perhaps into the night.

He trembled from the cold. He was hungry. Where was he going to find shelter?

The ravine ended with a cornered overhang. He spotted the black shadow of the overhang and headed for it. It looked large enough for him to crouch underneath. He could wait out the storm there.

He reached the overhang and crept under the rock. To his surprise, he found that the dark shadow extended back into the rock. It was a small cave. Pleased at his discovery, he pushed his way a little further and found that it was a narrow tunnel. A cool breeze blew on his face when he looked into the black tunnel. Air with a strong, earthy scent stung his nostrils. He wondered what was on the other side of the tunnel.

He waited awhile, but the rain poured down. He would not be going anywhere this day. Though he had no wood and no fire, under the overhang it was dry. The air was warm because it was summer, and he felt comfortable. After sitting and watching the rain for a while, he decided to explore further into the tunnel.

He pushed his spear ahead of him and crept through the narrow opening. Dusty debris and gravel littered the tunnel floor. He would have turned around, but the space was too small and the air touching his face smelled fresh. The tunnel would end soon.

And it did. He came out of the darkness into daylight. And into a large, scooped-out area that looked like it had been hand-carved out of the rock around it. But it was too big for men to carve, he saw, and then he chuckled to himself. A great clump of earth in the center showed him what had happened. It had once been a hollow cave and a part of the roof had collapsed, leaving a giant overhang and part of the walls standing.

Falcon crawled out of the tunnel and landed on the ground. The rain still beat down mercilessly but he was able to stay dry under the partial roof over the enclosure.

He glanced around at the walls and beheld a startling sight. He stared about him, whirling from first one painted beast to another.

Carved and painted on the exposed cave walls were strange animals, animals he had only heard about in stories told around the night fires by the old people. Animals his ancestors had hunted, but he had never seen.

Yet he recognized them—a painted mammoth, its long, waving trunk unmistakable. A sloth, its huge, meaty body bulging with spears. The old hunters must have enjoyed hunting sloths, he thought, for there were many on the walls.

And then his eye caught a dab of yellow ocher with dark spots—an animal that looked like a giant jaguar!

Drawn to it, he came closer. Though it looked like a jaguar, yet it was not one, for the canine teeth on it curved around and down. A fearsome-toothed animal, he thought, and then he remembered: a saber-tooth!

He stood in front of the painting. A saber-tooth! He had heard of them, knew the old ancestors had fought them. He was glad suddenly that he had never had to face one. No hunter he knew had. Yet they were here, on these walls.

The paintings looked very much alive.

A sheen of sweat broke out on his forehead as he stared at the likenesses.

Suddenly he realized how quiet it was in this place. Something tickled at the back of his mind. He had heard about this place, but where? When?

He prowled along the walls, scanning the pictures. With his finger, he traced the thick muscular neck of a huge bison.

But darkness was falling and he could not see the animals as well as before. He was feeling hungry and earlier he had spotted a berry bush where the cave's roof had collapsed. He went over and picked the fruit, eating in gulps. The berries tasted sweet and good.

He darted back under the roof. He would spend the night here. The rain pelted down.

He could sleep in the roofed area. And since the only opening into this place was the small tunnel he had entered through, he would be safe for the night. He still had his spear for protection.

He propped himself against a rock, his spear by his side, and fell asleep.

He awoke to an amazing sight.

Chapter Fifty-two

"This is the Cave of the Dead," said the man standing in front of Falcon.

Falcon gasped and sat up. "Who are you?" He reached for his spear.

"Do not fear," said the strangely garbed man. "I will not hurt you."

The man was dressed in soft, tanned skins and he had a glow of light surrounding him. On top of his head he wore a fierce saber-tooth head, the jaws open, the red mouth of the animal agape. The polished, yellow teeth of the saber-toothed tiger curved down over the man's forehead like small tusks.

"Who—?" began Falcon again and then he noticed that he was not actually speaking, but rather he was *thinking* his question. Before he could finish his question, Falcon knew where he had heard of this cave before: in the story Star had told about Darkstar. He had stumbled into the very cave that Star's ancestress had found!

The saber-tooth man responded. "The Great Spirit sent me."

"There is a Great Spirit?" asked Falcon.

"Of course," answered the saber-tooth angel.

"Where is he?" asked Falcon.

The saber-tooth angel laughed. "Ah, it is not your time to see him yet."

"I want to!"

But the saber-tooth figure merely smiled patiently.

Falcon liked him. Then the angel pointed to the walls, distracting him. "I was sent because you like jaguars."

"Yes, I do," acknowledged Falcon, "though I had to kill one not long ago."

"Yes," answered the angel and there was acceptance, not judgment, in his answer.

"Why are you here?" asked Falcon.

"To tell you that the Great Spirit heard your cries."

"That is all?"

"What more do you want?"

"I—I—" Falcon did not know what he wanted.

"Your son?" asked the angel.

"Oh, yes, I want to see my son! I love him so."

"Yes, you do." Behind the angel peeked out a little boy. He clutched the angel's leg but he would not come forward.

"Hawk?" cried Falcon. "Is it you?" He leapt to his feet and tears sprang to Falcon's eyes as he beheld his son.

The boy giggled and nodded, and Falcon saw

that it truly was Hawk. But a different Hawk. A Hawk whose eyes were clear, who understood what was said to him.

"Oh, Hawk, how I love you!" cried Falcon. The boy gave him a wide smile, then hid behind the angel again.

"He loves you, too." The angel laughed. "He has had much to teach you," added the angel, more soberly. "He had much wisdom to impart to you."

"Yes," said Falcon, "he did." Now he understood the purpose of Hawk's life. It was to allow Falcon and Tula to love someone who was unable to love them back.

"He brought you a gift," said the angel. "An unselfish gift."

"Yes," acknowledged Falcon sadly, "but I did not want his gift. I did not understand how important it was for me to love him as he was. I wanted him to hunt and run and speak. I thought *then* I would love him."

"You understand now?" said the saber-tooth angel.

"Yes."

"I wanted love for me, too," said Falcon. "I wanted it from Tula, from Star. I wanted it no matter what I did to anyone. I thought that love for me was important."

"It is. How can you love others if you do not love yourself? When you love yourself, you want to love others, too. It flows out of you."

It sounds so simple, thought Falcon.

"It is," agreed the angel.

"What about Tula? Did she learn to love?"

401

"Tula will learn, but in time," said the saber-tooth angel gently. "I am here for you."

By this, Falcon understood that the angel was reluctant to impart more about Tula.

"That is true," acknowledged the angel. "I can tell you only one thing more about Tula. And that is this: your son's sickness was caused by his long, difficult birth, not by anything you or Tula did. It is useless to further blame yourself. Or her.

"And the Great Spirit cut short your son's life to prevent further suffering for him. Hawk's sickness would have continued to get worse and he would have lived in much agony and pain. The Great Spirit did not want that for Hawk."

Falcon wanted to cry with gratitude. Now, *now* he understood. "I, too, love Hawk," he said. He heard a giggle from behind the angel's leg and was rewarded with another peek from those trusting brown eyes. Hawk beamed at him and then hid again.

Falcon smiled. Then his smile disappeared; there was something more he must ask.

"What is it?" asked the angel.

"What of Star?" asked Falcon at last. "I fear I have hurt her terribly. And—and what of our babe?" The thought was out before he could call it back.

"Ah, yes," said the angel. He stepped to one side. Standing behind him, holding Hawk's hand, was a little girl, her black hair down to her shoulders, her eyes bright with curiosity.

Love such as he had never known welled up in Falcon. "That is my child?" he breathed, but he

Broken Promise

knew the answer by the shy smile on her face.

"Yes, this is the child you and Star share."

The little girl pulled up Hawk's hand and covered her face, then peeped out between their entangled fingers at Falcon. She laughed mischievously.

"I love her," said Falcon.

The angel laughed. "Of course you do."

"And Star?" dared Falcon. "What of her?"

"You must find that out for yourself," said the angel gently.

Then, as Falcon watched and waited for more, the angel wavered in front of him and disappeared, taking both children with him.

"Come back!" cried Falcon. "Come back!"

There was no answer.

Falcon sat down, too overwhelmed by what he had seen and learned to get any more words out.

He woke up the next morning with a new feeling in his heart. He had something to live for now. He must find Star!

Chapter Fifty-three

Fall

Falcon sat outside the skin tent he had made, and breathed in the hot, pine-scented sunshine. The dried grass on the hills below him had turned brown and he had not seen his people since the night he had left them to run away to the Canyon of the Doves. He wondered how they fared. But more, he wondered how Star fared. He had not been able to find her or any sign of her Badger People.

Falcon sharpened the edges of a piece of obsidian he was shaping into a spear point. He had been fortunate to find a quarry of the precious stuff. He had set his tent in the shelter of the pine trees, next to the quarry. Whenever he needed more stone to shape he had but to walk over and pick it up.

Sitting in the sun warmed his body and brought sadness to his heart. He thought of his son, of his sorrow when Hawk died. He glanced around, satisfied himself that no animal was creeping up on him, and brushed a tear from his eye. Since his powerful vision, it had been easier to think of those he loved.

He had loved Hawk, wanted him to be able to hunt, to run and play as other children could do. He wanted the best for Hawk, but he had feared for him, too, feared that no one would hunt for Hawk when Falcon was too old.

Falcon had discovered that, in his heart, under all the guilt he had felt because his son had been crippled, under all the fear he had felt that it was something Falcon had done, and under all the sorrow he had felt since his son had died, there was a deep and abiding love for his son. It surprised Falcon that it was there. He had glimpsed it that night he had had the vision in the Cave of the Dead. But now he felt it: a strong, pure love for his son unmixed with guilt or sorrow or anger.

It was like the obsidian rock. After the sorrow and guilt and anger were flaked away, there was still a strong core. And for Falcon that core was love.

Why did I not face this before? he wondered. Why did I do everything I could to run away from my grief?

Because the sadness was difficult to bear, he realized. He had to face the death of his beloved son and the loss of Tula to another man. His grief at their loss at times overcame him so much that all he could do was huddle in the shelter of his tent.

But now Falcon could feel his grief. He had loved Hawk, and Hawk was gone. Nothing he could do could bring his son back. Ever.

And it was a sad shock to him the day he realized that he had loved Tula deeply, too. He had depended on her to remain faithful to him, and though she had not, he still wanted good things for her. But the time they had shared was long gone and would never return. There was nothing he could do to bring her back, either. She had chosen to be with Marmot and to have his child.

Falcon sighed heavily. No wonder he had not wanted to feel anything. This load of grief and sadness was much to bear.

As he had done for so many days, sitting in the hot sun and sharpening rock, he let the sadness flood his heart. Sometimes his hands sat idle because he could not see to chip the rock through the blur of his tears. After a while the sadness passed and he was able to chip the rock some more.

Yet besides the sadness in his life, something else strange was also happening. And he was aware of that, too. When he was not feeling the sadness, he had times of peace, real peace in his heart. Not the numbing, deathlike peace he had sought before, but a happy peace. At such times he could even wish Rapt, the shaman, well, and he could think of Betafor with gratitude for the food she had brought to him when he was alone in the cave.

And then at other times, the sadness would come over him again. He wondered if his grief was so great that it would never end.

But one night there came a time when he sat outside his tent and felt only restlessness. Where is this coming from? he wondered. He gazed up into the sky and he saw it: a bright, bright star. Darkstar, he thought. I wonder where my Star is this night? His grief for her loss he had not even dared to feel yet. It had been all he could do to cry for his son and Tula.

But the Darkstar shone brightly and he found he could not tear his eyes away. Where are you, Star? his heart cried out, and it was then that he knew that before him lay his biggest grief of all: mourning the loss of Star and their babe. For that was surely what the Great Spirit was telling him in his aimless wanderings: he should prepare himself for their loss. And yet he remembered the little dark-eyed daughter of his vision, and some part of him still hoped.

The next morning when he rose, he decided he had enough obsidian rock for spear points and knives. It was time to move on and continue his search for Star.

He had been weak from his time in the cave but now he was strong again. On hopeful days, when he believed he would find Star, he wondered if he should ask her to come back to him. On discouraged days, he thought he would search for her until he could but see her, nothing more. Yet always, his heart longed for her.

Sometimes he wondered if she had had the

babe . . . strange how he could not remember when the babe was due.

Whenever he thought of Star, hope always got mixed in with sorrow. I will go and see her, he thought as he followed a deer trail down into an oak tree–filled ravine. Then I can see if there is any hope for us or if I must let her go.

Guilt pierced him then. He had thrown her away. He had *wanted* to throw her away. Of course she would go on and make a life for herself, one without him. Of what use was it for him to hope?

And yet he did. It was there, nourished by his vision of the saber-tooth angel. Hope was a tiny flare that sparked in his chest.

Chapter Fifty-four

Late Fall

Star sorted serviceberries into three baskets on the grass near the tent she and her mother shared. The Badger People had moved to this place only two days ago and there were still berries in the area. She had filled two huge baskets. She was most pleased; serviceberries tasted good and could be added to deer meat or dried and pounded into loaves. They were a most tasty and useful fruit.

Her mother, Blue Jay, sat beside her and hummed happily as she sliced through a hind-quarter of fat antelope. Camel Stalker had killed the animal and given the haunch to them. A gift, he had said, but his eyes had lingered on Star and she knew the time was coming when she must decide if she would marry him or not.

"Camel Stalker is very generous to widows," said Blue Jay, looking up from the antelope and fixing Star with a glare. "And to unmarried pregnant women who take a long time to make up their minds."

Star winced.

"He is kind to old people, too," continued Blue Jay, returning to her job of slicing the meat. "He would doubtless be kind to little babies." She stopped her work to stare at Star's huge belly.

"Mmmm," Star murmured. She did not actually want to have to tell him yes or no. She knew her mother wanted her to accept Camel Stalker's joining offer, but Star was reluctant to do so. Yet what else could she do? She needed a man to help her survive in these harsh times.

She must not wait much longer to tell him her answer, whatever it would be. He had already brought them meat for three moons. He deserved an answer soon.

"It would be foolish for a woman not to marry him," said Blue Jay.

"Mmmm." The trouble was, how could Star forget a man like Falcon? To marry Camel Stalker would be wrong if her heart were still with Falcon. Which it was, she admitted sadly to herself.

"Especially a woman who is pregnant, and whose old mother cannot hunt. Who else is there in this camp for you to marry anyway? Tell me that!"

"Mmmm."

"Star! Listen to what I tell you," muttered her mother.

"Mmmm."

"Do what I tell you."

"No, Mother."

Blue Jay gave a wry chuckle. "Ha. You were listening after all! I would have told you to marry him."

"I know."

They laughed.

Blue Jay added, "Truly, daughter, I must tell you I want a happy life for you."

"I know you do, Mother."

"I worry about you. Who will hunt for you? I will not always be here for you. I will die some-day."

"Please, do not say—"

"It is true. And who will take care of you and your child? I cannot do it, even if I am here. Oh, I can dig roots and pick berries, but you need a husband to hunt for you. A husband to be your companion. You need a husband now, more than you need a mother." Her voice was sad.

"I already had a husband, Mother," answered Star. "I like you better." She chuckled.

Blue Jay just shook her head.

Blue Jay had invited Camel Stalker to join them for the evening meal. Star thought she could not protest the invitation since he had provided the meat.

Camel Stalker was quiet through the meal, though Star caught him watching her several times when he thought she was not looking. Once she surprised an angry look upon his face.

What does he have to be angry about? she wondered.

They had just finished eating the delicious antelope meat when Blue Jay jumped up, antelope scraps falling from her lap. One of the camp dogs ran off with a bone.

"Who is that?"

Star blinked twice as the tall stranger strode into the Badger camp. He carried a spear and he was naked to his waist. Leather trousers covered his long legs. His feet were bare. Long black hair fluttered past his shoulders.

She gasped and her hand went to her breast and she stood up. Why, he—he looked like Falcon. But surely it could not be he! He had left her; she had no expectation that he would return. And yet—

Tattooed on his shoulder was a black falcon in flight.

"Falcon!" she cried and ran toward him.

He swerved in her direction and she halted. Her hand went to her mouth to stifle her cry, but it was too late.

"Star?" He slowed when he saw her, then stopped. "Is that you?"

She flushed, but she would not let her embarrassment chase her away from her own camp. She knew she did not look as she had when he had first known her, but what did he expect? When a woman was pregnant and due to have the baby at any time, she looked like this!

"It is I," she answered, mustering as much dignity as she could.

Camel Stalker stood behind her. "What do you want?"

Falcon came closer. She saw his handsome face,

and she wanted to run to him. Her traitorous heart would have her go with him again! All he had to do was ask her.

What is wrong with me? she wondered miserably. This man has but to look at me and I follow him. Is it not enough that he left me—pregnant and alone? What does it take for me to realize that he is not good for me?

Camel Stalker stepped in front of her in a protective gesture. For the first time since he had returned to the Badger camp, Star felt grateful to him.

Falcon halted. "Who is this man?" he asked Star.

"I am Camel Stalker. Who are you?" Camel Stalker's jaw stuck out and his arms were folded across his chest. He looked grim. But then he had looked grim ever since his return from the Fish Eaters, Star reminded herself.

Just then the babe inside her kicked. The babe knows his father, thought Star.

Blue Jay ran up. "It is the Jaguar man." She stamped the grass several times, and then she spat. It was a very insulting Badger greeting.

"Star's Jaguar husband?" demanded Camel Stalker.

"The same." Contempt threaded Blue Jay's voice. "What do you want?"

Falcon's eyes were fixed on Star. "I came to see Star."

"You see that she is fine. Go home." Blue Jay stood next to Camel Stalker, her bulk blocking Star's view of Falcon.

Star shifted a little to the side, in time to catch

Falcon's easy smile. Her heartbeat quickened.

Falcon glanced around at the Badger tents set out in the grass. "A pleasant place to camp," he observed politely.

Camel Stalker said, "Go home, Jaguar. You are not wanted here."

"Who are you?" asked Falcon. "Star's husband?"

Star met his eyes as he waited for her answer. When she could no longer meet that bold, direct gaze, she forced herself to stare at Camel Stalker's broad back.

"So. She is not your wife."

Camel Stalker stiffened. "I provide meat for her."

"I thank you then," said Falcon with a nod.

"You thank me?" screeched Camel Stalker. He dropped his arms and glared at Falcon. "You *thank* me?"

"What are you saying?" cried Blue Jay.

"I thank you for caring for my wife while I was gone, but I am back now and I will provide meat for her." Falcon watched Camel Stalker out of cold, grim eyes.

Star's heart pounded in alarm. What was Falcon talking about? He had brought her back to her people. There was never any talk of his returning to see her. What did he mean, he would provide meat for her?

"You cannot just come and take her back," protested Blue Jay. "She is not like a carcass of deer meat you Jaguars stash in a tree and return to whenever there is nothing else to eat."

Star gazed at her mother's rigid back. The

woman was correct. She stood a little straighter.

"Let Star speak for herself," demanded Falcon.

Camel Stalker whirled on her. "Choose," he said. "Choose if you will marry me! Or do you join again with the man who left you alone and pregnant?"

Sweat stood on Star's brow. Her fists clenched and unclenched. What should she do?

Chapter Fifty-five

"I choose neither of you!"

"Neither?" exclaimed Camel Stalker. He looked pale.

"You have to choose," demanded Falcon. He looked stunned.

"You do," affirmed Blue Jay. She looked exasperated.

"I do not." Star crossed her arms on her breasts above her belly and peered at all three gaping fools. Her heart pounded but she would not be forced into making such an important decision at their behest. She must decide for herself who she would marry or if she would marry at all. And if it took her 20 seasons to decide, then so be it!

She would choose what was best for herself and her babe.

"Star, we must speak. Now!" demanded Blue Jay.

Camel Stalker leaned closer to hear.

"In our tent," stated Blue Jay.

She hurried Star away from the two men and in the direction of their tent. Behind her, Star could hear a heated, angry exchange of deep voices, but her mother kept her moving toward the tent.

They reached it and ducked inside. "Listen to me, daughter," said Blue Jay. "You now have two men wanting to marry you and you big with child! Never in my days have I heard of such a thing! Choose one and be done with it. Such good fortune will not come our way again!"

"Mother," said Star quietly, "I was married to Falcon. I do not know why he is here, or what he wants. As for Camel Stalker, yes, he is a good hunter and yes, he wants to join with me, but I do not love him."

She saw the disappointment in her mother's dark eyes. "I know you wish otherwise, but I cannot join with either man."

A shadow crossed her mother's lined face. "Star, I worry for you, for the babe. Who will look after you when I am gone?"

"I will look after myself. I have the Badger People. . . ."

Her mother waved a dismissive hand. "Pah! Badger hunters will only provide meat for you after their own children and wives are fed—"

Star gazed down at the pounded dirt floor of the tent. It was true. What should she do?

"Mother, I cannot go out there and choose one of those men! I do not know why Falcon is here.

And I know even less about Camel Stalker. Since he returned, he is a changed man."

Her mother frowned. "He does seem a little different. . . ."

"Very different, Mother. He is not the young man who first courted me. He is older, grimmer."

"Oh, come now, daughter. Not grimmer."

"Grimmer," said Star.

"Well," sighed her mother, "at least you do not want that Jaguar man!" She peered out of the tent. "Let us go and tell him to go home. You do not have to marry Camel Stalker yet. Take more time if you like. But let us get rid of that Falcon. I cannot stand the sight of him! When I think of what he did to you—dropping you off here like an old deer carcass, and you big with child—"

"Mother!"

"Forgive me, daughter, it is just that I do not like the man."

Star sighed. She could feel her little one kicking. The babe knows, she thought again. Knows his father is here . . .

They left the tent.

"Star has something to say," announced Blue Jay.

Falcon watched her, leaning on his spear. Camel Stalker waited, arms across his chest.

"I—I—" Star began. She caught Falcon's earnest gaze. "I want you to leave," she said to him.

Camel Stalker smiled in triumph at Falcon. "You heard her. Get out."

Star turned to Camel Stalker. "I need some

418

time before deciding to join with you."

Camel Stalker shrugged amiably. "Do not take too long. . . ." He eyed her belly. "Perhaps after the babe is born you will be able to decide."

Star smiled tremulously at him. She appreciated this glimmer of understanding from him.

"Do you truly want me to leave, Star?"

Falcon's voice drew her like nectar does a bee. She turned to him. "Yes," she whispered.

Falcon was confused. He had seen his little daughter in his vision, the child that Star carried. He had thought that meant he was supposed to be Star's husband. And now she was choosing this Badger man over him, the father of her child? What did this mean?

He did not want to go. He had wandered for a long, long time, trying to find her. Now that he had found her, he could not be turned away. He could not!

"She wants you to leave, Jaguar man," said Camel Stalker. He strode over and stood chest to chest with Falcon and glared at him.

I do not relish the thought of fighting this man, thought Falcon. He looks as if he would fight to the death. Yet I will fight him if I have to. Suddenly he remembered where he had seen this man before. He was Star's intended Badger husband, the one that had been captured by the slave catchers. *His time in slavery has made him harsh.* Aloud he said, "I heard her."

He shifted his gaze to Star. She looked strong and proud, her thick hair draped down her back as she stood watching him. He longed to plunge his hands into her hair, to hold her to him, to never let her go. Yet she stood waiting, waiting for him to leave her—to walk out of her life forever.

"Leave us," Camel Stalker warned. "She has chosen."

Chapter Fifty-six

Falcon wandered slowly beside the riverbank. He listened to the birds twittering as he wondered what to do. Some distance back, the way he had come, was the Badger camp. And Star.

Though he had left the Badger camp, he had not gone far at first. During the night, he had crept back to where Star's tent was set. If only he could get her to talk with him. But who should be lying in front of the tent but Camel Stalker, his spear beside him, guarding Star.

Falcon had left the camp then and followed the riverbank that meandered to the south and west. Across the river on the other side rose high cliffs, but on this side, where he walked, there was flatland and low brush. This had once been a wide riverbed, but now the river was not as wide, though it was still deeper than a tall man standing on his brother's shoulders. And it ran swiftly, too. The remains of the old riverbank could be seen as thick cliffs that rose up in rocky brown layers behind Falcon.

As he walked, he mused upon how he was going to meet Star and convince her that he wanted her back.

No idea presented itself and he decided to take a nap. He rounded a bend in the river's course and spied a tree in a thicket of brush. Any man who slept in the open was risking his life to lions and jaguars and any other predators that came to drink.

He settled himself in the thicket and fell asleep. When he awoke he yawned, and was just about to rise when he heard a muffled grunt and then a sharp cry. Slowly he moved his head and peered through the leaves of the thicket.

Around the bend, coming toward him, marched two men and a woman—a very pregnant woman. With long black hair.

Falcon sat up, careful not to disturb the interlacing branches and give away his position.

He watched as the men came closer. They were practically dragging the woman; she made no effort to walk.

As the heavyset men came closer, Falcon held his breath. Slave catchers! It was Hooknose and Red Jaw, the two deceitful slave catchers he had last seen at Claw's and Betafor's cave!

"What—?" he muttered. He picked up his spear and eased out of the thicket.

The three had not seen him. The burly men stopped at the water and waded in. Hooknose took several big gulps; then Red Jaw did the same. They ignored the woman they had left on the gravel beach.

Falcon could not take his eyes off her. She sat on the bank, her head drooping wearily. Star!

He crept out of the thicket and ran to where the three were. The men were looking across the water at the cliffs on the other side, and the woman's head still drooped.

Falcon ran up and speared Hooknose through the lower back. He fell into the water, and Falcon gave him a push out into deeper water where the current was stronger. Hooknose began to thrash weakly and float away, facedown.

Falcon whirled to fight Red Jaw. The two grappled in the shallows, Red Jaw howling in protest as they rolled over and over. Finally Falcon was able to hold Red Jaw's head down under the water. When his opponent no longer struggled, Falcon leapt to his feet. The current had carried Hooknose's body far down the river.

Falcon turned to Star. "Are you all right?"

She nodded weakly. She looked dazed.

He waded out of the water and went over to her. "Let me get you a drink of water," he said. "It will revive you."

She nodded and got to her feet, one hand supporting her belly. He led her to the water.

After several sips from his cupped hands, she said, "I do feel better."

"How did you come to be with them?" He nudged Red Jaw's body, floating in the shallows.

"They grabbed me. I was out berry picking and they came and dragged me off."

He frowned. "I wonder why they chose you.

It seems odd that they would steal a pregnant woman."

"They did it because they were still angry at you," she answered. "I overheard them talking. Tula told them to come and steal me."

"Tula!"

"She told them back at the Jaguar camp."

He nodded. "I saw them at Claw's cave."

"They were interested in trading me to the Fish Eaters because Hooknose wanted revenge on you. Said you'd stolen two children from him. My capture was supposed to be his revenge."

Falcon raised an eyebrow. "It is true I took Milky and Berry back."

"Yes, well, they did not like that."

"Hooknose has a long memory."

"It would seem so. As does Tula."

"Tula cannot hurt you now," said Falcon. He looked into her beautiful brown eyes. "How I have missed you." He sighed.

She turned away at his softly spoken words.

"I must go back to my people."

"Wait! Do not go yet."

She whirled to face him. "What is it you want, Falcon? What strange thing is this that you do? You tell me you do not want me for your wife. You bring me back to my people and leave me. Then you come back, looking for me. What is it you are doing?"

"I want you for my wife," he stated simply. "I was wrong to bring you back. I deeply regret it." He reached for her hands. "Star, come with me. Be my wife. We will raise our child together."

She pulled her hands out of his grasp and

turned her head away. He found himself staring at her long black hair.

"I cannot," she said. "I am too confused."

"What is it that confuses you?"

He did not hear her answer, because suddenly he was jerked by the throat and thrown to the ground.

Star's intended Badger husband, knife in hand, loomed over him. "You thought to steal her, Jaguar? Think again! I am here to defend her."

"No, Camel Stalker! He did not steal me!" cried Star.

"How is it that he is here then?" cried Camel Stalker, eyeing Falcon. "Get up," he snarled at Falcon. "Get up and fight. I will kill you and be rid of you for good!"

"No! Please, Camel Stalker, no!"

But Camel Stalker did not hear her. Falcon scrambled to his feet. Over by the water, out of reach, lay his spear. He grabbed for the obsidian knife he always kept at his side. Gone! It must have been lost in the fight with Red Jaw.

It was to be his bare hands against Camel Stalker's knife then. He leapt at Camel Stalker. The man swiped once and Falcon came away with a cut along the flesh of his ribs. He heard Star's shriek but he ignored her. Every part of him concentrated on the deadly man in front of him.

Camel Stalker lifted his knife and came at Falcon. Falcon tried to push him away, but the Badger man managed another long cut, this time on Falcon's side. Falcon winced at the pain. He grabbed the knife and yanked it out of Camel

Stalker's hand and flung it. He heard it splash in the river.

"Now we are evenly matched," gasped Falcon.

With a cry, Camel Stalker lunged at him, his hands grasping for Falcon's throat. The two went down on the gravel.

"Stop it!" screamed Star. "Stop it!"

The two men fought on, each struggling for a death grip on the other's throat.

Finally Falcon rolled on top of Camel Stalker. He sat on the man's chest and Camel Stalker's struggles were now too weak to dislodge Falcon. Falcon's two hands encircled Camel Stalker's throat.

"No!" cried Star.

Panting, Falcon glared down into Camel Stalker's eyes. "I do not want to kill you," he gasped. "But I will if you attack me again! Do you understand?"

Camel Stalker glared at him. "Kill me and be done with it, Jaguar!"

"No!" Star cried again.

Falcon stiffened. Something sharp poked him in the back. If he did not know better, he would think it was his own spear.

"Get up," hissed Star. "I will not have you killing him!"

When Falcon did not move, she pressed the weapon against him again—harder. Sweat broke out on his brow.

"Star," he said carefully. "Put the spear down."

"Not until you get off him!" He did not like the trembling in her voice. A frightened woman could do anything with a spear.

"Put it down, Star," he warned again. "I will get off him."

Below him, Camel Stalker was making a choking sound. Falcon glared at him. If he did not know any better, he would have thought Camel Stalker was laughing at him!

Slowly, carefully, he rose from his opponent's chest. The sharp spear was no longer at his back. Camel Stalker rose just as carefully, then scrambled out of Star's way.

"You two!" yelled Star. "Now look what you have done! You have brought on the baby!"

Chapter Fifty-seven

"It is going to be a girl," said Falcon, sitting calmly beside Star and holding her hand. Down by the river, Camel Stalker pushed Red Jaw's body farther out into the current, where it drifted swiftly downstream. When they could no longer see the body, he paced the riverbank.

"A boy," she panted. "It is going to be a boy!"

"You will see." After watching Camel Stalker pace for a time, Falcon suggested, "We should send Camel Stalker back to fetch your mother."

"Yes," grunted Star. "Do that."

After Camel Stalker disappeared around the bend of the river, Falcon leaned over and asked, "Are you thirsty?"

Star shook her head.

There was silence between them except for Star's heavy panting whenever the pains became strong.

"Did you stay with Tula while she gave birth?" asked Star when a quiet time came for her.

"No. Tula's mother and sister helped her. Among my people, men do not help with the birth."

"Among my people, they help," Star bit out.

Indeed, he was glad that Star did not know what courage it was taking for him to sit here and hold her hand. When the baby came, they would face it together. Because of his vision, he knew that whatever their daughter looked like physically, she had a beautiful, mischievous spirit.

Star gave a groan. "I wish my mother had told me more about giving birth," she moaned.

"You will do fine," Falcon lied.

Blue Jay and Camel Stalker arrived and with them came three other women, including Chokecherry, who was herself pregnant. Falcon marveled that she would want to see the ordeal that lay ahead of her.

Blue Jay pushed Falcon out of the way. "I will help her now," she said imperiously. "She does not need you."

"He saved me, Mother," gasped Star, "from the Slave Catchers."

"It is true?" Blue Jay looked as though she did not believe her daughter.

Falcon nodded.

Blue Jay snorted her disbelief.

"It is true," said Camel Stalker heavily.

Falcon glanced at him in surprise.

Camel Stalker nodded stiffly, then turned away.

"Hmph," snorted Blue Jay and propped a fur under her daughter's head. She and the other women spread bulrush mats around the laboring woman.

"Thank you," Blue Jay muttered out of the side of her mouth at Falcon. Then she ignored him.

The other women gathered wood for a fire. Chokecherry carried a burning brand and touched the tip of it to the wood. Tiny flames sprang up.

It was clear to Falcon that he was not needed with so many women to help, so he went to sit near the thicket where he had been hidden when the Slave Catchers arrived. He was trembling inside, but he did not think that Star had sensed it.

Please, Great Spirit, help her through the birth, he found himself praying. Help her and our child, too. Since his vision, it felt right to pray to the Great Spirit.

He could hear Star straining, and her low, guttural groans struck fear in his heart for her. Finally, he could stand it no longer. She had said that Badger men helped their women through childbirth; he could do the same. Anything was better than sitting by the thicket and imagining the worst.

He walked over and squatted down beside a sweating, straining Star.

"What do you want?" muttered Blue Jay.

"To sit with her."

"Go away," Blue Jay answered.

He rose.

"Mother! He stays!"

Falcon sat down and Star gripped his hand so tightly that her nails dug into his flesh.

Blue Jay's lips tightened, but she said nothing.

They sat like that, Blue Jay on one side, Falcon on the other, each holding one of Star's hands.

After some time, Falcon started to rise. He had to empty his bladder. "Do not go!" cried Star and yanked him back down.

"I will stay," he answered. "I will stay forever if you want me to." He sat back down, stolidly ignoring his bodily call and her frowning mother.

Star gazed at him, her brown eyes puzzled; then she closed her eyes, groaned, and her whole body shook.

"The babe comes soon," cried Star.

Blue Jay glanced at Falcon. "Will you help?"

He read the direct challenge in her gaze.

"Will you stay and help my daughter or will you run, Jaguar man?"

"I will stay," Falcon answered, his voice steady. "I was wrong to cast her aside. I was afraid— I—"

"The babe comes!" Star moved into a squatting position. She gave a huge grunt and her grip on Falcon was so strong that he winced.

"Ohhhhhhh!" she groaned.

"Help her," muttered Blue Jay.

Falcon propped Star up until she was squatting over the rush mats.

"Hold her," Blue Jay ordered Falcon, "from the front."

Chokecherry took his place propping Star's back, and Falcon went around and kneeled down

431

in front of Star. He leaned back on his heels so that she could brace herself with her hands on his shoulders.

"Aaaarghhh," groaned Star.

Falcon wanted to get up and flee but Star's weight on his shoulders pressed him in place.

"The baby is coming," instructed Blue Jay, "on the next wave of pain."

Star gave a guttural cry.

Falcon held one of her clenched fists. "You are doing well," he crooned. Another lie. If she survived this birth he would crawl back to the Badger camp on his knees until his flesh was bloody in tribute to the Great Spirit. He would!

"The babe comes!" cried Star.

The other women ran over to see. "He comes!" cried Chokecherry.

"I see his head!" announced Blue Jay.

Falcon did not dare look down to see what was happening. He stared into Star's beautiful face, her head thrown back, her breath coming in quick pants, her naked breasts slick with sweat. "I love you," he whispered.

She opened her eyes but she did not see him.

"Ahrrrrrrgh," she groaned.

"You are doing very well," he encouraged. Perhaps he did not lie after all. The women acted as if this were an accepted way to birth a child. Was it?

"The babe is here," cried a jubilant Blue Jay.

"Oh!" cried Chokecherry.

Falcon held Star, his arms supporting her. He held her until Blue Jay could pull the child out from under her.

"A knife, a knife!" cried Blue Jay. "I need a knife to cut the cord!"

The women fluttered about. Falcon handed his obsidian knife to her.

Blue Jay's dark eyes met his. "Thank you," she said, and he thought she was doing more than thanking him for the knife.

Star lay back down on the mats and held out her arms. Blue Jay put the long, thin baby into them. "My babe," Star muttered, exhausted. She beamed at the child. Falcon brushed Star's hair back from her wet forehead.

"It is a girl," she said in surprise.

Falcon took a breath, willing himself not to turn from the twisted body. Willing himself to smile upon the sickly features. He would do it. For Star. And he would stand by Star until her death. Or for as long as she would let him.

He looked at the child. Her face was small, her eyes closed. At that moment she opened them and he gazed into clear brown eyes. He jerked back, startled. Her face looked—looked—

His eyes flew along her body. Strong little legs kicked and jerked. Little fists shook in the air. She was strong. She was healthy!

He gasped. His babe was born whole and healthy! He stared at Star, stared at the babe. His child, his daughter, alive, strong . . .

He covered his face with his hands and he wept.

Chapter Fifty-eight

Night had fallen but Star could easily see her babe by the fire's cheerful light. Star smiled as the baby nursed at her breast. "She knows what she wants," murmured Star proudly. "See how she seeks the nipple? She knows she must do that to survive."

Falcon sat beside her and watched the babe, but he said nothing.

Happiness coursed through Star. She was so happy her beautiful babe was born at last. Ah, but her life was good.

She admired her child for a long while, then glanced at Falcon. Knowing how he never liked to talk about anything important, she nevertheless had something to ask him. And though she now risked losing her newfound calmness, she must know the answer, for her sake and for her beautiful daughter's. "Tell me, Falcon, why did you return?"

His dark gaze held hers. "To see you."

"You have seen me. Are you going to leave?"

"No."

She frowned, surprised. "I remember, during the birth, that you said you would stay with me forever. What did you mean?" She held her breath.

"I meant it. I will stay with you as long as you want me to."

She lifted a brow. "That is very different from what you told me before. When you brought me back to my people."

She heard the accusing note in her own voice. At any moment he would get up and say he had to leave or go hunting. She braced herself.

He shook his head slowly. "I was a fool."

She stared at him in surprise. "Falcon?"

"Yes?"

"What has happened to you?"

Around them, the women waded in the water or gathered wood. Chokecherry and Blue Jay laughed beside the water. Camel Stalker sharpened a knife blade. Falcon leaned closer to Star. "After you told me you were pregnant, I greatly feared that you would give birth to a sickly child."

"And if I had?"

"That is why I came back. To help you with a sickly child."

"She does not look sick," observed Star, eyeing the baby asleep at her breast. "She looks healthy."

"She does." There was something in his voice she did not understand. His scar was white against his cheek.

"I—I thought that it would be like it was with Tula," he added. "A long, difficult birth, a sickly child who would later die, and then I thought you would turn against me."

She frowned. "Like Tula?"

"Yes." He stared at the river.

"But why would I do that?"

He shrugged. "I thought you would."

She thought about that. "I am not like Tula," she said at last.

He laughed. "No, you are not." He appeared cheerful at the thought. "That is what Betafor told me, too."

"Betafor?"

He smiled ruefully. "She told me much to think upon." Then he grew solemn again. "I thought you would stop loving me if our child died. I could not bear to see your love turn to hatred, too."

"So you sent me away."

He nodded and sighed. "I thought I could not face such pain again. It was very difficult for me, Star."

"It was very difficult for me, too," she whispered. She remembered the nights she had cried herself to sleep. The days she had hoped for a glimpse of him. She glanced away, unwilling to let him see her tears.

He reached for her chin and gently turned her face back to him. "I love you, Star," he murmured, kissing each tear that rolled down her cheeks. "I want to be a good husband to you, and a good father to our child."

She closed her eyes. How she had longed

to hear those words from him. Did she dare trust him?

"You said you did not want to face such pain again, and yet you came and sought me out at the Badger camp. What changed you?"

He shrugged and was silent for a time. "I realized finally that I loved you and wanted to be with you. If it meant helping you with our sickly child, so be it. I came to help."

She smiled sadly. "It is not like you to talk like this," she admitted. "I am surprised you have not jumped up to go hunting."

He laughed. So did she.

She kissed the top of her sleeping daughter's little head. "If we become husband and wife again, there may be more children, Falcon. Will you run each time I am pregnant?"

"I hope not." He laughed, but ceased when he saw her watching him.

"I could not bear it, Falcon." Tears blurred her sight of him.

"Ah, Star," he murmured. "Do not cry, dear one." He kissed her lips softly. When he drew back, he said, "I have had much to think upon, these last seasons without you. It was my grief at losing my son and then losing Tula that made me so unreasoning. I thought my life was over.

"And then you, a mud-covered, long-legged heron, came into my life. I could not believe that you could love me. Or that I could love you. I did not think I deserved such happiness." He shook his head. "I did not even recognize your love in our home."

"And now you do?"

He sighed. "It took a long time, but now I do."

She thought about his words. A feeling of hope stirred in her heart.

"Do—do you still love me, Star?"

"Yes," she whispered.

"And I love you. Let us start anew in our lives," he urged, taking her hands in his. "Let us face our problems together. We can talk about them. Together, we can overcome our fear and anything that awaits us."

"Falcon, I hardly know you," she marveled. "Is that *you* saying we can talk?"

He looked sheepish for a moment. "Perhaps I should go hunting now," he said and started to rise.

"Falcon, do not!" she cried and tried to sit up. The baby on her breast squirmed and woke up and started rooting for the nipple.

Falcon laughed and plopped himself back down beside her. "I will stay, Star. I did but joke."

"Come here, Jaguar man," she said and pulled his head toward her. She gave him a long kiss. "I love you, but you put me through much agony."

"Can you find it in your heart to trust me again, Star?"

She gazed into his obsidian eyes for a long, long time. Without him, her life would be easily planned, things done just as she wanted them. Without him, she would have calmness and peace in her tent.

And without him, she realized as she felt herself falling into those black, black eyes, she would have a terrible emptiness in her life.

"I can," she whispered.

"I love you," he murmured. "No more broken promises between us, wife."

"None," she answered as their lips met.

Above them, the Darkstar winked brightly.

Epilogue

Four years later

"What is this place?" asked Star, glancing up. "I have been here before, I think."

Falcon and Star and their little daughter stood at the foot of a steep gravel slope. Old Blue Jay sat resting nearby on a bison robe. The long trek from the Badger camp had wearied her.

Falcon answered, "This place is called the Canyon of the Doves."

"Canyon of the Doves," repeated Star, puzzled. "Why did you bring us here?"

"I have something important to do," he said. He reached out his arms. "I will carry Hope now."

His little daughter went into his arms with a squeal of delight.

Star laughed. "She wants her father to carry

her! Are you tired of Mama carrying you, little one?"

"Now that you carry our second child in your belly, we must be careful not to tire you," said Falcon.

"I am not weary," Star assured him, warmed by his concern for her.

They started up the steep hillside, pausing many times to rest. She had brought along extra strips of dried meat and three water bladders so that no one suffered from hunger or thirst on this journey.

At last they reached the top of the slope. Star gazed down into the canyon on the other side. "It is a long way down," she observed, stepping back from the edge.

"It is," he agreed. Young Hope squirmed in his arms. "Be still, my child. I have something to show you." He lifted her arm and pointed out the directions, just as his father had done before him.

Star watched her husband and daughter and a wave of love burst over her. How she loved him, this man who was so different from her in his ways. That he loved her and their child had been proved over and over. Ever since he had stayed with her through Hope's birth, a bond had been tied between them, a strong bond, stronger than leather, one that could not be cut.

Star no longer feared he would cast her aside. And no longer did he pretend that nothing mattered. Now many things mattered to him and he was unashamed to tell her.

She loved him, this Jaguar man of hers. And

he loved her. He told her so every night. And showed her.

She listened to Hope's murmurs as she repeated her father's words. Perhaps Hope was still too young to understand what he said, perhaps not. But knowing this husband of hers as well as she did, Star knew he would bring his daughter here many times again and explain the land to her.

Star smiled as she watched them pointing at the hills and valleys below.

"And you will pick thick bulrushes in that river bottom."

Her life had turned out very different from what she had planned or expected. But the life she had now was wonderful, much better than she could have ever planned.

Joy filled her as she gazed up at the blue bowl of sky above their heads. There was Someone who could be trusted to guide human lives, after all.

"You will butcher big deer in those hills."

Hope nodded solemnly at her father's words.

"You are a fine daughter, and all this land is yours. I, and my father before me, stood on this place. It is Jaguar land. Good land. Someday you will stand here again and look out over the land, your land."

Star smiled at the solemn looks on both their faces.

"It is good, this land. It is for you, and your daughters and your sons."

Hope was very still, as if she understood what her father told her.

Star smiled to herself at her daughter's wisdom.

Suddenly Falcon glanced at Star. She met those bold dark eyes and her heart leapt with happiness.

"It is time to return, wife," he said, and his low voice sent thrills through her.

How she loved him! She gave one last, shivery look down into the canyon, then fell into step as they carefully climbed back down the steep slope.

When they reached the bottom, Blue Jay was waiting for them. "I will carry her," she said, holding her arms out to Hope. Falcon handed the child to his mother-in-law.

Then, together, he and his beloved wife walked hand in hand along the trail toward the Jaguar lands.

REFERENCES:

Cahalane, Victor C. *Mammals of North America*. New York: MacMillan, 1964.

Dixon, E. James. *Quest for the Origins of the First Americans*. Albuquerque: University of New Mexico Press, 1993.

Driver, Harold E. *Indians of North America*. Chicago: University of Chicago Press, 1970.

Fryxell, Roald and Bennie C. Keel. "Emergency Salvage Excavations for the Recovery of Early Human Remains and Related Scientific Materials from the Marmes Rockshelter Archaeological Site, Southeastern Washington, May 3-December 15, 1968." A final report to U.S. Army Engineer District, Walla Walla, Corps of Engineers. Washington State University, 1969.

Fryxell, Roald, Tadeusz Bielicki, Richard D. Daugherty, Carl E. Gustafson, Henry T. Irwin, and Bennie C. Keel. "A Human Skeleton from Sediments of Mid-Pinedale Age in Southeastern Washington." *American Antiquity* 1968: 33, pp. 511-514.

Grady, Denise. "Death at the Corners." *Discover*, Dec. 1993: Vol. 14, no. 12, pp. 82-91.

Gustafson, Carl Eugene. "Faunal Remains from the Marmes Rockshelter and Related Archaeological Sites in the Columbia Basin." PhD. thesis. Dept. of Zoology, Washington State University, Pullman, WA, 1972.

Hoeffecker, John F.W., Roger Powers, Ted Goebel. "The Colonization of Beringia and the Peopling of the New World." *Science,* Jan. 1993: Vol. 259, pp. 46-53.

Jelinek, Arthur J. "Perspectives from the Old World on the Habitation of the New." *American Antiquity* 1992: 57(2), pp. 345-347.

Kelly, Robert L. and Lawrence C. Todd. "Coming Into the Country: Early Paleoindian Hunting and Mobility." *American Antiquity* 1988: 53(2) pp. 231-244.

Krantz, Grover S. "Oldest Human Remains from the Marmes Site." Washington Sate University. Pullman, WA, circa 1975.

Meltzer, David J. "Why Don't We Know When the Firsst People Came to North America?" *American Antiquity* 1989: 54(3), pp. 471-490.

Rice, David G. "Preliminary Report. Marmes Rockshelter Archaeological Site. Southern Columbia Plateau." Washington State University, Pullman, WA, 1969.

Schurr, Theodore G., Scott W. Ballinger, Yik-Yuen Gan, Judith A. Hodge, D. Andrew Merriwether, Dale N. Lawrence, William C. Knowler, Kenneth M. Weiss, and Douglas C. Wallace. "Amerindian Mitochondrial DNAs Have Rare Asian Mutations at High Frequencies, Suggesting They Derived from Four Primary Maternal Lineages." *American Journal of Genetics* 1990: 46 pp. 613-623.

Sheppard, John C., Peter E. Wigand, Carl E. Gustafson, and Meyer Rubin. "A Reevaluation of the Marmes Rockshelter Radiocarbon Chronology." *American Antiquity* 1987: 52(1), 118-125.

Torroni, Antonio, Theodore G. Schurr, Chi-Chuan Yang, Emoke J.E. Szathmary, Robert C. Williams, Moses S. Schanfield, Gary A. Troup, William C. Knowler, Dale N. Lawrence, Kenneth M. Weiss, and Douglas C. Wallace. "Native American Mitochondrial DNA Analysis Indicates That the Amerind and the Nadene Populations Were Founded by Two Independent Migrations." *Genetics* 1992: 130, pp. 153-162.

Trafzer, Clifford E. and Richard D. Scheuerman. "Renegade Tribe: The Palouse Indians and the Invasion of the Inland Pacific Northwest." Washington State University Press, Pullman, WA, 1986.

Turner, Christy G. II. "The First Americans: The Dental Evidence." *National Geographic Research* 1986: Vol. 2(1) pp. 37-46.

Wallace, Douglas C., Katherine Garrison, and William C. Knowler. "Dramatic Founder Effects in Amerindian Mitochondrial DNA." *American Journal of Physical Anthropology* 1985: Vol. 68, pp. 149-155.

Whitley, David S. and Ronald I. Dorn. "New Perspectives on the Clovis vs. Pre-Clovis Controversy." *American Antiquity* 1993: 58(4), pp. 626-647.

HUNTERS OF THE ICE AGE

THERESA SCOTT

At the dawn of time, a proud people battled for survival, at one with the harsh beauty of the land and its primal rhythms.

Dark Renegade. Talon has stalked the great beasts of the plain, but he has never found prey more elusive than Summer, the woman he has stolen from his enemies. A terrible betrayal turns Talon against her—only a bond stronger than love itself can subdue the captor and make him surrender to Summer's sweet, gentle fury.

_51952-6 $4.99 US/$5.99 CAN

Yesterday's Dawn. Mamut has proven his strength and courage time and again. But when it comes to subduing one helpless female captive, he finds himself at a distinct disadvantage. He claims he will make the stolen woman his slave, but he soon learns he will never enjoy her alluring body unless he can first win her elusive heart.

_51920-8 $4.99 US/$5.99 CAN

BRIDE OF DESIRE

THERESA SCOTT

"More than an Indian romance, more than a Viking tale, *Bride Of Desire* is a unique combination of both. Enjoyable and satisfying!"

—*Romantic Times*

To beautiful, ebony-haired Winsome, the tall blond stranger who has taken her captive seems an entirely different breed of male from the men of her tribe. Though Brand treats her gently, his ways are nothing like the customs of her people. She has been taught that a man and a maiden may not join together until elaborate courting rituals are performed, but when Brand crushes her against his hard-muscled body, it is only too clear that he has no intention of waiting for anything. Weak with wanting, Winsome longs to surrender, but she will insist on a wedding ceremony first. When Brand finally claims her innocence, she will be the bride of his heart, as well as a bride of desire.

_3610-X $4.99 US/$5.99 CAN